FOUND

FOUND

The FOUND Series, Volume 1

Ellie Katz

Published by Ellie Katz, 2024.

FOUND

First edition. September 24, 2024.

ISBN: 979-8224025497

Written by Ellie Katz.

For Kit - We've found where we belong, together

For Hallie - Soulmates since the beginning

Content Warning

This novel contains adult erotica and explicit sexual situations including, but not limited to, the following:

- Voyeurism
- Exhibitionism
- Anal play & penetration
- Cunnilingus
- Vaginal fisting
- Blowjobs & deep-throating
- Gagging
- Bondage & BDSM content
- Power play
- Shibari
- Use of sex toys
- Group sex
- Spanking & impact play
- Role play
- Mention of sexual assault
- Threesomes
- Masturbation
- Humiliation
- LGBTQ content, including FF, MM, FFM, FFMM

Intended for mature readers only.
Not suitable for readers under the age of 18.

Prologue

Parker

Here I am.
Once more.

The Ceremony.

It's not my first time; I'm not a virgin by any means.

But this time, things are different.

Instead of my world revolving around her - my every breath relying on her command - this time, I'm in control. I make the rules. I enforce them. I decide the consequences.

It truly is the best arrangement I can think of.

I stand, waiting, my body still. No nerves. A picture of cool composure. I'm dressed to impress in my best navy-blue suit. My sleek, blonde curls are combed and styled just so. My eyes peer through my black-rimmed glasses, watching for her arrival. I'm ready to see her. I fold my hands together, fingers intertwined. My mind is calm.

The door opens, at last, and she takes her first step toward me. A wave of hot air forces goosebumps and sweat to decorate the surface of my skin. My eyes penetrate hers, seeing past the dress, past the spectators, past the technicalities of the present moment. My gaze bores into her, hungry to devour her in the commitment she's about to make.

A slow smile spreads across my lips.

I can't wait.

Part One
Iris

One

The shrill chime of the alarm on my phone reverberates off the walls of my bedroom. The sound pierces my eardrums and snakes into them, tunneling deep into the caverns of my brain. The peaceful sleep that I had known just seconds ago seems a distant memory. I blink rapidly, as if to prime my eyes to the daylight by allowing slivers of brightness in. I tap the screen of my Apple watch, only to have what I already know to be true confirmed: the battery is dead. So much for the slow and pleasant wakeup of a silent alarm. I kick my legs out of the heavy sheets of my bed and feel the coolness of the morning envelop them. A light breeze sneaks in through my cracked window and flutters around my body. I breathe it in and center myself, the cool California air dancing in my nostrils and invading my brain. I run my fingers up my body in a long stretch and let out a squeak. I settle into the plush of my blankets, pushing myself back into them as I ready myself to begin the day in the best way I know.

I take a deep breath in and close my eyes. My mind flickers with images of inspiration from the usuals: Chris Hemsworth, Scarlett Johansson, Rihanna. I ultimately decide on a fantasy involving Tom Felton, in which he pins me up against the wall, and I yelp under the surprising force of his touch. I sneak my hands under my shirt and imagine his are grasping at my breasts and pinching my nipples. Writhing against the sheets of my bed, I slip my fingers along the lips of my pussy, teasing myself as I imagine him tormenting me. I stroke at the apex of my opening, allowing my fingers to play with the sensitive nub at its entrance. My body tingles with sweat and warmth; I wiggle and moan. His lips meet mine, and I envision our kiss blooming and deepening as he yanks on the locks of my wavy hair. My shallow pants quicken, and I crave release. But he teases me more, moving slowly then quickly, even stopping completely at times. It's an agonizing edging game that goes on longer than I have time for, but the indulgence is overpowering. Besides, who am I to rush Tom Felton? He plunges his fingers inside of me, moving them rhythmically as his thumb circles my clit. I pant as he pushes me to the precipice, then over. An exhilarating wave of warmth courses through my entire body as I succumb to the sweet surrender of my orgasm. My heart bounces in my chest as I work to steady my breath.

Whew.

Good morning.

It's Tuesday: my favorite day of the week. Most recently, Tuesdays are to me what Mondays are to most others - the start of the work week. Sure, I love weekends, but, even more, I love the transition back into a familiar routine. The predictability is profoundly comforting.

It's early spring: my favorite time of the year. With the mornings still refreshingly cool, I greedily bask in a hot, sudsy shower. I rustle through the pile of scrubs still waiting to be folded in my heaped laundry basket and choose a fresh, clean top. Today, I opt for a bright yellow one decorated with cartoon snails and spring blooms. Cheery and cute. I pair it with navy bottoms, then run a brush through the auburn strands of my unruly hair. Almost ready to go, I grab the library book on my bedside table and toss it into my tote bag. I catch a quick glance of myself in the mirror of my closet door and fiddle with my bangs. Ready at last.

I lock my apartment door and head down the flight of stairs to the front gate of the building. Throwing my bag over my shoulder, I skip across the street and make my way down two blocks and along another street until I'm within view of Nuance Plaza: my second home. The parking lot has about two dozen cars parked, several coming, and a few going. I smile. The predictability of the day is already pleasing me.

Time to caffeinate. I step inside of my usual morning haunt, a locally-owned coffee shop called Urban Grind. Already, the place is bustling. Omar and Lane are working double time to create the many unique caffeine concoctions demanded by coffee snobs abound. Behind the register, Simone catches my eye and gives me a nod. I join the line of five others, also itching for their morning fix. I reach inside my bag to find my power bank and check if my watch is charged yet, only to realize that it's not charging at all. My power bank and watch are both dead. I roll my eyes, irritated with myself for starting my week this way. I shrug it off and move up in line. A fresh, plump blueberry muffin sprinkled with large granules of sugar looks like exactly what I need right now. When my turn comes a moment later, I order two: one for me, and one for Maria, my morning shift co-worker. Simone hands me my double Americano with four pumps of vanilla and a splash of milk, and I thank her for the sugary fuel to get my day started.

With my hot coffee and breakfast cupcake in hand, I sneak down and behind the plaza, across a tree-lined pathway, and over to the river. Hidden within the urban sprawl, this secret green space is my sanctuary. I settle down on a stump next to the damp, dewy grass of the riverbank and savor the warmth of my coffee. I watch as the steam leaks out of the crevices of the lid, weaving with the cool air surrounding it. Turning my attention forward, I watch the water flow. The river is bloated from the snow melting north in the mountains. The trickle of it sings in my ears. Local birds splash and dive into the water, their feathers slick with cool morning dew. I hum. There's such comfort in the beauty and rawness of nature. I take several satisfying sips of my coffee, close my eyes, and breathe deeply. A breeze gusts over the river, carrying the cool reminder of winter with it. My body shudders at the perfect contrast.

I pull my phone from the front pocket of my sage tote and check the time: 7:43 a.m. Just about fifteen minutes before my shift begins. I tuck my phone back in its place, take another large gulp of coffee, and reach for my book. My latest read is a detective novel set in the post-World War II era. I crack it open and turn to my bookmarked page about a third of the way through. I read one page, then another, then another. This is my fifth or sixth detective book in a row, and I can't get enough of them. I read compulsively, devouring each word and digesting the clues. Engrossed in my read, I almost don't notice the weak buzz coming from inside my bag. I pull out my phone and turn off the five-minutes-before-work-starts alarm. Where would I be without modern technology? Late. I'd be very late.

I slide my book back into my bag and take one more perfect sip of my coffee. Getting to my feet, I stand up to stretch, twist my body, and reach my arms toward the sky. Ready to go. I bend down to grab my bag, but clumsily lose my balance on the slick edges of the riverbank.

What ensues is a slow-motion spectacle of shame.

I slide down the mucky edge, my legs slipping and kicking up behind me. I fall to my hands and hopelessly grab at the roots and loose leaves on the ground around me, desperate to stay out of the water and regain my footing on dry land. Thankfully, my feet catch on the rocky edge of the riverbed and save me from going for a morning dip. My bag, however, is not so lucky. The blueberry muffins escape from inside of it and roll like snowballs over the edge. They immediately turn to mush in the shallow water. My library book also slips out, sliding steadily right between my legs. A slow dribble of the last drops of my coffee trails behind.

If it wasn't happening to me, it probably would've been hilarious to witness. Which is why the next thing I hear is laughter.

From him.

I fling my disheveled hair out of my eyes and glance up, realizing only now that I am practically doing downward dog in front of... oh, shit, there are a lot of people here. The river trail is usually quite busy in the mornings, with people on their a.m. jog or taking their dog out for a walk before work. Today is no exception. My eyes dart around, fueled by a mixture of caffeine and public humiliation, as I search my surroundings for the comedic culprit.

There he is, just a few feet from me, standing with his arms crossed and a smug grin painted on his face.

"Hi," he says, raspy and confident. His blonde curls bounce in the breeze.

"Hi," I exhale, agitation in my throat. I push myself up to standing, unsuccessfully brush the dirt from my hands, and mirror him with crossed arms.

He lets out a chuckle and walks toward me. He reaches down, his body long and lean, and grabs my book. It's in an unfortunate state.

"Here," he offers, clutching the corner of the book. "You dropped this." I don't like the mockery in his voice.

Or maybe I do.

"Yeah. Thanks," I snap, ripping the mud- and coffee-infused book from his grasp.

"That's quite the way to start your day. I'm sorry about your coffee," he says, his voice gentler this time. "And your book."

"It's okay. I really like this book, so even though I'll have to pay for a replacement, I get to keep this copy. Which is good. I'll read it again." I wave the book around, like a maniac. "And I drank most of my coffee. It was practically empty anyway. So, yeah." I'm not sure why I'm over-sharing about my coffee. Or the book. It's at this exact moment that I wish I could shrink down to the size of a small pebble and get kicked into the river.

"In that case, I guess I don't need to offer to buy you a new one." His voice cracks. He clears his throat. "Coffee, I mean."

I giggle. Pausing, I wrinkle my eyebrows and examine him. My honey-brown eyes flutter as I blink, drinking him in. He's taller than me, probably around six feet is my guess. His arms are magnificently toned, and beneath his plain, white tee, his figure is slim and athletic. He has those beautiful blonde curls that are the perfect combination of messy and manicured, and his dark jeans hug his hips delightfully so. I can't stop myself from noticing a seemingly adequate bulge at his center. He has a charming smile despite the satisfied smirk taunting me, and with an intriguing squint, his bright blue eyes bore into me, infecting me with their potion. A rush of heat ricochets in the space dividing us.

"Hmm..." I feign thoughtfulness. "Not coffee," I begin, breathing deeply. "But. I could use a drink later," I state boldly.

"Maybe you should tell me your name first," he replies, rubbing his finger and thumb over his groomed stubble.

"I'm Iris."

"Nice to meet you, Iris." He reaches his hand forward. A jolt of electricity spikes through me as we touch for the first time. And an undeniable pulsing throb pangs between my thighs. "I'm Parker." My cheeks burn pink as I admire him.

"Hi, Parker," I say, tasting his name in my mouth.

"Hi, Iris," he mocks. Again. "How about I get you that drink tonight?"

My heart flutters.

My insides clench.

I'm in trouble with this one.

Two

Just a few doors down from Urban Grind is my workplace: Dr. Val's PetVet. Sprawling several units across the wood-and-brick building, the veterinary clinic is well-lit with bright, floor-to-ceiling windows lining the front. I've worked here for a number of years now. I love everything about it: the proximity to my apartment, the people I work with, and the clients we serve. The coffee shop down the way is a huge bonus, too.

"Good morning, Iris," Maria greets me as I prance through the front door. She's busily typing away on the intake computer, setting up the system for the day.

"Good morning!" I reply, probably more enthusiastically than 8 a.m. calls for.

"Huh, you've got quite the smile on," Maria teases me. She studies me with suspicious eyes. "What happened to you this morning?" She raises her eyebrows. "Look at how flushed your cheeks are!"

My hands instinctively shoot up to cover the grin spreading across my face.

"Look at you, all smitten," she sings. "You met someone, didn't you?"

"I diiiiiddddd," I drawl, falling into the reception chair beside her.

"Details, details!" she hollers, snapping her fingers and stretching her eyes wide.

"It was stupid, really," I begin. "I was reading my book by the river and slipped when I stood up. I looked like an idiot. Such a mess. I'm still so embarrassed." The sting of shame remains fresh between my legs.

"Are you okay?" Maria asks, alarmed. Her mother instincts kick into full gear.

"Oh, ha! Physically, I'm fine. My ego, though, is pretty bruised. This guy started laughing at me."

"Oh, I'm sure it wasn't as bad as you think. Wait. Wait, what? Someone laughed at you?" I nod. "Please don't tell me this is the guy."

"What?"

"You cannot go out with a guy whose first instinct is to laugh at you in a weak moment!"

"Well... it sort of... maybe... it might be."

"No, Iris, no. Any guy who finds enjoyment in your embarrassment is not a good human." Oh, Maria, if you even knew me. I open my mouth to defend myself, but instead let out a hearty sigh. Maria drones on. "No, no, no. Any man of yours should be there to support you, to lift you up!"

"Well, he did," I reply in his defense. "He helped me up and offered to get me another coffee after mine became carnage."

"It's the least he could do!" Maria huffs.

"Well, yeah, I guess. Anyway, I told him no thanks. To the coffee anyway."

"For the best. He doesn't deserve you."

"But... we are going out for drinks tonight."

The shock on Maria's face makes me shriek with laughter. Her disapproval is wildly entertaining. The two of us have been working together for a couple of years now. Although Maria is six years younger than me, she is vastly more mature, having met her husband in her early twenties, gotten married, and already had two children. Having come into marriage and parenthood with great ease, she rightfully has a natural air of superiority concerning relationships and family life. She's loud, opinionated, and devoutly realistic. We have a great working relationship. We chat and gossip about our personal lives, and Maria is always excited to share the latest on each member of her exceptionally large extended Mexican family with someone who is removed from it. She's an excellent storyteller, so I'm certain she embellishes here and there. I'm much more private than she is, but I do occasionally share stories of life as a single thirty-something, which Maria has admitted she is equally captivated and horrified by. *"So glad I'm not single!"* she reminds me almost daily.

While Maria keeps busy at the front of the clinic, I make my way into the back. I check on our overnight patients, set up the iPads in each examination room, and do a quick wipe down of all the working surfaces. While I'm administering Brumble the cat's morning medication, our owner and head veterinarian Dr. Val waltzes in, carrying a large mug of black coffee. It's heavenly aroma perfumes throughout the room, and I immediately regret having not taken Parker up on a second cup.

"Good morning, Dr. Val," I greet as I gently urge Brumble back into his kennel.

"Good morning, Iris. How are you, my dear?" he asks, gently reaching for my hand and squeezing my fingers in his.

"Good, good." I pause. "How about yourself?"

"Wonderful," Dr. Val answers between sips of coffee. His silver-gray waves are neatly combed back. His facial hair is smooth and groomed, and recently trimmed, I can tell - his lips are now visible instead of hidden beneath. "Ruby is going to be in again today. She'll shadow me for the morning, then, this afternoon, Dr. Caroline will take over so I can catch up on the paperwork in the back," he informs me.

"Sounds good," I say, nodding in acknowledgment.

With students finishing up their studies and getting ready to enter the working world, Dr. Val has been taking on a number of trainees. Also, with his retirement approaching, he's cut back his hours a lot. Dr. Caroline is our main veterinarian now, with Dr. Amar and Dr. Vincent also working limited hours at the clinic.

As for the vet techs, our staff has faced some recent turnover. Charlie and his aspiring artist boyfriend moved to San Francisco last month, and Petra returned to Colorado to care for her terminally ill mother a few months ago. Daisy, who ghosted us back in January, had been cryptically talking for a while about making a big life change. We suppose that she was especially inspired by the New Year and took the leap. To fill the void left by the three of them, we've all been working a lot of overtime. There are also a few newbies shadowing us as we look for suitable replacements.

The clinic is a busy place, but I love it. Being around animals all day is immensely healing, and Dr. Val fosters a very warm and inclusive working environment. One of the best parts about my job is that PetCation, a short- and long-term boarding facility, is located just next door. Dr. Val and PetCation's owner, Sherry, have formed a friendly working relationship over the years, and about a year ago, the two businesses made the mutual decision to merge together. While I'm employed by the clinic, I do occasionally sneak away to PetCation and spend time with the critters there.

Will and Stefanie appear a moment later and help me finish up the morning dosage duties. I scurry back to the reception area and assist Maria in welcoming the first few clients of the day.

We are open for business.

Three

E leven hours later, I'm panicking. A flurry of fabric explodes on my bed as I dig through my closet, throwing aside shirts and skirts and dresses and jeans. There has to be something here. I check my watch, which is charged at last, and wish for time to slow down.

As I was getting ready to clock out, Dr. Caroline asked if I would mind staying a little longer and taking Hugo, a curly-haired terrier staying at PetCation, for a walk before I left. I couldn't resist. So, I ended up staying almost an hour late at work, and I couldn't shake my acute need to confess to Tess the Librarian that I had defiled my book. I shamefully paid the damage fee and borrowed another two books to add to my bedside pile. The library detour took over an hour, too, so, home now, I have less than thirty minutes before my date with the handsome and mysterious Parker.

I don't regard myself as vain, but, considering the fact that during our first encounter I was dressed in scrubs and mucky swamp dirt, I do feel the need to step up my game just a tad. I finally decide on a pair of dark wash, high rise skinny jeans and my favorite black sweater. I barely have time to run a brush through my hair before throwing on a pair of simple black heels and running out the door. Thankfully, I'm not really one for makeup.

I pull my phone from its spot in my tote and type in the address to Parker's suggested meeting place. It's a twenty-minute walk. I need to get moving. I pop in my earbuds, put on an upbeat Spotify playlist, and allow the nice lady of Google maps to guide me on my journey. Anticipation setting my pace, I glide along the sidewalk and jog across several busy intersections. Finally, after nothing but houses and apartments for nearly forever, a cluster of commercial buildings becomes visible. The plaza ahead stretches several blocks long and is occupied mostly by larger shops and mainstream businesses. My eyes dart around as I search for our meeting spot: Pearl Wines & Eatery. Labeled in muted, thin lettering that blends into the building that houses it, Pearl is, seemingly, a hidden gem.

I'm relieved to have made it just on time. I let out the breath I didn't realize I was holding and slow my pace. As I approach the door, my heart flutters at the possibility of what could be.

I replay our first meeting in my mind yet again, the embarrassment still fresh and nagging in the pit of my stomach. It swells and moves lower, the humiliation playing a torturous, erotic game. I sigh heavily as the warm surge of arousal blooms through me.

I'm definitely in trouble with this one.

• • • •

I'M GOING TO DO IT right this time. I'm going to be upfront, raw, honest. No excuses. Absolute truth. I will show Parker all the facets that make me who I am. No holding back. Not this time.

It's been a good three months since my last relationship, if you can call it that. I admit - I'm not very good with commitment. My last flame asked me to a family holiday dinner, and I all but dropped dead. That's the last time we saw each other. Sorry, not sorry. I'm not the Christmas-family-dinner type.

I've grown a lot in the time since, and the biggest thing I've come to terms with is my need to be true to myself. I'm done with hiding. I'm done with running. It doesn't keep me safe; it just prolongs the inevitable. If my past exploits have taught me anything, it's that I need to live my truth. Honesty is the best policy. Especially with myself.

It's hard to be vulnerable, though. I'm not like other people. I never have been. I don't share the values of mainstream society; I'm different.

The truth can be scary, but I vow that the next person I date will know all of me. I will bare all my quirks, kinks, and unique perspectives. Maybe, as proverbially foretold, the truth will at last set me free.

But now, with the prospect of that new partner before me, I doubt my fortitude.

No.

I can't hide anymore. I *have* to be honest. And, with that sly look Parker had on his face, it's possible he'll understand. Let's hope he can keep an open mind.

• • • •

I TAKE A DEEP BREATH and pull the corkscrew-shaped handle on the door. Stepping inside, I'm in awe. This place is much larger than it looks from the outside, stretching long and breaking off to either side to form a T-shape. Impeccably stylish, the restaurant is decorated in rich, warm tones of red and accented with blush drapery and just a touch of gold. Glancing down at my jeans and casual black sweater, I feel immensely underdressed. Of course I'm making a fool of myself *again*. Is this going to be the pattern with this guy?

Part of me hopes so.

It's just after 8 p.m. now, and the place is surprisingly bustling. I wait for several couples ahead of me to check in with the hostess before it's my turn. With warm cheeks and flawless, dark skin, she smiles at me, a hint of knowing in her eyes. She invites me to follow her, and I do so, trailing behind like a lost puppy. She leads me to the right of the restaurant, past the main bar, and over into a smaller area decorated with several high-top tables and crates of wines from various vineyards around the world.

Parker is sitting at a table hidden in the far corner. His eyes find mine, and everything shifts. The world blurs in slow motion, just as it did the first time Parker came into my life. He stands tall and approaches me, reaching for my hand and kissing the back of it in greeting. The touch of his lips against my skin makes my cheeks burn with a redness that's richer than the color of the tablecloth. I'm speechless. It's as though we've been transported back into the 1940s, where even the slightest touch is overwhelmingly sensual. The hostess bows in our presence, as if to show some form of secret respect, then takes her leave.

Parker smiles, his lips stretched wide and welcoming. He's wearing glasses tonight - a pair of round, black frames that emphasize the color of his eyes and make their blue look even sharper. It pierces right through me. He's dressed in a pair of gray slacks that fit him all too well. With a black button-down and thin, black necktie, he's smart, dapper, and goddamn irresistible. The front of his hair is whipped back messily, making my mind wander... thinking about just how much messier I could make it. I work hard to keep myself from drooling. He radiates class and elegance, with just a sprinkling of naughty. I'm hopelessly intrigued.

And incredibly turned on.

"Iris," he coos, "so wonderful to see you." He takes both my hands in his, running his thumb along my knuckles. The feeling of our skin rubbing together makes me flush, and I wonder how the hell I'm going to make it through this meal without images of naked Parker dominating my thoughts. I clear my throat.

"Ahem, yes, hi, good to see you," I manage. *Get it together, Iris.*

"You look beautiful," he offers. I know he's fucking with me. The servers are dressed nicer than I am.

"Thanks," I mutter. "You wear glasses?" I'm a fucking idiot. Of course he wears glasses. He's wearing glasses. My skin smolders as embarrassment charges through my body, releasing a gush of wanton need.

"Ha," he chuckles, "yes, I do, sometimes." He releases the hold on my hands and takes his glasses off to inspect them. His eyes. They are intensely captivating - with glasses, or without.

Realizing we are awkwardly still standing beside the table, Parker motions for us to sit. I sink into my chair and clear my throat, resolving to ignore my deep carnal desire to rip Parker's clothes off and fuck him on the table.

"How was the rest of your day?" he purrs. His voice is hypnotic.

"It was fine," I sigh. "I work at a vet clinic. It was a bit of a busy day, but," I pause. "I got through it!" Triumphant. "What do you do?"

Before Parker has the opportunity to answer, a sleekly dressed, middle-aged man with just the right amount of gray speckled through his jet-black hair interrupts us.

"Good evening." He greets us with a friendly and polite smile. "Thank you for joining us here at Pearl. My name is Jeremy, and I'm pleased to be of assistance to you tonight. May I get you two started with a bottle of wine?"

"Yes, please. Whatever you recommend." Parker takes the lead.

"Brilliant, Sir. May I suggest the Pearl Vineyards Cabernet Sauvignon? Or, if you'd prefer, the Pearl Vineyards Chardonnay is excellent as well."

Both look to me for guidance. I decide to have them wait for a moment while I appear to mull it over. But the truth is, I'm not particularly picky when it comes to red vs. white; it depends on my mood. And my mood tonight is definitely red. Still, it's fun to make them wait.

"The red would be lovely," I decide at last.

"Excellent choice, Madame. I'll be back momentarily." Jeremy glides away from the table.

"The Cab Sav. I'm surprised. I took you for a Chardonnay type." Parker thinks he has me all figured out. Cute.

"I'll keep you on your toes," I tease. Parker smirks and raises the menu.

"Share an appetizer?" he suggests. His fingers wrap firmly around the thick leather binding of the menu. His eyes scan the options. He reads me the list of choices, and I listen intently to the beat of his voice. It's beautiful, a strong and certain symphony of sounds that sucks me right in. We decide on a plate of crispy Brussels sprouts and potatoes with maple bacon dip as well as grilled beef and vegetable kabobs.

Jeremy returns with our wine and delicately pours us each a taste before filling our glasses properly. The velvety first sips bring a welcome calm to my nerves.

First dates unfold in one of two ways.

Option one: The Interview. The Interview is exactly as it sounds - you ask your date about themselves, and they give you a list of credentials that qualifies them as a potential partner. You pry and interrogate, all in an effort to determine if this person is compatible with you, who you are, and what you want.

Option two: The Organic Connection. For those who are easygoing and patient, the Organic Connection is for you. This is a laid-back approach that allows the energy of the interaction to dictate the conversation, connection, and outcome.

I have not a single laid-back bone in my body; therefore, I always go into first dates with a list of questions I'm hungry for answers to. For me, though, these questions are not, *where do you see yourself in five years?* and *what do you think is the most important quality in a lasting relationship?* Instead, I focus more on questions like, *what are your preferred sexual positions?* and *name your top three favorite sex toys and why?*

Of course I care about the goals and dreams of the person I'm with. I want us to be compatible in our worldviews; however, sexual compatibility is equally important. And it's most often overlooked. If you ask me, the easiest way to discover a person's deepest, darkest self is simply by learning what they are sexually aroused by. Sure, I'm a bit of a hedonist, but I believe that discussions on sexual chemistry are a better predictor of relationship success than mundane conversations about likes and dislikes. It's forward, I know. But if Parker can't handle questions such as these, there's no hope for him in managing what I have in store for him later.

Given the cringeworthy unsexiness of our first encounter, I wasn't sure how Parker would handle getting to know me. But, to my surprise, my candor doesn't catch him off guard. He conquers everything I throw at him. He has a suave seduction about him that mingles effortlessly with my vibe. Our energies match, and the conversation flows like water. It's a happy surprise, but undercut with uncertainty. I feel my walls coming down, and that never happens on the first date.

Who the fuck is this guy? Where did he come from?

"Is there a limit?" Parker responds to my question regarding how often he enjoys fucking.

"Excellent answer," I reply, licking the final drops of my first glass of wine from my lips. His eyes trace my every move. I feel exposed, vulnerable, and undeniably aroused by his unwavering gaze. "What about fetishes?" I raise my eyebrows.

"What about them?" Parker exhales. He stretches his arms above his head. They are magnificently toned, the muscles straining against the cotton of his shirt. He folds his hands in front of him, and I imagine the grip of his fingers around my neck while he whispers depraved words into my ears.

I clear my throat. "Tell me yours."

"I prefer to show than to tell," he deadpans. I gulp.

My mind swirls with obscene imagery. With wide eyes, I return Parker's gaze, and I'm certain he can read my thoughts. That stupid smirk of knowing taunts me. He's memorizing my imagined indulgences, making note of my kinks. I study him.

"I have very eclectic tastes," he offers at last. "There isn't much I won't do. Or try." He reaches for the bottle of wine and refills our glasses. The earthy smell of the liquid pulls me in, and I take a hearty sip. "The limits of my consent are quite far-reaching."

"Me, too," I blurt out, too loudly and too eagerly. The sting of the wine (or perhaps my humiliation) burns in the back of my throat. "I mean..." I stumble. "I mean, I'm very experimental. Open to new things."

Parker nods weakly. "Well, then."

Our food arrives a moment later. I overfill my plate with potatoes and Brussels sprouts, then grab a whole kebab and stack it on top. I dig into my feast, not aware until several bites in that Parker has not only left the food untouched, but also has not moved his sight from my full mouth.

"You ought to grab some for yourself, before I devour the entire thing," I laugh, hiding my stuffed mouth and accompanying shame behind one hand.

Parker seamlessly reaches across the table and tucks a loose hair behind my left ear.

"You're beautiful," he breathes. I clench my teeth... and the ache between my legs. "I can't wait to fuck you." His eyes are locked on mine.

I almost choke on my potato.

I imagine it's Parker's cock.

Shit. Shit shit shit. I am so very, truly, fucked. I grab my water glass and chug back several gulps to clear my throat and my mind.

I regain my composure.

"Aw, poor you," I whine. "You'll have to wait. Unlucky for you, I'm not a fuck-on-the-first-date kind of girl." I force a smile, knowing beneath it that I am, very much, a fuck-on-the-first-date kind of girl. I'm not going to waste weeks getting to know someone who can't fuck me how I want to be fucked. I'm toying with Parker, and I'm eager to find out if he will play.

"Unfortunately for you, I usually get what I want." So sure of himself.

"As do I," I respond playfully.

"Well," Parker sighs, stretching his hands overhead. "It's started raining outside. You walked here, right?"

I nod, but wrinkle my eyebrows in confusion. How does he know I walked? And there isn't a single window near us. Today's forecast said nothing about rain - there's no way it started raining outside. But, I will admit, it certainly is getting damp between my legs.

"So, being the kind gentleman I am, I will offer you a ride home." I see where this is going.

"I suppose I have no choice but to accept your obscenely generous offer," I sigh dramatically.

"That's right. No choice," he echoes.

"Mm," I hum. I'm certainly enjoying this.

Parker signals for Jeremy, and he dashes over to our table. Parker requests a couple of boxes to pack up our nearly untouched appetizers, and Jeremy brings them over without delay. Parker chivalrously pays the bill, that sly grin still etched on his face.

"Thank you."

"It's been a pleasure... so far. I'm sure there's more to come."

"Is that so?"

"That's so."

The suggestive edge to our banter is doing me in. My skin breaks out in warm prickles.

Parker politely directs me toward the exit, and I lead the way out of the dining room and into the main entrance of the restaurant. He hops in front of me to open the door, and I glide ahead of him into the perfectly rain-free outdoors.

"This way." Parker guides me a few doors down to a large, black truck. Unlocking the passenger side, he opens the door and I hop into the cab. Inside, the truck is impressively clean with that new-car smell still apparent. I breathe it in. Parker jumps into the driver's seat and a new silence descends around us. It's not awkward or uncomfortable; in fact, it's quite the opposite. It's thick and full of promise. Parker clears his throat. "So. Where are we headed, Miss Iris?" His voice is strong and comforting. I pull it inside myself.

"My address is 112 Griantido Ave. I'll direct you."

"Yes, ma'am."

Parker starts the engine and maneuvers out of the parking lot. Unfortunately for me, I do not own a car and rarely drive in one. For this reason, I know my way around the city via walking paths and neighborhood shortcuts. This does not, as I learn in this precise moment, translate when, in fact, driving in a vehicle.

We get lost.

A twenty-minute walk can't be more than a five-minute drive, and yet, here we are, and I've managed to get us lost. Embarrassment creeps back into my chest, heavy and hot. I try to dismiss it, blaming Parker and his lackluster job of keeping his eyes on the road. I'm not even entirely sure how he managed to focus on driving when I felt his gaze drilling into me the entire time.

"Can't find your way home," Parker harasses, playing into it. "Tsk tsk tsk. Whatever shall we do with you?" My libidinous desire for him grows with every word. I glance over and sneak a look at his bottom half, finding relief and deep satisfaction in knowing that he, too, is finding enjoyment in our banter. He notices my gaze but I keep it steady, the bulge beneath his slacks growing as I part my lips.

Parker pulls over, and the tension is so thick that I struggle to breathe. I half expect him to pounce on me, our mouths joining together at last and our hands hastily exploring each other's bodies. I gape at him, my lips open and my eyes wide with lust. His arms prickle with goosebumps as his erection begs to be let free. He bites his bottom lip and lets out an immense sigh while scratching the back of his neck. He's working hard to hold back, I can feel it.

Admitting defeat in both my ability to navigate and to seduce Parker, I pull out my phone. I open Google maps and find directions home via car instead of my default setting via foot. We are only two minutes and a few left turns away from my apartment. I turn on the directions, allowing the satellite navigation to take the lead. Moments later, we pull up in front of my building. I'm on the second of three floors, sandwiched between old man Clyde on street level and newlyweds Martina & Harry on top.

"Home at last," I say dreamily. Parker cuts the engine, and the stark silence in the air is deafening. I hear my own labored breath, short and quick and dripping with want. "Care to walk me inside?" I suggest, my cheeks warm with the anticipation of what's to come. I can taste my heart in my throat.

"Of course, I wouldn't be a proper gentleman if I didn't ensure you get inside safely." He raises his eyebrows. "Let me get the door for you." He hops out of the truck and comes around to free me. I take his hand and step out.

His touch makes me jittery. It fires through me and buzzes under my skin. I can't hold on a second longer. I need to taste him.

I grab a hold of Parker's flaccid tie and pull him into me. At last, our lips meet and sink into each other, their softness melding together in a sweet kiss that's all our own. His hands find my hips, and the feeling of them on me is divine. I yank his tie harder, forcing his mouth closer to mine and deepening our kiss. I push my body against his, and my nipples harden at the closeness of his chest. Parker slides his hands down around to the back of my jeans and cups my ass. He spreads his fingers widely and squeezes, triggering a blissful inhale from me. I feel the outline of his cock against my belly button and crave its freedom. He moves his tongue into my mouth. I moan, drowning in lust. I loosen the grip on his tie and run my fingers down the center of his chest. His muscles are firm, and my fingertips trail along them, eager to explore their shape. Even hidden under a layer of clothing, Parker feels incredible. My hands move to his waistline, and I hover above the clasp of his slacks, toying with the button against my fingernails. How tempting it is to rip it off.

I break our kiss and shove him backwards. He stumbles a step or two, and I stare at him, drinking in his impassioned fervor. He looks wild, animalistic, and profoundly dissatisfied at the sudden end to our kiss.

"Good night, Parker," I pant.

He stands before me, stunned. The confusion on his face makes me want to laugh. I almost do. I love a good game. I bite the tip of my finger to hide my sadistic smile beneath. I blow him a kiss, then break out into a slow jog as I head for the apartment entry gate. I feel the soft locks of my auburn hair swinging behind me, brushing against the nape of my neck and arousing my already overstimulated skin. I shiver. Reaching into my back pocket, I feel around for my keys.

They aren't there.

My stomach lurches. How the fuck did I lose my keys?

And then I realize - congratulations are in order.

Well played, Parker. Well played.

I spin around to go after him, but he's already here, a smug grin plastered onto his face. He lifts his left hand and my keys dangle from it.

"I said I'd walk you in. Not to the curb," he jokes, shaking his head. A new wave of desire overcomes me. My cheeks flush as I feel the staggering humiliation of being beaten at my own game.

Parker waltzes past me and unlocks the entry gate. He directs me in first, following closely behind. So close, in fact, that I can smell the sweetness of his skin.

I begin up the stairs on the left, still sensing Parker trailing behind, when he suddenly slides his hand into mine and takes his place beside me. His touch once again sends a shock through my system, and I wonder if I will always be this responsive to his every touch.

I certainly hope so.

Up the first flight of stairs, we turn right and then right again, to the corner unit at the very end: my home, number 5. I dig into my pocket for my key again, only to foolishly recall the second I do so that I do not, in fact, have it.

With an arrogant smirk, Parker forges ahead to unlock the door. He might think he's outsmarted me, but we are only just getting started. The lock clicks.

Our moment is here.

I present my palm to Parker, demanding my keys back. He acquiesces. Good boy.

"Thank you for a great evening," I beam, proud and pleasantly entertained by the surprises of our date.

"Thank you, Iris. I have truly enjoyed the pleasure of your company." Parker shuffles to the side, and for a moment, I think he is going to leave. I'm not ready for him to, not yet. I'm not done playing.

"I appreciate you seeing me to my door," I blurt out, before he has the opportunity to turn his back.

"Ah," he hums, facing me directly. "Yes, to your door. But I do believe you had asked me to walk you inside. So," he nods at the door. "Inside." His voice is condescending, firm, and profoundly seductive. I hear my heartbeat in my ears.

He has me there.

I stand before him, our eyes locked. With the knob behind my back, I reach around and turn it, my eyebrows raised contemptuously. The door gives, and I slowly step backwards into my apartment. Parker closes in on me. The heat of his body sears onto mine. I can almost taste him, his skin just inches away. I hunger for it.

At last, we both cross the threshold.

Game on.

Four

B efore I even have time to shut the door behind us, Parker's mouth is back on mine. With desire at the forefront of his mind (and his pants), he thrusts his tongue between my lips. Our tongues dance together, passionately caressing and challenging one another. I push into him, squeezing my breasts against his chest. It's as though he's touching me without touching me and the tantalizing truth hardens my nipples under the chunky fabric of my sweater. The same is true for Parker's cock - firm and swollen against my middle. Arousal aches in my core. I run my hands through Parker's hair, captivated by the soft chaos of it. The way he smells - distinctly woodsy - and tastes - sweet and warm - hollows out my stomach. My center gushes with wetness.

Parker's hands seize my body, and his fingertips explore my shape. My neck, my shoulders, my arms, my chest, my stomach, my hips. His touch makes my breath ragged. His fingers linger on my backside, intentionally distracting me once again, no doubt. They run in circles along the back pockets of my jeans, and he firmly grips the bottom of my supple ass with wide fingers. An impassioned squeak escapes from my lips. Then his fingers move between my legs, where they glide from front to back. I pant under the sweet torment. The ache is almost too much to bear.

Clothes off. Now.

I loosen the knot on Parker's tie and slip it off effortlessly. I tackle his shirt next, but am instantly met with bitter frustration. I wrestle for what seems like eternity trying to undo the fucking buttons on his shirt. He seemingly finds enjoyment in my struggle, snickering at my failed efforts. At last, I have three of them undone and scratch my nails below the surface, dragging them along the muscles of his chest. His skin is magnetic. I yank the bottom of his shirt from his waist and pull up, forcing it over his head.

My eyes take him in. His body is defined, trim, and clean, with next to no body hair. His chest and arm muscles are gently defined; he has the body of a man who takes care of himself, but doesn't spend every free moment lifting at the gym. I hopelessly try not to drool.

I realize I've been gawking, and that Parker has been entertained in watching me do so. I raise my eyebrows at him and flash a sly grin. I bite my lip. I shift my attention to my own clothing and seductively undo the oversized buttons on my sweater to allow it to hang open. Peeking out from beneath is the white lace of my bralette, which immediately piques Parker's interest. We spend a moment lost in admiration, touching each other with nothing but our eyes. The profound intimacy of it captivates us. I shrug my sweater further off my shoulders, and it falls down my arms and lands behind me. My jeans are the next to go. I unclasp the button, pull down the zipper, and wiggle them off. Taking two steps toward Parker, I offer myself to him.

Parker's lips curl into a wide grin of approval.

"Beautiful."

I turn away from him to flash the white lacy thong traveling up between my rear cheeks. I imagine his smirk at the sight of my bare ass teasing him as I widen the distance between us. As I move past the kitchen, along the hall, and toward the couch, I hear the shuffle of clothing, and a belt buckle jingles. I fight the urge to glance over my shoulder to catch a glimpse of my prize. My face burns with the anticipation of it. I abruptly stop in the living room, sensing Parker closing in.

I hop onto the couch and bend my knees, then shift my feet beside me so that, turning the corner, Parker will get a peek at my exposed rear once more.

Exposed is right.

To my shock and delight, Parker has shed every ounce of clothing he had on. His erection is at last free, stretched out and greeting me from afar. My mouth hangs open - both in surprise at the length of his cock, but also in the primal hunger I feel to take it in my mouth.

"Wow."

"Wow, you," he echoes.

I push myself up from the couch and drop the straps of my bra down my shoulders.

"Help me with this, would you?" I beg playfully.

"My pleasure."

I bet.

I step toward him and swing around so he is once again faced with my backside. His fingers graze my shoulders before moving to my back, where, expecting him to unclasp my bra, his touch is lost. It immediately sends shivers through my body - desperate and wanton. I crave him - his mouth, his hands, his skin. My mind swims, too lost in lust to predict what will happen next.

WHACK!

Parker's hand fiercely smacks the tender skin of my ass. I yelp, feeling the immediate prickle and reddening of my sensitive skin. He lets out a raspy grunt.

"Fuck," I whine.

WHACK!

Again.

WHACK!

And then again. With each strike, the wetness between my thighs pools, growing in a desperate plea for attention. I'm barely able to catch my breath.

A stillness descends around us, the air silent save for our raw pants of desire. Then Parker's mouth finds my shoulder. He kisses and nibbles my neck, and I lean into him. His hands move to unclasp my bra, and my breasts finally spring free from their lacy confines. Parker immediately cups them, his hands overflowing with their generous size. His skin, although warm, feels cool compared to the heat released by my body from the spanking. I purr. Slipping off my thong, I step out of it and spin to face Parker once more.

It's his turn to examine my exposed body. His blue eyes drink me in, devouring every detail of my naked skin. The vulnerability of it is profoundly erotic.

My hands reach for his cock, and I finally feel the length of him in my grasp. I tease my fingers at his base, running my fingertips down and around to the fullness of his sack. His wanton exhale fuels me, propelling a surge of exhilaration through my body. I bend to my knees, eager to familiarize myself with Parker's lengthy appendage, but he pulls me up and instead cups my face in his hands. His touch is soft and delicate. Our eyes blaze into one another.

"You are truly stunning," he whispers.

"You don't look too shabby yourself," I joke in response. I lean into him, and our lips graze for a brief moment. The desire is thick and concupiscent. "So fuck me," I tell him.

He doesn't disappoint.

Parker tosses me back onto the couch and pries me open. He parts my legs with his arms, and I toss my head back, already overloaded with anticipatory pleasure. The first thing I feel is the warmth of his mouth as he kisses the insides of my thighs. Then his hands are on me, caressing the delicate skin of my folds. My entire body tingles. He falls into a rhythm of touch - soft then rough then soft then rough again and again. The constant back and forth in tempo nearly sends me over the edge. I squirm with need. At last his fingers enter me, sliding in easily, and he wiggles them inside, exploring the hidden details of my crevice. I wail and moan, writhing under his intimate touch. At last, his mouth finds my center. His tongue moves expertly over my clit, and I lose myself in unfathomable depths of pleasure. I'm dangerously close to release. I pull into myself and hold my breath in a desperate attempt to prolong the sweet bliss, but I'm powerless to stop it. My climax erupts in a giant wave, cascading over my entire body. I give into it, into him. I quiver as the delectable rhapsody of release floods through me. Parker groans in satisfaction as my inner walls grip around his fingers in the height of my orgasm. I pant, breathless and weak.

But he's not done.

"You feel fucking incredible," Parker gasps.

His fingers remain inside of me while his thumb, slick with my cum, slides over my mound. He rubs and flicks, forcing raw, feral yelps from deep inside me. Parker's satisfied hums echo in my ears; he's proud of the effect he has on me. I feel his cock, firm and ready, waiting impatiently against my leg. Warm, wet juices leak from its tip as he continues to finger my pussy. I reach for his length, eager to give it the thorough attention it deserves, but Parker won't allow it. He shifts his body and moves his mouth to my breasts, where he spends liberal time worshiping the tender skin around my nipples. Red speckles of heat decorate my skin as I moan.

Parker lifts my left leg into the air and removes his fingers from my folds. With my hip now raised, he rocks his fingers along my openings, front to back. A forbidden satisfaction gushes through me. His mouth returns to my clit, where he effortlessly brings me to the brink and over once more. I breathe in heavy exhales.

Parker continues to gratify me, intent on making me come until I ache. His fingers enter me again, and his tongue joins them in a lewd dance of persuasion. His other hand fondles my breasts, and he squeezes my nipples, rolling and pinching them between clasped fingertips. I squirm uncontrollably, the heavy stimulation of my most sensitive parts overwhelming my system. Wailing in agony, I instinctively tense my legs together.

Parker won't have that.

His resolve is doubled, and with a final lick and flick of his tongue at the sopping folds of my pussy, I come, my body trembling at his will.

I struggle to catch my breath. I roll onto my side, panting in ethereal ecstasy. Parker disappears for a moment, and my ears perk up at the clink of his belt as he sources a condom from the pocket of his pants. He rips the packet open and slides it onto his length. Revitalized by what's to come, I leap toward him. We enter into a deep, harsh kiss. I melt into him, my body teeming with endorphins. Parker nibbles on my bottom lip and reignites my inner fire. Our mouths lock in a passionate kiss, and I shuffle backward until I feel the soft fabric of the couch against the back of my calves. I balance on the armrest, steadying myself, and spread my legs, inviting Parker to enter me. His tip teases at my entrance. Moaning, I hunger for more. My fingernails dig into the thick skin of his back as I urge him forward. He is no doubt craving his release by now - he certainly is impressing me with his restraint. I pull on his hips, but he holds firm. I let out a heavy sigh, and in that moment, Parker plunges into me at last. He fills me to the brim, the deepness of his thrusts entering into a new part of me. I whimper. With a slow and tantalizing rhythm, Parker's torment is palpable. He grunts and moans, feral sounds coming from the back of his throat. I ache for his release as much as he does. I tilt my hips and work them against his core, throwing in the pull of a Kegel or two for good measure. He picks up his pace, and I throw my head back. My breasts bounce under the new momentum.

"Fuck, fuck," Parker lets out under his breath.

I throw my arms around him and whisper into his ear. "You can do better."

Immediately Parker retreats, pulling out and leaving me mournfully empty. Toppling off the couch, I turn to lean over the armrest. I shake my hips, provoking him with my bare ass just lying there, in front of him, begging for attention.

He bites.

WHACK!

My ass stings with the pang of his harsh blow. Fueled by venereal need, it burns more than the others that came before it.

"Fuck!" I yell.

"Is that better?" he asks, his voice thick with mockery.

His cock delves into me before I can utter a single word in response. Instead, I wail in pleasure as Parker's cock penetrates me from behind. I revel in the sensation of fullness as his balls knock into the back of my thighs with each thrust. Parker slaps my ass again, then grasps my tender cheeks in his hands. He digs his fingernails into my flesh and spreads my cheeks apart. Revealing my forbidden hole, he groans in approval and runs his thumb over it. My body becomes limp under his touch.

"Much better," I manage under my breath.

Heaving into me even faster, Parker plunges into my G-spot. The buildup is so immediate that I almost don't realize I'm coming until I already have. Parker calls out, his voice fierce and deep, as he finally reaches his climax, too.

Together, we collapse onto the soft give of my couch and ride the euphoric wave of our shared pleasure.

That was some of the best sex I've ever had.

And I've had a lot of sex.

Five

Parker is unexpected. His initial confidence and tenacity intrigue me, but also make me wonder if we will do nothing but butt heads. The power struggle seems imminent, lurking in the background, waiting to pounce on us.

But it doesn't.

He makes it easy. He laps up everything I throw at him. Our physical and sexual chemistries score freakishly high, of course. But, admittedly, there's an emotional magnetism between us that is undeniable. Parker is hypnotic. He asks me real questions about myself and gives me real answers about himself. We reach an emotional depth that's new to me, getting to know each other in a genuine way that I have never experienced before.

Who would've thought?

I devour every little detail about him and what makes him who he is. Like an addict, I can't get enough of him.

Parker had an interesting upbringing as the only child of adoptive parents. He had a healthy and positive childhood overall, but struggled to feel like he ever belonged in the life he was thrust into. His parents cared for him and have always loved him in the best way they know how, but there's always been a certain void - a spark that's missing from his life. My heart aches for him. I can only imagine the hardships he faced growing up in an adoptive home. The way I look at it, though, is that his parents *chose* him. They made a deliberate choice to bring him into their lives. That, right there, is the essence of love.

Feeling out of place, though, I can definitely empathize with.

Parker's parents are in their sixties now, still living in the same house they brought him up in the Inland Empire. He has love for them and appreciates them for the opportunities they have given him, but, like me, he left home at a young age to discover and craft his authentic self.

He moved into housing at UCLA for college, where he followed in his father's footsteps and studied finance with a minor in math. He's passionate about his job as a Senior Executive with Olahoni Financial, a startup that has made it big in recent years. He's ambitious in his career... and I would say the same is true for in the bedroom.

Expecting him to be a stereotypical nerd who reads the Wall Street Journal and does math puzzles for fun in his spare time, it's surprising to learn that he is also extremely outdoorsy. He spent a lot of time outdoors as a child, exploring the local hikes and riding his bike with his friends around town. He credits nature with keeping him sane; no matter what, he always feels at home when he's outside in the fresh air. He enjoys hiking in the mountains on the weekends and fishing with his buddies in the summer. The damn man even keeps his own garden.

As time passes, I come to the heavy realization that I really, really like Parker. The incredible sex is one thing, but it's the person he is - his true, most real self - that seals the deal for me.

I'm no fool. I know these are the beginnings of falling in love.

Goddammit.

Something about this one makes me want it to last.

Neither of us considers ourselves much of a cook, so takeout rapidly becomes our norm. Korean, Indian, Thai - we both like exotic, ethnic foods. Parker watches me eat, which makes me aware of how I eat, which makes me insecure of how I eat. I feel more exposed eating in front of Parker than I ever do fucking him. I begin to notice the sounds I make as I eat - lots of moans and chirps of content, how far I open my mouth - wide, how big the bites I take are - I would fail etiquette class. It shatters my defenses. Parker knows this, and still he observes me, the shadow of a smile on his face, reveling in my humiliation. While the shame burns in my cheeks, the slickness between my legs grows. It's all part of our provocative game.

On Fridays, we order in dinner and chase it down with a bottle of wine. With our veins and brains warm from good food and drink, our bodies meld together like putty. We sink into each other, wrap our legs together, and he slips into me, passionately thrusting as I moan under him. My heart beats fast, my vision blurs, and I give in to my innermost hunger. We become one, connected in our primitive desire for each other.

Parker and I get to know each surface of my apartment, fucking over and over all over it - against the kitchen counter, on the couch, in the shower, in front of the window overlooking the balcony. My personal favorite is being pushed up against the wall in my bedroom facing the mirror, with my wrists bound in his one hand and my neck in his other. It feels excruciatingly wonderful to experience such deep euphoria while simultaneously being unable to make any noise at all.

When we are satiated, Parker watches me as I change back into my clothes, carefully layering on each garment. He finds it just as enticing as undressing, he tells me, as I tuck my ample breasts back into a black, lacy bra. His eyes trace my every move. It invigorates me in the most exotic, intoxicating way.

I love it.

I hate it.

I hate that I love it.

I love that I hate it.

I become profoundly aware of a carnal longing I have for Parker. I want him; I crave him. At first, our schedules conflict, making it frustratingly difficult to indulge my needs. Gradually, though, work becomes more stable. We get the trainees attuned to the ways of Dr. Val's PetVet, and Parker and I find our stride. My schedule adjusts back to a predictable Monday through Friday. The weekends belong to us, and I vow to enjoy every moment of our effusive honeymoon phase.

It quickly becomes apparent that Parker and I make a great team. We aren't ashamed to share whatever is on our minds, and we are open and receptive to each other's thoughts and opinions. We aren't defensive or accusatory. We banter, of course. It's our signature kink. But it's never in a toxic way. We've established a rooting of respect that has allowed us to deeply trust each other. Besides, Parker knows what makes me tick, and trust is essential in what makes me tick.

Parker is observant and attentive. He can read me - what I'm thinking, what I need from him - and it excites me. It really excites me. But he can be intense. His stare - those piercing, blue eyes - drive right into me. He has an edge to him that always keeps me on my toes, and it feels good, and bad, all at once. At times he makes comments that leave me feeling simultaneously uneasy and aroused, that deep burning in the pit of my stomach, like there's something there, hidden just below the surface.

It's a baited hook I'm desperate, but reluctant, to bite. Yet, somehow, his intensity perfectly complements those darker parts of me.

Everyone has secrets. Parker and I are still fresh. We don't know everything about each other yet, nor do I expect us to. The mystery is part of the draw. But to say that what Parker and I have is a fully transparent, honest relationship is... well.

It's a lie.

Six

W e wake up late on a Sunday morning, lazing in bed and scrolling through all the things we had missed on our phones while we were busy worshiping each other's bodies the night before.

"Did we have plans for next Friday?" Parker asks me. "I mean the Friday after that. So, two Fridays from now."

I pause. Opening the calendar app on my phone, I check my schedule. "I work. But after that, no, I don't think we have anything set in stone," I answer. "Why?"

"I just got an email... a fun idea for a Friday night date." He hesitates. I wait for him to elaborate. "Seven or nine-thirty?"

"Seven is kind of tight depending on whether or not I need to work OT again next week. This week I'll be working until six-thirty every day. I have to help cover while we're training the newbies. Still."

"Okay, nine-thirty it is."

"You gonna tell me what this is, or just keep it to yourself, Mister?"

"Nah, I think you can wait," he says, smirking. "But when you find out... it'll be hilarious," he giggles.

"Uh, huh," I roll my eyes, elbow him in the side, and return my attention to my phone.

I have several texts waiting for a reply. I add *Secretive Thing with Parker* to my calendar for two Fridays from now at 9:30 p.m. Close enough for me to overthink what it could be, but far enough away for me to likelier forget about it.

It's the little things.

I exit the calendar and open my messages.

MOM
Hi honey! How was your week? Wondering if you
have some time to come by this week and take a look
at your boxes? I'm having your brother empty out
his as well. Moving day is coming up pretty quickly,
and I need these things sorted out. Thanks, honey!
I love you!

I take a deep breath and dig within me to find the patience to reply to my mom without sounding like a dismissive bitch.

ME
Hi mom! Week was good, pretty busy at the clinic.
Covering some extra shifts this coming week,
but the following, I can come by and go through my
boxes. Shouldn't take me long,
I don't think I have much left.

There, short and to the point. I sigh loudly.

My mom. How do I even begin to explain our relationship? I'll put it simply: we just don't get along. The most important thing in the world to my mom is being well-liked and accepted by those around her. She is always molding and changing herself and her personality in a desperate attempt to fit in wherever she can. Truth is, I guess I don't really know *who* my mom is, because she is always someone new. I resent her for it. With dad, who was an Imagineer, she became a Disney fanatic. When dad died, she met Charles. Charles was a big-deal real estate developer. Suddenly, mom was interested in interior design. When that imploded, Bill was it for her. Mom became mesmerized by all the latest tech that Bill, a computer genius, obsessed over.

My mom's need to be liked is repulsive to me. I cannot stand it. I've always thought of her as a relationship chameleon: a master of camouflage, shifting from one relationship to the next, constantly blending into her surroundings, desperate for affection, acceptance, and love. And she always coats everything in sugar.

As soon as I graduated high school, I knew I needed out. I got a shitty job where I worked ten-hour shifts making just above minimum wage until I could afford my own, shitty apartment. I was exhausted, overworked, underpaid, and living in a dive, but being independent was a high. Some years later, I had saved up enough so I could put myself through the vet tech program at Windsor College.

I take care of myself. I am accountable to myself. I am proudly me.

But.

As much as it agonizes me to admit it, sometimes, when I look in the mirror, I can see the insecurities that have shaped my mom staring right back at me. While I pride myself on being who I am, while I embrace what makes me different from everyone else, there are parts that I keep hidden. Secrets. And the deeper I fall down the rabbit hole with Parker, the more those secrets are nagging at me.

I know I need to be honest with Parker. And I need to do it soon.

My mom's latest squeeze is Willard, a retired pilot with a thirst for travel and adventure. He's been all over the world, and mom can't get enough of his stories. She listens to his retellings over and over again, eyes wide and hungry for more. Willard is filthy rich and, having the financial capabilities to retire early, has elected to do so. He entertained numerous possibilities for retirement: overseas, there was Croatia, Greece, Portugal; or he could choose an island in the Caribbean - there were so many options. Eventually, though, he settled on staying in the States, choosing Hawaii as his retirement landing pad, his reasoning being that it would be easier to visit his three adult children and growing brood of eight grandchildren. He and mom have been together for a few years now, around three, I think, so when he asked my mom if she would join him on this new adventure, of course she said she would.

The following weekend, her house was on the market.

Don't get me wrong, I'm not mad. I'm definitely not jealous. I'm irritated. Because virtually everything my mom does irritates me. Whoever she's with says jump, and she says how high? She isn't her own person, and that makes me very sad for her.

So, here she is, throwing out everything, or selling it, or putting it in an overpriced storage unit. My brother, Zach, and I are being forced to go through the boxes housing our childhood memories and treasures. Maybe I lied to my mom when I said I didn't have much to go through. The truth is that I left tons there when I moved out. More than I care to revisit. A trip down memory lane is not something I want to voluntarily indulge in.

Onto the next text.

VIENNA
Sad news... My uncle passed away last night.

I know it's late notice, but any chance you can watch
Sir Snowball this week? I have to fly out tomorrow for
the funeral. Should be back next Sunday xxx

Horrible. I type an immediate response:

ME

V! I'm so sorry for your loss.
Of course I can watch your man.
Here for anything you need. My condolences.
Thinking of you and your family. Sending love xxx

"I have to watch Vienna's cat this week," I announce. "Her uncle just died."

"Oh my God, I'm sorry. How tragic. What happened?" Parker asks.

"He's been battling lung cancer for a while," I explain. "He quit smoking ages ago, but you can't undo that damage." I hate cigarettes. Vapes. Chew. Any tobacco. Smokers disgust me. Such a stupid way to die, if you ask me. Downright preventable.

"Yikes. I'm sorry. Good of you to watch over her cat."

"Yeah, I'm happy to. I love him, his name is Sir Snowball. He looks exactly like his name sounds," I laugh, picturing his white, fluffy body.

I don't have any pets. I love animals, which is why I choose to work with them for a living. But, unfortunately, my line of work is a double-edged sword. Sure, I get lots of time with adorable and sweet critters. I also face the burden of working with those who are not in good health, and some who are on death's doorstep. It is an emotionally challenging job. But my love for animals outweighs the pain, even if I do feel those hard moments more intensely than I care to admit.

I open my calendar app. My week sure is filling up. I add in my cat-sitting responsibility and click on each day to review what's ahead:

Monday
all day clean up for carpet cleaners! Coming tomorrow!
8 a.m. - 6:30 p.m.: Work + OT - Training Robbie / Dog Walking
6:30 p.m.: Vienna's
7:30 - 8:30 p.m.: MMM BC @ Library

Tuesday
9 a.m.: Carpet cleaners - Leave door unlocked!
10 a.m. - 6:30 p.m.: Work - Training Robbie
6:30 p.m.: Vienna's
8 p.m.: Dinner with Ben? *To Be Confirmed*

Wednesday
8 a.m. - 6:30 p.m.: Work + OT - Training Robbie / Cat Duty
6:30 p.m.: Vienna's

Thursday
10 a.m. - 6:30 p.m.: Work - Training Robbie
6:30 p.m.: Vienna's

Friday
8 a.m. - 6:30 p.m.: Work + OT - Training Robbie / Dog Walking
P.M.: Parker leaves for Expo
6:30 p.m.: Vienna's
7:30 - 8:30 p.m.: FFN BC @ Library

Saturday
all day Parker Away
6:30 p.m.: Vienna's

Sunday
all day Vienna returns
P.M.: Parker Returns

I do have a lot on my plate. I have the tendency to overcommit myself; I guess it comes with having a lot of energy and love for being around people. And I'll admit: I'm a bit of a yes-woman. So maybe I wasn't stretching the truth when I told mom it's a busy week. I realize that next weekend Parker will be away on his trip to Nevada, and the thought makes me sad. I drop my phone down on the bedside table, pull up the soft, velvety cover of the comforter around my chin, and lean into Parker. I let out a deep breath and close my eyes.

Parker reads me so well. He mirrors me and puts his phone away, too. He pulls the blanket up around his previously exposed shoulders, and wraps his arms around me. We lay there, nestled together under the sheets, simply relishing in the moment. There's something so intimate about simply existing there, together, our bodies and hearts weaved, as we share our time in the stark silence.

Mid-day creeps up on us. We shower together, taking turns under the streaming, steaming water. Parker dumps a glob of vanilla-scented body wash on my loofah and the pungent, sweet aroma perfumes around us. He stands behind me and cascades the soapy sponge over my body, paying special attention to the sensitive skin of my hardening nipples. His touch is like a drug. I stretch my head backwards, humming, until my lips meet his. His free hand finds my slick, damp hair, and, pulling it down, he deepens our kiss. His tongue invades my mouth, and I open wider, eager for it. He tightens his grip on my hair, pulling it down still, until our lips break and my knees give way. I spin around and come face-to-face with his engorged cock. My tongue dances around the tip, teasing its sensitivity. I open wide and welcome it in. Its full length slides into my mouth. I rhythmically bob my head, taking it all the way into the back of my throat and out again. Occasionally, I add a tickle of my tongue against his sack, and Parker lets out an exasperated moan. I love to see - and hear - him enjoying himself. I feel his eyes on me the entire time. His watchful gaze takes in the sight of me, his muse, worshiping his manhood. I proudly take this cock deeper, letting it slide all the way in as far as it can go. I gag. Parker's lips twist, a primitive groan escaping them. It seems he and I both find immense pleasure in my deep-throating capabilities. The wetness between my legs pulses and I ache for Parker's touch. I move my tongue around his balls again, sucking on them and trying to fit the entirety of his swollen sack into my mouth. Then I bring his cock into my mouth once more, pushing it far into my throat, urging his length to glide all the way in. Parker's body convulses in pleasure, and I worry he's about to come.

We can't have that.

Not yet.

I quickly jump up and turn my back to him. I bend over and brace myself against the marbled shower wall.

Parker heaves himself inside me. I yelp as his erection fills me up. He holds my hips and gives several gentle thrusts, groaning in enjoyment. The slickness of my pussy is making it easy for him. I reach behind and dig my fingernails into the muscular flesh of Parker's ass. I adjust my position, pulling myself up slightly, and Parker's cock slides into place, caressing the most tender, responsive part inside of me. I quiver in my heightened pleasure. Parker chuckles, no doubt feeling the clench of my insides and the corresponding wave of shared satisfaction. He suddenly pulls himself out of me and lays two rough slaps on my ass, one on each cheek, making me leap. The heat of the water streaming down on us makes my skin even more tender. Parker sinks his fingertips into my reddened cheeks, forcing a rush of masochistic energy through me. He bends down and unexpectedly bites my ass. His teeth sink into my hot flesh.

"Fuck, ah! That fucking hurts!" I protest in short, labored breaths. It does hurt; an admittedly agonizing pleasure.

"I know," Parker says dismissively. "But I can't help myself. So delectable."

Something about Parker's obsession with my body, with how he can't get enough of it, with how he can't get enough of *me* - it's exhilarating. I give into it, our individual gratifications intertwined as one. He begins running his fingers back and forth between my legs, and I allow them to sink into my crevice. As he explores my opening with his hands, he buries his face into my ass. His tongue glides in and around my rear opening, and I instinctively throw my head back.

A primal energy takes over. I yelp and reach for something to brace myself on, but find only the slippery wall. It's hopeless. My body defenselessly shakes with each forbidden lick. Parker hums, relishing in the power he has over me.

"I'm going to fuck your ass," he breathes into my ear. A declaration, not a suggestion. I can barely see straight.

Parker reaches beside us for the bottle of silicone-based lubricant that resides in the shower niche. I use this momentary pause to my advantage, and once again pull Parker's cock into my mouth. I push my face into him as far as it can go, deep-throating his entire length and holding my breath for as long as I can. Parker releases a bout of soft, libidinous moans that make me proud of my distinct skill set. I choke, and Parker leans himself into me deeper before grabbing hold of a fistful of my hair and yanking me off of him.

"You're so fucking good," he exhales, pleased with me.

"I love having you in my mouth. I bet I'll love having you in my ass, too."

With my hair still in his fist, Parker pulls me in for a rough kiss. His tongue pushes into my mouth, and he bites my bottom lip.

"Bend over. Spread that ass for me," he demands.

I do as instructed, pulling my cheeks apart so my back hole is exposed. Parker globs the lube onto his length and teases my opening with his tip. The rush is intensely, terribly pleasurable. He works his cock into my ass, taking it slow so I can feel every inch of him enter me. I imagine how it looks from his perspective - watching his cock disappear into the most taboo part of my body. I'm breathless as he fills me up. My heart jolts in my chest. He moves his hips forward and pulls me into him. With his cock fully inside my ass, Parker lifts me against his chest and grips my breasts in his palms.

"You feel fucking amazing, Iris," he breathes. Incoherent in my aroused state, I whimper in response. "Look at you, taking my cock all the way into your tight little hole."

Parker's words ring in my ears and make me dizzy. Raw, wanton moans escape from my lips as he moves in and out of me, finding his rhythm. He quickens his pace, and my body is flooded with desire. His hands dance along the edges of my neck, thrusting me further and further down the rabbit hole. Then he wraps his fingers around my throat and gently squeezes. My body quivers. I hold my breath, tantalizingly close to the edge.

"I want you to come for me," he whispers. "I want to feel you come while I fuck your ass." Bucking his hips, he pummels deep inside my back hole, boring into me, thrusting without mercy. I squeal, my undoing imminent. "Come for me."

I do. There's no stopping it. I scream out as my body completely surrenders to the bliss of my release. My pussy clenches and I squirt, spewing liquid from its depths. I wail as my body trembles, weak in the empowerment of one of the best orgasms of my life.

"Ah! Fuck, yes!" Parker groans, feeling the muscles of my insides tense and squeeze. Panting, he continues to plunge inside of me until at last his own climax finds him. In one final movement, he pumps his hips and fills my ass with his cum. I feel like I'm floating, the sensation so overwhelmingly glorious that it carries me off into another world.

For just a moment, time stops, and nothing exists but the two of us in our shared euphoria. Parker gently slides out of my back hole and pulls me in close to him. I rest my head on his chest and listen to the pounding of his heart beneath his skin. My breath slows, and I meld into him.

What I would give to spend all our days in this lustful state.

But, reality does, always and eventually, catch up. I reluctantly peel myself from Parker's embrace and pull the glass slider of the shower open to hop out. I towel myself off from our rendezvous and pat my skin dry with a freshly laundered and fluffy, blue towel. I pay special attention to the tender skin of my rear, which is still red and hot. I wrap my hair in the towel and throw it on the top of my head. Meanwhile, Parker finishes up in the shower, running a bar of soap over his stomach and chest. I glance over to him with an enamored smile. He's been watching me, I realize, since the moment I exited the shower. My cheeks turn pink with the reminder that he always seems to have his eyes on me. It's profoundly invasive... and welcome. He has an insatiable hunger for me. The way he craves me - it's an addiction for both of us. It churns my stomach and thuds in my heart; a distinct combination of thrill and shame.

I love it.

I hate it.

I love that I hate it.

I hate that I love it.

By the time I finish combing through my hair (which is incredibly matted due to Parker's roughness with it), Parker has dried off, dressed, and returned a work call. He's still on the phone when I emerge from the bathroom and plop down beside him on the couch. To my surprise, he immediately pops up from his seat, gives me a *this will just be a moment* hand signal, and heads to the balcony door. He slides it open and steps out, then shuts it firmly behind him. I remain on the couch. With my stomach grumbling and a headache coming on from caffeine withdrawal, I really, really hope it *will* just be a moment.

It isn't.

Parker stays outside for probably close to twenty minutes. To distract my hunger, I open up the mystery novel I got out of the library a few days ago. The opening has me hooked, and I need to finish it up today if I plan on attending the Murder Mystery Monday Book Club meeting at the library tomorrow.

Yes, I'm so book-obsessed I attend a book club.

But I can't fight the burst of anxiety plaguing me as I wait for Parker to wrap up his call. I understand we are in the midst of tax season, but I don't see how he could possibly have a work call this lengthy on a Sunday. I drop my book down into my lap and inch to the other side of the couch where I hope to covertly catch a glimpse of him. He's pacing as he talks, wandering in circles, smiling, and even throwing his head back in laughter. This doesn't look like a work call. I decide that I can't wait any longer and walk over to the slider. Parker immediately sees me approach and raises his *one moment* finger again. I shake my head, done with being dismissed, and knock on the glass. I soundlessly mouth *let's go!* and head to the front door. I slip on my white converse and grab my blue sweater hanging on the wall. I'm about to very well leave without him, when at last Parker emerges from his hilarious work conversation on my balcony.

"Sorry, that took longer than I intended," Parker apologizes as he slides and locks the balcony door.

"It's almost one-thirty," I tell him, looking at my watch. "I'm starving. Come on, let's go eat something."

"Sounds good. I'm hungry, too. Just going to grab my stuff." He disappears into my bedroom and hurries to grab his overnight belongings and return them to the backpack they came from. I wait, tapping my foot. I feel tremendously put out.

Or maybe I'm simply hangry and this situation wouldn't normally bother me.

"I'm going to head across the street and grab us a table at River's Edge," I holler to him. "I'm leaving my key here on the hook. Lock up and meet me there, okay?"

"No need!" Parker bellows. "I'm ready to go!"

He meanders over to meet me at the door and leans in for a kiss. I'm so irritable I almost dodge it. I allow a quick peck.

"Let's go, now," I order.

"If it pleases you," Parker bows, ushering me out of the door first.

Seven

Across the street, I'm relieved to discover we've missed the lunchtime rush. River's Edge is a small, local haunt decorated in a quaint, cabin-esque manner. It's fairly new, having opened only a few years ago. I've come to know most of the staff and am pleased to see Sven is here today. He seats us near the back at a table overlooking the river. It's my favorite spot in the whole place - the view is stunning. Sven knows my vibe and immediately delivers a pot of coffee to our table. I am so appreciative that I almost reach over and pull him in for a kiss.

I greedily suck back my first cup of joe and am half done my second before I even look at the menu. Being a weekend, River's Edge honors all-day breakfast, and I decided even before we sat down that I'm going to take advantage of it. My eyes scan the brown, antique-looking menu. Hmm... what to have? When it comes to eating out, I'm not one to order *the usual*; I almost always get something different.

Variety is the spice of life, after all.

I decide on a big plate of Belgian waffles with triple berries and extra whip. Oh, and a side of scrambled eggs, please. Parker orders fish and chips. And more coffee.

"You okay, Iris?" Parker asks timidly. "I'm really sorry my call took so long."

"I honestly think I'm just hungry. And needed my caffeine fix," I explain as a guilty laugh finds its way out of my throat. I'm relieved now that my brain feels infinitely clearer after several cups of coffee. "I'm sorry for being impatient. You didn't deserve that."

"No, no. I realize I shouldn't have made you wait while I was on that call. You are my priority, Iris. Other things can wait." He reaches across the table and we join hands. "When I'm with you, that time is ours. That time is special to me and I could've - and should have - finished that call with Laura later."

"It's okay, really," I brush it off. I take a moment to digest what Parker has just said to me. "Actually," I begin, gathering my thoughts (and my courage), "I want to say thank you. Thank you for communicating this to me. This sounds really pathetic, but in all my previous relationships, never has my partner taken a moment to discuss things with me like this. I'm sorry I was grumpy about your work call. And while I appreciate that you view our time like that - I do, too - I also understand you have a life outside of our relationship. I know you have commitments to your job. I guess it's just how you dismissed me, saying you'd just be a minute. I don't think it's wrong of me to interpret that as you'd be wrapping up soon. But you didn't. I waited for close to thirty minutes. So, I guess it wasn't that you took the work call so much as you kept me waiting and misled me about how long it was going to be." I'm droning on, but Parker doesn't interrupt. Not once. Not to try to explain himself, or challenge me in the validity of my feelings. He listens intently to my every word, his eyes following the movement of my lips, his hands gently cradling mine. "This is kind of a ridiculous example of it, but I guess above all else in a relationship, I value honesty. Even if it's honesty I don't like. I'd rather it be true and upsetting than false and convenient. I need an honest partner."

Parker's eyes shine bright in the midday sun pouring through the window. A smile spreads across his cheeks, and he breaks into a cheery grin. I can't help but mirror it.

"Iris. This is everything I want, too," he assures me. "This is still fresh. We are still getting to know each other. It doesn't happen overnight. I found you. That's the first step. I want to learn everything there is to know about you. Don't hold anything back."

I shudder. Did I really just call Parker out for being dishonest when I am holding back an enormous part of myself from him? What a hypocrite I am. I feel exposed - it's as though Parker can see right through me. My chest tightens and the weight of my secrets bear down on me. I should reassure him, but my words are caught in my throat.

I'm a fake.

"And I want to do the same," he adds. "We'll get there. I know we will. In time. And every moment we have together is building the path. And that is a real treasure to me."

I melt. His words, his mannerisms, his persistent stare - somehow everything about Parker dives into me and disintegrates my defenses.

"Parker," I whine in lust.

"Communication is hard. Trusting someone to be receptive to all you have to say means being vulnerable. But I'm here for it. I'm here for you." He leaves his seat and scoots onto my side of the booth. His mouth finds my ear. He leans in, his whisper hot and full. "I have secrets, too," he promises. "I can't wait to share them with you."

I let out a stammering exhale, and, with it, heat cakes my skin. A throbbing wetness hits between my legs. There's a darkness to Parker. It's intriguing, provocative, and tempting beyond measure. I wrap my fingers in the loose curls of his hair and sink my lips into his.

Our kiss grows, beginning light and slow, then deepening. The passion is potent. It seeps into me; I can taste it. The desire between us is heavy and unrelenting. I am desperate to consume every ounce of it, ravenous for Parker and all that he is. As our tongues dance together, I realize that I am, without a doubt, positively captivated by this man.

Three o'clock hits, and the sadness creeps in. Our time together is coming to an end. Our romantic bubble of infatuation is about to burst, soon to be replaced by the dark hole that is adult drudgery.

This weekend has been a big one for me and Parker. The honeymoon phase, while still very much alive, is shifting. Those pockets of reality are weaving themselves into our relationship. We discuss the week ahead, scrolling through our calendars in an effort to find mutual availability. It's about as unromantic as it gets. Parker and I are business partners, working to set up a meeting we can both attend. I don't like the way it feels, but modern life is excessively committed so we truly have no other choice.

It's partly my fault, partly his. We both stretch ourselves too thin.

I'm pleased that our schedule remains pretty consistent as of late: Tuesday nights, Friday and Saturday nights, and some of Sunday. But this week, I'm planning on dinner with Ben on Tuesday night, and Parker reluctantly reminds me that next weekend is his Sporting Convention in Vegas. I pout in protest. Parker nibbles on my puffed lower lip and slides his hand along the back of my neck. I fall under his spell. Like putty in his hands, he could ask anything of me and I would obey without hesitation.

"Don't be so sad, my sweet pet," he purrs.

"But I'll be so lonely without you. How will I have my needs met while you're away?" I whine, leaning into our game. I can think of a couple of ways. But I can't mention them. Not yet.

"Hmm..." Parker hums. "I have an idea about that."

Eight

Time flies when you're having fun. When you're not, time crawls slower than the pace of a geriatric snail. That about sums up the week I'm having. Monday, although a blur of busy, drags on and on. And on. This is probably due to the fact that I hate cleaning, and I have to make sure every carpeted surface of my apartment is spotless for the carpet cleaners. There is also the unpleasant conversation with my mother, in which she further threatens her impending move in an effort to guilt me into seeing her. I tell her I'll stop by for a quick breakfast before work Thursday. I'm dreading it.

I do finish my book for the book club meeting, but my Monday disappointments continue when I learn that Maisie, the librarian who typically hosts the meetings, has been officially replaced. Maisie has been MIA for several months now, so it's not a surprise, just a letdown. Our new host, Gemma, explains that Maisie is instead hosting the Friday Fright Night Book Club discussions, due to a complex adjustment in scheduling. Unfortunately, I almost never go to those. Horror isn't my favorite genre, and, well, Fridays. I usually have social commitments.

I love reading, and books are my truest companion. But I am willing to admit that part of the draw in attending the Monday meetings was because of Maisie. She's close to my age, and, from the numerous discussions we've had after club meets, we share many of the same interests. Especially in books. Maisie is a joy to be around. She's polite, playful, excellent at directing discussions, and incredibly insightful. She also has an edge to her that I find very alluring. Not to say there's anything inherently wrong with Gemma. She's perfectly fine, if not a solid twenty years older than me and infinitely more severe.

The only thing I am looking forward to this week is dinner with Ben, but, in usual fickle fashion, he delays. He gives me a quick call in place of our dinner date, solemnly swearing that we will gorge ourselves at Giuseppe's next week. I can tell from this tone that he's going through it, so I come to terms with our canceled plans. He spends most of our call venting about computer programmers and how lazy they are, what with cutting corners and writing shitty code that inevitably breaks the entire system and is Ben's unfortunate job to repair. I understand about 1% of it. Still, I voice my unwavering support for his upset, reassuring him he is totally justified in his anger toward those incompetent tech assholes. He briefly asks me how I'm doing with my new *boy toy*, and I go pink.

I suppose I can't rightfully say that looking forward to seeing Ben is the only light in the dark workweek tunnel. Spending time with Sir Snowball (or Snowy, as I affectionately call him) is a true treat. His impossibly soft, pure white fur provides comfort beyond measure. He loves to be groomed, so I'm sure to give him a nice brush during every visit. I'm certain I get as much enjoyment out of it as he does. You get what you give.

Vienna lives in a cozy studio apartment a quick five-minute walk from mine. I'm glad for our closeness, considering how exhausted I am from the long hours I'm putting in at work this week. I think back to a year ago, when Vienna lived almost forty minutes away, and feel grateful for now having to stroll just down the street. I'm in a crabby mood and need to snap out of it.

Vienna and I have a unique relationship. We met under strange circumstances, each of us dating one of a pair of best friends who shared an apartment together: the infamous Nick Daily and Greg Warners. Vienna was already seeing Nick for a few weeks by the time I entered the scene. It was the middle of the week, and I sauntered into the bar down the road after work, aching for a fix. Greg quickly sought me out, our eyes making contact from the table he sat at with both Nick and Vienna. He approached me with swagger, his crooked grin sucking me in right away. He ordered me a stiff Jack and coke and said all the right things. I've always considered Greg to be a certifiable expert when it comes to hitting on women. Or, maybe more likely, it was my desperation for a hookup that made him seem so suave. His green eyes were my weakness. Staring into those, I would agree to anything. Drinks led to kissing, kissing led to making out, and, after a short Uber ride back to their place, making out led to a very steamy sexual exchange.

Dating Greg was different. Different than any other connection I'd had before it. Our relationship was unconventional, to say the least, because dating Greg was a lot like dating Nick. And Vienna. We were a fierce foursome. It was fun while it lasted. A lot of fun. Unfortunately, though, at that time in my life, I wasn't very good at committing for longer than a few months. I wasn't ready to. Sometimes I think back to things with Greg, and Nick, and Vienna, and wonder, had the timing been different, could that have been everything I ever wanted?

Regardless of how things ended, Vienna and I really got on, so we stayed in touch. We wouldn't see each other often, given how far away she lived, but in the months since she relocated, we've been spending more time together.

Vienna travels a lot for work as a brand consultant for KeyFit, a fitness products and accessories company. I've become Snowy's second mom, watching after him while she's away. I have a key to her place, even.

My friendship with Vienna is a win-win.

I check my watch and realize it's closing in on 8:30 p.m. I'm drowsy and peckish, so I decide to order delivery and lay down beside Snowy for a quick rest while I wait for food to arrive. In addition to having the softest cat in the universe, Vienna also has the most luxe bed. I sink into the plush of her white comforter and pull up Snowy's cat bed next to my chest. I pet him slowly until he settles into a neat ball of poof. I rest my hand on him, my fingers sinking into the warmth of his heavenly softness.

I doze off.

It's always in my lightest state of sleep that I have the strangest, most erotic dreams. They almost always involve a beach, beach house, or summer home, and a large orgy composed primarily of men. Unlike my preference in reality, I am usually the observer, although occasionally I play the role of a willing participant.

This time, I'm a guest at the home of a seemingly important and grossly affluent woman (I assume based on her flowy, sheer-tinged clothing, high heels, and hugely impressive house). She is tall and blonde, with a booming voice that cuts through the background chatter of the guests gathered in her home. The house is enormous, as you expect all rich homes to be, but hers is unique in its modernistic lack of, well, things. In fact, there are virtually no permanent fixtures, furniture, or decorations anywhere at all. The house is bustling with people of various talents - hairdressers, makeup artists, wardrobe stylists, photographers, directors - all of whom bring their own chairs, tables, and light setups, as though to create their own temporary workspace within the home. The house smells distinctly of hair spray and mint chocolate chip ice cream.

The woman has gathered a group of a dozen or so recruits, of which I am one. I wonder if we were all auditioning for a role in an adult film, or maybe we are hoping to be the next big star to come out of whatever business it is that this woman is running. I'm at the waxing station, having my pussy ripped clean of hair by a man who has no tact and a distinct lack of care for the condition of my vagina after he's done with it. I'm eating a cookie, and chip my tooth on a walnut as Mr. Couldn't-Care-Less yanks a strip of wax from between my lower lips. I go on next to the dressing area, where a woman identical to Effie from *The Hunger Games* makes me her Barbie doll. She wraps me in strips of ragged fabric in such a way that I look more like an Egyptian mummy than a sex goddess. Having had enough of these shenanigans, I resolve to complain to the woman in charge, when I hear footsteps approaching Vienna's front door and shoot awake.

I'm a dreadfully light sleeper.

I pop up, fumble in my disoriented state, and nearly flatten Snowy. I mumble heartfelt apologies as I struggle to settle back into the present. I blink rapidly as Snowy disappears into the safe space of his living room cat condo. I open the apartment door and grab the white, plastic *THANK YOU* bag waiting for me on the porch. I grunt. I should've ordered a coffee, too.

I carry the bag into Vienna's modest kitchen, where I set it down on the beige, tiled countertop. Before I even consider tackling the army of knots keeping my dinner hostage within the bag, I pour myself a large glass of water. Still in a tizzy from my dream, my mind is foggy and disconnected. I gratefully chug the water down, finding the slick coolness of it immediately hydrating.

The bag is triple knotted, and I cannot for the life of me untie it. I give up and grab scissors out of the knife block. I slice my way through the plastic to release my yellow curry and jasmine rice. Dumping a little of each into a bowl, I chow down, the distinct spice of the curry rousing my brain. Snowy has decided it's his dinner time, too, and is munching loudly on his kibble on the floor beside me.

I send Vienna a check-in text to let her know that Sir Snowball has been sufficiently cuddled and fed. I spoon the last few scoops of dinner into my mouth, slurp down one more glass of water, and decide it's time to head home. After a few final scratches under Snowy's chin, I gather up my things and head out.

I'm just about to walk in the door of my apartment when my phone rings.

It's Parker. God, I miss him.

"Hey, you," I sing.

"Hi, beautiful." His voice gets me every time. "How'd your day go?"

"Well, I'm just getting in from Vienna's. This week is long."

"Tell me about it."

I sigh. "How was your day?"

"Pretty ordinary. Nothing to report."

"Hmm," I hum, feigning interest. "Oh, I wanted to ask you. Tomorrow morning..." I realize I've started talking before I've even allowed my brain to process the repercussions of the scenario I'm about to suggest. Fuck. Fuck fuck fuck.

"Tomorrow morning?" Parker echoes into the sudden silence.

Shit. Do I? Well, I've already started. I don't really have a choice now.

"Tomorrow morning. What time are you going into the office?" I ask, stalling for time.

"Well," Parker lets out a weak laugh. "I'm pretty senior now. I can go in whenever I want."

He sees right through me.

"It's just that..." I falter. "Well, any chance you could get away for an hour before you go in?" Parker is silent, listening intently. "My mom guilt-tripped me into having breakfast with her. It would be a lot less awful if I had you there. With me. To, uh, be there with me."

This is a first. I've never brought home someone for my mom to meet. I haven't been in the kind of relationship that warrants a meet-the-parents, nor do my mom and I have that kind of meet-the-parents relationship dynamic. But, with Parker, it's different. Even though we've been seeing each other for just a few weeks, I feel safe with him. Understood. Accepted.

And in love.

There, I admit it. I'm in love with Parker.

Here's my heart. Please, don't destroy it.

"Of course. I'd love to have breakfast with you and your mom tomorrow," he accepts, matter-of-fact. It sends a mixture of relief and anticipatory anxiety through me. "Iris, thank you for this. It means a lot to me."

Why are tears forming at the corners of my eyes? Stop. STOP. I sniff.

"Oh. Okay, great!" I reply, gulping back my emotions. "Meet at my place here around eight-thirty? I know it's early but I work at ten."

"No problem. Looking forward to it."

I am not.

Nine

At exactly 8 a.m., my phone rings. Parker is early. Quite early. I've just gotten out of the shower so I rush to throw on some clothes, then race down the stairs to open the gate.

"Hey," I say breathless in my hurried state.

"Good morning." He offers two bouquets in my direction; one of roses, the other of lilies. My mouth drops open. How does he know lilies are my favorite? I swear this man is custom built for me.

"Parker! What? You didn't need to. This is... too much." He ushers them toward me, and I take them from his outstretched hand. My wrist buckles under the weight. The bouquets are full and bright and probably cost a small fortune each. "They are absolutely stunning." They are.

Parker follows me up the stairs and back into my apartment.

"I couldn't show up empty handed," Parker insists. "One for you, one for your mother."

"Thank you," I gush, leaning in for a grateful kiss. I intentionally keep it light and quick, for I know otherwise we would be naked and fucking in under thirty seconds. I place the bouquets on the kitchen counter and dig through my cabinets in search of a vase.

"You're most welcome." Parker wanders over to the couch and sits while I fiddle with the flowers. "I brought something else, too," he reveals mysteriously.

"Did you now?" I raise my eyebrows, intrigued. I drop the lilies into their vase and fill it with water. I bring them over to the coffee table and position the gorgeous arrangement down in front of Parker. "They're so beautiful. This was really thoughtful of you, Parker. Thank you so much." I take a seat next to him and push my body into his. We kiss again, and Parker pulls me in close. Desire spikes through me.

I slip my hands along the band of his pants, fighting against the tightness of his belt to free his tucked button-down. I slide my nails along the soft skin of his exposed back. Parker moans, and I push my claws in deeper. His mouth is on my neck now, and he nips at the tender flesh along my throat.

"Fuck," I gulp, unraveling. I can't fight it. I can't fight him.

"Ready for your little surprise?" he whispers into my ear. His tongue flicks my earlobe.

"I thought *this* was my surprise," I reply, coy, reaching my hand to cup his generous bulge. He did arrive much earlier than I told him to, after all.

"Tsk tsk tsk. Not yet, you naughty thing," he scolds. He wags his finger at me and pulls his body away from mine.

This surprise had better be good.

"Alright, what is it?" I ask, more than a little annoyed that my advances have been dismissed.

Parker nods toward the coffee table. Distracted by the flowers, I failed to notice that Parker has placed a brown paper gift bag there as well. With a pleased grin, I eagerly pull out the red tissue paper and reach inside. Parker's wide-eyed, expectant stare traces my movement. He's waiting for my reaction. I raise my eyebrows. My hands grip a box inside, and I pull the mystery item into view: a sleek, black vibrator.

I inspect the box, turning it over in my hands.

Smart Pair with iOS or Android devices
Intimacy from afar
Scan to download our Play Away app!

This isn't your average toy. A very satisfying gift indeed.

"It pairs to my phone through an app," Parker tells me, his voice precise. "So... no matter where I am," he breathes, "I can play with you." A pool of wetness floods my center.

"Oh, can you?" I smirk and let out a schoolgirl giggle, trying hopelessly to hide my arousal.

"It should be all set up," Parker explains. "But you can't use it yet!" He grabs the box from me as I try to slide the lid off. "I want to try it out this weekend, while I'm away." My face flushes as the sudden, absurd realization of what he is proposing sinks in. Excitement simmers inside me.

"You want to play while you're at your expo," I deadpan. Parker nods. I tuck my lips between my teeth to try to keep from breaking into a wide grin. I clear my throat. "Don't you think we ought to test it out before you go?" I suggest, taking the control back. I really have to stop letting Parker catch me off guard. "I mean, just to make sure it works. Ahem. Properly." I cough. My cheeks burn as heat cloaks my skin.

"No."

Firm.

And unacceptable.

I playfully reach across him to grab the box back. He grins, amused at my pathetic attempt to overtake him.

"Come on," Parker ushers, getting to his feet and slipping the vibrator box back into its brown bag. He glances at his watch. "Your mom is expecting us soon."

I scoff. Where does he get off being all concerned with punctuality?

Parker stands up and re-tucks his shirt. Dejected, I return to my room and rifle through my closet for something to wear. I decide on a pair of black jeans and maroon, scoop-neck Henley layered on top of a basic black bra and panties. I lay them out on the bed and peel off my oversized navy tee and pajama boxer shorts. Parker watches me intently from the doorway, leaned against it with his arms crossed. I turn to undress within his view, wiggling my hips and glancing seductively over my shoulder as I drop my shorts. I am absolutely trying to provoke him. But, like a statue, he stays put with an entertained and enduring smirk.

"Get dressed," Parker demands. "I won't tell you again."

Oh, so we're onto threats now. I let out an infuriated exhale and get dressed speedily instead of taking it slow as Parker prefers - an empowering *fuck you* to his cold shoulder.

Knowing what awaits me this weekend makes our lack of a sex session before breakfast even more maddening. I'll be on edge during breakfast, no doubt about it.

I lock up my apartment and start down the street. Parker calls me back, pointing to his truck and offering to drive. I shake my head and remind him that driving means signing up for an extra hour of time with my mom, since the walk to my childhood home is around thirty minutes each way.

"Get in the car, Iris," he demands. "Don't make me force you."

"Fine," I concede. Even though a big part of me does want him to force me. My stomach flutters.

On the drive over, my world tips sideways. Instead of preparing Parker for what he's about to walk into, I become quiet and guarded. I grow increasingly selfish as we draw closer, worrying about my own self-preservation rather than about how Parker will fare against my mother. What was I thinking inviting him? I can handle my mom's guilt trips, but it doesn't feel right dragging Parker into this.

"Why don't you just drop me off?" I blurt.

"Drop you off?" he asks, puzzled.

"Yeah, I mean, just drop me off. You don't have to come. You shouldn't come. I haven't told my mom about you. She doesn't know I'm seeing anyone. And I'm not sure this is a good idea. It's not you... oh, God, that sounds so cliché, but really, it's not. I want you to come, but - oh, fuck. Oh, shit. I'm not feeling good. I'm so out of sorts right now. Just pull over right here. My mom's house is around the corner. I'll walk. Yep, right here. Just stop the car, okay? I'm getting out now. I'll call you later. I need to go. Oh, God, I'm sorry!" It spills out of my mouth like word vomit. I fling my body out of the car door as Parker pulls up to the curb. I take off in a jog, my brain swirling with embarrassment. But the farther I get from Parker, the worse I feel. The regret rises in my throat. I gulp and try to push it back down, but my anxiety defeats me. I lean over a garbage can overflowing with little baggies of dog shit and barf my guts out. My mouth fizzes with the taste of stomach acid and last night's Thai. I wince, disgusted with myself.

Parker appears and rubs my back. "It's okay. You're okay," he coos in my ear. His gentle voice burrows into my brain. This moment reminds me too much of my twenties, when Ben would comfort me after a long night of drinking and a rough morning of regret. Shame overwhelms me.

"Hey," he mutters. "You're okay." Smooth. Reassuring. Loving.

"I wish you didn't see this," I admit, my voice thick with remorse.

"Iris. You mean everything to me. I'm here for you through all of it," he promises. "Even barfing in a garbage can before nine a.m." He chuckles to lighten the mood.

It doesn't work. Somehow my stomach drops so low inside me I feel like it's going to fall right out. My heart vibrates in my chest. I want to cry and laugh and smile and kiss Parker all at the same time. I let out a low grunt. I slump down beside the wiry exterior of the garbage can in defeat.

"Any chance you have an Altoid?" I beg, my voice pitiful.

"Sure do. Be right back." He dashes off to his truck and returns with the familiar metal container. He opens the lid and I gratefully grab two. I pop them in my mouth. The potency of the mints somehow calms me, steadying me after my spiral.

"Feel better?" he asks, crouching down beside me. His hand is on my thigh, his touch electric.

I shrug my shoulders. "It's just a lot - things with my mom. With Willard. With the whole move and everything."

"I get it. Family stuff is hard. It's complicated. Not really easy for someone on the outside to comprehend. I'm here for you, though. I want you to know that. When you're ready, that is. We can do things at your pace," Parker reassures me. "I'm here for whatever you need - Altoids and all!"

I laugh in spite of myself. Tears gather behind my eyes, but I snort them back. I've already barfed in a public trashcan - let's not add sobbing beside said garbage pile to my list of today's early-morning accomplishments. I push into Parker and sink into his chest. He wraps his arms around me and squeezes, activating a charge of nurturing comfort that penetrates my every molecule. I breathe deeply, wafting in the fumes of pine-scented soap still lingering from his morning shower. For a brief time, reality disappears and it's just me and Parker, together, in this shared moment of closeness.

It's a kind of intimacy that couldn't be clearer: this is love.

Fuck. I have to tell him.

Soon. Very, very soon.

I owe it to him.

But, more than that, I know I owe it to myself.

And just like that, the present returns. Parker helps me up, and we wander back over to his truck. He opens the cab and reaches behind the front seat to grab me a spare bottle of water. The refreshing sting of the mints travels down my throat with each sip.

Exactly one minute past nine, my watch vibrates with an incoming call from my mom. I'm late for our breakfast date. I shake my head and answer the phone.

"Hi mom," I sigh.

"Hi honey! Almost here? Willard is out grabbing the pastries, and I've just finished the scrambled eggs. They can't sit out for long or they'll get soggy, you know how it is. Oh! And the sausages have been done for a while now too, so I hope you're close by. We can expect you soon, then?" she pauses, finally allowing me to speak.

"I was on my way, but, I'm sorry, mom, I'm going home," I blurt out, talking quickly so as to be able to say my piece before she dominates the conversation again. "I just threw up on the way over. I'm not feeling well."

"Oh, Iris! That's awful! A stomach bug? Oh, it could be the flu. Gina's son's family had a bad bout of something rip through their household. Martha had said her daughter's entire family got a really bad stomach bug and everyone was in bed for three days! Well, in bed but also in the bathroom, you know how it goes with stomach bugs. Truly awful, what a horrible thing to have to go through. Let me know how you're feeling tomorrow. I hope you'll be able to get some good rest and be feeling better soon so you can go through those boxes next week like you promised!"

I narrow my eyes. "Okay, mom, will do. I have to go. I'll talk to you later."

"Yes, of course. Take care of yourself, honey! Willard wishes you well, too!"

"Thanks, mom. Bye."

I call into work, leaving a very flustered-sounding Maria sounding even more flustered knowing I won't be coming in. Parker drives me home and tucks me into the soft sheets of my bed. He kisses my forehead, tells me he'll call me later, and leaves to begin his workday. Within minutes, I fall into a deep sleep.

Not a single erotic dream to be had.

It's a restorative disappointment.

Ten

I sleep until late afternoon, get up to drink water and go to the bathroom, then snuggle back into my mound of blankets for the remainder of the day. Just after midnight I wake up again, feeling infinitely better. My brain is still a blur, but my stomach has settled and my nerves have calmed. I dig my phone out from my tote bag and see several missed messages from Zach, mom, Ben, Vienna, and Parker. There are also two voicemails from Dr. Val's - it's poor Maria begging me to come in even if I feel an ounce better. I can't decide if it's comforting to have that many people checking in on me, or debilitating to have that many people nagging for my attention. Succumbing to the latter, I drop my phone onto the bedside table and return to my blanket cave.

The next morning, I wake up obscenely early. It's just before five, but I feel incredible - renewed, rested, revitalized. I may as well have spent an entire day at the spa. Shocking what a good, solid sleep will do for your body, mind, and soul. I hop out of bed, brush my teeth, and lather my body in the alpine-scented soap Parker left in the shower. I breathe it in, missing him desperately.

Once dressed in my star-patterned, navy scrubs, I decide to tackle my phone. I call Parker, yearning to hear his voice.

He doesn't answer.

Disappointed, I sigh and text him instead.

ME
Good morning!
Feeling so much better today.
Not sure what that was.
Thanks for taking care of me xx
See you tonight before you go?

Next up is Vienna.

VIENNA
Hey girl, just checking in! Thanks so much
again for taking good care of Sir Snowball!

Love the pictures you're sending! I appreciate
you xxx

I type up a quick reply.

ME
Happy to do it! He's been such a snuggly boy!
I'll head over this morning just before
work for kibble and cuddles.
You doing okay? Sending hugs

Funerals are no fun - I would know. I hope Vienna is holding up. Her
two older sisters are there with her, so I'm sure they're taking good care of
her. The three of them are very close.

Next, I send a quick message responding to Ben's request for my
opinion on potential outfit options for his date with Leo this weekend.

ME
The purple, duh!

I let my mom know that I'm feeling much better, which I immediately
regret. If only I had thought it through, I could've stretched this thing out
a little longer and avoided the whole *go through your boxes, Iris!* ordeal.

Zach has sent me a digital invitation to Molly's art show at the end of
next month. I instinctively type out a response declining, then promptly
delete it and force myself to send a more agreeable reply. My finger hovers
over the RSVP options for a moment before I tap the *maybe. I'll do my best
to make it!* I type out in the comments.

Just then, a reply from Parker pops in.

PARKER
Glad to hear it. Take it easy today.
Picking the guys up then heading out around 6:30.
I'll swing by to give you a goodbye kiss on the way out.
xxx

I blush. A thousand responses run through my head, but I inevitably
decide on the simplest one.

ME
xxx

Snowy doesn't disappoint in his snuggly softness this morning. He rubs his nose into my leg and his soft fur tickles my bare ankles. I give him an extra scoop of wet food as an apology for missing him yesterday due to my mystery illness. He greedily laps it up.

I take some time to play with him and flash the red dot of a laser pointer along the tiled floor. Snowy leaps and jumps on a wild hunt to destroy it. I laugh as he scurries along, his fluffy butt wiggling as he prepares for the ultimate attack. He tires out pretty quickly, and I reward his excellent hunting skills with chin scratches, a head-to-toe groom, and plenty of cuddles.

Off to work next, I fall back into my usual routine and stop for coffee. Urban Grind is just as busy as always, and I'm pleased to see Simone's smiling face greet me as I walk in. With a nod, she lets me know she's preparing my drink, and I wait patiently for my turn to hand over my dollars to Lane.

As I settle beside the river with my coffee in hand, I reflect on what an incredible day it's turning out to be. I'm well-rested, I've already had some pet therapy time with Snowy, and my coffee tastes like perfection.

But Parker is leaving tonight. He won't be far - just Vegas - but the Camping Expo he's going to will keep him away right through Sunday. I can't help but feel like the weekend is being taken from us. I'll need to keep myself busy in his absence. As I pull my latest read from my tote bag, I'm reminded of Friday Fright Night Book Club, and consider attending that tonight. It would be nice to see Maisie and catch up; it's been months now since our paths have crossed. And I could also grab a couple of new books and return the three I devoured already this week. I decide it's a date.

Dr. Val isn't in today, but Dr. Amar is, followed by a shadow of two interns: Roy and Ruby. Even with the air of superiority engulfing every step Roy takes, I manage to get through the day with minimal conflict. I spend most of my shift at the front with Robbie, training him on manning the reception desk. Robbie is incredibly friendly with a broad smile. His positivity is contagious, which makes for numerous pleasant interactions with pet parents.

As I wander home from work, I realize it's been a month since Parker and I met. That time has passed in a bawdy blur of bliss. My mind sifts through the memories of our first month, the corners of my mouth wrinkling on my walk down memory lane. This weekend apart from Parker will be good, I tell myself. Absence makes the heart grow fonder.

Although I am already terribly fond of him.

I struggle to find the appeal of an entire weekend looking at tents, portable stoves, and hiking shoes, especially when the alternative is fucking each other too many times to count. Despite this, I vow to be supportive of Parker's weekend away with the guys, and even make a quick stop off at the liquor store on my way home. My eyes eagerly select a bottle of *Sale!* wine for me and a 24-pack of beer for the guys. I carefully place the wine bottle in my tote bag, but hauling the box of beer home is another story. Even with good intentions (maybe mostly to impress the friends I haven't yet met), it was foolish to think I could carry it. With each step, the box grows increasingly heavy. A harsh regret burns into me as the cardboard handle cuts into my fingers. I wiggle so the handle sits on fresh skin, but my fingers pulse in discomfort. Dropping the box onto a green electrical box beside the sidewalk, I rearrange and grasp the box in my arms instead. They, too, rapidly become weary, but I push through in the name of love.

At last, I trudge toward my apartment gate. The bottle of white jabs into my armpit, but I remind myself that soon it will be my prize. Wrestling the beer box onto the other side of the gate, I opt to leave it at the bottom of the stairs until my arms have had a moment's rest. I unlock my apartment and rush inside, eager to put down my tote bag. I wash my hands, the soap burning my raw fingers, then fill a large wine glass with ice. The cubes clink loudly and ring in my ears. I wrap my wounded fingers around the glass, the coolness bringing a welcome relief as it penetrates my sore skin. A moment later, I reach for the wine opener in its home beside the forks and knives and greedily rip out the cork from my $7 Chardonnay. The crisp liquid glugs as it invades the glass, spreading to fill every crevice between the ice cubes. I take a hearty sip. The sweet liquid is a soothing reward after my struggle. I hum in contentment. A couple more sips, and I'm ready to tackle that troublesome beer box.

I gallop down the stairs to retrieve my nemesis.

"Hi, beautiful," rings a familiar voice.

"Oh! Hi! You're here already!" I sing. I leap toward Parker and lean through the gate for a quick peck. He looks incredible in a loose black tee and dark-wash jeans. I want to rip them off and ravage his body.

"Didn't take you for a beer drinker," he teases.

"Ha! Right. This is for you. And your buddies. Because I'm a *good* girlfriend," I emphasize. I pull the gate open and kick the box toward Parker.

"You're a *great* girlfriend," he replies, sinking his lips into mine once more. I melt into him, my heart jumping with infatuation. I pull away. No. I won't give him the satisfaction. Not right before he abandons me for three days. I'm taking my power back. Damn right.

Parker's eyes search for a reason, studying my gaze and the expression on my face. But I don't give him one. Instead, I flash a snide grin.

"Harsh," he whines.

"You made your bed..." I shrug. Reaching for the gate, I securely latch it to create a barrier between us.

It's only then that I realize his truck parked on the street is already loaded up with everything from his overnight bag to... his friends. Shit. Shit shit shit. My cheeks turn red in embarrassment. I should go say hi, introduce myself, be friendly. Parker raises his eyebrows, entertained by my shame.

"Care to say hello? I've told them a lot about you." He leans into it.

I let out an awkward laugh, half genuinely amused by how Parker has played me, and half terrified at the thought that he's shared secrets from between the sheets.

"You ass."

Pulling the gate open a second time, I pinch his arm in retaliation as I take his side. He smirks, and I'm certain I see the bulge in his pants swell. I feel flushed. And absolutely humiliated that I didn't take a moment to compose myself and change into something more becoming than star-patterned scrubs.

Parker guides me to his truck, his fingers twirling in gentle circles against the small of my back. Will those butterflies ever fly away? The thrill has never lasted this long before. It does the opposite of grounding me - it sends a jolt down my spine and my heart thuds in my chest. My head feels airy, and I can do nothing but hope I'll somehow be able to string a coherent sentence together in the presence of Parker's closest childhood friends.

We draw nearer. I scan the truck to catch a glimpse of the faces I'm about to meet. Staring through the open window of the front passenger seat is a man with plump, full lips. His beautiful dark skin is etched with stubble along his chin and cheeks. His large eyes smile at me, and, even in my insecure state, I return his gaze with a friendly grin.

"Iris, this is Devin. Devin, meet Iris." Parker continues to guide me forward.

"Wonderful to finally meet you, Iris," Devin hums. His voice is effortlessly seductive. "How rude of me. Here, let me hop out and give you a proper greeting!" He pushes open the door of the truck and bends his head low to exit.

Standing before me, Devin is immensely tall, dwarfing even 6'2" Parker. He hugs me, engulfing my entire body in his arms alone. Just then, the back door of the truck swings open and another of Parker's friends joins us. Unlike Devin and Parker, he is quite short, although still slightly taller than me, with a sharp, rugged look to him. His dirty blonde hair is in disarray, almost as though he was napping until Devin woke him by opening the door.

"Nice of you to join us," Parker jokes, patting his friend on the back. "This is my buddy, Rafe."

Reluctantly breaking my embrace with Devin, I turn to greet Rafe. "Good to meet you," I squeak. Rafe nods politely and avoids eye contact. I smile, but behind it is an obvious discomfort. Rafe is withdrawn, a little offbeat. An introvert, likely adopted by outgoing friends such as Parker and Devin and thrust into the social world that he would otherwise avoid if left to his own devices.

"Well, boys, we can thank my lovely Iris here for the drinks we will enjoy tonight!" Parker howls. He hauls the beer box up off the concrete and tosses it into the bed of his truck.

"Thank you, Iris," Devin sings, his voice like velvet. I blush, and my mind wanders... imagining the incredible thrill of being entangled between the limbs of both Parker and Devin.

"What did I tell you guys? She's the best!" Parker proclaims. His voice brings me back to the present, but the heat of my reverie clings to me, and my skin prickles with sweat.

Parker notices.

Of course he does - he notices everything. He watches me squirm, my mind a blur of arousal, his eyes tracing my face, studying it. I clear my throat.

"Well, it was so great to meet you both. I won't keep you. I know you have a lot of driving ahead," I ramble whilst taking several steps backward toward the safety of my apartment. "Have fun at the expo!"

"We'll take good care of Parker, don't you worry now," Devin promises with a devilish grin.

Rafe keeps his head down and tucks himself back into the truck. Not a word.

Parker walks with me back to the apartment gate and leans into my ear. His mouth hovers, so close to my skin that it aches.

"I don't know how I'll get through the weekend without fucking you," he whispers. An immediate rush of need pools at my center. "Oh, wait. I do..." he exhales, his breath hot on my skin. I'm breathless at the reminder of my gift. "I can't wait to try it out. I hope it'll do the trick, for now."

I hum at the promise of many wonderful orgasms to be had. I lean in to Parker, desperately closing the gap between us. Our lips join in a soft, fleeting kiss.

"How dare you," Parker gasps, displeased, once again.

"You don't want to keep your guys waiting, do you?" I blink innocently, my eyes wide with tempt.

"You vixen."

Parker leans in and snatches my lower lip between his teeth. I gasp and snap my hand up to my lip, shocked by the pain. It stings, but the arousal burns hotter. Parker turns to leave, and I do the same, forcing myself to move without turning to catch one last glance before he's gone. I let myself in through the gate and run up the stairs.

Maybe I can't use my new toy yet, but Parker said nothing about playing without him.

So, in the meantime...

• • • •

NESTLED BACK IN THE confines of my apartment, I take a grateful swig of wine, but swallow it with regret. It's watered down now, having sat waiting while I met Devin and Rafe. I empty it into the sink and pour a fresh glass with much less ice this time. Bringing it with me into my bedroom, I rifle through my bedside table in search of a toy that will help to release the lubricious energy cloaking my body. Deciding between one of my rabbit or G-spot vibrators, I select the latter - a sleek purple one with just the right curve. I toss off my scrubs and slink out of my undergarments. Admiring my naked body in the mirror of my closet door, I imagine Parker's eyes are on me, tracing the lines of my body and memorizing my shape. I turn the vibrator on and play with it around my nipples. Parker's voice chimes in my head, instructing me what to do next. I listen carefully, taking my time and moaning as the pleasure builds. I lean over the edge of my bed and carefully slip the toy inside of me, yelping gleefully as it slides into place. I greedily turn it to the second-highest setting, my breath hitching as I give into my need for carnal gratification. The movement of the vibrator urges me instinctively to tilt and wriggle my hips. My body and brain are lost in pleasure, and the wetness between my legs grows still. In a manner that would be most pleasing to Parker, I coat my fingers in my slick juices and lick them off, my tongue grateful to take part in our provocative game. I switch to the highest speed and angle the toy so it relentlessly strikes my most tender and wanton part. Drilling into my G-spot, the shaft pushes me to the edge. I spill over and into oblivion, wailing in my euphoric release.

I study my red-speckled skin in the mirror and smile. Parker would be most pleased, indeed.

I could go for more.

But I don't.

Although maybe I should. What else am I supposed to do on a lonely Friday night?

I think of many things I *could* do. It's been a month now. This weekend would've been the perfect scenario for a test-drive, had Parker already known. I feel a wave of guilt spread across my cheeks. My mind goes wild with visions of what could've been, had I told him.

But I didn't.

My stomach drops, the promise I made to myself nagging at me. It taunts me in its imminence.

My internal battle is momentarily paused when my wrist buzzes with an incoming call. Without taking a millisecond to read who it is, I regretfully answer the call on my watch.

"Hello?" Shit. Shit. Why the fuck did I just answer a call when I'm literally naked with a vibrator in my hand? Where the hell is my brain?

"Iris! Hi honey! Oh, I'm so glad you answered. I was worried I'd get your voicemail - you are terribly hard to get a hold of, you know? Well anyway, I'm so glad I caught you. Well -"

"Can I call you back?" I interrupt. "Sorry, I'm just in the middle of something. Should be five minutes..."

"Uh, well..." My mom's hesitancy immediately makes me feel like a horrible daughter.

"It's just... well, you're on my watch. I need to find my phone. Give me just a few."

"Alright. Don't forget to call me back though!" She laughs maniacally.

The relief I feel hanging up on that call almost matches the relief from my orgasm just minutes ago.

Almost.

I run into the bathroom and turn on the shower. I bring my toy in with me, lather it in soap, and scrub it clean. I rinse off my body next, fighting the urge to rub another one out. I towel off and throw on a pair of black sweats and loose gray tee. Loungewear for the win. Not a second later, my wrist buzzes again. Can she not give a woman a minute? In a frenzy, I race to the front door, dig into my bag, and at last locate my phone.

"Hi. Hi, I'm here. What's wrong?" I ask, realizing only after I said it that I've deeply offended my mom. She hates negativity. *How are you?* or *What can I do for you?* are totally appropriate, but, *What's wrong?* is blasphemy.

"Wrong? Nothing is *wrong*, honey," she rebuffs. Grunting, she finds resolve in her voice. "Listen, Iris, the moving truck is coming next weekend. I called to remind you. The rest of your things need to be cleared out," she demands. "We are having the Salvation Army come Monday. Anything left behind is going to be donated." It almost sounds like a threat. "I know you're always so busy during the week, and impossible to get a hold of, so since I have you on the phone here now, you really should come over this weekend before the movers come."

"This weekend?"

"Yes. Tomorrow. Come over. In the morning. You can spend the day with us! We can have lunch to make up for the breakfast you missed. While you were sick." Why does my mother have this way of making me feel like I do nothing but let her down? "Willie would love to have you over, too!"

Oh, my fucking God. I can't stand when she calls him *Willie*. All I see is an old man's wrinkly ball sack and tiny, shriveled-up penis. I recoil at the thought, trying to shake the horrible imagery that hits me every time she calls him by his pet name.

Aaand, she's still talking.

"Willie would just love to spend some time with you before moving day. Oh, you know what? This will be so great! I'll give Zach a call and see if he and Molly can make it for dinner tomorrow. We can have a whole family get-together just before the big moving day!" She fake-sobs into the phone.

I don't even have a chance to plead my case before my mom commits me to a weekend consisting of all the elements of my own personal hell: my childhood home, boxes of my past, my family, and elderly-penis man.

"Uh..." I ponder the excuses I can use to get out of this. I'm definitely not still trapped in a vision of elderly dicks. "Uh..." Okay, I am. Fuck. While my mind is in a panic, desperate for an out, my mouth can't put an intelligible sentence together.

"You're welcome back on Sunday, too, of course. I'm sure you won't be able to get through everything tomorrow with the big family get-together going on now!" So now there's a party tomorrow. Good. Lord. "The house is under contract so," she continues, sniffing, "this is our final moment!" She pauses, and I hear indiscernible chatter in the background. Willard is in her ear, no doubt egging her on and feeding her the script. "There is a new family coming in and they need to do inspections, make plans for moving, all of that." Her tone shifts. "So, I need you to come tomorrow. And Sunday. And whatever is left by the end of the weekend will go out to charity on Monday."

I raise my eyebrows and start pacing in the kitchen. I have an entire weekend to get through without Parker, so I suppose the distraction of boxes is... fine. Not fine, fine. But the kind of fine where it's not really fine but you have no choice but to accept it, fine. It's excuse enough to keep busy.

I'm dreading going through those boxes. Some people love to reminisce and indulge in the memories of old. I am not some people. Yes, I have a past, everyone does, but things are better now. In the present. I don't want to be reminded of my childhood years spent trying to figure out who I was - the uncertainty of identity, of belonging, of everything, really.

"Um, yeah, yeah, okay, mom," I begrudgingly agree. "I guess I'll head over in the morning."

"Great! Wonderful! Can't wait to have you home, honey!" The background whisper picks up again. "Oh, oh, that's right. Willie and I have plans to meet with Debbie and Donnie in the morning," she pauses. "Let yourself in, we'll see you back here for lunch!" she finishes, too enthusiastically.

"Okay mom, tomorrow," I exhale, relieved to know that I'll be alone in the morning, without mom hovering over me, either (a) criticizing every item I opt to keep, or (b) criticizing every item I opt to toss.

"Love you, bye honey!"

"Love you too, mom. Bye."

Immediately upon ending the call with my mom, my phone buzzes with a text. Already irritated beyond measure at having my weekend conscripted, my phone feels like another unwanted task nagging at me. But, to my delight, it's a message from my favorite person.

Ben.

BEN
Girrlll what a week. I know it's late but I'm just
about to duck out of here. Up for meeting at
Giuseppe's in 30?

I smile, immediate calm flooding my veins. My time with Ben always re-centers me. I love him deeply.

ME
Yes yes yes! xxx

The timing is perfection.

Eleven

Giuseppe's is a second-generation family-owned Italian restaurant with the best carbohydrate-dense and gluten-heavy food in the state. And although I consider myself a pretty basic bitch, I must agree with Ben in that the $95 bottle of red imported from the Giuseppe family vineyard is one of the best things to have ever entered my mouth.

The irony.

I wait patiently at a small table in the back, staring out the window, hoping to catch sight of Ben's arrival. The dinner crowd is thinning out now, and only a few couples remain, littered throughout the dining room. My stomach gurgles and growls as overwhelming hunger hits me. I selfishly dive into the basket of warm bread that Lorenzo, the twenty-something son of one of the owners, has placed in front of me. Its sweet scent is too tempting to resist. I drench a chunk of bread in oil and balsamic, so much so that it tastes more like the dip than bread. I hum with immediate satiation at the first taste. I break off another chunk of the bread, dipping it to my soppy satisfaction, then chase it with a sip of hearty red wine. Just a glass of the house blend tonight - I don't want the commitment of a full bottle when I have to shamefully trod off to my mom's in the morning. The wine is fruity and deep with flavor, and it hits me just right. A few more voracious bites and the bread is almost gone. As though Lorenzo was watching me and senses my insecurity in finishing the basket before my date arrives, he swoops in with a fresh batch and carefully tops up the oil and balsamic. My savior. And just on cue.

The next moment, Ben waltzes through the door, looking dapper and fresh. He spots me immediately, and I jump up to meet his outstretched arms.

"My queen! Iris!" he announces, embracing me flamboyantly.

"*My* queen!" I echo, my body immediately relaxing in his embrace. Nestled in his strong arms, I feel invincible and protected.

"I have so much to unpack!" he squeals as he releases me. He places his hands on my shoulders so as to hold me at an arm's-distance and lets out a deep exhale. "You look fantastic, by the way! Look at that glow on your cheeks!"

I toss my hair back and give a smug grin. Before heading out to meet Ben, I traded my sweats for a plum button-down and pair of light jeans. I couldn't meet my best-dressed friend looking like a bum.

Ben is undeniably handsome. His body is the perfect mix of gentle and toned. Tonight, he's wearing a beautiful brown sweater with a white shirt tucked underneath. His light eyes glow a warm, earthy shade of brown, and his hair is swept back. Usually groomed, I notice that, tonight, it's a little on the messy side. In a wispy wave of blonde and light brown, it's a beautiful, chaotic cocktail of colors. Ben's best accessory, though, is always his radiant smile.

Ben moves to sit opposite me, taking his seat to face the rear of the restaurant.

"Fill me in. I hope your trip wasn't pure hell," I say, although I'm admittedly afraid of his response.

"It pretty well was!" he exclaims. "I don't know why I always hold out hope that maybe - just maybe - this time will be different. That this is the day my family will accept me as I am!" he acts out dramatically, with the back of his hand on his forehead, a damsel in distress awaiting rescue.

"Fuck them!" I declare.

"I know. But. They are family. Aaand I'm a softy."

Yes, Ben is a softy. It's his biggest flaw.

Ben grew up in South Florida, in the smallish town of Jupiter. "From another planet!" he always jokes. He moved to the west coast after high school, leaving behind his teenage years spent being bullied by homophobes, young and old. His family, while they try to *understand* (understand what, exactly, *I'll* never *understand*), have settled on his gayness as being a phase, regardless of how long it lasts. They pray for him nightly, believing that, at one point or another, Ben will see God's plan, meet a nice girl, get all the warm feelings, marry her, grow a family, and live a traditional, good, Christian life.

Ben is a gentle soul. Although firmly asserting himself over the years, he's grown weary of defending his sexuality. It's easier for his family to believe the story they tell themselves. In a strange way, it gives Ben a sense of power to know he knows better than they do, that he is more in touch with reality than they are. I always feel a combination of disgust and regret when it comes to his family. Such a pity that they have such a wonderful son, brother, nephew, and grandson who they refuse to ever truly see. I ache for Ben. While he is strong and refuses to be anything but himself, he is also much too forgiving.

I met Ben in college. He studied computer science and ran a side hustle tutoring for different tech programs. One of my second-year classes was especially challenging, so I reached out for some help with a database project. I fell in love with Ben immediately, and he has since been my best and closest friend.

Ben has it all: a beautiful mind, heart, soul, and body.

How sad it is that so many judge and dismiss him.

Ben purges his heart out, filling me in on all the details of his time back home. I'm glad to hear that he got to see his sister, Charla, for the first time in nearly four years. She is among the few members of his family who love Ben for Ben. Charla has moved time and time again all over the country with her military husband, Dan. She rarely makes it home for their annual reunion - traveling is hard when you have 3 children under the age of 3. She and her brood are doing well, and she is finally settling in in Maine, where Dan is stationed for the next while. Ben's dad is keeping busy in his semi-retirement, still working a few days a week at the bank and filling the others volunteering at the church. Ben's mom is a classroom aide at the elementary school. She always has boundless energy, and takes on more than I ever could. She is also fostering a new litter of kittens from the humane society while they wait for their time to be spayed and neutered. I smile, making various *aw!* sounds while looking through photos of the clumsy babies, walking over each other and bumping into everything. They remind me of late-night drunks wandering blindly in the dark. I chuckle at a sweet black kitten with a Mohawk that climbs over its siblings in pursuit of a bowl of slop. Baby animals are so carefree. Facing Ben's aunts, uncles, and cousins was the hardest part of his trip. His Uncle Eugine is the local pastor, so every interaction with him was highly unpleasant. He's too hard on Ben's soft heart, preaching hate in a manipulative way disguised as love.

Ben sobs as we walk through the memory of it. My eyes well up in solidarity. Our hearts ache together for the acceptance of the things that make us *us*.

I share what's new with me, feeling a pang of guilt when I bring up Parker and how I feel about him. Ben is climbing the ladder in IT, and his hours are notoriously unpredictable. This makes it hard to cement plans - or to date, he always reminds me. Ben is happily attached at that moment, but his relationship is new. He met Leo just before his trip back South. They've been on several dates, and the infatuation is there, but it's still blooming. Leo might or might not be it for Ben; whereas, I know in the depths of heart that Parker is, without a doubt, the one for me.

Two hours, two bowls of linguine carbonara, and a shared plate of tiramisu later, our bellies are stuffed and our hearts are full. We split the bill, leaving a hefty tip for Lorenzo, then waddle out of Giuseppe's, hand-in-hand.

Home again, I sleep soundly. My time with Ben has brought me such a sense of peace. We know and trust each other with our deepest secrets and most authentic selves.

Sometimes I wonder if our soulmates aren't our partners in life, but our truest friends.

Twelve

During the week, I'm used to the time without Parker. Work inevitably fills the minutes that I would otherwise spend pining over him. But the weekends - every weekend since we first met - we have shared together. Every Friday night, every Saturday night, as predictable as can be. I like planned monotony. But this weekend is different.

It's impossible to overlook the void.

Waking up alone is like being single again, and the burn of last night's heavy feast bubbles in my stomach, making me queasy. I listen to the wind dancing through the trees outside my open window. Staring at the knockdown pattern on the ceiling, my mind creates shapes and images that I quickly get lost in.

I have a lot on my mind: the dread of a family-filled weekend, the anxiety of the conversation I need to have with Parker. Parker. My skin glows at the thought of him. Then my heart shakes. I'm not questioning myself, but I am torturing myself over the unknown of his reaction. My mother always says that worrying doesn't change anything, it's like riding a stationary bike - a lot of work that gets you nowhere. She is right, but only about this one thing, ever. Yet, here I am, worrying. I can control a lot, but I can't control how he will respond to my confession - to my ultimatum. But then again, I know him well enough to know that he will be supportive. We will be on the same page. He will accept me; I know he will. He will.

Will he?

Then there's the dreaded L-word. The acute vulnerability of it. But I do, I do love him. I love Parker. But I can't - I won't - sacrifice or ignore who I am and what I need simply in the name of love. Yes, I love him. But but but... I also love me. And I have to live with me for the rest of my life. I am staying true to myself this time.

At all costs.

I vow to stop wallowing right now and get my sad, lonely ass up and out the door.

Coffee first. Nothing like a sugar-laced caffeinated beverage to reset the mood.

Simone never lets me down. She's the light of my day, halting all other tasks to prepare my drink the moment I walk through the door. Her hair is down today, flowy brown strands cascading over her shoulders. Her smile weaves into me. We chat briefly despite the growing line of impatient customers - it's just me and her in a world of our own, even just for a moment. Our voices dance off one another's, making the air sing with warmth around us. I know we linger a beat too long.

Next, Vienna's.

There's nothing like the softness of Snowy to put me immediately at ease. His sweet, high-pitched mew sinks into me, and, in this moment of need, I almost crave a cat of my own. Especially after Ben's sweet stories of the baby kittens his mom is fostering. My heart sings.

Has Parker's absence really turned me into a crazy cat lady?

I shake off the thought and pull out my book. My impromptu dinner with Ben took precedence over book club last night, but thankfully I still have this week's Murder Mystery Monday read to finish. I flip it open and get lost in the tale about a bachelorette party gone wrong. Set in the deep woods, the maid of honor is found dead the morning of the wedding. I'm almost done and feel pretty confident in my guess as to whodunit. I sip my coffee and lay with Snowy curled in a soft pile of warmth on my lap, intent on finishing the last chapters.

I guessed right: the jealous ex-best friend.

Having devoured my coffee all too quickly, I brew another in Vienna's Keurig. I rinse out my to-go cup in the sink and refill it with the fresh brew. I breathe it in; the scent invades my nostrils and intoxicates my brain. Here's hoping that all the caffeine coursing through my veins will be the anchor in getting me through what's ahead. I sink my fingers into Snowy's fur and scratch between his ears. He purrs with his tail wrapped around my arm.

"Wish me luck," I whisper into his coat.

• • • •

MOM'S HOUSE IS A BRISK 30-minute walk from my apartment, and just under that from Vienna's. With a little pit-stop to grab a poppyseed muffin (and say a quick hello to Simone again), I arrive in just around 40 minutes. The sun shines brightly in the sky, gleaming over the peak of the roof that houses my childhood bedroom. I blink under the rays as they assault my naked eyes. I take a deep breath, then fiddle through the keys hanging on my cat-themed lanyard to find the one that unlocks my past.

The house is quiet. Thankfully, mom and Willard are still out for their senior's brunch. I find my pile of boxes neatly arranged against the side wall of the empty closet in the main floor guest room. Disappointingly, there are more than I expected or remembered - probably close to fifteen in total. I take a swig of my coffee and come to the harrowing realization that there is no way this is getting completely done today. I have to be as productive as possible, though, before mom gets home hovers over me, narrating my poor choices, old and new. I can't put it off any longer. Start at the top and work my way down, I guess.

The first few boxes go relatively quickly (as does my second coffee). It isn't until box four that it really hits me. My mom is moving away, to an island, in the Pacific, selling our childhood home, and leaving me and Zach behind.

This stupid pile of old birthday cards is the trigger.

Birthdays: the smell of cake wafting through the house, the piles of presents stacked on the table, the balloons and decorations themed to your most recent obsession decorating the halls. The best part about your birthday is that it is entirely yours. It's your special day to be doted upon, all eyes on you. That's the wonder of birthdays - for most people. For me, it's never been my day. It's never been a special day where I've been the center of attention. My birthday hasn't even ever been mine. It's been *ours*. Mine, but not all mine, because I share it with Zach.

November 16, 1990 - Happy Birthday, Zach! Oh, and Iris, too. Happy Birthday, Both of You!

Possibly even worse than having a brother whose birthday is the same as yours, is having a twin who you can always count on to one-up you, outshine you, and overshadow you in every corner of your life. There came a point, around when I was fifteen, when I decided that I had had enough. I'd had enough of being a twin, of being compared to my brother simply because we were born together, of being held to a special standard of performance that never met the bar he set. I wish I could say I hate Zach, but the truth is I never really have. I've hated society, and all of its nonsensical rules and standards that govern our existence.

So, in my late-teen years, I made a pact with myself. Fuck society. I am going to live my life by my own rules and make my own decisions based on what I want for me. No making choices to please others or do what I'm supposed to according to *society's* obscure expectations.

I am going to live a passionate life that is meaningful and fulfilling to *me*.

I'm not entirely there, but I'm working towards it.

As kids, Zach and I got along well enough. We didn't incessantly bicker and fight; we mutually respected each other and accepted the bitter truth that we would forever be bound together. In our early years, we were never without a playmate, which I suppose both helped in the future as well as set me up for failure, because I had a hard time forming connections with people that, well, simply, weren't Zach. Maybe it was because we knew each other so well, or maybe it was because I am, admittedly, a strong personality, and making friends who really understand me and all my uniqueness has never been my strong suit.

We grew up, and Zach went on to university to study business and become a big deal banker. He focused on building up his career and, by the time I graduated from minimum wage to a salary with benefits, Zach was making six figures. In the next breath, he met Molly, got married in a majestic hotel, bought a mansion, and popped out two kids in two years. Now, much to the delight of my mom, they are expecting their third, due in August.

Conversely, I went to community college and floundered around for a couple of years before landing on the path to become a veterinary technician. I spent more years than one should living in a shitty apartment barely being able to afford to feed oneself, and I have no Molly. I plan to stay on birth control until the day comes when the risk of blood clots is too high and I must instead march myself off to get a hysterectomy. I know myself well enough to know that motherhood is not for me. My heart is plenty full of the wonders of childhood simply from having gone through it myself.

Damn right, society. I do not want children. Or marriage. Or to follow any of the other, antiquated laws you demand of me.

Staring at the pile in my hand, I have no idea why I kept this wad of birthday cards. They aren't even mine. Every single one is stamped with a *Dear Zach & Iris*. I wrap an elastic band around them and walk them over to the kitchen, where I decide they are Zach's to deal with. My heart pangs as I have a sudden longing for him. I miss him. I miss us. I hate how sentimental I'm already feeling, goddammit. I pull out my phone and send Zach a quick message.

ME
Hey, just at mom's.
Found some old birthday cards from back
in the day. I guess you can go through
them tonight when you come over?
Otherwise, I can recycle them...?
Not sure of the appropriate course of
action when dealing with such sentimental
items being ousted from their resting
place in our childhood home.

I take a deep breath and rip back the paper of the bag containing my muffin. I gobble the entire thing up in a few indulgent bites. Shaking the crumbs off me and onto the dark, cherry floor below, I feel my mom's ghost of disapproval.

These boxes are making me sad, but the thought of their contents and memories going to Goodwill does, reluctantly, make me sadder. Box after box, I'm forced to confront countless memories. Some bring smiles, like my sixth-grade science paper on Jaguars. The cover art is gloriously childish and brave, featuring a family of jaguars inside of a heart and a hunter with a big X eliminating him. The paper itself is confident and optimistic, outlining all the good being done to conserve big wild cats. My passion really shines though.

I find a Ziploc bag full of all sorts of stubs and knickknacks: tickets from the movies I saw at the theater in senior year, shiny coins, a name tag from my first job as an *inventory specialist* (aka kid who stocked shelves) at the local CVS. Why did I keep all this meaningless junk?

Other items are harder to confront. I come across a wristband from a music festival I went to when I was nineteen. Immediately, I'm overcome with horror at having kept it. My friend, June, was sexually assaulted on that trip. Repulsed by the memory, I toss it aside into the garbage pile, shuddering, the feeling of bile filling my throat. Desperate for a glass of water, I jog into the kitchen and chug back a full cup. It does nothing to wash away the memories. I grab the garbage can from under the sink and pull it behind me back to the guest room. Tossing piles of worthless items - and the wristband - into the trash, I feel fueled to push through this process as quickly as possible.

I open the flaps of a new box: paperwork. Pushing through the piles with minimal emotional strain, I find a reprieve. Shuffling through old school papers, I become annoyed with myself for keeping math and English worksheets from as far back as grade four. There is, however, relief to be found in dealing with items so easy to categorize as garbage.

Then there are the folders, binders, scratch pads, looseleaf. And the notebooks. So many notebooks. Looking down into a deep box filled exclusively with journals and diaries, I'm faced with the blatant truth that I, Iris Gladwell, am a hoarder of paper.

There are at least twenty notebooks, each etched to the brim with the words of my past: memories, feelings, birthdays, first crushes, first times. Dating from 1998 to 2015, these notebooks span almost two decades of my life. It's overwhelming to consider that I have kept such a record. In a way, I'm proud of myself for it, but in another, I'm deeply ashamed of the harsh realities contained within them.

I first flip through a basic Five-Star coil-bound with 120 pages and a blue cover. 2002-2004. The awkward era of middle school, when hormones are raging and everyone is hell-bent on being either entirely popular and well-liked, or entirely unique and different from everyone else. Middle school was horrible. (Isn't it for everyone?) Past the milestone of first crushes and having a general sense of how the world works, middle school is very much a time for navigating social rules and trying to find that sweet spot of belonging. I was a passive middle schooler, standing in the background most of the time and trying to float through unnoticed. Zach was popular and well-liked, and as a result of this, most of the kids in his inner circle tolerated my existence. I continued to struggle with processing dad's death, even years later, so admittedly, this was one of the only times I welcomed living in Zach's shadow.

But, seeing all these notebooks with the years written on them makes the memories feel tangible and fresh. I flashback to 1999, when Zach and I were just kids. We always thought we had the coolest dad, because when you are in elementary school and your dad is an Imagineer at Disney, nothing is cooler than that. Dad was fun and creative and had a magic charisma about him that would charm even the grumpiest of people. We were lucky kids - spending our weekends at Disneyland and riding the teacups over and over until we felt like we were going to be sick. Sometimes, on really special days, dad would even let us go *behind the scenes* so we could peek in on what he was creating next. I'm sure he was never supposed to share the secret plans of the Boss Mouse, but he always confided in us, and the thrill Zach and I got from feeling so special as to be entrusted with such secrets was true magic. We knew years ahead of everyone else, right down to the little details. Zach and I are irrefutably excellent secret-keepers.

Dad was energetic and full of life. He had a gift for vision, creativity, and crafting fantasy into reality. It destroyed our family when we lost him. It destroyed me.

With hot tears marching down my cheeks, I sniff into the sleeves of my oversized hoodie and roughly wipe them off. This is fucking hard. I try to dig deep and hold onto all the good parts, but that's the thing with memories - try as we might, it's the bad bits that stick. Desperate for a happy memory to prove that I am, actually, very wrong about this, I pull out a notebook from a time I know good things happened: my late teen years. A time of transition, this is when I started to learn who I am, and, equally important, who I'm not.

And then there was Alba.

Alba.

Alba was the catalyst launching me into a world of self-discovery. She was the one who first opened me up to my own sexuality.

She was also my first great love.

My experiences with Alba taught me everything about myself. That thrill I get from vulnerability, that rush from humiliation, that craving to be watched and desired - it all stems from her. We were best friends, so we kept our sexual involvement a secret, and, at the time, it felt right. These were intimate pieces of each other that only we had the privilege of knowing. Alba was grossly popular in the dating world and found herself bouncing from boyfriend to boyfriend. Everyone wanted her. I understood - she was captivating. It never bothered me, really, that she was involved with other people. Because what we had was special - and it was all ours. I understood her need for attention. Our relationship was sacred, and I felt confident and comfortable in that.

Just before my twentieth birthday, Alba made the difficult decision to move back to Indonesia, where her dad was from. I was completely heartbroken. The thought of living without her made my soul ache; she had become a part of me, woven into the fabric of who I was. But Alba wouldn't let me get down on myself. In our final goodbye, she talked me up, reminding me of how kind and sweet and beautiful and smart and amazing I am and the fact that I'm different - that *we're* different - is a true gift.

"How lucky the world is to have you in it, Iris," she said as our lips met for the last time.

Alba inspired me. She made me feel like I owed it to her to be the person she believed I was. And so, moving forward in my life, I strive to find my place, my place of belonging, and share it with someone the way I did with Alba.

Thinking about her now makes my heart glow.

We didn't keep in touch after she left. Our experience together was perfect in my eyes, and I didn't want to taint it by attempting a long-distance... friendship.

I sloppily wipe the tears welling in my eyes with my sleeves again, which are now humiliatingly damp. I sniff back the snot and the memories. I toss the notebooks aside and find another one dated 2012 on the top of the pile. I contemplate opening it. I run my fingers along the side, playing with its ragged edges. I think back to 2012 and consider that time. 2012. The year Zach graduated from college. The year I applied for the vet program. The year of Jennie. And Cal. And Derek. And Rose.

I put the notebook back into the box and pile the remaining ones on top. The final one is dated 2015. That was a better year. I flip it open.

May 19, 2015

I am so proud of myself. I'm finally on the home stretch! I'll be graduating soon, and I'm so excited to already have a job lined up! Dr. Val had the nicest things to say about my internship. He said my dedication, compassion, and hard work were unmatched and he generously offered me a staff position! I honestly can't believe it. I'm going to be a real working human with a real working job! Look at me go, world.

I keep flipping.

August 10, 2015

Things with Braden are fucking amazing! He's so fucking hot - I'm honestly getting wet just thinking about him. He's so sure of himself and not afraid to really push me. We met at the best time. I really needed some hardcore sex to keep my mind off of things, and, boy, he is delivering. The other night he bound me to his St. Andrew's Cross and went to town on me. He licked me from top to bottom with that amazing tongue of his. OH! MY! GOD! He ate me out like a fucking ravenous dog, sucking and licking and rubbing all over my pussy. Mm! I swear he has magic hands. He made me come so many times I was getting dizzy. Okay, well, this was fun, but now I have to go and grab my vibrator because I've gone and turned myself on!

My cheeks burn with redness. Mm, Braden. We fucked *a lot*. He had a knack for kink, and knew exactly how to challenge me and how far to push. There wasn't anything Braden wouldn't try. We did a lot of crazy shit together; role play was one of our favorites.

Reliving the memories of Alba, Braden, and all the flames in between floods my mind with graphic images of Parker. He invades my thoughts and snakes into my brain. I recall one of our most recent indiscretions, when Parker couldn't wait to be inside of me after we shared dessert at Dulce. He whispered in my ear how he wanted to fill me up and watch his cum drip out of me, just as the vanilla ice cream melted and pooled at the bottom of the plate. Sprawled in the backseat, he fucked me in his parked truck. I was certain we would attract an audience. With each of Parker's enthusiastic thrusts, the truck rocked and shook. I yelped loudly, the thought of a crowd assembling exciting me.

I sigh, wishing I could relive that moment, instead of the ones I'm forced to confront with each new item I pull from the boxes. With a heavy exhale, I take one last look at my pile of notebooks. I return them to the dark space from which they came and close the cardboard flaps above them. A tranquilizing relief permeates through the room.

The next few boxes are primarily items I had hoarded as a child - favorite toys and stuffed animals I shared my bed with. One box is entirely Barbie dolls, clothes, and accessories. I'm certain I had the most chicly-styled Barbies of the '90s. Having no use for them now, or, ever, for that matter, I decide to offer the bulk of my childhood things to Zach and his growing posse of littles. I pull out my phone once more. No reply from Zach. I send another message.

ME
Also found a few boxes of old toys
that the kids might like. Lily would love
all the Barbie dolls I found.
They're yours if you want them!

Then there is a clunk and the sound shuffling.

Fuck. My solace has come to an end; mom and Willard are home. My mom turns the corner as I finish shoving a few unwanted papers into the stolen kitchen garbage can.

"Hi, honey!" she shouts, her voice shrill.

"Hi, mom," I say nonchalantly, looking up briefly before returning to the box. "Just chugging along."

"Wonderful! I always love going through old things," she muses, leaning against the wall and dragging her fingertips against the flaps of a box. "It's such a delight to take a trip down memory lane. Don't you think?"

"Uh, yeah," I humor her. "Well, I've made good progress, but still have a lot to do. Better get back to it," I say dismissively.

"Oh, of course!" mom exclaims, her piercing voice echoing in my ears. She wanders over to me, arms outstretched. I reluctantly stand up and succumb to her embrace. "I sure will miss you. And Zach. Both of you. Promise me you'll visit? Hawaii is so beautiful at any time of year. Willie and I can't wait to host you!" She's tearing up now, her eyes pink around the edges.

"Aw, mom, don't cry! Of course I'll visit," I lie. Even if I wanted to, my bank account won't allow it. "I'm sure Zach will be around soon. He travels for work," I remind her in a desperate attempt to comfort her.

"Oh, honey, you didn't have one of those dreaded, ultra-processed muffins and consider that your breakfast, did you?"

And there it is. The judgment. I twirl around, break free of my mother, and scoop up the crumby muffin bag and empty coffee cup.

"It was just a little something to tide me over. I had a gift card from one of the dog moms I sat for. I think it was going to expire soon," I over-explain in an elaborate fib. "Anyway, I'm going to get back at it." I plop down in front of a box and will my mom away.

"Alright, honey. Well, Willie and I are just going to give Zach a call and finalize plans for tonight. Then I'll make you a proper breakfast with some eggs, sausages, and fresh strawberries. How does that sound?"

Condescending. "Really nice. Thanks, mom."

• • • •

I CLOSE THE DOOR TO block out the existence of my mom and Willard, who are jauntily chit-chatting in the kitchen as my mom prepares me a meal acceptable by her standards. Their voices echo off the walls and give me chills. It's impossible for me to concentrate now. I have two-thirds of my boxes left and zero stamina to guide me through. I dig through my tote bag and pull out my earbuds. I pop them in and choose the *Mood Booster* playlist on Spotify, hoping that it will make good on its promise to *Get happy with today's dose of feel-good songs!* Turning the volume up higher than what my mom would approve of, I breathe deeply and delve into the next box of my past.

One box blends into the next, an endless string of *then*. I become much less invested in the process as time marches on and opt to toss close to three quarters of what I encounter. My brain turns into mush, my eyes are puffy from strain, and by the time dinner rolls around, I question how I'll find the strength to endure this over-the-top family feast.

Nearing six o'clock, the babbles and whines of the grandchildren, intermixed with gleeful squeals from my mom, ring outside the door. There comes a bark or two as well, and I'm surprised my mom has allowed Zach and Molly to bring their family dog, Remi (short for Rembrandt, a nod to one of Molly's favorite classical artists), with them. It's utter chaos out there.

A knock comes on the door to my box room, and my stomach drops.

Zach peers in, his charming smile (identical to dad's) brightening the room. I want to resist it, but even more than that, I want to hug him tightly and never let go.

"Hiya, sis!" he greets. His voice is light and warm, like the steam coming off a freshly-baked pie. "So good to see you."

"Hey," I muster. My throat is coated with emotion that I'm struggling to keep contained.

"I've missed you. It's been months!" he reminds me. "How are the boxes coming?" He glances down at them, then back up at me. "You look like you've been crying. Are you okay? I know it's not easy to revisit the past. I'm here for you."

And there it is. All the reasons I love my brother so deeply. He is kind, compassionate, empathetic, and supportive. He pulls me in for that hug I'm craving. I breathe him in and begin to cry. I can't stop it. The tears come uncontrollably, flowing in a hot stream of salt and snot. He holds me close. Zach allows me to be me; he welcomes me, accepts me. It's too much to bear. I collapse into him, wondering if I'm borderline insane.

I know I'm not.

I'm human. I've struggled. I've been broken.

But I'm still here.

I'm still me.

Zach is still with me.

"I love you," Zach whispers into my mess of hair, and I hear the emotion in his voice, too.

My ears throb with the heat of my vulnerability as I fall apart in my brother's arms. I'm ashamed knowing that my mom, Willard, Molly, and the little girls are all just outside that door, undoubtedly within earshot of my breakdown. The shame fuels me somehow. I sob harder, pulling Zach closer, until I'm empty. Zach continues to hold me, and I flash back to the aftermath of our dad's death. A numbness overcomes me.

"I've got you," Zach assures me. "I had a hard time with my things, too," he empathizes.

"It's hell," I bluntly state. We both laugh weakly. "Thank you."

"You never have to thank me, Iris. When you are hurting, I hurt, too. Something about twins, you know, it's like we're genetically identical," he jokes.

We stay together in the room, and time stops. We talk like we used to, and in a bizarre, backwards way. An absurd rush of gratitude spikes through me. It's almost worth having endured the pain of the past to get to this moment.

This special, divine moment of connection between me and my twin brother.

Thirteen

Zach has a certain Midas touch - he effortlessly transforms my pain with his unconditional love. I'm certain I wouldn't have the strength to get through the remainder of the evening without him. Thank you, Zach.

As mom does with all things when it comes to impressing her partner, she prepares an extravagant feast of roasted chicken, twice-baked potatoes, a fresh salad, and a hearty, home-made mac and cheese. Thankfully, my mom's dedication in the kitchen keeps her sufficiently occupied for the short time I exist outside my box jail and in the living room with the rest of the family. Molly buzzes around with her, helping to stir when instructed and add a pinch of salt where needed.

That leaves me stuck in the living room with Willard and Zach's two young girls, Lily and Nora. But, thankfully, Willard has naturally come right into his role as doting Grandfather and is quietly supervising one-year old Nora as she stretches and slices Play-Doh. Lily, although only just two, is playing on her own, lost in the world of Barbie and her various adventures. I smile, my heart warm, as I see the joy that the toys of my past are bringing Lily in the present.

Remi sits outside on the back porch, his leash tied to one of the patio chairs. I look over at him longingly, fighting the urge to find my place beside him. I've always felt more at home in the company of animals. They don't ask questions and use the answers to silently tally up my worth.

Zach finishes up on a work call then fills me in on how things are going at the office. He uses words to describe the financial market that I've never fully understood or even cared to, for that matter. But I'm proud to say I comprehend a lot more now since having listened to Parker occasionally drone on about his work. I almost, almost mention something about Parker to Zach, but given my fragile emotional state at the moment, I elect not to.

Lily jumps on Zach and asks when her "baybee sisserr" is coming, and Zach glows at the mention of it.

"Still a while," he tells her, his voice obscenely patient and gentle.

"Too mush wait," Lily replies, then abruptly launches herself off of Zach and back over to her Barbie land.

Zach tells me how excited Lily is about the baby. He and Molly are hard at work getting the nursery ready, and Lily peeks in often, expecting the baby to magically appear within it.

As an artist, Molly is in her element when it comes to decorating their grossly large home. They recently moved Nora into a new room with a toddler bed, and Molly went to town on theming it with custom art featuring Nora's most favorite thing in the world: tigers. Zach flips through photos on his phone, showing off the impressive wall mural Molly hand-painted. There are trees and vines and flowers all tangled in a lush jungle scene, with several cartoonish tigers lounging throughout. Along another wall is a group of tigers with the names of each member of the family above it: Daddy, Mommy, Lily, Nora, and a little baby tiger labeled Felicity.

"Felicity! That's a beautiful name," I gush admiringly.

"Yeah, thanks! Molly chose it. It was her grandmother's name. We want to call her Cici," Zach explains.

"I love that, too."

"Another girl. Can you believe it?" Zach asks in awe. He's beaming with pride.

"I'm really happy for you. You make a wonderful father. Dad would be so proud," I say, my voice cracking.

"That means a lot, Iris. You know, dad would be really proud of you, too. Your passion for animals is something so beautiful, and I know he always admired you for that. You worked really hard to get where you are."

Relishing in Zach's kind words, I lean into him for another hug. Our hearts beat in unison.

Having avoided interaction with my mom for long enough, I join her and Molly in the kitchen. I offer a hand, and mom is just as glad to give me a task as I am to receive one. I set the table and take drink orders, making sure I pour a glass of chocolate milk "indo da bijjer growshup cup" for Lily. Her red hair and matching cheeks remind me of me as a child. My emotions creep back in. It takes immense fortitude, but I push them away. Again.

We sit at last, and Willard politely leads the family in saying grace. Lily garnishes a laugh from me and Zach as she belts out, "wuz a grashe?" just as Willard attempts his speech of holy thankfulness. Molly looks equal parts petrified and humiliated. Lily's outspokenness once again mirrors mine. Zach apologizes to both Willard and Molly, whispering to Lily to remember her manners and that he'll explain it to her later. Willard is understanding, but Molly is so uptight it looks like she's about to explode from shame. I secretly savor it.

Despite how harshly I criticize my mom, she is an excellent cook. The meal is delectable. We each devour our overfilled plates, and I even go in for seconds. I keep my mouth full in hopes of avoiding conversation, but my mom has a disease when it comes to prying and smoking out my secrets. I do my best to be amiable. But when she comments on how puffy my eyes are and asks what face cream I'm using, and oh Belinda recommended this amazing new formula that I really ought to try out because honestly, I should be looking my absolute best, the thirties are when the signs of aging really creep in and no man is going to want a puffy-eyed, wrinkled hag. I summarize, but that's the gist. Tempted to defend myself in revealing that I do indeed have a partner and up yours, mom, I instead smile and nod, agreeing to try some of Belinda's miraculous anti-aging eye cream of the Gods.

Molly gushes about her upcoming art show at the gallery in a desperate attempt to save face after Lily's show of ignorance. Mom makes a show of her own in theatrically expressing her deep regret and sadness of missing it because they'll have just arrived in Hawaii and they really ought to get settled before making the long trek back here again especially since it's going to be a big move and there's so much to consider with blending two families together, you know. She asks if I'll be going (slash tells me I must go), and I politely respond the same as I did to Zach's text invitation: I'll do my best to make it. As expected, this provokes my mom to berate me over how I need to be a better sister and I should support my brother's beautiful, pregnant wife no matter what because really what do I have going on in my sad, single life, and isn't Molly wonderful in all that she does for her growing family, and on top of it she manages to maintain a successful art career, and really, she expects more from me.

It takes everything in me at that moment to not lash out. My mother is the only person in the world I ever allow myself to be treated so badly by, and in this moment of tension, I search deep, asking myself why.

Is it because I know she's secretly hurting too? She keeps those deep emotional wounds protected by harsh words and judgments. She abuses me with them. I think in some ways she projects the disappointments she's had onto me. It makes me angry, of course it does. But underneath it all, she's drowning in insecurity. The ugly thing plagues her.

My mom doesn't know most things about me. I've carefully crafted a version of me that she does know, and I'm sure that if I was to reveal even a little beyond the small glimpse she has into my real life, she would like me even less. So, I hold my ground, not allowing her to shake it.

Willard allows my mom to talk to me the way she does, which only reflects onto his own character. He has a strong personality, his candor hitting with a boorish edge, but my mom thrives on it. To her, it's simply another opportunity for her to prove how wonderful she is and how perfectly she complements Willard in his elderly life. I don't doubt that he had a word or two with my mom prior to our meal in which he took his own jabs at me. His calculated influence morphs my mom into exactly the person Willard wants by his side.

I understand that she wants companionship, but at what cost?

A sour, repugnant rush of shame crashes down on me. My stomach lurches in the hypocrisy of it all.

Once more, I'm forced to confront it: I haven't told Parker the truth.

I make a vow to myself. Next weekend, no matter what, we are having the conversation.

At all costs.

I excuse myself to use the restroom, where a red-faced, puffy-eyed reflection glares back at me. My mom was right: I do look like shit. I dig in the cabinet under the sink to find a clean facecloth and dampen it with cold water. I sit on the toilet lid and lay my head back against the wall. I drape the facecloth across my closed eyes and turn off my brain. In direct contrast to the heat of my agitated skin, the cloth is cold as ice. I let it sink in. It's refreshing. And somehow pacifying.

A few minutes later, I pull out my phone. I missed a message from Parker.

PARKER
Passed a mountain climbing booth that I don't
know how anyone can walk by without thinking
of all the things you can do with that rope...
Hope you're up for playing tonight. 10 p.m.?

I can't do a damn thing to stop the stupid grin that breaks out on my face.

ME
Yes! Grateful for the excuse to
get out of here... been stuck at my
mom's all day going through my crap,
now dinner with the whole fam.
It's been torture.

An immediate response buzzes in.

PARKER
10.

I contemplate leaving it at that, and forgetting about the message I had intended to send.
But I don't.
He needs to know where I stand.

ME
Next weekend I have something
I really need to talk to you about.

I bite my nails as the dots that show he's typing a response dance before my eyes.

PARKER
I do, too.

What?

What the fuck does that mean? *I do, too.* That's cryptic as fuck. Fucking great. Now in addition to my own secrets eating me alive, I have Parker's, too.

PARKER
10 p.m. Have the device on and ready to go.
That's an order.

My mind swims with the possibilities of Parker's secret. As infuriated as I am by it, I can't deny the draw. It's a puzzle I love to hate solving. I pick at my nails and bite my lip. I chomp down too hard in my contemplation, and my lip starts to bleed, a chunk of flesh in the corner of my mouth cut out. The redness pools as it burns. But something about it is soothing, a certain release of sorts.

I think of another release that could be quite helpful in this moment.

I imagine tonight, at 10 p.m., as I'm lying in bed with my vibrator at the ready. My naked body is sprawled out on the soft sheets as I wait patiently for directions. My phone rings with an incoming Facetime from Parker, and I excitedly answer, tastefully keeping the video above my shoulders. To my shock, Parker, Devin, and even quiet Rafe are all in on the call together. I'm caught completely off guard. I don't know how to respond, but my body decides for me, a pool of wetness surging at the thought of the three of them watching me as I get off. Parker reassures me that he wants this.

I know I do, too.

He instructs me to prop up my phone and stand so he and his friends can get a good look at me. My cheeks burn scarlet, the shame of how much I know I'll enjoy this churning inside me. I do as told and stand. My breasts are plump and my nipples erect, and I shiver when several drops of my excitement drip down my thigh. I slowly turn, showing off all angles of my body, and the sounds of approval coming from my observers fuel me. My imagined audience tells me how incredible I am and how fucking lucky they are to have me entertain them. Parker uses his app to turn the vibrator on to the lowest setting, and it buzzes in my grasp. I use it first on my nipples, gently teasing them. I moan in pleasure. The men take turns holding the phone to watch me, and I notice as it gets passed around, they have all undressed. The four of us are naked together, indulging in this passionate moment. At Devin's direction, I force the toy into my mouth and press it along my cheek. He moves the camera down so his cock is the star of the screen, and its length takes my breath away. He tells me to move the shaft into my throat. I choke and cough as I imagine it's Devin's cock. He begins to stroke his member in rhythm with my movement as I thrust the toy in and out of my mouth. He moans in approval. Parker pushes into view and orders me to bring the vibrator lower. He adjusts it to a higher speed, and I slide the toy along my creases. It glides and slips easily in the dampness of my pussy. I get lost in the pleasure, almost forgetting about my audience. I bring my phone lower and prop it against a pillow, yelping as Parker distracts me with constantly adjusting the toy's speed. Directed to focus on my clit, I run the vibrator around my pink bud. I throw my head back and writhe under the sweet stimulation of it. Satisfied voices coo in my ears. I close my eyes and indulge in the exhilarating nearness of my orgasm. I'm on the brink. My insides tighten and my breath becomes erratic. My hands grasp at the sheets and I whimper loudly. Suddenly, a thundering voice orders me to stop. Shocked and rattled, I'm forced to leave the promise of release behind. My eyes refocus on the screen. Rafe has taken control. I realize only now that this is the first time I've heard him speak. His voice is commanding and harsh. My heart pounds.

"Fuck yourself with it," he demands.

My folds are sopping in my sensual juices, and I easily swipe the toy in and out of my slit. Rafe watches as I fuck myself for our communal pleasure. I maintain eye contact, Rafe's green eyes boring into mine, as he greedily pumps his own cock in his hands. Then Devin comes into view; he's worshiping Rafe's testicles, taking them in and out of his mouth and sucking on them. His lips are lush and delectable. The sight of it sends a rush of heat through my body, and I move the toy along my nub, aching for my climax. Parker then takes control of the phone and whispers words of encouragement, telling me how fucking bad I am and how it's too good. He rapidly swipes his fist up and down the shaft of his elongated, swollen cock. I hold my breath, frozen in the swell of pleasure overcoming us all. I come at last, the ecstasy of my orgasm making my entire body quiver in release.

There's a knock at the door.

"Iris? Are you nearly done? It's just that Lily really needs to use the restroom." It's Molly. Her sad, whiny voice rings in my hot ears.

Fuck. Fuck fuck fuck. I'm breathlessly thrust back into the reality of the present. I fumble with my jeans, nearly falling off the toilet lid as I struggle to pull them up. I clear my throat. "Uh, yeah, um, sorry, just finishing up, sorry." I wash the cum from my hand and grin at myself in the mirror. My indulgence still fresh, I feel lightheaded and airy. I rinse the facecloth in a fresh stream of cold water and dab it along my hairline. My face is flushed from my little game, my cheeks pink and spotty.

"Iris? We're doing the potty dance out here!" Molly warns.

I pull the door open and slink out of the bathroom, leaving a thick trail of shame behind me.

Mom has cleared the table of our dinner dishes and now whips out an array of desserts. The smell of baked sugar and chocolate wafts through the air. In the mood to spoil myself, I fill my plate with several chocolates and a big scoop of strawberry ice cream. Zach and Willard are deep in conversation over the top travel destinations where you can get the most for your dollar. I nod as they look to me for an opinion, but considering how devastatingly poor I've been for the bulk of my adult life, I have nothing to offer in terms of travel experience. Mom takes the opportunity to yet again point out that I really should do more with my life, get out there and see the world and such, so I satiate her in saying that of course I will be glad to visit her and Willard in their island paradise. I neglect to disclose that this might be in ten years, after I've paid off my school loans and likely treated myself to my first car.

Nora yawns five times in succession, sending the signal to Zach and Molly that it's bedtime. I take this opportunity to excuse myself as well, but not before mom cries and hugs me and Zach at least a hundred times each.

"My two babies!" she hollers. "I will miss you both so much! Oh, and my grandbabies! I cannot wait to meet this new little one!" She pets Molly's stomach like it's a soft rabbit.

"We will of course set up a guest room for the two of you anytime you'd like to visit," Molly offers, referring to one of the seven or eight empty bedrooms in their mansion. Her eyes sparkle at my mom, surely in a fake display of affection. "Our home is your home." The perfect daughter-in-law.

Molly's faux warmth sends my mom into a frenzy. She completely loses it. Willard and I both share the same smirk of disgust, and, this being the only time we've ever agreed on anything, it feels like we've bonded. Strange how misery loves company.

"We really ought to let the little ones get off to bed," Willard encourages, wrapping his hesitant arms around my mom so as to pull her sad, pathetic ass away from the front door.

"We'll stop by next week before you leave, mom, don't worry," Zach reminds her as he steps over the threshold and out the door, sweet Nora's sleepy head nestled into his neck.

"Night, mom," I say, waving awkwardly as I trace Zach's steps.

"Oh, Iris," my mom sniffs, "will you please make it over for breakfast tomorrow? I'll make some cinnamon buns from scratch? Let your mother cook for you one last time!"

"Thanks, mom." I nod, even though I have no intention of coming back tomorrow. I'll break the news over text so as to avoid worsening this theatrical farewell.

The walk home is exactly what I need. The air is crisp, just enough to make my nose turn a little red by the time I reach my apartment. My deep inhales refreshingly sting.

At exactly 10 p.m., my wrist buzzes with a message from Parker.

PARKER
Ready when you are...

I take my position on the bed and unleash the toy from its box.

ME
Let's do it.

The vibrator suddenly clicks on. I nearly jump - a large part of me wasn't entirely sure that it would work. But work it does; a pleasant surprise indeed.

Parker relays his orders to me through text. First, I tease my opening, moving the vibrator in circles. It slides easily along my creases and quickly becomes wet. My invented fantasy from earlier is still playing in a loop in my mind. My mound throbs and releases a slick liquid as I envision Devin and Rafe there with Parker, helping to direct my pleasure. Inspired, I bring the vibrator to my mouth and move my tongue along the shaft. A wonderful surge of shame shoots through me for finding such arousal in the sweet taste of my own unique elixir. I text Parker to tell him I've taken initiative. *You dirty slut,* he replies. The edges of my mouth curl upward into a sly grin. *Sorry, not sorry,* I reply.

Parker instructs me to play with my breasts, and I carefully graze the delicate skin of my nipples with the tip of the vibrator. They are immediately responsive to the stimulation, and I moan in arousal. My body melts into the mattress below me. I move the toy, at an accelerated pace now, back down between my thighs. As the tip sweeps across my clit, I yelp out. It hasn't even entered me yet and my system is already swimming in ecstasy.

I really am insatiable today.

As we play, I find myself craving Parker's touch more than I ever have. I wish he could see me and watch as I revel in the gratification that he controls. I imagine his eyes on me, tracing my body as I squirm under the intensity of the vibrations that are still focused on my clit. I buck under its power, each moment an exhilarating rush. Suddenly the vibrations stop, and Parker orders me still. But the wait is too much to take. I thrust the black shaft inside of me and angle it to hit my G-spot. Parker activates the movement again and, as it wiggles inside of me, the sensation pulses under my skin. I wrap my fingers around my neck and hold my breath, the euphoria of my release imminent. At last I come, surrendering to the astonishing capabilities of modern technology. My legs quake in the aftermath, and I work hard to regulate my breath. The room smells distinctly of my arousal; the fluids from my pussy have dampened the blankets beneath me.

ME
I just came so hard, it's all over the sheets
So. Fucking. Good.

PARKER
You can do better.

Still reeling from my release, it takes almost no time or effort for me to come again. And again. I breathe in deep exhales, riding wave after wave of intoxicating bliss. I feel bad for men - single orgasms are so unfortunate.

My body grows heavy.

The euphoria is wonderfully paralyzing.

Fourteen

Never has a Sunday been so agonizingly long.

I spend the first minutes of my day doing damage control with my mom. I explain that I've gone through everything (a stretch, but a necessary one) and will come by tomorrow after work with an Uber to load up what I'm keeping. She doesn't take it well, but I don't have it in me to endure more hours in my memories. I sigh. With that fire sufficiently put out, I send a message to Vienna to check that her flight got in okay this morning. She confirms that she's home safe and sound, and thanks me once more for taking care of Sir Snowball.

I almost take her up on her offer to come over for lunch, but profoundly aware of my fragile sexual state, I decline.

Rolling out of bed, I wander into the kitchen and scour my cupboards for sustenance. I can't rationalize buying myself even a bagel when I recall how much Ben and I spent at Giuseppe's two nights ago. I find cereal in the cupboard, but have no milk, so I gnaw on dry Cheerios like a toddler. Lily would approve. Thankfully, I have a full tub of coffee, which I'm not surprised about, since I never make it at home. Except for today. I make myself a cup, drink half, and am reminded of why I have a full tub - instant coffee sucks. I pour more Cheerios into my blue bowl, and, as I chew them, decide that six dollars for coffee is always, always worth it.

As I sit on the patio outside Urban Grind with a steaming cup of my usual brew in my hand, I breathe in the sunshine of a new day. With the hardest part of the weekend behind me, things are looking up. Yet still my mind swirls, the conversation that I need to have with Parker - and that he needs to have with me - bubbling in my brain. If the time we've had apart this weekend has done anything, it has absolutely solidified for me the validity of who I am. Yet, here I am, chasing one sugary sip with the next, my thoughts running on a hamster wheel. I desperately try to distract myself in the pages of a book.

Somewhere in the late stages of conflict between the two main characters of my latest read, Simone's shift ends and she finds herself at my table.

"Hey. Mind if I sit?" she asks. Her hair is thick and shiny. I want to run my fingers through it.

"Hey! Yeah, of course."

"Thanks. What are you reading?" She pulls out the wooden chair and settles in it across from me.

"Oh, it's a mystery. Pretty intriguing, actually. Almost finished."

"Cool, cool." There's an expectant pause. "Hey, listen. I was wondering if you wanted to grab lunch sometime this week? You know, catch up. It's been a minute."

My cheeks turn red. "I would love to," I reply. "Let me just... hold on." I pull my phone from its pocket in my tote and check my schedule. "Best time for me is Wednesday. I could do Thursday, too."

"Let's do Wednesday first. After that, we can decide if we want to do Thursday, too," Simone suggests. Her eyes are dark and bright all at the same time.

I sink into my chair as a lusty warmth washes over me. It's hopeless to fight the stupid grin plastered on my face. "Sounds like a plan," I giggle. I'm an idiot.

"Noon work for you?"

"Sure. I'll be here. And by here, I mean there. At work." I awkwardly contort my body to point down the plaza towards my building.

"Right. Well. I'll see you tomorrow morning?" I look at Simone, puzzled. "I'll have your coffee ready for you, seven-thirty," she laughs, sensing my confusion.

"Yes, thank you." I tilt my head. Simone gets up, ready to make her leave. "Hey, tomorrow," I start, just as she's about to walk away. She turns back to me, her beautiful mouth upturned in amusement. "Can you make me something a little different?" I request. "You know, surprise me."

"I didn't know you like surprises."

"I think you do."

My mind flashes back to a few months ago, when Simone and I hooked up. We were at a party. I don't remember whose, I don't remember what for, but I do remember she smelled like lavender and vanilla. She immediately caught my eye from across the room, a shy smile at the corner of her mouth. I approached her. It wasn't like our eyes didn't meet almost every day at

Urban Grind, or that our hands never grazed when she passed me my coffee, or that we didn't feel the unspoken spark pulling us toward each other.

I knew she felt it, too.

"Hi," I said.

"Hi."

And I kissed her. It was 80% attraction, 20% Tequila. She tasted amazing. Her lips were lush and full, and our mouths sunk into each other, fitting just right. Her skin was sleek and soft and all I wanted to do was run my hands over every inch of her. I started to, but she stopped me.

"Let's get out of here," she suggested.

Seeing as we were two blocks from my apartment, it was the most sensible option.

I pushed her against the back of my door and laid my body into hers. Our kiss changed, from infatuated to hungry. She bit my lips, and I wailed in dizzying enjoyment.

"You have to know something, first," Simone breathed into my mouth, her voice hazy and hesitant.

"Mm hmm." It was all I could muster as I licked and kissed her neck. I ran my fingers along her chest and kneaded her perky breasts in my hands. They were perfect.

As I went to pull off her shirt, she stopped me, her body suddenly rigid.

"What is it? You okay?" I asked, sort of panicked.

"You need to know. I'm actually... well... I'm trans," she said, her voice cracking. She cleared her throat. "I'm transitioning," she clarified. "So..." she looked down at her waist. "I'm not... not yet."

I smiled, so widely, I probably looked like a maniac. Because I always knew there was something exceptionally unique about Simone. Her voice is hearty but soft, her skin dewy, but thick. One thing is certain though: she's strikingly beautiful.

"Okay," I said.

"Okay?" she gulped.

"Very okay," I insisted.

Then I pulled off her shirt, nestled my face in between her two perfect, new-to-her breasts, and relished the beauty of her body, scars and all.

She was hesitant, though, and pulled away before either of us got our fill.

But she had hooked me, drawn me in. Since then, we've remained friendly, and, at least on my end, the attraction is still there.

Which makes me wonder if I should *not* go on this lunch date.

"Actually," I blurt, just as Simone is about to take her leave. "Do you mind if we push lunch back until the following week? I have some family stuff going on this week that's demanding more of my attention than I'd care to give it." Not an entirely untrue excuse.

"Sure."

I can tell she's disappointed. I am, too. I hope my postponement isn't in perpetuity.

To escape the discomfort of having to keep Simone at arm's length, I launch back into my book. I finish it, but immediately regret doing so, as I don't have another to fill its void. And the library is closed on Sundays. I make the ethically challenging decision to go to the bookstore, start a new read there, and pick up a copy of it at the library tomorrow while I'm there for book club. I'm sure I'm not the only one who has ever done this. Right?

. . . .

BOOKSTORES NEVER SMELL the same as libraries. Book stores are new, untouched, virginal, almost. Libraries are full of memories, of times enjoyed over and over, of late nights and early mornings. I am a library person. However, I am grateful Books on Main is open 7 days a week, so I can haul my sad, book-less ass over there to find a placeholder. I'm combing through the NEW ON SHELVES section when I see a familiar figure.

A brown bob with bangs, green eyes, pale skin, and freckles: it's Maisie, the librarian. I guess I'm not the only bookworm missing home on the weekends.

"Iris! Hi!" she sings, her voice warm and light.

"Hi! Oh, my God, so funny running into you here!" I yell, leaning in for a weird, should-we-hug-or-not-because-our-relationship-is-not-really-a-hugging-one-but-still-I-feel-like-we-should-hug-oh-God-I'm-sorry-I'm-so-awkward hug. "I just finished the book for book club tomorrow."

"Oh, nice! I'm sad to not be doing Mondays anymore," she whines.

"Yeah, I'm sad, too. I mean, Gemma is fine, but I like you a lot more!"

"Aw, you're going to make me blush! I miss the Monday group. Lots of interesting opinions there."

"We miss you! Come back to us, please!" I beg, like a child asking mommy for ice cream before dinner. *Please???*

If only our schedules aligned.

"I feel kind of like a traitor at the bookstore right now," I admit.

Maisie laughs, her giggle filling the air and making everything around us seem inconsequential.

"I'm just picking up a few new ones for the library," she explains, wiggling her armful of books.

"Any recommendations I should look into?" I ask. My eyes wander to the pile in her arms.

Maisie exhales and awkwardly shifts, twisting her pile almost as if trying to avert my gaze from it. My presence suddenly feels invasive, and I consider impaling myself on the nearest bookshelf so as to escape the tension of this moment.

When it comes to the relationship between me and Maisie, it doesn't really extend beyond the professional realm. She's the librarian, I'm the book-obsessed patron. But, in the vast number of book clubs Maisie's hosted and I've participated in, I've noticed it. Her voice changes - a faint breathlessness - when our discussions cover those of a *sensitive* nature. Her body language speaks volumes; skin reddening, pulse quickening. There's a sensual warmth to her. Perhaps Maisie and I have more in common than a love for books.

"You know," she says, after a seemingly endless pause, "I'm going to try giving this one a go." She pulls out a black-and-white hardcover from her pile. "I've read so many mysteries and horrors for book club. I thought I'd switch gears and try non-fiction." A memoir. Interesting choice. I study the cover, feigning intrigue when really, I'm trying to catch a proper glimpse of the other books in her arms.

Maisie's phone rings at just the right time, she excuses herself politely, and runs off to the checkout, leaving me book-less (still), and (newly) intrigued by whatever secrets she has.

I eventually decide on a smutty romance novel, inspired by Maisie's aspiration to try something different. It's an easy read, and in just a few hours, I'm nearly done. It's predictable, but funny and light. Everything I need after a tough weekend.

. . . .

TURNS OUT IT'S REAL: that whole butterflies-in-your-stomach, fluttery feeling depicted in all the clichéd romance stories (including the one I just consumed). Parker's name pops up on my phone, and my cheeks immediately turn a humiliating shade of pink. My stomach churns in delightful anguish.

"Hi."

"Hi." The sound of his voice - good God. Two pathetic letters and I'm coming apart.

"How was your trip?" I ask. My heart rate spikes and adrenaline floods every particle in my body.

"Good! It was good. But fuck, Iris," he groans, "I missed you. Being away from you - it was torture."

You're telling me, I think. "Eh. Missed you a bit."

"Right. Just a bit." He laughs. "I'm just heading home from dropping off Rafe." I can't help but flash to Rafe's imagined cock and feel my skin tingle. "I was planning on a quick shower then..." he pauses, drawing it out.

"Then come and see me," I finish his thought for him.

"I was planning on it. But. We got in later than I expected to. And I have a few work things that need my attention pretty urgently."

"You're joking, right?" He's playing with me. He has to be.

"I wish I was. I'm sorry, Iris. Tuesday, though. Tuesday's ours."

Those butterflies I had just a moment ago are replaced by rocks - heavy, pointy rocks sitting in a grotesque pile at the bottom of my gut. I'm in such a state of disbelief. And confusion. Sure, Parker and I don't usually spend Sunday evenings together, but given the fact that he's been away during our *designated* time makes me feel robbed. Schedules schedules, commitments commitments. There's always something getting in the way. And, just like the time Parker was *on a work call* on my balcony, smiling all cheerily on a

Sunday morning, I find it outrageously difficult to believe *work* needs his urgent attention on a Sunday night. Yes, it's nearing the end of the month, which means he's no doubt drowning in paperwork. April is a notoriously busy time for him, but. Something isn't adding up.

The rocks inside me swirl.

Next weekend I have something I really need to talk to you about, I had texted.

I do, too, he had replied.

What secrets is he keeping?

Fifteen

Aching from rejection, I fall into bed and vow to spend the night thinking of anything but him.

But I don't. I can't. I can't stop thinking about him. Parker has seeped into me. The mere thought of his existence, somewhere in the universe, no matter how far from me, makes me jittery and flushed. I can't fight this truth. I'm so in love, so spellbound by this man, that it seems impossible to deny that he is a part of me, weaved into who I am.

I think of him while I fold laundry. I think of him while I stress-clean the kitchen. I think of him while I undress for bed and spread my naked body across the cool sheets of my mattress. I think of him while I pinch my nipples in the tips of my fingers and thrust my favorite black vibrator in and out of my slick folds. I think of him while I come, imagining he's there, watching me.

I think of him even as I doze off to sleep, a blanket of love and resentment carrying me off into my dreams.

• • • •

BY SOME MIRACLE, I sleep peacefully and wake clear-headed. I stretch my body, pointing my toes and raising my arms above my head as I take in a deep morning breath. The promise of a new day. I shower and scrub head to toe. I pull on a comfortable bra and panties, then layer my bright Bluey scrubs on top. I feel fresh.

My phone is waiting for me, fully charged, in the kitchen. Countless notifications bombard the screen, but my heart skips a beat when I see a message from Parker. Just like that, the bitterness melts away. I smile and open the text.

It's a simple *Good morning* message accompanied by a gif of a couple playing with ropes and bondage. Mm. A familiar warmth threatens between my thighs. My heart flutters, then a profound ache replaces it. I have to wait until tomorrow to see him. It feels like an eternity has passed since I've felt him close.

I reply with a heart-eyed emoji and a drop of water. Immature, but appropriate.

I'm grateful to have a full Monday to distract me from all the things I want to do with Parker when I see him. My first stop is Urban Grind, where I'm guiltily glad to see Simone promptly at 7:30 a.m. with my promised mystery beverage. I take two sips and allow the alien flavor to dance on my tastebuds.

I hate it. I have no idea what it is, but it's awful. Too creamy, not sweet enough, a strange aftertaste. My face says it all.

It can be good to try something new, but sometimes you just know what you like, and that's that.

Simone laughs heartily. "I had a feeling it would be a flop! Made this just in case." She immediately presents me with my usual. I give her a grateful hug over the counter threshold. We linger a beat too long, and our cheeks graze as we break our embrace. Her skin is electric against mine. That spark.

I add an everything bagel to my order, then grab a seat on the patio today instead of retreating to my usual spot by the river. I pull out my phone in absence of a book to read, take a few bites of my bagel, and scroll. Just a moment later, I'm interrupted by a tap on my shoulder. I look up, my eyes meeting those of my disruptor.

My breath hitches.

"Hey, I'm really sorry to bother you," he whispers, rubbing the stubble on his chin. "But you're here, and I'm here, and I figure I may as well ask. I just feel like you'll be able to help me." He exhales cryptically, the sweetness of his breath hanging in the air. He towers over me, with broad shoulders and thick muscles fighting against the confines of his shirt. His voice is deep and dark, matching his flawless skin. I can't stop myself from doing a head-to-toe. He's stunning. "Do you work at the vet clinic at the other end of this plaza?" He leans in to me. I look up into his dark eyes.

"I do," I answer, cautioning myself. I clear my throat.

"Oh, great," he sighs. He retreats from the space of my personal bubble and takes the seat to my right. "I hope you can help me." He settles in the chair, putting his large coffee on the table beside mine. He's dressed to impress in gray slacks and a white dress shirt, with the top few buttons undone in the absence of a tie. He licks his lips. He is so beautiful that I immediately feel like a ridiculous joke in my childish Bluey scrubs. I stare at him, captivated.

"My grandmother's dog isn't doing well. Does your office make house calls? She is very reluctant to take him to the vet. So, I was thinking maybe if you - well, not you, but someone from your office - or maybe you, if you're the vet - well, you know." He's adorable, tripping over his words. "I'm just wondering if your office makes house calls?" he finishes.

I chuckle, charmed by him. "I know what you're trying to say," I giggle again. "Yes, actually, we do make house calls. I'm not the vet - that would be Dr. Val. He's wonderful. I suppose I'm sort of biased, but I personally do truly believe he is a good human. We also have several other pet docs in the office. Here..." I reach down into my tote bag and rummage through to find a piece of paper. The best I can do is the receipt from Giuseppe's on Friday. My embarrassment continues. I jot down Dr. Val's PetVet's number. "Give us a call, and we can provide you with scheduling, fees, and that sort of thing." I transform into business-mode, trying to save face in awe of him.

"Thank you." He reaches out and grabs the receipt, our fingers just grazing. His skin feels rough. The stimulation against mine is a welcome sensation. "I appreciate this," he says as he slips the paper into his breast pocket. Then he jumps up, grabs his coffee, and with a "bye," he's gone.

My heart races and my mouth feels dry. Such a simple interaction, yet the heat of it lingers in the air.

I decide there are too many distractions around here. I retreat to the river, breathing in the freshness of the day as I stroll along the pathway. Parker immediately invades my brain. For so many reasons. I chug down several sips of my coffee and glide along the path, willing the caffeine to saturate my veins.

I arrive at work just on time. Maria and Robbie are already in, getting reception ready for a new day. Robbie is mostly trained now, so it's a relief to know he'll be mostly self-sufficient. I glide into the back, where I'm planning on spending most of the day. Focused on our kenneled critters and their care, I relish in the warm adorableness of their little furry bodies.

Dr. Val is in today, and he stays for the duration of my shift. I always enjoy working with him. He's compassionate, grossly intelligent, and has an excellent bedside manner. He has always treated me and the other techs with respect and appreciation, and, on a day like today, I'm reminded how much I love my job.

I don't tell him to expect an inquiry about a house call. I know my cheeks will immediately tighten and go pink at the mention of the sexy coffee shop man. I push him out, electing to focus on Simba the ginger cat and his asthma medication.

It's Parker who overtakes my thoughts.

I imagine his soft lips and the feel of his disheveled hair. I think of his smell and breathe it in. I fantasize he's watching me. The entire day, his blue eyes study and follow my every move: as I pick up a burger for lunch, while I'm out taking the dogs for their afternoon stroll, when I slice my finger on a pile of papers and suck on the dot of blood pouring from the cut. I don't know why I fight it.

Love has a strange way of holding on and not letting go.

• • • •

I'M ELATED TO WALK into the library after work. I've missed you, dear friend. I have about half an hour before book club, and I spend every second of it soaking in the pages of books, new and old. I check out my copy of the book for next week's club meeting and three others. Should last me until the end of the week. I hope. I wander into the meeting room and settle into my chair between two of the usual suspects - Olga and Nancy. We chat briefly about our thoughts on the book before the meeting officially begins, and the three of us share the opinion that it was a tad too predictable, although it had excellent pacing. One other joins us - a new attendee named Carl - before Gemma begins discussions.

It's probably the worst book club meeting I've ever gone to. Maybe because the book wasn't great, maybe because Gemma really is no Maisie, or maybe because Carl, although somewhat shy, has ruthless commentary when he does speak. I can't wait to get out of here, and, having just received a text from Ben, I excuse myself early to call him.

It isn't good news.

Leo has ended things. Just now. Literally seconds before. Ben is a wreck.

I order an Uber and go to his apartment, which is a harrowing thirty-five-minute drive away. When I finally arrive, Ben falls into my arms and I wrap him up, safe and loved. He cries. I cry. We basically bathe in each other's snot. It's ugly and horrible, yet beautiful and validating. I never got to meet Leo, but Ben has nothing but love for him. Even now, in his distraught state, he can't say a bad thing about him.

It's in that instant that I decipher that the culprit: the vile monster that is unrequited love.

I want to cut my heart open and pull Ben inside. He's the best human I know, and his pain ripples in my bones. It isn't fair. It isn't right. This poor man has faced more rejection than any one person should.

We order pizza and eat the entire thing between us. Ben cries some more. I take a soft blanket, gray and inconceivably plush, and wrap him in it on his bed. His breathing stills as I rub his back. His eyes close.

He's going to be okay. My brave, beautiful Ben.

It's nearing 10 p.m. now, and my exhaustion is heavy. I'm about to order an Uber home when my stomach drops. On the premise of self-preservation, I had silenced notifications from my mom, and in doing so missed five calls and over a dozen texts from her. I scroll through them, terror streaming in my blood.

A bittersweet relief hits when I realize everything is okay, it's only that I promised I'd pick up my boxes from her house today. Talk about dramatic.

But also, fuck. Fuck fuck fuck.

I'm not in a good headspace for this. But then again, is there really a *good* headspace for the last time I'll ever visit my childhood home? I reluctantly adjust the Uber destination from my address to my mom's. And choose an XL that can hopefully fit my boxes into its trunk.

By some miracle, mom and Willard are out. Who knew old people had a life on a Monday night? I have the Uber wait while I attempt to pull the boxes containing my journals, a few childhood knickknacks, and a couple of stuffies out to it. The driver, a young mom named Cindy who says she drives part time to supplement her wife's income, witnesses my struggle and hops out to help me. I'm deeply appreciative - it not only cuts down on the difficulty of it all (emotionally and physically), but we get to chatting, and I don't think about Ben or Parker for the entirety of it. I don't even really think about the fact that this is the last time I'll ever be able to call this house my home.

Like spies, we get in and out undetected. Mission complete.

Cindy goes above and beyond by helping me haul the boxes from her SUV up to my apartment door. It's closing in on midnight. I pull out my wallet and give her a twenty, which I feel like is not really enough to express my gratitude, but I'm broke. She thanks me effusively, even though I insist she's the one who needs thanking, and we go our separate ways.

I text my mom to let her know the boxes are gone.

I text Ben to let him know how much he's loved.

I text Parker to let him know I miss him.

Sixteen

It's finally Tuesday. At last.

I wake up to a string of depressive texts from Ben. His sadness is asphyxiating. Despite my heavy heart, I dig deep to find strength for him. He called in sick to work, he tells me, and plans on taking the day to rewatch the most recent seasons of Love is Blind and eat every last bag of chips in his pantry. I give him my full support, and offer to bring him takeout tomorrow night. He says that he'll think on it.

Parker grows increasingly naughty on our text thread. He sends me a message detailing the many things he wishes to do to me tonight. It's cute, the way he thinks he gets to call the shots. Cute, and ignorant.

I can't wait to feel his skin on mine.

The anticipation makes the day excessively drawn out. Roy is in this morning. He's shadowing Dr. Caroline, who is taking things painstakingly slow, thereby causing a backlog of impatient pet parents in the waiting room. Robbie continues to impress me with his tenacity. He turns on the charm and circles the room, surprising each pet with a special treat for their patience. I watch him with admiration and know we made the right choice in adding him to our permanent staff roster.

Dr. Caroline sends me over to PetCation for a couple of hours near the end of my shift, and I am more than happy to spend time tossing tennis balls for the pups in the playroom. I giggle, thinking of Parker, his balls, and all the playing we have to do.

I'm such a deviant.

• • • •

JUST BEFORE SEVEN-THIRTY, Parker messages me that he's here. I throw open my apartment door, run downstairs with shameful enthusiasm, and turn the corner.

The moment my eyes land on him, the world around us melts away. Our attraction is magnetic, and I'm propelled toward him. I throw the gate open and lay my lips on his, kissing him more deeply than I ever have. I get lost in it, the hypnotism, the draw. It's ethereal. He sucks me in, my body

121

melding into his. My tongue invades his mouth. I'm ravenous for him; I want to devour every part of him. He tastes of spice and warmth and it comforts my deep ache for him. We breathe each other in and our bodies tangle together in mutual longing.

We don't talk. There are no words. Pure, carnal desire dictates our every move. We fuck over the kitchen table. Then on the couch. Then we go into the bedroom, where Parker gets on his knees and eats me out. He worships my pussy with his tongue, lunging his fingers into my slit. I'm thrust into oblivion, again and again, the sweetness of release launching me into another plane of pleasure.

In a state of pure bliss, we lay in bed. I'm wrapped in Parker's arms.

It's the perfect nest of love and comfort.

• • • •

IT TURNS OUT THAT THE expo weekend was a success. Parker relays the details, which I admittedly only half listen to. It all sounds rather dull to me, but then again, camping is never something I would ever willingly participate in. The boys had a memorable time, though, and even fit in ax throwing on Saturday afternoon.

"The place was really quaint. I bet you'd like it. We ordered a couple of rounds and gave it a go. Rafe completely whooped our asses." Parker recalls. "He was a natural. I struggled the most. Devin didn't do too bad."

"Who knew you were amongst ax throwing Gods?" I laugh. "Why is the image of Rafe wielding an ax bizarrely turning me on?" I joke. A sting of embarrassment hits as I process the potential repercussions of my brazen comment. My heart sinks.

"Turning you on, huh?" Parker teases, pulling me in closer and fondling my naked chest. He laughs it off and bites my neck. Relief hits me, and the horrible yo-yo of self-doubt vanishes as if it never existed.

I fall further under his spell.

"I should have a shower." I break free of his grasp and raise my eyebrows at him. "Care to join me?" We are both caked in sweat and cum.

Parker smiles. "Hmm... do... I... need... a... shower..." he ruminates.

"You need a shower," I command.

"You need a shower," he echoes. "Just look at you. Your hair."

He grabs a tuft of it and holds me at arm's length. My heart skips a beat. His eyes examine me, tracing the shape of my face and the lines along my eyes. He yanks on the fistful of my hair, harder this time. It hurts so good, and I yelp in response. My body reacts similarly, releasing a slick liquid in the creases of my pussy.

"A disgrace," he continues. He threads his fingers through my disheveled locks, pulling on knots and causing me to wince. "Unacceptable," he mutters. "Unacceptable," he repeats, more loudly this time.

The power struggle is almost as hot as the sex that follows.

"I'm sorry," I play into it. "I have a hairbrush in the bathroom."

Parker says nothing. His eyes sear into me, his gaze sinking into my skin. Without warning, he grabs my arm and rushes me into the bathroom. He slams the door, then shoves me into the shower. I lean against the shower wall, the cool tile a refreshing sensation against the heat of my body. Parker turns the faucet on, immediately showering me with a gushing stream of cold water. It takes my breath away. I shiver.

"Turn around," he orders. I do as told, facing the wall of the shower. A quiet fills the room for a moment. The only sound is my labored breath blended into the falling water.

The wait just about kills me. I would say it's the unknown, but that would be a lie. I have an inkling. It's the anticipation that's torture.

WHACK!

Parker smacks the smooth back of my paddle brush against the tender flesh of my ass. I let out a breathless howl. It gleefully stings.

WHACK! Again.

WHACK! Again. My heels shoot up, my ass burning, cheeks clenched to brace for more.

WHACK! The final time.

I hear the brush fall to the floor with a clink. Parker climbs inside the shower with me and grabs hold of my hips. He thrusts inside of me. The feeling of him filling me up is like a drug. It intoxicates me, making me weak and powerful all at once. He wraps his arms around me and fills his hands with my supple breasts. The humid bathroom air forms a smoky mist around our bodies. I can smell it, taste it, even. The arousal is thick. Parker lays into me, fucking me as he bucks his hips mercilessly. He reaches for my wrists and grasps them tightly against the wall. I'm helpless. It's exhilarating, giving up control like this. I'm hungry for it - for him, for my climax.

Next thing I know, I'm on my knees with Parker's erect cock before me. He orders me to take it into my mouth.

"Slowly," he commands.

But I'm ravenous. I eagerly pull him into my mouth, and his hand blasts across my cheek in an impossible motion, so fast, so unexpected. I gasp. He's never slapped me before.

But... I like it.

My cheek burns, and I instinctively raise my hand to touch where his was.

"I said, slowly," he repeats, a taunting smirk painted on his face.

I start over, slowly sliding him in, through my lips, past my teeth, and along my tongue. I bring him in as far as I can, allowing the tip of his dick to sit against the back of my throat. I hold my breath, waiting for instructions, fighting the urge to bob my head along his full length.

The surprises continue. Parker presents a second cock, this one a black dildo, and forces it next to his. I cough, unable to make space for even an inch of the toy with Parker lodged in my throat. I pull back, my mouth nearly empty, as I make room for the second shaft. The two barely fit, their tips sliding just past my lips.

"Aw, is it too much for you, Iris?" Parker whines, humiliating me. "Can't take it, can you?"

His words fuel me. I open wider, and wider still, desperate to prove myself. But my mouth is only as big as it is, and my jaw seizes up. I shamefully admit defeat.

Parker tuts in disappointment. "That just won't do. Now, what am I going to do with you?"

I thrust his length into my mouth, dedicating my full attention to it. Parker pulls away.

"That's not what I told you I wanted," he chastises. "Bad. Very bad."

I kneel before him, shame surging through me. It makes me so hot that I think I'll explode. I'm desperate for his approval. It takes everything in me to wait for him, to wait for his next direction. He's testing me - torturing me; he knows my patience fuse is short.

He shakes his head, turns away from me, and steps out of the shower. He's gone. I wait. He doesn't come back. I wait some more. Still, alone. I stand under the water as it beats down on me, a warm hug embracing me where Parker isn't.

I emerge from the bathroom in a flurry of confusion. Parker is on the couch, fully dressed, texting on his phone. We were playing our game. What happened? What went wrong?

"You okay?" I mutter, my words disjointed by the glass in my throat.

"Hmm? Uh, yeah. Sorry, just have a couple of emails I need to answer." He doesn't look up.

It's the first time ever that I've felt a divide between us. This isn't him. He's never this removed, this distracted.

"I was waiting for you. In the shower."

"Uh..." silence. More silence. Beads of water drip from my damp hair and splash onto the floor. "Yes." He finally puts his phone down. "Yes, I... sorry, my phone rang. I had an urgent matter." He pulls off his glasses and rubs his eyes.

What in the fuck is with all these *urgent matters*?

"You need to tell me these things. Remember?" I prompt, hoping he'll make the connection to our previous conversation just a week ago. "Communicate. Tell me what to expect. Don't leave me hanging like that." My tone is sassy, but I'm proud of myself for calling him out.

"I know. I'm sorry. I'm stretched so thin right now, between work, you, o... other commitments," he stutters.

"Well, I don't mean to be a burden," I say, more passive aggressively than I intend.

"Iris."

"I didn't mean it like that. I just... we barely get time together. You really left me hanging there, right in the heat of the moment. At first, I thought it was part of the game, you ignoring me. But you didn't come back. Then I come out here, and you're... working? Like, what? What the fuck?"

Parker laughs. He laughs heartily, amused by my humiliation. My stomach swirls, and I sink to the floor.

"You're smart as a whip, you know that?" He leans over the back of the couch and pets my head. I lean into him. I can't help it, with that ridiculous L-word hanging in the balance. "I was punishing you. I really got to you, huh?" he coos, a little shard of regret apparent in his voice. My lips hang open.

"You fucker," I mutter.

I shoot up and go to slap him back. He grabs my wrist, as though he was expecting it. My hand burns, my wrist fights him, and he lets go. I slap him, hard, his cheek turning the same pink hue as mine had. It doesn't feel as good as I hoped it would. I lick my lips, the desire to kiss him all better setting them on fire.

Parker stares at me, his eyes digging deep. He's reading my thoughts. I can't resist him. He has hold of me, like the roots of a one-hundred-year-old tree entrenched in the dirt below.

"Let's go to bed. I want to hold you close."

My heart melts.

Seventeen

I sleep like a dream, nestled in my cocoon of blankets, entangled in Parker's arms. Complete contentment.

Parker leaves early the next morning - he's out of bed before 4:30 a.m. I'm barely coherent as he gives me a quick peck and whispers something in my ear, which now, replaying retrospectively, might have been those three little words. More likely, though, that's wishful thinking.

I fly through my library books in the passing days, finishing next week's club read and half of another in just a day. Hopped up on too much caffeine and the buzz of Parker in my blood, my energy is intense. I'm peppy at work, pleasant with the staff and customers, and happy to stay late on Thursday when Dr. Caroline requests an extra hand with a diabetic cat named Who.

Each day is a stepping stone getting me closer to Friday, when I finally see Parker again. I check my calendar and recall it's our mysterious date night. I have no idea what Parker has in store, but I know what I do. I mull it over - the expectations for the night ahead. In typical Iris fashion, I form an organized list in my mind of my three goals for the evening.

1. Tell Parker my secret. Okay, *secrets*. Two, about me; One, about us. Try not to die in the vulnerability of it all.
2. Find out what exactly he's been hiding from me. We both need to be transparent to move forward in this.
3. Keep it together. And hope that by the end of all these adult conversations, our relationship stays intact. Because I do really, *really* love him.

I can do this. I'm a mature, adult human ready to have mature, adult human conversations. On my end, I suppose I'm as ready as I'll ever be to reveal my truth. But it's Parker's unknown reaction to my plan that sours it. It slowly festers in my mind, corrupting my ability to do anything but obsess over it. Those easy moments of focus and positivity seem a distant memory as Friday hits. Fuck. Fuck fuck fuck. The torture is sickening. My morning coffee swirls in my throat and burns in my brain. The unspoken facts cloud my mind.

My wrist buzzes with a text from Parker. He really is embedded in me.

PARKER
Be ready, 8 p.m.

ME
Yup.
Can you tell me where we're going yet?

PARKER
Nope
But, like I said...
When you find out...
It'll be hilarious.

Eighteen

I smile and let out a pathetic laugh. I whack Parker on the arm with my black clutch, aggravated by his stupid joke, and also by the fact that he was right - it will be hilarious.

We stand in front of a wide building decorated with oversized marquee letters. They shine brightly against the black of the exterior. Laugh Lane. A comedy club. Of course Parker is taking me to a comedy club.

I grab onto his arm, shaking my head.

"You're ridiculous, you know."

My tall heels clip-clop along the sidewalk as we glide toward the entrance. The burly man at the door scans the tickets on Parker's phone, and we walk down a dimly lit hall. Reaching the end, we turn right. There's a coat check and, a little further down, a bar. A beautiful woman dressed in a short black skirt and sheer blank tank makes her way over to us. She's young, probably just of legal age, but she knows how to mix a drink. Parker orders us each the house special: a sweet, fruity cocktail called the Naked Lady.

I look around and take the place in. It's shocking this colossal room is hidden within the walls of the black building. At first glance, the exterior doesn't seem large enough. The ceiling is high and open, with pipes, air conditioning vents, and electrical conduit running along it. At the front of the room sits the stage, lined by a row of rectangular tables first, then square ones behind that. Our seats are on the left in the next row, in a series of half-circle tables outfitted with plush, leather benches horseshoed around them. Behind us are more rows of the same, then the square ones, then the rectangles. The seating continues in a dizzying pattern of shapes that stretches on and on.

We take our seats and clink our drinks together. I sip, allowing the sweetness of the cocktail to slide down my throat. It smells bitter, but tastes the opposite, and I soon find myself with an empty glass. We peruse the food menu, and I decide on a hearty bowl of spaghetti, while Parker chooses a classic burger and fries. We order another round from our handsome server, Janeel, and our hands lightly graze as I pass him my empty glass. I feel a flutter in my stomach. Does Parker notice me smack my lips in an attempt to hide my lustful grin?

I'm sure he does.

And in that moment, I ponder if he has known this entire time. If I'm only fooling myself in thinking he hasn't yet discovered my secret.

I dart my head around in an attempt to locate the bathroom. I notice the crowd around us growing, and the room is filling up. What's the capacity of this place, I wonder? Five hundred people? One thousand? This place is so massive, it's beginning to make me uneasy. My head spins as I try to comprehend all the bodies swirling around us. Having noticed the edge of a neon sign lit up at the far left of the room, I take a chance and excuse myself, hoping it will direct me to the bathroom.

Thankfully, it does.

I travel down another dimly lit hall opposite the entrance. Also an expansive space, the bathroom itself appears large enough to house a show of its own. I wash my hands and splash a few drops of water over my forehead and cheeks. The coldness is welcome. I can feel my body heating up from all the energy that's gyrating within it. I examine my image in the mirror, tracing my eyes from top to bottom. I focus on the pointy ends of my auburn hair, which, in a rare occasion, I straightened, the plunging neckline of my crimson blouse that exposes just a hint of cleavage, my hips, securely nestled in an overly expensive pair of black jeans I scored on clearance at Nordstrom rack a year ago. My honey-brown eyes are bright and wide, framed by black mascara I swiped on for this occasion. I take a deep breath and reluctantly remind myself of my list. I can't put it off much longer.

I shake off the anticipation of what's to come and take a deep breath. First things first. I'm going to enjoy this date with Parker. We'll laugh, joke, and bask in the happiness that fills us up when we're together. The rest can wait.

Making my way back to our table, I notice there are new faces. Parker is chatting with a short-haired blonde in a stunning blue number who has plopped down next to him. Beside her is a clean-shaven mammoth of a man tucked into neat slacks and a crisp white button-down. They are, without a doubt, a very attractive couple. I hesitate a moment, my eyes drinking them in, then I slide into my seat. Parker immediately disrupts the conversation to introduce me.

"There you are," he says, lifting his arm above my head and sliding it down my back. "Iris, this is Betty and Steven. They just sat down."

"Hi, nice to meet you," I offer politely.

"Hi!" chirps Betty.

"Hi." Steven is less enthusiastic. He is so gargantuan, I can only imagine his discomfort in being stuffed into a tight seating arrangement such as this.

"Our drinks came." Parker nudges mine toward me. "I was just telling these two that they might have more luck getting a drink up at the bar."

"Mm," I mumble, a fresh sip of Naked Lady on my lips. "Yeah, this place is really filling up." My eyes wander briefly, but I immediately return my stare to our tablemates. My body flashes with heat as I study them. I feel like I'm somehow being tested, my wherewithal being evaluated. Betty is perky with huge eyes, a bright smile, and, yes, ample cleavage that's too inviting to my gaze. Stephen is a colossus in his own right. My mind slips away as I imagine him, a Hulk, offering his massive cock before Betty's petite mouth. I doubt she could take him in very far. I could do better. A devious grin glides across my face.

I snap out of it as I notice the two of them heed Parker's advice and make their way over to the main bar.

"See something you like?" Parker teases, leaning back and stretching himself out in the space made by Betty and Steven's departure.

"What? I mean, well, yeah..." I blush and clear my throat. "They're quite the couple."

"Uh, huh."

Thankfully Janeel swoops in and saves me. He positions our plates in front of us, and I eagerly dig in. Parker eyes me as I scoop the spaghetti into my mouth. The sauce is tangy and a bit runny, so I struggle to keep from splattering it all over my face. As it always is when Parker watches me, I feel a murky mix of naked vulnerability and exhilaration. And then there's Betty. And Steven. And Janeel, even. My throat tightens.

"How is it?" Parker asks, knowing full well how it is.

"Messy!" I exclaim. I pat my face with the black fabric napkins laid before us.

"I see that." His mouth forms into a slick grin.

"You going to eat that?" I ask, motioning toward his untouched plate. He glances at it briefly, but then his eyes snap back and collide with mine. I stare into them, challenging him. The corners of his lips turn up ever so slightly, but his gaze stays, unwavering.

It appears we are at a stalemate.

But of course he wins. I melt under his stare. I always melt under him. The depth of his blue eyes sucks me in, weakening every bone in my body. My stomach feels like it's falling away. My cheeks ache as I hopelessly work to suppress the urge to break into a wide smile.

"I love you, Iris."

His words enter the air like a caged bird finally freed. The world around us vanishes. I'm breathless. My lips part slightly as his hands reach for mine and our eyes are once more locked. We are connected in a way beyond understanding; it's intense, feral, and teeming with sensuality.

"I do. I love you. You are the most stunning, fearless, alluring woman I have ever encountered. You've captured my heart, Iris. It's yours. I'm yours."

I search for my voice but cannot find it. I'm paralyzed. I yearn to echo his words. I'm aching to tell Parker I love him, too. Because I *do* love him, too. But hearing his profession overwhelms me with guilt. I can't ignore it. Down in my depths, a heavy shame swirls like a tempest. Parker can't love me. Not all of me. He doesn't know all of me. Not yet.

I had intended to tell him tonight, after the show, but now I find myself cornered. This is all wrong. This isn't how it's supposed to go.

I worry that I've waited too long.

Parker's eyes remain on me, waiting expectantly. His words echo in my mind, and I use them to steady my breath. My heart slowly calms. In his gaze, I feel safe. Parker is it for me. He's my person. My face flushes and my cheeks give way to a giddy grin. A fresh surge of courage spikes through my veins.

"I love you, too, Parker!" I shout into the world. Of course I do. He has been too easy to fall in love with.

One secret down. The easiest one. Two to go.

Parker heaves himself onto me. We share our first kiss as two people openly in love. There's an electric spark as our lips join. Our tongues mingle and dance in the heat of our affection. I push myself into him. I want to conquer his body and climb on top of him. I don't care where we are. I want to fuck his brains out.

We are flung back to reality with the return of Betty and Steven, who comment on how perhaps they should sit at another table.

Parker cavalierly responds with a blunt, "You're welcome to watch." I turn a humiliating shade of red. I shrug back into my seat and sink into it, my shoulders collapsing. Then Parker leans toward Steven and whispers something into his ear that I can only speculate was suggestive.

Soon, the first comedian takes the stage. We sit through the warm-up act, surprised to find ourselves laughing at the cracks of a fresh-faced twenty-something, who is admittedly on the autism spectrum. His voice is fast and brusque and his jokes have an undeniable veracity to them.

Comedian Paulina Gonzalez appears immediately following. Single and closing in on her forties, her humor is more on the crass side of things, although extremely relatable. She has strong stage presence and puts on an entertaining show. She carries herself with confidence, tossing her thick, long black hair around enthusiastically to add emphasis. She claims to be a serially single Latina, making fun of how this has been true her entire life since she grew up as an only child.

"I'm so single that I didn't even have a sibling growing up. Alone, alone. Always alone. Don't get me wrong, my parents TRIED to have more kids. I mean, come on... you see I'm Mexican, right? But no! No. I am destined for single life, from my literal birth to the day I DIE."

She's spicy with plenty of stories crafted to entertain. Parker and I find ourselves laughing indulgently, and when the show ends, there's a thick desire for more lingering in the air.

Paulina Gonzalez may be single, but she certainly knows how to bait and hook you.

Nineteen

The drive back to my apartment proves to be quite precarious. In a bubble of freshly proclaimed love, we struggle to keep our hands off each other, and Parker's eyes on the road. His fingers tease at the apex of my thighs and gently brush the material of my blouse against my hardening nipples. I reach into his lap and stroke the fabric suppressing his member as it bulges against the fly of his jeans, begging me to set it free. Feeling rather brazen, I fiddle with his belt and unbuckle it. Parker shuffles in his seat, and I release his cock from its hiding place. It springs free, already hard as it anticipates my touch. I make a show of licking my hand, then I lean into his lap. My hand pumps up and down, petting his length. Parker's lips part. At the stop light, I unbuckle my seatbelt and crawl across him. His swollen length fills my mouth. I welcome it, allowing his cock to slide further into my throat, and I gag. Oh, fuck. I've missed choking on it. Parker wiggles under me, letting out exasperated groans of divided attention. I bob my head and throw in the occasional deep throat to satiate the both of us. He's about to come - I know from the careful tilt of his hips and erratic breath. I wait for it, urging it on with greedy licks around the tip of his cock. He's so close now. I can't wait to taste his cum.

He shoves me off.

"Fuck, Iris," he breathes, ragged. "Fuck. You're so bad. So good, but so bad."

"Why did you do that?" I ask with exaggerated puppy eyes.

"I can wait," he sings playfully, and I realize that edging isn't a game just for me. "It's Friday night. Let's make the most of it."

When we finally make it back to my apartment, desire reeks in the air between us. It takes everything in me to not rip my clothes off, fall to my knees, and beg Parker to fuck me sideways.

But I can't. Not yet.

It's finally here. The time to be completely, totally honest.

At all costs.

Sitting on the couch with my legs draped over Parker, I make the beginnings of my confession.

Item one: secrets. I swallow deep in my throat and blurt it out.

"Parker, there are some things you need to know about me."

He nods his chin while showering mine with gentle pecks. It's somehow easier to say it without him looking at me.

"I'm bi." The relief is immediate. It's finally out there.

"Of course you are." He doesn't miss a beat.

"What?" I pull away. "You knew?" My relief is ousted by shock.

"Of course I knew. You're not that discreet." He laughs. Again, at my expense. This time, though, it's liberating. A secret I've held in for so long now set free, and discredited as a secret all together.

"And you're... okay with that?" I ask, needing confirmation of his acceptance.

"Very okay with that." His laughter echoes through the apartment.

"Well, okay. Great. But..." I begin, "there's more." When did I become a horrid infomercial? I want to shrink down into the carpet and get stepped on.

Parker pulls my hands into his. He stares into me, his gaze saturated with seduction. Having his attention fills me with anxiety.

It would be so much easier to forget it and fuck him right now.

But I can't. I turn into myself, calculating how to say what I want to say. I can't fuck this up. I don't want to lose him. I run it through my mind.

What is at the core of all relationships? Attraction. Basic, animal attraction. When you meet someone, you're either attracted to them, or you're not. And, when the person you find attractive is also attracted to you, that's the catalyst for the possibility of interaction.

There are different types of interaction. For some, interaction is a romantic date, or a casual hookup, or even just time spent in the company of another. For others, interaction spans across all aspects of life. This interaction makes the leap into the realm of committed relationship. These people want more: love, longevity. The promise of a future, shared together. Then, there are still others, who want both.

I am one of the others.

I want the comfort and commitment of a relationship. The stability of someone who I'm invested in deeply, and who is invested in me the same.

Our relationship, sacred. I want to commit to that person. My person. The person I'll always love and who will always love me.

But.

But I can't be caged. I thirst to explore interactions with other people, outside of my committed relationship.

I'm an insatiable flirt.

Parker is it for me. He is my person - the person I want to spend all the good times with and suffer through all the worst alongside. I am confident in our connection. I trust him, and he can trust me. So much so, that I can explore interactions outside of *us*. He needs to know that I will always come home to him in both my mind and my heart.

Non-monogamy.

Or, known more commonly as, an open relationship.

That's all he hears. That's all Parker hears. He wants me, all of me. And I tell him that this is a part of the whole me. A part that I'm not willing to compromise on.

I'm voracious.

Over the past weekend when Parker was out of town, he wasn't here to fulfill my needs. Nor was I there to look after him. A non-monogamous arrangement entails the kind of understanding where we *both* can ensure we are getting what we need. What we desire. I believe in us, together, as a couple. We have what it takes. I love Parker. My heart belongs to him. I accept him, with all his quirks and kinks, with all his mundane and dull, and especially with all his passion and fire.

I trust in him.

I trust in us.

Parker isn't convinced.

His stare sears into me harder than it ever has. My eyes search them for understanding. Then his lips move. He calls me a lot of names. Deviant. Greedy slut. Insatiable whore. My heart falls into my feet. My ears burn as the insults bore into them. My cheeks redden.

Just like that, the relationship between me and Parker as we know it, is over.

Just like that.

Over.

Part Two

Iris

Twenty

I'm proud of myself.

I'm proud of myself for being honest with Parker, but even more so for being honest with myself. It can hurt to be who you are, but what of the agony of hiding it? After my conversation with Parker, I do feel like my truth really has set me free.

So cliché.

I won't allow myself to be distraught. I push myself to move past it quickly. I can't sit in my apartment, looking at all the surfaces in my place, replaying the imagery of me and Parker having sex on all of them. I need to form new memories. I need to be hopeful of finding a connection with someone new.

. . . .

I TAKE A WEEK AFTER things with Parker before I put myself back out there. A lot happens in that week. Mom and Willard move to Hawaii, I cry over the regret (and also freedom) of unloading my past to Goodwill, and I binge every season of Schitt's Creek on Netflix. With Ben. We are so in sync, it's a sickening comfort.

I spend a lot of time at the library, consuming one book after the next, lost in stories and worlds a far cry from my own. With my Friday night now gapingly open, I am able to join Maisie for book club. I even drag Ben with me.

Misery loves company.

This week's book is a post-apocalyptic horror that was a thrilling read. I engage in the conversation wholeheartedly, excited to share my thoughts and absorb all the commentary from the group. Showcasing her superiority as the meeting organizer, Maisie orchestrates discussions that keep the conversation flowing like water. Just the right mix of sweet and spicy, she captivates us with her charm and ferocity. I find myself chatting with her at length following the meeting, while Ben gets lost in the science fiction section until I've had my fill.

Serendipity, it turns out, is real. While wandering in his wait, Ben meets Kai, a six-foot-three high school math teacher. The spark between them is immediate.

In the days that follow, Ben becomes blissfully enamored with his new flame. The happiness wafts from his skin, cascading around him and blanketing him in a cloud of lust. I can't help but smile. I'm truly overjoyed for him.

Inspired by Ben and Kai's tale of new love, I decide I'm not going to waste another second pining over Parker. Out into the dating world I go.

• • • •

SATURDAY NIGHT IS THE perfect night to find another person as desperate for a hookup as I am. I decide to extend my pool of prospects by heading to a bar I haven't gone to more than a couple of times. It's a bit of a walk, but turns out to be well worth the trek.

That's where I meet them: a man and a woman, sitting together at the bar, drinks in their hands. Sensing my gaze, they catch my eye. My skin lights up. The woman reeks of sensuality, with rich, olive skin that glows under the dim overhead lighting. Her navy dress plunges deep into her cleavage, teasing the plump, perky breasts that hide beneath.

How coincidental I decided on a blouse of the same shade.

The man is equally captivating, with beautiful thick curls that remind me of Parker's. His skin is a delicious deep mocha, with his gray V-neck tee exposing just a tasting of his chest. He rubs fingers along his chin and through his goatee, as though he's deep in thought. I toss my hair back behind my shoulders and tease my bangs.

I take a seat two chairs down from them. The bartender approaches me expediently. I point to the mysterious couple, and order *whatever they're having*.

With a whiskey neat in hand, we raise our glasses.

"Cheers," I mouth.

I take a swig. Whew - it hits hard. My throat prickles and my mouth burns. The aftertaste is delicious, though, with notes of cherry and oak. But it is very, very strong.

I notice the man smile in the corner of his mouth, and the two of them relocate, taking seats on either side of me. An Iris sandwich.

"Hi," he greets.

"Hi," I echo.

"What's your name?" she asks, her voice thick and full.

"I'm Iris."

"Pleasure to meet you, Iris. I'm Nina." She offers her hand, but I decline it. Feeling bold, I lean into her, planting a soft kiss on her lips.

"The pleasure's all mine," I whisper into her mouth. I turn away from her and take a sip of courage from my glass. It burns, and I struggle to keep from coughing.

"Iris. What a beautiful name." His fingertips graze my arm. "I'm G."

I lean into him. "Nice to meet you, G." I lick his ear.

"A pleasure, indeed" he coos, raising his glass and giving mine a light clink.

"Mm, this is good," I compliment. "Nice choice." The inevitable cough exposes my cover.

He chuckles. "Not a whiskey drinker?"

"Not usually, but I'm always up for trying new things." I turn to Nina. "I like to experiment."

"Oh, do you?" Nina licks her lips. "We do, too."

In my mind, Nina pushes me against the bartop and straddles me. She forces her tongue into my mouth, kissing me deeply, as she unbuttons the front of my blouse. My hands push into her chest, eager to explore the shape of her body. G watches in delight as we touch and moan and rub against each other.

Needless to say, I'm not entirely focused on the conversation. Every move G makes is clever play in a sensual game of chess. He takes lead, using humor and suggestive innuendos. I watch him speak, his lush lips dancing beautifully to form words. I soak in the hint of exoticism in his accent. I can't wait to taste his mouth.

Nina uses the power of touch to hypnotize me. Just a graze of her fingertips along my shoulder, and I'm cast under her seductive spell. The distinct floral smell of her perfume invades my nostrils and draws me in.

I shiver. Each passing moment feels like an eternity - the buildup is an unimaginable anticipation.

And Nina and G know very well the power of anticipation. They walk me out of the bar, G's hand on the small of my back. His touch sends shocks down my spine. With wide eyes, I look to Nina, eager for an invitation to continue our connection elsewhere.

It doesn't come.

They politely wait by my side until my Uber arrives. A black Prius with the license plate matching that in the app approaches.

"That's me," I admit disappointingly.

G smiles at me, his full lips looking too inviting to resist. With one hand on my hip, he reaches the other across my cheek. His fingers brush my skin, sending a shock through my body. Goosebumps break out all over my arms and chest. I clench as I feel a wave of wetness flow between my legs. He tucks the loose strands of my hair behind my ear and pulls me in to him. The world slows as our lips graze. I breathe him in. I lean in, craving a deeper kiss, wanting more, but G won't let me have it. A brief peck is all he allows for the time being. A grave disappointment.

"You'll hear from us soon, Iris," G promises. He releases his hold on me.

Nina takes his place and pulls me in for a hug. The bulge of her breasts against mine is too much to take. I squeeze into her, the layers of fabric between us only intensifying the arousal. "See you soon, Iris," her voice rings in my ear.

I fall into the Uber, deflated. The surge of desire I clung to all evening dissipates like a balloon leaking helium.

Some rebound.

Twenty-One

Never have I ever been so begrudgingly let down and simultaneously hooked by an interaction. Our initial meeting has me aching with want. I mull it over, wondering if it's nothing more than a planned strategy on their behalf. As though they want to torture me.

How do they know what I like?

I hear from G on Tuesday. It's agonizingly familiar.

The following night, he treats me to dinner and dessert at a fancy restaurant called Savor. I have never heard of it. I had no idea it even existed because it's so out of my price range. Even in the classiest dress I own - a little black dress with cap sleeves and a tasteful neckline - I feel genuinely out of my league. G fits into this place naturally, with his incredible good looks and classic black suit.

With the specialty of Savor being a variety of global foods, G orders several dishes for us to share. I quietly nurse a glass of crisp white wine while G takes the lead on the conversation once again, the beauty of his voice tunneling inside my ears.

Nina is working tonight, so it's just the two of us. This time.

Everything about G is interesting. He moved to America from Bangladesh with his mother, father, sister, and brother when he was six. His dad traveled a lot while he was growing up, leaving his mom to care for them almost exclusively. He has a great relationship with his mother and younger sister, but doesn't really see eye to eye with his brother or father. He wanted to do something important with his life, so G joined the military at 18, was discharged from service at 25, and has since joined the police force. He is incredibly intelligent, with an air of knowing surrounding him. His keen eye for observation is especially intriguing. Much like Parker, I can feel G's eyes constantly on me, surveying my every move.

A thin, young man with bushy eyebrows delivers our food at last. Each bite is absolutely decadent. The combination of sultry atmosphere and exotic food sets the scene for my unraveling. G feeds me little bites off his fork, directing me in how to taste and chew my food. It's profoundly erotic. His gaze barrels into me, and his fingers graze the fabric of my shoulders.

It's somehow even more arousing with the fabric of my dress acting as a barrier to his touch.

At last, G leans into me and kisses the tender skin of my neck alongside my jaw. My heartbeat quickens, and I forget to breathe. His mouth is on me, finally. Playfully, he licks my lower lip and his tongue slowly teases its way into my mouth. I can't take it another second. I push into him, uniting our lips together. I wrap my arms around him, desperate to feel the closeness of our bodies as one.

As is the pattern with G, I get only a taste.

• • • •

A COUPLE OF DAYS LATER, Nina arranges a wine tasting for the three of us. At a private bar owned by a dear friend of hers, we get close while sniffing and swirling various wines. My hosts are just as intoxicating as the drinks. We nibble on fine meats and cheeses to keep our minds from spinning.

It doesn't work.

In this intimate setting, I'm easily seduced by them both. Nina is eager to learn about me in a similar way that I enjoy learning about her - the primary focus on bedroom interests and kinks. Having been raised in a very conservative Catholic home, Nina has fought for her own sexual liberation since puberty. She speaks highly of G and their unconventional relationship, particularly in regards to the *long leash* (her words, not mine) that G keeps her on. The way she speaks of their connection gives me hope that I, too, can build a relationship with that deep level of trust and enlightenment.

Of all things, Nina grew up to be a sex therapist. Somehow knowing her gaze is evaluating and analyzing me makes me want to be more myself than ever. I don't hold back. Possibly from the wine, but more likely from my attraction to Nina, I openly admit my sexual identity and deep disdain for monogamy.

Nina moves close into me and gives me a gentle, light peck.

"You're going to be perfect," she whispers into my mouth.

I pull her in for a deep kiss, our lips locked for a blissful moment. My fingertips dig into her scalp. She smells of a sensual mixture of citrus and spice, and I hungrily drink her scent in. Her lips part and I glide my tongue inside, tasting her. G is behind me, his mouth on my neck, his hands on my chest. Nina pulls him into me, and I feel the distinct bulge of his cock pushing against my back. The sweetness of Nina, the smell of her perfume, the heaviness of G on me, the way his fingers are teasing my nipples - it's hypnotic. The three of us blend into one, moving and moaning in our shared indulgence.

But that's as far as it goes.

And it continues like this for another week. This agonizing game of cat and mouse. Everything we do only leaves me starved for more.

More skin.

More touching.

More.

I know the buildup is all part of the game. And it is proving to be satisfying in its own right. But.

Can we just fuck already?

. . . .

THE FOLLOWING WEEK, I anticipate the wait is over. G invites me over to his place for dinner with the two of them. If I was Goldilocks scouting out three different houses, I would say that G's is just right. A 2-story, 3-bed/2-bath with just the right amount of things inside of it to make it feel homey, but not cluttered. It's clean and comfortable with light beige walls and a bold, dark-wood kitchen. The surfaces throughout are mostly clear, save for a few photos of friends and family, stacks of books, and candles. I'm immediately drawn to the pile of books on the coffee table. I plop comfortably onto the sectional sofa and reach for one. They're not what I expect: three fantasy novels and a non-fiction thrown in. I didn't take G for a dreamer of far-off worlds. Intrigued, I leaf through one about a futuristic sex cult making a new planet their home. I raise my eyebrows. Kinky.

While I peruse his collection, G is busy in the kitchen pouring drinks and gathering the ingredients for homemade linguine. Unlike Parker, G is quite the cook. He often helped his mom and sister in the kitchen growing up, and he's become quite fond of the culinary arts. I'm a few pages into the story when G strolls out of the kitchen and makes his way over to me at the couch. Handing me a glass of fine Zinfandel, he takes a seat beside me.

"What did you find?" he inquires.

"You have quite a collection of books over here. I couldn't help myself. Have you read this one?" I ask, closing the book so G can see the cover.

"Yes, actually, a few times. It was a gift from Nina."

Of course it was.

We sit for a while, catching up on the past week while we wait for Nina to join us. I listen intently, as does G. His eyes never leave me. In this moment, he reminds me so much of Parker that it's as if I can feel his presence.

I push Parker from my mind. G and Nina are my focus now. They challenge me, playing deep into my sexual cravings, baiting me and leaving me hanging. It's all a game. A wonderful game of torment. It does the trick, fills the void.

For now.

G retreats to the kitchen, where the pot of water he had put on begins to boil. I trail after him with our empty glasses. I carefully refill them, promising myself to go slower on the next glass. I'm already buzzed. The kitchen is soon filled with decadent smells of fresh herbs and ripe tomatoes. I offer a hand, but G politely declines, recalling I had earlier professed to being a horrific cook. It's a smart move.

Nina strolls in just moments later, her long legs exposed in a tortuously short pair of jean shorts. Her hair is down, dark locks cascading down her back. Her lips look especially kissable today. She flocks to G and gives him a deep kiss, of which I'm instantly envious. G's hands move to her ass, which he grasps firmly in his palms, and Nina makes the most erotic exhale I'm certain I've ever heard.

I'm immediately wet.

I can't take it another second.

I grab Nina's hair in my fingers and pull her away from G, breaking their kiss, and replace G's lips with mine. Nina breathes into me, a little wail of surprise at my audacity. She folds into me, and our kiss quickly intensifies. Her hands are on me now, fingertips dancing along the waistline of my jeans. I can feel my nipples hardening under my dark green tee. My pussy throbs with desire, slickness growing with each passing second. I pull her close, positioning my leg between hers. I invite her to rock her hips against it. I squeeze my hands on her ass, massaging her thick cheeks in my palms. She fights it at first, not yet willing to give in, but then G is behind her, urging her into me. Nina complies, and I moan as she sways her hips and slides herself along my thigh. Her noises send me into a state of hysteria.

I have to make her come.

I pull her tee over her head and unclasp her bra, exposing her bare chest at last. I take her dark nipples into my mouth. I'm hungry for them - their taste, their sensitive response to my touch. But more than anything it's the sounds Nina makes that charge me. The noises of her enjoyment fill a void in my sexual repertoire I never knew existed. Each moan, gasp, grunt - they infect me, crashing over me with raw, primitive need.

G unbuttons her shorts for me, and she quickly slips out of them. We stumble, lust coursing through our veins, over to the couch in the living room. I push Nina back and she falls onto the plush cushions below, letting out a soft yelp that rings in my ears. I pull off her panties and my fingertips trace the outlines of her pussy. Her tender skin is moist with wetness. Her intimate smell invades my brain, the sweetness of it intoxicating me. I can't wait to devour her.

I slide my tongue between her folds. Nina moans, and my desire to pleasure her is more potent than ever. I delve my fingers inside of her, eliciting another sweet gasp. I suck on her clit and fuck her with my fingers. She wiggles under my touch. Her breathing becomes short and fast, and I sense she's almost at her climax. I continue the rhythm, desperate in my own selfish need to pleasure her. She wails into the air around us and digs her fingernails into the cushions below. Her body convulses as she hits her peak. Her insides squeeze my fingers tightly. I continue to lick her, lapping up her fresh fluids. Her cum tastes incredible. She howls, her body aching in overstimulation.

"You feel fucking amazing," I tell her. Because she does. Her essence consumes me.

I lean into her, craving more, but she wiggles away from me. G is seated across from us in an oversized armchair, I notice, with a wide smile and approving eyebrows.

I'm not done.

I crawl over to G, eager to give him the same treatment bestowed unto Nina. I slither up his body and kiss my way from his chin to his lips. The prickliness of his goatee is a harsh contrast to the softness of the skin at Nina's center. Still, I savor it, running my fingers along his pronounced jawline. He allows me a deep kiss, but rejects my further advances (much to the dismay of the hearty bulge in his jeans.)

G returns to the kitchen to attend to our meal, leaving me and Nina (sadly dressed again) to nurse our glasses of wine in the living room. The ghost of our shared moment haunts the room. I try hopelessly to focus on Nina as she speaks, to hear her words, but my ears echo with the sounds of her pleasure, drilled deep into the drums.

Soon the pasta is cooked, the sauce is simmering, and the house is caked in the smell of hearty spices.

We leave the comfort of the couch and its memories behind to take our seats at the dining room table. Matching the cabinets, the chairs are a dark brown, but the table top is a rich shade of cherry. I wait patiently, eyes on Nina, captivated by her. G dishes our plates and serves them as though we are in a five-star restaurant. The linguine is twisted into a neat circle, its interior decorated with a generous scoop of decadent homemade tomato sauce and garnished with bright green, fresh basil leaves. My mouth drops open in astonishment.

"Wow," I breathe.

"Bon appétit, mes chers!" G exclaims with a showy bow.

"So fancy! You are no joke quite the cook."

"Don't say that until you try it," G laughs. He settles into the seat opposite me, beside Nina, and raises his glass.

"Well, the presentation gets a ten out of ten," I compliment.

"Fully agree," Nina offers.

"Cheers," we say in unison, clinking our glasses and indulging in a sip.

Without question, the meal is heavenly. Every bite is more scrumptious than the last. I scoop the noodles into my mouth, chewing contentedly as the tang of the sauce hits my taste buds just right. My stomach fills quickly, to my disappointment; I wish I had room for seconds. With a full belly, my head feels clearer.

"It's incredible, G. Thank you for the delightful meal." Savoring the last bite, I wipe my mouth with a napkin and notice G has barely had half his plate. "Aren't you hungry?"

"Very," he laughs. He and Nina share a knowing glance. "It's you. Your enjoyment. The noises you're making. Fuck, Iris. Just look at you." He breathes in deeply, his fingers rubbing the prickles of his chin. It's a disturbing reminder of the exact way Parker felt about me when I ate. I want to laugh in my humiliation, laced with equal arousal and discomfort, but then I realize I felt the exact same during my encounter with Nina on the couch. I suppose it's not that unique of a kink to enjoy the sounds of others enjoying themselves. G leans over the table and whispers into my ear. "You're quite the treasure."

"G, stop," I demand playfully, certain I'm turning several shades of red. I chuckle through my embarrassment.

G tosses back the remainder of his second glass of wine and pushes his chair back. He struts over to me. I sit, frozen in place, a slim grin failing to hide beneath my reddened cheeks.

"Turn to me," G demands.

I do as told, swiveling my body to the left. I am face-to-face with the bulge beneath G's black jeans. Finally. All I want is to unbutton them and allow his cock to bounce free. I look up at G, awaiting his next instruction. He smiles, as though he can read my mind, and revels in my obedience.

He raises his hand and glances at his Apple watch, which feels strange and out of place in the heat of the moment. I stare at him, quizzically. Must be work, I think to myself, strangely reminded of Parker once again. He nods to Nina, who leaves her seat and scurries away. Maybe not work, then? Stretching his neck side to side, he refocuses on the task at hand.

"Where were we?" he rhetorically asks. "Oh right, dessert. Let me hear how much you enjoy it."

I smile and bite my lip. My time to shine.

I pull open the buttons of G's pants with such fervor that I carelessly smack my hand against the table. It stings, G laughs, and I use it as fuel to prove myself. I yank his briefs down, allowing his luscious cock to spring free. Tasting G's cock at last feels as good for me as I'm sure it does for him. I proudly worship him with an eager tongue and desirous hands. G pushes my bangs back and stares into my eyes, thirsty to watch me serve him. I lick the underside of his length and test his tolerance for perineum play. G gives me the green light with a hearty moan of pleasure as I flick my tongue against his tender area. I find my own satisfaction in doing so - Parker did not enjoy having this area stimulated. I revel in G's moans, licking with more vigor now, dancing my tongue in a series of circles and flicks. I suck on his balls next, bringing them into my mouth to taste them.

My nails dig into G's ass as I lick his underside. Little dribbles of excitement leak from the tip of his cock and fall onto my shoulder. He scoops it off and feeds his juices to me, and I lap them up devoutly. I fill my mouth with his full length, sliding his cock all the way into the back of my throat, then all the way out to my lips, over and over until I find my pace. The buildup is all too wonderful. I bob my head in rhythm with G's pleasurable moans, feeling my own arousal thudding at my center.

I want to fuck.

I pull away from him, leaving G an agitated mess of want. I remove my shirt, step out of my pants, and strip naked before him. I push our dinner plates out of my way and lean back onto the table. I want him in me. Now.

G bends down and reaches inside the pocket of his jeans, giving my pulsing mound a tantalizing lick as he does so. He rips open the packet and slides on a condom. I feel primal, waiting for him, desperate to have my hole filled.

At last, he pounds into me, his cock invading the slick space of my pussy. I writhe under him. He strokes my sensitive nub and thrusts, keeping a steady, predictable pace. It builds. The arousal between us radiates in sparks of heat and sweat. Release is imminent. I cling to him, my hands wrapped around the firm muscles of his arms, fingernails digging in. Our eyes bore into one another.

Suddenly, he pulls away, leaving me empty, but only for a moment. He's on his knees now, tongue and fingers inside me, pushing into my slit and tickling my clit. My fullness returns; G's fist is inside of me now, striking against my G-spot. My body quakes. I pant, my breath shallow, the smell of sex suffocating me. The pleasure is overwhelming, forcing me into oblivion, my climax hitting like a brick wall. It literally takes my breath away. I shake and wail, my insides squeezing around G's fist, his wrist covered in my cum. My body is heavy with satiation. I don't want to move, I feel frozen.

But it's G's turn.

He flips me over and I lay on my stomach, my legs dangling below the table. He enters me once more, my body welcoming him in, pulling him deep. His rapid thrusts tunnel into me, pushing my overstimulated body to the edge once again. I yelp as he smacks my ass, the heat of it spreading through me like wildfire. He grabs my hair into a ponytail with one hand, and continues spanking me with the other, all the while quickening his pace. Release taunts us. G groans as he nears his undoing, his hips bucking and twitching in sweet delight. We come together, our whimpers an indulgent, primal sound. G folds into me and my body pulls him in, that surge of bliss joining us in our mutual gratification.

"My turn," Nina pleads, presenting her naked body before us.

In her hand, she's holding a long, curved, glass toy that I immediately recognize as a double dildo. A slow smile spreads across my lips.

I trail behind Nina as she seductively canters into the living room. We return to the familiar couch, where she takes a seat and spreads her legs in front of me. She inserts one end of the glass toy into her slit, making irresistible noises as she does so. I watch her with wide eyes as she begins to fuck herself with it. Her pussy swallows it up and releases it, over and over.

"Come play with me," she sings.

I straddle Nina and lower myself onto the other end of the toy. It fills me up, the glass pushing against my insides without mercy. Nina leans into it. The tender skin of our slick openings finally touch. We moan together as we move, our bodies dancing in ecstasy.

I'm lost in the bliss, in the deep sensuality of our connection. Shocks zap through me every time the lips of our pussies graze. I toss my head back, possessed by pleasure. Nina groans, whining incoherently to herself in her aroused state. G appears and joins us, caressing my clit with one hand and Nina's with the other. That's all I need to be thrust into oblivion once more.

My orgasm overcomes me in a heavy, sticky wave. I sink deeper onto the toy, melting into Nina, as I ride the aftershocks of my release. My body trembles and I struggle to steady my breath. Nina screams as G quickens his pace. He strokes her nub with fierce ambition and yanks her nipples with the hand that was on me just a moment ago. I watch Nina as she holds her breath. Her body tingles with goosebumps and her skin reddens. G shows her no mercy as he twists her nipple in his grasp, a passionate look of power in his eyes. At last Nina's climax finds her, and she exhales the most glorious sound. I pull the glass cock out from both of us and push my fingers into her, feeling her muscles contract against them as she comes.

G leans down to kiss Nina, then me, then Nina's lips meet mine one more time.

Holy fuck.

I could do that again.

Twenty-Two

D inner (and dessert) with Nina and G is exactly what I needed. The sexual tension between us, and its incredible release thereafter, brings comfort and satiation that I have been hopelessly desperate for. It stays with me for the rest of the weekend. I'm satisfied. For now, at least. G and Nina are good for me. What we share is low pressure, the three of us just fucking around without wanting anything serious to come out of it. We aren't going to be life partners. We aren't going to fall in love. The purpose of our interactions is to play, fuck, and have fun with each other's bodies. That's all I want from them.

Monday comes, and, along with it, the predictability of the workweek. My morning routine remains unchanged: shower, coffee, river, book. I sit with my newest read in my lap, savoring the sugary sips of Simone's perfect blend, breathing in the heat of summer days to come. With my nose down in my book, I cling to the calm that this routine used to bring me. But it's elusive. Ghosts are hard to avoid, and Parker's follows me through the most basic steps of my every day. I remember how we met, in the most ridiculous way, right here, and my heart aches for him. Loneliness creeps in; a desperate longing for him.

I can still feel Parker's eyes on me. I can sense him here; I can catch glances of him out of the corner of my eye. His presence is a thrilling torment in the back of my mind.

I read ten pages of my book before closing the cover and reinserting the bookmark where it was when I started. I didn't absorb a word of it. My mind is preoccupied. I decide to check in with Nina and G to make plans for our next date.

ME
Hey hey! Wondering when you guys are free this week?
Could go for some more dinner & dessert... xx

An immediate reply pops up.

155

NINA
Tomorrow. Coffee @ 11?

My middle throbs at the thought. I entertain it for a moment, considering the fantasy of a mid-day romp with Nina. But in the name of workplace discretion and boundaries, I decide that mixing business and pleasure is probably a bad call.

Look at me! So mature. I reluctantly decline.

ME
Can't, after work instead? I'm off at 5:30.

G
Work has me on a new case. Can't get away
until late.

ME
Late works for me!

G
10 p.m. Wednesday? Come over for a night cap.

NINA
I'll be out of town Weds - Sun, have fun for me xx

ME
Wednesday it is! We'll be thinking of you, Nina xx

I look at my calendar on my phone and am disappointed to see I have almost nothing going on this week. My first instinct is to message Ben, but every second of his free time has been willed away to Kai. I can't be mad about it - they seem to be really hitting it off. I sigh a sigh of admiration... laced with admittedly a hint of envy.

I scroll through my contacts, on the hunt for someone I can count on to have zero going on. A B C... Cora. Perfect. I send her a message with the usual spiel of *oh it's been so long, we are due to catch up!* and to my delight, she eats it up. We make plans for coffee and a stroll along the river tomorrow after work.

I realize that Friday is the art gallery gala that Zach invited me to weeks ago. I initially gagged at the thought of having to endure such a pretentious interaction with Molly and her stuffy art folk, but when I learn that Nina will be out of town and G tells me he has a work thing, I feel relieved to have something to fill the hours. Even if I just eat free appetizers and sip expensive champagne for an hour, that's win enough to warrant making an appearance. I send a message to Zach confirming that I will be able to attend Friday's art soiree. I'll hit up book club, run home to change, and head to the gala fashionably late. It's a plan.

I run the week through my head. Today, I have book club after work. Tuesday, Wednesday, and Friday are now booked. Taking a deep breath, I feel better. I finish the last sips of my coffee, throw my book back into my bag, and stand up. As I brush off pieces of grass and leaves knocked down by feisty squirrels, I most certainly do not casually glance around me, desperately hopeful that Parker is, indeed, hiding in the shadows.

• • • •

DR. VAL AND DR. CAROLINE are both out today, leaving Dr. Amar to run the clinic. I haven't worked much with him prior, but after today, I can confidently say that his energy and mine do not mix. I can get along with most people, but Dr. Amar is among the few I cannot. I leave work in a huff, not having enjoyed a day so little in my entire career. Feeling belittled, inferior, and unlikeable, I retreat to the warm walls of the library.

It's much too early for book club, but, being the outrageous nerd I am, I'm all too happy to spend an extra hour or two meshed between the comforting pages of a good read.

As I'm heading in through the sliding doors of the library, Maisie is heading out. It's bittersweet seeing her - a friendly face after a day of drudgery - knowing our schedules no longer match up. We share no more than a meager *Hi!* as we pass by. It feels incomplete. I shrug it off and find a table hidden near the back of the Q-S fiction section. I review the content for tonight's book club, refreshing my mind. I read it almost a week ago. Being such a quick reader is both a gift and a curse - I can power through a lot of content quickly, but that also means consuming in such haste that

I bounce from one book to the next, the meat of one never really sticking unless it's exceptional. Typical for a bookworm, I think. We devour books; some parts stay with us, others are lost forever, hidden somewhere in our depths.

Tuesday tastes like regret. I chastise myself for reaching out to Cora. How could I forget how pathetic and whiny she is? That seems mean, but it's not if it's the truth. And it's the truth. She's always complaining and victimizing herself, and our conversation is borderline intolerable. I wish we had met for drinks instead, so at least I could take the edge off with some alcohol, because the caffeine in our coffees is making her more dramatic and me less tolerant. Cora is an architect assistant, forced into the field because her father was an architect himself. After his untimely death as she was just about to graduate high school, she made the obligatory choice to honor him by studying architecture. She hates it. She's miserable, lusting after the career in fashion design that she had always dreamed of. I feel like her therapist, having to listen to her lament over the guilt she feels for hating architecture and how it's somehow an insult to her late father to feel as she does about it. I say very little, mostly because she's constantly rambling, but also because I'm not sure I really want to share anything that's going on in my life with someone who can't stop talking. Right around an hour is all I can take before I feign an emergency phone call and book it out of there.

Wednesday finally comes. Another day in work jail with Dr. Amar, and my disappointment with the week continues as G cancels our plans. Apparently this new case is *highly intensive*, and he is pretty well spent from all the hours and energy he's putting into it. I try to hide my disappointment, but in truth I'm more annoyed than anything. Work work work.

Is history repeating itself?

It's ironic, isn't it? To have a casual, open arrangement with another couple, only to find myself in exactly the situation I was in when I didn't have such an arrangement. I can't stop my mind from entertaining the idea of expanding my circle of interaction. G is too busy for me. Nina is out of town and unavailable to me. I need someone who is here, now, to fill the void in lieu of them. Convenience is a big component of what draws me to non-monogamy. I sigh, coming to terms with the bitter truth that I'm not going to abracadabra a fuck buddy right here, right now. I shuffle through my nightstand and find a sleek purple vibrator to help me through this moment.

I pull my white tee over my head and slip off my blue jeans, exposing a playful pair of black boyshorts and my naked chest. The gray sheets below me are cool and soft against my skin, drawing out goosebumps as I shimmy down into a comfortable position on my back. I start with the vibrator on the lowest setting, rubbing it between my thighs but over my panties. I take a breath and blow a stream of air across my nipples, focusing on the sensation as they prickle and harden. If Parker were here, he would tell me I'm too easy, already getting excited with so little stimulation. The mere thought causes a gush of satisfaction, and my toy begins to slide more easily, even with the barrier of my panties. I hum, the fantasy of Parker narrating as he watches me vivid in my mind. I turn up the speed on the vibrator and pull my thighs together to hold it in place. Then, I focus on my nipples and rub them between my thumb and index finger. My head pushes into the pillow beneath me as I wiggle, basking in the pleasure of it. I move my hands down to my hips, and seductively wiggle off my panties. My pussy is slick with the wetness pooled at its opening. I slither the toy all around, readying it by soaking it in my juices. Parker demands I fuck myself with it. I plunge it inside my slit and let out an exasperated moan. The blissful feeling of fullness I've longed for overcomes me. I wiggle it inside of me, finding a rhythm as I imagine it's Parker's cock. I concentrate on my clit now, brushing my sensitive nub with the tips of my fingers while the buzzing inside me continues. The buildup drives me mad. My body quivers. As I know Parker would demand so close to my unraveling, I remove the cock from inside me and watch as my wetness drips off of it. I smirk, knowing this would please him. I drive the slippery shaft into my mouth and down my throat, gagging on it for his enjoyment. Back into my pussy, then my throat, over and over in a delicious dance of torment. At last, I work the shaft in circles inside of me, pushing against the most tender parts of my core. I moan and shiver as my entire body floods with pleasure. At last, I come, yelping into the darkness of my room. With my skin covered in a thick layer of sweat, my heart thuds in my chest.

Good, but not good enough.

I reach for my phone and send a woeful text.

> ME
> Hey V, any chance you're around tonight?
> Feeling lonely and could use... some company

I tap my fingers along the plastic case of my phone, impatiently awaiting a reply from Vienna. Seconds stretch into minutes. After twenty-five of them, I regretfully accept the disappointing truth that I am destined for solitude tonight.

I decide to shower before heading to bed. Still left wanting, I greedily bring my vibrator with me. I shampoo my hair, scrub my body, and satisfyingly come twice more. I slather the ends of my hair in a lavender-infused conditioner and let it sit. In deep breaths, I drink in the relaxing scent, hoping it will usher me into a sleepy state.

It doesn't.

Vienna does message me back, though. She's out with some work colleagues tonight, but extends a rain check.

> VIENNA
> Tomorrow - any time after 7 xxx

> ME
> It's a date
> xxx

I lay in bed for nearly two hours, which is productive when it comes to finishing one book and beginning another, but quite the opposite when it comes to restorative sleep. Closing in on one a.m., I force myself to close my eyes, willing sleep to find me. Some time later, it does.

The morning comes early. I lay in bed for a long while after my alarm, squeezing my eyes closed to ignore the beams of light pouring through the shutters. The snooze goes off for the third or fourth time, and I admit defeat. Time to get up. I slump into the bathroom and peel off my pajamas. I grab my toothbrush and slather on a wad of toothpaste, my eyes heavy as I brush my pearly whites. I feel hungover. I run a comb through my still-damp hair and opt for a simple low bun. I pick out my most comfortable (which also happen to be my ugliest) bra and panties, then toss on plain black scrubs. Coffee. That will make everything better.

I stroll into Urban Grind a few minutes later than usual. Simone isn't in today. A strange disappointment hits. I realize I never followed up with her on the lunch date I pushed back until I had *the talk* with Parker. It didn't go as planned, and I've been caught up in my own emotions since. It's a bad excuse. I decide that the next time I see her, I'll make good on my promise of lunch.

In Simone's absence, I entrust Lane with creating my usual concoction, but with an extra espresso shot for good measure. The moment the sweet elixir hits my lips, I sigh with cathartic relief. It's so good, I have to keep myself from leaping behind the counter and laying a big one on Lane's thin lips.

Before I allow my mind to sabotage the day ahead, I make a beeline for my spot by the river. It's already pretty warm out, with the sun's rays showing no mercy this morning, so I shift over from my usual place on the bank to one in the shade. I pull out the book I read most of last night, and fall right into it. I'm grateful to the eccentric characters in the pages for keeping my brain from bubbling over.

Dr. Val pops in for a brief moment first thing in the morning, but Dr. Caroline is running the show today. She's wonderful, and, sensing my exhaustion, allows me to self-direct my role today. I decide to finish up the scheduling for the coming month. I make a quick call to Stefanie to double-check on her availability (she did mention going up to San Francisco to visit her dad), then get moving on it. The sense of accomplishment I have after completing the schedule for all of June and most of July is heavenly. I love progress.

Spiked with energy from my coffee and my productivity, my mood improves. I offer to take a couple of the pooches in long-term care at PetCation for a walk, and Dr. Caroline is more than happy to indulge me. Getting out in the fresh air does wonders. With Stover the corgi, David the Maltese, and Bella the pug underfoot, I take an extended stroll along the river pathway. The sun kisses my cheeks and I breathe in the warmth.

Maybe Parker was onto something - the outdoors really does have the power to heal.

I spend the rest of my shift finishing up some billing, assisting Dr. Caroline with a biopsy, and running a couple of lab tests on a German Shepard's blood and urine samples. It's good news - with a week-long regimen of antibiotics and rest, she'll be good as new.

I have a spring in my step as I leave work, relieved to have had the day surprise me. And I have even more in store to look forward to.

Vienna.

We haven't hooked up in almost a year, and the last time we did, Vienna was the one who reached out. We are excellent friends, and I think that our mutual disdain for traditional values keeps our relationship strong. It's pretty great that we are able to connect sexually without letting it fuck up a perfectly healthy friendship. We're mature about it. Having a friend like Vienna gives me hope that there are others like me - like us - out there.

I go home, let my hair down, throw on a casual outfit, and let Vienna know I'll be over around 8.

Grateful she lives so close now, I wait until the last second to head over. I don't want to seem too eager, even though I've been obsessing over seeing her for the last hour. Or two. I push open my apartment gate and waltz down the walkway.

And that's when I see him.

Across the street, parked in his truck, with a beautiful brunette in the passenger seat beside him. Parker. My stomach churns, a dizzying chaos of thoughts and feelings running amok. After I pull up my chin from its trip down to the ground in shock, my throat tightens. I long for him. My skin, my heart, my eyes, my mouth, my body - all of me feels a deep, aching, longing for him.

I squint, studying the scene before me. Parker's back is turned to me, with his blonde locks shining in the glow of the setting sun. They beg to have my fingers run through them, and I feel my hand twitch at the muscle memory of it. I watch the woman beside him, with her captivating smile, as she animatedly talks and laughs, relaying her story to him. Parker watches her with the same intent focus he watched me. Then, they kiss. It's a deep, passionate kiss that Parker and I, too, have shared.

I want to be mad. I want to be furiously mad. But, even digging into the deepest, most vulnerable parts of me, it's not there. There's no anger, or upset, or hate. The love I have for Parker is still very much there. Instead of a heavy heart, I find great relief.

Parker has found a connection with this beautiful mystery woman.

My only wish is that he would come home to me afterward.

I turn away and carry on to Vienna's.

Sir Snowball greets me at the door in a flurry of meows as he brushes against my leg. Vienna welcomes me with a big hug. She gives me a *just a sec* hand gesture as she finishes up on a phone call. It's frustratingly familiar.

Snowy and I cuddle up on the couch. I stroke under his chin, finding great comfort in the fairytale fluffiness of his fur. His low, growling purr hums in the background. I pull out my phone and fall into the scrolling trap, lost in stories and posts I've missed over the last week. Maybe two. I almost never check my social media.

"Sorry about that!" Vienna reappears. She comes over to me for a proper welcome. Trapped under Snowy, Vienna leans down for a quick peck, then plops down in the armchair beside me.

"No worries. Thanks for having me over. It's been a week."

"Ugh, you're telling me. I found out today they're sending me to Chicago *again* in a couple of weeks. I'm so done with all the conferences and product training seminars."

"Need me to watch this guy?" I brush my fingers through Snowy's tail.

"Would you mind? Ugh, girl, I appreciate you so much. I don't know what I'd do without you!"

"Anytime. He's such a treat."

"Shall I make margaritas? I got some fresh limes from a coworker. She pretty much has a citrus orchard in her backyard."

"Ooh! Yes! That sounds wonderful."

Vienna shuffles around in the kitchen and my eyes take in the sight of her. Her luscious curves are accented in a sleek crop top and skinny jeans. I can't wait to rip them off her body. Her hair is in a high ponytail, with long, cherry-red locks flowing down her back. I watch as her thin eyes concentrate on a finicky gadget that is supposed to help squeeze every last drop of juice from the limes. She fiddles with it for a moment before tossing it into the sink and using her bare hands. They do the job. Oh, I know they do the job.

Vienna's energetic voice echoes in the air around us as she fills me in on the latest. She tells me a completely nuts story about a guy she recently hooked up with who ended up being a biter... and not in a good way.

"He fucking chomped down on my leg! It hurt so bad, my eyes started to well up. And girl! I was bleeding! It got so swollen, I had to ice it for days afterward, and I still have a horrible bruise. It'll probably scar." She unbuttons her pants and pulls them down, revealing an adorable pair of daisy panties. She shows me the mark on her upper thigh, which is every bit as horrifying as she made it out to be.

"Holy shit! Did you see a doctor? That's some kind of fucked!" I take a long sip of her delicious tequila concoction.

"Right! I'm low key wondering if I should've gotten tested for rabies."

I almost spit out my margarita. I feel the alcohol burn in my nose as I gulp it back. The giggles take over, and we both laugh and laugh. Snowy spooks and scurries off.

With Vienna's jeans hanging at her knees, I grab them and pull her over to me. I run my fingers around her injured skin. "This is really bad, V. Does it still hurt?"

"Not so much anymore. It's just taking its time healing." She runs her fingers through my hair.

I lean in to kiss it better. Probably as a result of the trauma of having her thigh gnawed on, she twitches and backs away.

"Too soon?" I laugh.

She pulls me up to her. I smile at her, grateful that we have the sort of relationship where we can be friends but also more. I lean into her and our lips join in a soft kiss. She tastes like the incredible zing of lime. I pull her in close, feeling her body relax into mine. She hums. I gently tug at her ponytail and run my fingertips along the back of her neck. Her hands rest on my hips, and we enjoy the warm tingles of our first shared kiss in some time.

Vienna steps out of her jeans as we relocate to her bedroom. I pull my black tee over my head and allow my jeans the same discarded fate as hers. In our skivvies now, our bodies become entangled on the plush blankets of her bed. She touches me first, her fingertips brushing along the fabric of my black panties as I lustfully pant. My lips loiter at the crook of her neck, and I breathe her in. Vienna slips her fingers past my panties and into my folds, which are already humiliatingly moist. I instinctively rock my hips as she thrusts her fingers in and out of my slit. I use my teeth to pull down the straps of her top, moaning as I do so. I playfully nip at her shoulder, and she squeaks in response, then delves her fingers more deeply into me. I can barely focus; I'm lost in my own pleasure, my gasps ringing in my ears.

But I'm desperate to touch Vienna's body. I reach for her and yank her top over her head. Her chest exposed to me at last, my hands explore the shape of her beautiful breasts. They are the perfect handful. Her nipples are wonderfully responsive to my touch and harden as I alternate blowing on and licking them.

But Vienna is a giver. She quickens her pace, setting a rhythm destined to end in my blissful release. I fall onto my back and she rolls on top of me. My breath becomes erratic as I give into the movement of Vienna's fingers inside my pussy. She pushes my bra up to expose my chest and harshly pinches my nipples between her fingers. I wail, the sensation releasing an immediate gush of wetness at my center. She does it again to the same result. I pant in ecstasy.

Vienna removes her fingers and licks them, tasting me. "You were getting close, weren't you?" she teases. "Mm. You taste incredible."

I throw Vienna off of me and pin her down, ass in the air, face in the blankets. I pull her panties to her knees and admire the tight hole of her behind. I swipe my tongue, quickly, from the dripping crevice of her pussy to the forbidden hole of her ass. She yelps, her body shuddering each time I tease my touch. Her noises barrel into my ears, wrapping my brain in a warm blanket of lust. I move myself under her and suck on her sweet nub. She wriggles over me. I lap her up, my tongue praising the center of her femininity. Her taste is intoxicating.

I plunge my fingers into her, and she wails. I twist them inside of her, the warmth of her insides swallowing me up. My tongue moves to her rear opening, and I worship her delicate hole with my mouth. My fingers drum against her G-spot. Vienna squirms, squealing and moaning while I fuck her with my fingers.

"Fuck, yeah," I pant. "Feels good, huh?"

I push my face into her ass and lick her hole again and again. She yells out, her body agonized in euphoria. She comes against my fingers, the carnal throbbing of her insides pulling me in.

Vienna folds into a ball under me, and I push my naked body into her. My slick pussy slides against her ass as I work towards my release. I rock into her, the soft exhales of her orgasm still dancing in my eardrums.

Vienna flips over and grabs my neck in her hands. She looks at me with deep, wanton eyes and squeezes. I hold my breath against her grasp.

"Your hands are fucking magic. Let me see you come with them," she demands.

I slide my hand down to my pussy and begin to stroke it. I use the same hand that was inside of Vienna just a moment before, and our intimate fluids blend together. They create the most heavenly scent; it diffuses around us, perfuming the room and sinking into my skin. Vienna's eyes drill into mine. She clutches my neck tightly, holding me firmly at her mercy. I rub and tease my nub, which is already heavily stimulated, and I shake and groan in the agonizing pleasure of it. Vienna's eyes follow the movement of my fingers, entranced.

"Come," she demands, shaking her hand and yanking my neck.

I grab onto her wrist with my free hand to steady myself, certain I'm just a moment from oblivion. It builds. And builds. My eyes roll back as my orgasm hits. My body shakes, and Vienna plunges her hand into my creases. My muscles seize and pull her fingers in.

"That's fucking right!" Vienna announces around us. She releases her hold on my neck, and I fall into her. I pant against her, my body shaking in the aftershocks of my orgasm. She pets my hair and plays with my bangs.

A few moments later, Vienna retrieves our half-consumed margaritas from the living room, and we lounge beside each other, sipping on them. The distinct scent of sex hangs in the air around us, sweet and hypnotic.

Twenty-Three

The next day, the art gallery event unfolds exactly as I expect it to. I enter an obscenely modern building, made more of glass windows than anything else, just steps from the beach. Cue the horde of rich, snotty, entitled, pretentious, well-dressed people all gathered in one large, acoustically-sound room. They analyze and discuss the many pictures and paintings adorning the walls, using words like *stunning, visionary*, and *complex*. It's so cliché that I want to barf. (The three glasses of champagne I down doesn't help with the wanting to barf thing, but it's mostly the people.) Even Molly, who I had hoped had grown awkward and ripe and highly gargantuan in the past weeks, looks *stunning* and bright and glowing, like a rare breed of pregnant woman I thought only existed in airbrushed magazine photos. Her strawberry blonde hair is perfectly styled in a half-updo, and her long, sparkly black dress looks like something a celebrity would wear to the Met Gala. The large, silver bow perched on her left shoulder is an art piece in its own right, garnishing an endless string of compliments from the wealthy patrons that I'm sure do, in fact, attend said Gala.

I eye the grossly expensive artwork, smile, and say mostly agreeable things. I check my watch thirteen times before making the call that my appearance has been sufficient as to show support for my brother and his perfect, art genius wife. Finally, my wrist buzzes to notify me that my Uber has arrived, and I stumble toward the gallery door and push it open. The cool evening air hits me in a refreshing wave.

That's when I see him.

I see... them.

My head feels light and tingly from the champagne. My eyes must be playing tricks on me. I blink several times and rub them. I refocus.

It can't be him, though. This is just another one of my imaginary circumstances.

Isn't it?

It has to be.

In what world would they both be here, late on a Friday, across the street from my sickeningly successful sister-in-law's art gallery? G is out on assignment, immersed in his new case. Parker is, well, wherever Parker is. Probably doing some *highly urgent* work thing. He's most definitely not here with the brunette from yesterday. And G.

This has to be a cruel trick of the mind.

My body shudders. I shake my head to push the possibility away, get into my evening chariot (a generic, white Toyota Camry), and immediately message G. *What are you doing?* I type, then add, *I'm missing you, xxx* in an effort to sound more caring and less accusatory. My heart thuds as I wait for his reply. Jimmy the driver puts on his signal and shoulder checks, ready to leave, but I shout out to him, more loudly and snappy than I had intended, to please just wait a moment. I stare out the window, eyes glued to G's impersonator, waiting for him to react to my text. Parker and his new flame stand side-by-side, laughing at a joke I feel desperate to be included in. They turn away from me now, facing the building opposite. G also has his back to me now.

It makes the hairs on the back of my neck stand up. I feel the blood rush into my fingers. I stare at the black screen of my phone.

No response comes.

My heart beats faster and faster. I feel defeated, confused... and played. Jimmy, feeling similarly I assume, reaches his patience threshold and sets off.

I don't stop him.

I need bed.

Part Three

Iris

Twenty-Four

N on-monogamy; an open relationship.
        I trust in him.

I trust in us.

Parker isn't convinced.

His stare sears into me harder than it ever has. My eyes search them for understanding. Then his lips move. He calls me a lot of names. Deviant. Greedy slut. Insatiable whore. My heart falls into my feet. My ears burn as the insults bore into them. My cheeks redden.

Every insult is fuel to my libidinous fire. I love it, every bit of it. It turns me on in a way I can't explain - the rawness of it. The humiliation is an agonizing aphrodisiac.

Just like that, the relationship between me and Parker as we know it, is over.

Just like that.

Over.

As we know it.

This changes everything.

Parker grabs me by my hair and spits in my face.

"You greedy little slut," he whispers, pulling my ear to his mouth. Its warmth makes me shiver. "Greedy. So fucking greedy. So pathetically sleazy, aren't you? You would fucking love that, wouldn't you? To be passed around and fucked by whoever wants to have their way with you. Have your holes filled and used. You would fucking love that," he repeats. He licks my cheek. I'm breathless, my chest on fire. "Wouldn't you?" He looks at me, his blue eyes peering into my soul from behind his black frames. I'm frozen in arousal. "Wouldn't you, Iris? My beautiful fucking deviant."

"I would fucking love it," I exhale into his mouth, so quiet it's almost silent. It's also the truth.

Parker releases his grasp on my hair and takes my face in his hands. My pussy throbs between my legs.

"I would fucking love it," he echoes. Glancing down at the firm outline in his jeans, it is abundantly clear that yes, yes, he would. I smile, knowing this

is all part of our game. "You know how I feel about you, Iris." The tenderness in his tone grows. "I have never felt this way about anyone. I can't explain it. You're everything to me."

"I feel the same way," I admit. "I love you, Parker. I do. I love you so deeply. I want to share myself with you. And that means being brutally honest. We've been together for long enough now that I knew you could handle it." My eyes begin to well up with hot tears. "I didn't mean to keep it from you - truthfully, I didn't. It's just so awkward to bring it up."

"I've always known, Iris."

"Y-y-you have?" I stutter.

"You're an easy read!" Parker laughs.

I think back to all the hints I had dropped, unintentionally or not. I am not the most talented at pretending to be anything other than myself.

And Parker knew. He knew the entire time.

Which means he accepts me. He accepts me!

We really are the perfect match.

"Now, where were we? Oh yes, I was reminding you what a filthy slut you are," Parker grins, getting back into character.

I hum and bite the tip of my thumbnail, welcoming his regression back into the scene. "As we were," I state, tossing my hair and inviting him to reach for it again.

He does.

In all my glorious humiliation, the wetness between my legs pulses. Still clinging to my hair, Parker grips his other hand around my neck. My heart pounds as my pussy gushes with slickness. I reach for his waist in an attempt to unbutton his jeans, but he beats me to it. He throws me down and whips off his pants. Then, in a flurry of clothing, he removes mine and pulls me in closely. His hand invades me, lunging into my damp folds.

"You're so fucking wet, aren't you, my little slut?" he calls into my ear.

I whimper in response.

"Look at how wet you are. You're so fucking easy," he insults, working his fingers in and out of me.

I lean into him, kissing him deeply. Our tongues weave together. Parker continues to fuck me with his fingers, drumming them against my tender insides. I rock my hips, moaning in pleasure, edging closer and closer to release.

My skin is coated in sweat as my body moves by its own volition. I'm on the cusp, my climax tortuously near, when Parker removes his fingers and steps back.

"On your knees, you filthy whore," he orders. He shoves his dripping fingers into my mouth and pushes me down. I choke on them in the back of my throat as I fall to the floor. "That's right. Taste them. Eat your cum." I moan, finding deplorable enjoyment in it.

Parker pulls his hand away and slaps me with it. I gasp, wondering if I can come simply from being so insanely aroused.

He heaves his whole length into my mouth, immediately making me gag. Again. I start to salivate, coughing in my throat.

"Oh, what? Is it too much for you? I thought your whore mouth can take it," he scolds. "Open up," he commands, "take it all in." He pulls my head back and pushes himself into my mouth again. Deeper.

Most of it is a mind game, when it comes to deep-throating. I focus on relaxing my muscles and allow him in. I like holding my breath, and he likes when he can thrust all the way into my throat, deepen his push, and hear me choke. I crave the air; I feel desperate to breathe. It's an edgy, licentious game of chicken. I want him to push me harder, make me hold my breath for longer, but he won't, not yet. He's just warming up, testing how far he can go today. Some days I can deep-throat forever; others, I just can't stop gagging. And, likewise, some days Parker loves to make me gag; others he just wants to fuck my throat silently.

Our game is intense, but underlying it all is trust. And I trust Parker wholeheartedly. We have rules and limits, and we always communicate, even when speaking isn't possible. Parker and I respect and trust each other's boundaries.

Today, I'm not giving him what he's craving. Parker groans and exhales, his body growing speckled with sweat. I cough again and again, and his frustration grows.

"Sounds to me like you need a lesson in following my commands," Parker teases as he pulls his cock from the depths of my throat. "Get up. On the couch. Spread your legs, like the whore you are."

I cling to his words, feeling shamefully turned on by them. Parker disappears from view, turning the corner and going into my room. He appears a moment later with a surprise in hand. I'm spreadeagled before him, willingly helpless.

"Keep your legs open. If you try to close them, I'll have no choice but to use this." Parker slides the coarse fibers of rope against my thigh. It makes me shiver. "Or maybe I'll just use the rope anyway," he sighs nonchalantly. I gulp with need.

This isn't our first time using rope, but Parker surprises me with how well-versed he is in complicated knots and ties. He makes quick work of binding my thighs to my arms, forcing my legs to stay widely open. With every movement, no matter how slight, the rough texture of the rope burns against my skin. My breathing becomes increasingly erratic as Parker tightens the complicated knots. My center floods with desire.

Parker reaches down to my abandoned panties on the floor and shoves them into my mouth.

"Can you taste yourself on them? Hmm, not quite wet enough, are they?" Just as quickly as he pushed them into my mouth, he removes them. "Let's get some of your filthy juices on them, then you can have a proper taste."

Parker strokes the lacy fabric of my panties against my opening. He runs them over my clit and around my creases, swirling them in the moisture that has pooled there. My body yearns to wiggle in response, but the rope makes it nearly impossible to even twitch. It's torture. Incredible, welcome torture.

Parker licks my clit and moans, which provokes my own symphony of sounds. He uses his fingers to carefully nudge my panties into the lips of my pussy, and they immediately become damp. He then thrusts them inside of me and I gasp.

"Let's make these nice and wet for you."

Parker's fingers tuck the fabric into my crevice. They squelch in the dampness. It's utterly humiliating, and arousing as fuck. Then his mouth is on me, sucking at my nub. I gasp in surprise of it, and pleasure overwhelms my body. The rope burns as my body shakes. My skin is blanketed in goosebumps. Parker's fingers dance inside of me, swirling my panties and tapping against my walls. As he flicks his tongue against my bud, I whimper in the sweetness of my impending release. Reading me, Parker stops just as I'm on the cusp. His fingers dig inside me, reaching for my panties. He slowly pulls them from my slit, groaning as my pussy releases them from their prison. He pulls them to his nose and smells them, making me gush with embarrassment.

"Perfect," he mumbles, as if intoxicated by my intimate aroma.

In one swift movement, Parker plunges his cock into me and crams the panties into my mouth. Then he covers my lips with his hand and shushes me. His hips buck wildly into me, and his length fills me up, pounding into the depths of my pussy. I let out a soft whimper in my throat, strangled by ecstasy. Parker pinches my nipples. I turn into myself and focus on the sensation of his every touch: the soft skin of his hand against my mouth, the strong muscles of his legs against my thighs, the shaft of his cock stroking against the walls of my insides. I clamp down on my panties, holding them between my teeth, and savor the taste of my own femininity. Parker's other hand finds my clit, and there's no hope left for me. I wail out beneath him, my body trembling as I succumb to my climax. He smacks my nipples then wraps his hand around my throat. Quaking and grunting, Parker's eyes bore into mine as his release overcomes him, too.

Twenty-Five

In my champagne-induced inebriated state, I fall into a deep sleep as soon as my head hits the pillow. I don't hear Parker enter my apartment - he slides in undetected sometime after midnight.

It feels incredible the next morning, waking up wrapped in his arms. Parker tightens his hold on me, pulling me close to his warm chest. I'm wonderfully trapped.

"I love you," I whisper, digging my nose into his neck. All the worry of the night before has melted away, a seemingly distant memory - a fabricated fantasy, even.

"I love you, Iris," he echoes, squeezing me tight. He sighs. "I'm so lucky to have found you. I'm so excited for our future. To do this," he pauses, gathering his thoughts. I smile in my weighty bliss. "Watching you... God, I love watching you, it gives me some sort of high. You're so beautiful, and everything you do is so fucking seductive. I get hard just thinking about it." I lower my hand to his belly button, listening intently. I trace circles on his abdomen, teasing him, before reaching down and firmly grasping his cock.

"Everything? How about this?" I innocently ask, fluttering my eyelashes.

"Especially that." He exhales, releases me, and pushes me below the covers.

There's no doubt about it: I'm love drunk.

• • • •

WHAT A WAY TO START the day. I give Parker a world-class blow job, then his expert fingers bring me to the brink and over three wonderful times. He leaves in a bit of a hurry, though, rushing to finish something for work before our *official reunion* as a non-monogamous, happy couple tonight.

God, I've missed him. The time we've had apart has been fulfilling in its own right, but not without its challenges. It has tested me in countless ways. Including last night. My mind wanders back, confusion creeping in. I need answers.

What the actual fuck were G and Parker doing together last night?

I consider the terms of our game. Parker and I agreed on a time frame: three weeks. I met Nina and G, and we would play for three weeks. (My little hookup with Vienna was just an added bonus.)

Time's up.

Of course I know who the brunette is - Parker also selected a playmate for our time apart. They know each other from work, he tells me, and this isn't the first time they've hooked up. I believe it - her smile alone has me wondering what else her lips are good at.

I roll out of bed, wander over to my phone in the kitchen, and text Parker.

He beat me to it.

PARKER
Good morning, beautiful!
Sorry I had to rush off. Can't wait to see you
tonight. I have a surprise for you
(And no, it's not *just* my hard cock)

He's included a gif of a gangbang.
My soulmate.

ME
I do hope the gif is a true representation of my surprise
But really... what was going on last night?
I saw you outside of Molly's gallery with G...?!

As soon as I send it, regret thuds in my chest. Maybe it really was all the champagne fucking with my head. In the absence of an immediate reply, I shake it off and begin my day.

After a shower, I head for coffee. I decide to make good on my vow to follow up on lunch with Simone. Thankfully, she is there this morning.

"Hey," she says, her voice full and earthy. "Morning."

"Hey," I reply, giving her a flirty smile. "Hey. I'm sorry I never planned that lunch date with you." I run countless excuses through my mind, entertaining each one. But I decide that Simone deserves better than some generic, *oh, so sorry, been hella busy.* "I was a jerk. I'm sorry. I really would love to have lunch with you. Dessert. Drinks. Whatever you're up for. If you'll still have me."

She blinks at me, a slow grin blooming across her face. She exhales in a cute half laugh, then looks me straight in the eyes. "I will still have you," she says, and we both giggle.

We make plans for lunch on Wednesday next week, at the pho place across the street. As Simone hands me my usual brew, our touch lingers, fingertips grazing each other. I boldly lean across the counter, and she doesn't stop me. I kiss her gently, pull my coffee from her grasp, and walk out the door.

With my cheeks erupting pink, I pop in my earbuds and select a peppy Spotify playlist to deviate my focus away from Simone's impossibly kissable mouth. I set off for the library, even though I was there just yesterday for book club. I would live there if I could. After yesterday's meeting, Maisie and I got caught up in discussing our favorite thrillers. The more we chat, the more I enjoy her company. Like me, she reads almost anything, but her true love are those books that really make her think. She recommended a couple books to me, but I didn't have time to check out anything last night before heading to the art gallery. So today, I make it my mission to investigate her suggested list.

Libraries are generally pretty busy on the weekend, and today is no exception. Most of the tables are occupied, so I decide to find my books, check them out, and retreat to my couch to read them. My first steps into the world of books makes my mind immediately clearer and calmer. I pull out my phone. Still no message from Parker. I open the notes app and find the list of books Maisie mentioned. I check the library catalog on my phone, but only one of the three is available. The other two aren't stocked by any of the local libraries. Strange.

For now, the one book will have to do. I browse the shelves and find another two to add to my pile; these ones are mysteries. I also grab the book for Monday's book club, which I haven't read yet, but will easily finish over the weekend.

As I hop out of the library with my fresh stack of books, I decide to call Parker and check in.

Thankfully, he answers.

"Hi, beautiful." Oh God, here I go again, coming apart in two words.

"Hey," I whine.

"I miss you. I miss you so fucking much. This morning wasn't enough. I can't wait to see you. I'm just finishing up a couple of things here, then... I'll head over."

"Fuck, I miss you." So pathetic, but it's all I can muster.

"Give me an hour. I'll bring lunch."

• • • •

JUST PAST ONE, I HEAR Parker's truck pull up outside my building. I rush down to meet him and throw open the gate, racing toward him. I leap into his arms, and he scoops me up against his chest. I hear his heart, a steady thumping that takes my breath away. Electricity zaps through my veins as our lips join in a deep kiss. I'm intoxicated by his taste. We drift into another world all our own.

"God, that felt impossible. Three weeks. Fucking felt like three months."

"Is this real?" I gasp, holding myself back from sobbing. I have the love of my life. I have a non-monogamous relationship. It's all I've ever dreamed of. Pinch me.

"Very real." Parker smiles. "Did you have fun?" he asks, knowing full well I most definitely did.

"Ha!" I laugh. "Too much fun. But it was so hard to stay away from you that long," I say, pouring on the pout. "Especially with catching glances of you everywhere. It was borderline torture." Delightful torture.

"That's all part of the game, my love," he reminds me.

It is.

"I need to ask you about last night, though," I say, my voice becoming somber. I clear my throat. "What were you and G doing there? Do you two know each other?" My voice cracks.

"Yes, we do. Iris, I have a lot to discuss with you. Let's go inside."

My heart leaps into my throat.

Twenty-Six

S ettled onto my couch with overfilled bowls from Chipotle, Parker and
I munch in silence. It's deafening.

I can't wait any longer. It's finally time for him to reveal his secrets to
me.

"To address your question about last night, yes, I do know G. And
Nina, too. And my coworker? Georgina. She's a mutual friend. We are all
sort of, well, I guess you could say, we all run in the same circle." I nod,
wiping the last bite of my rice bowl from my lips. I wrinkle my eyebrows,
hanging on Parker's every word. "I hope you're ready for this. I know you
are," he says more to himself than to me. "It's been a long wait."

Parker tosses his still-full bowl onto the coffee table and turns to me.
I want to spit out the bite I just took; his eyes are blazing into me. I gulp
it back, almost gagging, then put my bowl beside Parker's. He takes a deep
breath, pulling my hands into his. I might barf.

"When you met Nina and G that night, it was, well... we had planned
it. It was all part of something... bigger."

I definitely feel like I might barf. My stomach drops into my feet and
my heart rattles in my chest. Despite himself, Parker's smiling, the look of a
giddy teenager in his eyes.

"What?" I mumble. My brain swirls with questions. Parker has never
been so cryptic.

"I'm not making sense. I'm sorry. Here. Let me just... I'm just going to
grab something." He gives me a light peck on the forehead before making
his way over to the front door. He reaches inside his black coat and takes
something out from its pocket.

"Before I give this to you," Parker begins, "I just want to say..." he trails
off, emotion gathering behind his eyes. He sits back down beside me, so
close that our thighs are touching. With a big inhale, he continues. "Iris.
I have never met anyone like you. I am so in love with you. I feel grateful
for you every day of my life. I know that, in you, I have found my match."
He touches my cheek and brushes my bangs across my forehead. A surge of

warmth courses through me, and my eyes begin to prickle. "You allow me to be me, and I have never felt so validated and so... *seen*. I love you deeply."

"I love you, Parker," I reply, sniffling. "You mean everything to me." My voice cracks. This man has me utterly captivated.

I trust in him.

I trust in us.

Parker is now convinced.

"So..." he clears his throat. "It's my honor to present you with this. Now that our game with Nina and G is over, we can move onto other things. Open it. Then we can talk more." He passes me a mysterious black envelope.

It's heavy and thick. I turn it over in my hands. Across the front, written in fine gold lettering, is my name: Iris. I look to Parker, hoping his eyes will give a clue. But he's stoic, watching me expectantly. I flip the envelope over. The back is sealed with a golden, circular emblem inset with the silhouette of a tree. I look up at Parker again. Anxious energy radiates from his pores. Enough delay. I rip across the seal.

Inside is a thick, stark white note card. Golden vines and leaves snake around the words inscribed, framing them at the center. I study them. The bold, black lettering seduces my eyes.

Dearest Iris,

It is with Our deepest honor that we invite you to join us.
It is with Our sincerest pleasure that we accept you as one of Our own.
It is with Our shared joy that we hope you find your place.

Our Family is a lifestyle organization that embraces and enriches the unique and distinct indulgences of Our Members.
You have been nominated for membership.
You have excelled at your test for entry.
We now passionately await your response.

Please reply within twenty-four hours
Through Our contact,
Parker Douglas.
It is with Our abundant enthusiasm that we eagerly anticipate your acceptance.

Congratulations. We are so glad to have found you.

Truly yours,
Desi Harold
Our Family, Head of Branch 29

NDA Encl.

I go over the wording, crinkling my eyes to decipher the hidden meaning. It's seductively cryptic. My cheeks burn as the muscles work to suppress the smile spreading across my lips. Lifestyle organization. I have a pretty good idea of what that means. But it doesn't seem trashy and cliché in the way I always imagined an organized group like this would be.

I'm intrigued.

"So..." I begin, my mind swirling. "A lifestyle organization? Like... a swinger's club?" I ask, trying not to turn red at taste of the words as they roll off my tongue. Parker's ears turn pink. His cheeks flush. Maybe for the first time ever.

"Ha! Well, essentially... yes. We avoid that term, though." he answers defensively. "Is it a club? Yes. Do we swing? Yes. But it's so much more than that!" he exclaims.

"Tell me." My eyes widen as I study him. He's giddy, glowing.

"I want to. Fuck, Iris, you have no idea how much I want to. But first you have to submit the NDA," Parker explains. "Then, if you accept the invitation, we can talk about it in more detail."

I raise my eyebrows. "An NDA? Sounds hardcore."

"It's not," he puts simply. "Every organization has them to protect the privacy of their sensitive interests." Back to business mode.

"Okay," I concede. I reach back into the envelope and pull out a wad of paper that was wedged beside the note card. "This is it, I assume?"

"That's it."

I unfold it. The document is long. Horrifically long. Parker hands me a black pen, and I begin reading.

At first, my eyes and brain are focused and eager, fueled by provocative promise. But my attention quickly wanes. I suppose I expect some seductive little nuances since I'm signing off on a swinger's club, but, in reality, there is nothing sexy about an NDA. With awkward wording and cryptic vernacular, I struggle to get through the six pages, front and back, of water-tight disclosures. I scan it, running my eyes and fingers along the words, taking note of the seemingly most important terms, such as ESSENTIAL, UNDER NO CIRCUMSTANCES, and NOTWITH-STANDING. I deem that effort sufficient enough. I raise the pen and sign my life away inside the neat signature box at the bottom of the final page.

"All done!" I announce proudly. I pass the paperwork over to Parker.

"Great. I'll just send this off to Mallory." Parker takes the document and lays it down on the coffee table. With the signature page facing up, he snaps a photo and forwards it to this Mallory person. "Okay. Next. Give me your phone."

"Uh, why?" I ask, taken aback.

Parker responds in his own sassy tone. "You want to know more or not? I'm going to set up the info on your phone for you. If you please." Snarky and playful. I wish I could say I'm not insanely turned on.

"Here." I spin around and allow him to pull my phone from the left back pocket of my dark-wash jeans.

Parker gets started, typing and tapping away. Sitting by his side in silence, the anticipation nags at me, and I feel displaced. I pick up the note card invitation and reread it again, and again. My mind spins as I try to assemble the pieces together. I analyze the words, working to absorb and decipher them. *Nominated for membership* and *your test for entry*. Then it hits - a salacious blend of shameful ignorance and sensual excitement - as I succumb to the realization.

I have been played.

It seems congratulations are in order. Well done, Parker. I scoff.

The loudness in my brain and the silence of the room collide. I can't take it. I need to know more.

"So, you're a Member?" I pry. The burn of pathetic desperation coats my throat.

"Yes. I've been a Member for almost a decade now."

My jaw drops open. "A decade? Holy fuck!" Holy fuck is an understatement.

Parker laughs, finding enjoyment over and over in my pitiful ignorance. "Here. All done." He passes me my phone. "I've downloaded and set up the app."

"App? This swinger's club has an app?"

"Lifestyle organization," Parker corrects. "And, yes. Everyone who's anyone has an app these days. It's 2023. Get with the times, Iris," he teases. "The main thing you'll want to look at is the Rulebook. You'll probably have a couple of messages as well, likely from Desi and Mallory."

"Who are...?"

"Desi is the Head of Our Branch. Mallory is one of Our Members - she's the Communications Officer."

"How many Members are there?"

"In Our Branch, you'll be number sixteen. There are seven other couples in addition to us," he clarifies. "That's *if* you accept."

"Do I even have to think about it?" I joke playfully.

Even with the limited information I have, I already know that I've never been better suited for membership in anything in my entire life.

Twenty-Seven

The Our Family app icon is entirely black with the same emblem as was on the envelope: a golden circle inset with the silhouette of a rooted tree. My heart skips a beat. I know monogamy is not for me, but swinging as a couple is something that I thought could be a reality only in my wildest dreams. A deep excitement bubbles in my core as I entertain the possibilities that could be. I lick my lips and clamp my mouth shut. I take a deep breath in through my nose to steady my racing thoughts, then click on the icon.

After a sobering experience setting up face ID verification to allow me access to the highly confidential inner workings of Our Family, I am finally able to view the content within. On the home page, I'm greeted with a digital version of the same invitation Parker had presented me with. The only difference is at the bottom, where **NDA RECORDED AND ACCEPTED** floats in bold.

My heart beats in my ears, the thudding of it cutting. I can't wait to explore everything that awaits me. I eagerly chomp down on my fingernails, my nerves directing my unconscious movements. I readjust to sink further into the couch. Parker wraps his arms around me, nestling me in a cocoon of comfort. I lift my chin up to look at him, and he gives me a deep kiss that radiates through my entire body. I melt into him, breathing in his glorious scent, a mix of spice and wood.

"Go on!" he urges.

I tap outside of the invitation, and the screen glows with a *Welcome, Iris* floating in the middle. Along the bottom of the screen, there are several symbolic icons identifying the different sections of the app. My fingers tremble with anticipation as I ponder where to even begin. My ears burn hot as I bite my lips. I decide to go through them in order.

I click on the first: a notebook icon. It reveals the *Basic Policies & Information Rulebook*. Never in my life have I been so excited to read a policy manual.

BASIC POLICIES & INFORMATION RULEBOOK

Introduction

Congratulations on winning membership into Our Family. You have excelled at your test, you have been invited as a Member, and we are now proud to welcome you as one of Our own. Please review the following as soon as possible. It is essential that all Members of Our Family understand and agree to uphold, at all costs, the set of rules laid forth in this document. It is of equal importance that all Members are steadfast in upholding their Responsibilities.

Background

Our Family was originally founded by Lucie DuValenteau in 1908. It is with pride that Our Members have maintained the values of Our Family and ensured its survival for over a century. Your membership in Our Family is not to be taken lightly. While it will require great discretion in the eyes of many, there is tremendous pleasure to be found within it.

Structure - Branch Level

Our Family consists of many Branches. Each Branch is governed by a Head. The Head of your Branch oversees the requirements of your continued dedication to Our Family.

Recruitment & New Membership

- New Members are admitted on a recruitment basis only.
- No Member will be admitted any other way; absolutely NO exceptions.
- All new Members undergo a thorough vetting period of investigation and evaluation.
- All new Members undergo testing as the final step in recruitment.
- New Members are admitted only upon completion and approval of this recruitment process.

Membership Policies - Branch Level

- Partnership
  - All Members in Our Family exist within a two-person partnership.
  - Partnerships are composed in one of the following ways:
    - Two Members who have been recruited in tandem and exist as a couple;
    - Two Members who have been recruited independently,

but now exist as a couple;

- Two Members who have been recruited independently and have been assigned partners by Our Family;
- Two Members who have been recruited independently and have requested partnership with each other

  - Partnerships are NOT permanent.
  - Partnership designations can change at any time after an initial two-month 'locked in' period.
    - Our Family approval is required for all partnership adjustments and changes.

- Transfers
  - Membership exists exclusively in the Branch for which recruitment occurs.
  - Branch transfers are permitted only after a period of membership in the current Branch of at least two months.
  - Applications for Branch transfers must be submitted by one or more partners requesting the transfer.
  - Branch transfers are not guaranteed.
- Length of membership
  - Initially, the length of membership in Our Family is limited to a one-year term; however, it is subject to evaluation and scrutiny at any time.
  - At the expiration of the initial one-year term, a request for extension may be submitted. If granted, membership will be lengthened for another 1-5 years, as determined and approved by Our Family.
- Dues
  - There is a $1,500 annual due for membership.
    - Dues must be paid directly to the Head of your Branch.
    - Dues must be paid in full on the first of January each year.
    - Memberships acquired mid-year are prorated and dues will be collected upon Membership Confirmation.

Termination

- Membership may be terminated AT ANY TIME FOR ANY REASON at the discretion of Our Family.
- Requests from individuals for membership termination will be considered on a case-by-case basis; however, it is with confidence we trust all Members will fulfill their commitment to Our Family as rendered upon Membership Confirmation.

Rules for Branch 29 (Harold)

General Information:

1. Branch No.: 29
2. Branch Head: Desi Harold
3. Active Members: 15; Proposed Members: 1
4. Active Partnerships:
    a. Desi Harold & Marc Harold
    b. Julia Wellgrint & Thom Wellgrint
    c. Scarlett Sharvista & Aki Tanaka
    d. Mallory Chambers & Davis Grenner
    e. Marie Rivers & Evan Rivers
    f. Bea Fox & Riley Irving
    g. Sunny Bahatti & Wyatt Richards
    h. **(PROPOSED)** Iris Gladwell & Parker Douglas
5. Arrangement: Full swap

Branch Mixers & Policies:

1. Mixers are held once monthly, at the minimum, or once weekly, at the maximum.
2. Mixers are an overnight commitment. Overnight accommodations are provided by the host at the Mixer location.
3. Mixers require participation of all Members. Participation refers to both attendance at the Mixer and active engagement in Mixer activities.
    a. If you are unable to attend, you must submit a Request for Absence. Failure to do so will result in a Consequence.

      i. Denial of your Request will also result in a Consequence.

      ii. Consequences are determined by the Branch Head and must also be approved by your partner.

      iii. Consequences must be completed within 30 calendar days of the event in question.

4. Mixers constitute a variety of proceedings. Activities may include, but are not limited to, the following:

    a. Cocktail hour & socialization

    b. Formal or informal dining

    c. Partner exchanges

    d. Group engagement

    e. Kink play at the discretion of participants (and as consented to), including, but not limited to, the following:

      i. BDSM

      ii. Anal

      iii. Toy play

      iv. Fetish play

5. All personal devices, including mobile phones, smart watches, tablets, and laptops, are prohibited from Mixers.

    a. All devices must be surrendered upon entry to the Mixer. Failure to do so will result in membership suspension, or, in serious cases, expulsion.

Private Exchanges:

1. Private exchanges occurring between two or more Members of any Branches are permitted and encouraged.

2. Private exchanges occur on a voluntary basis only.

3. All private exchanges must be documented.

    a. Involved parties must report the following to the Head(s) of the Branch(es) concerned within 24 hours of the private exchange via Our app:

      i. Exchange date

      ii. Exchange location

      iii. Participating Members and corresponding Branch No.

<u>Inter-Branch Mixers & Events:</u>

1. Our Family is proud to encourage Members of various Branches to interact.
2. Our Family consistently offers two Inter-Branch Mixers per calendar year:
    a. Annual Spring Soiree - Mid-April
        i. Inter-Branch event consisting of at least four Branches
    b. Annual Masquerade Ball - Mid-October
        i. Inter-Branch event consisting of at least three Branches
3. Additionally, Branches are encouraged to organize their own Inter-Branch Mixers at least once per year at the discretion of the Branch Heads; however, this is a recommendation only and not a requirement.

<u>Surveillance:</u>

1. All Branch Mixers and other Our Family engagements are recorded for the safety - and pleasure - of Our Members.
2. Recordings are limited in availability to your unique Branch of membership only.
    a. Exceptions exist in the Executive Branch.
    b. Exceptions apply to Inter-Branch interactions.
3. Access to Recordings begins following participation in your first Mixer.
4. Partners will discuss, at their own discretion, the adoption of Recordings in private spaces.
    a. If desired, Members must submit an application to Our Family for approval.
    b. If approved, any Recordings obtained within the private space will be available as previously outlined.
5. Recordings may be accessed through the Recordings portal in the Our Family app.

My jaw is on the floor. My throat aches, a tight dryness restricting my breath. It somehow makes my heart thump even faster. Parker lays his hand across my chest to steady it. Like magic, his touch sends a rush of calm over me.

As my eyes cross each word, the initial shock of it is immediately overshadowed by arousal. It grows with each new shred of information. The more I read, the further I fall down the rabbit hole. This is a world I never dreamed could exist in reality. Parker is walking me along a glorious, dark, wonderfully provocative path. I excitedly forge ahead.

Confidentiality, Consent, & Communication:

1. All Members must sign and agree to a Non-Disclosure Agreement (NDA).
2. All Members must sign and agree to a Consent Form.
   a. Our Family recognizes that all individuals have sexual, social, and personal limits and boundaries. Members are required to complete and submit preferences and limits as soon as possible using the Consent Form.
   b. Changes and adjustments may be made to consent at any time.
   c. Safe words are a requirement of consent and participation. Each Branch has their own method of instituting this requirement.
      i. Branch 29 safe words are: Five Bear Circle, or FBC (abbreviated, if preferred).
      ii. Before engaging in play with a partner where verbal communication is not possible, nonverbal consent limits MUST be discussed and agreed upon.
   d. Our Family offers both soft swap and full swap opportunities.
      i. As previously stated, Branch 29 is a **full swap** Branch. Full Swap describes full sexual exchange, including oral sex, vaginal intercourse, and anal intercourse (as consented to).
3. Communication between active partners is vital to ensuring consent is respected, upheld, and enforced. Thus, communication is an **essential** responsibility of all Members.
   a. It is the responsibility of all Members to vocalize, communicate, and discuss tenets of consent with all partners interaction occurs with.
   b. As a reminder, communicating with the use of safe words is a requirement.
4. All required documents are available through the Responsibilities portal of the Our Family app.
5. All communication between active Members will occur through the Our

Family application ONLY.

    a. All Members will communicate through this app and this app only. Failure to do so will result in a Consequence.

    b. Exceptions apply only among Member partnerships that exist outside of Our Family.

6. Communication between Members and the use of the Our Family app must occur in private, discreet spaces, such as your home or private vehicle.

7. Under no circumstances are messages to be opened in public spaces such as, but not limited to, workplaces and other social spaces.

(A) External Confidentiality:

1. All matters relating to Our Family are to be absolutely confidential and never discussed, alluded to, or mentioned with any Non-Members. This includes, but is not limited to, the following:

    a. Mention of Our Family with Non-Members, including the existence of the organization, what it stands for, the activities of the organization, and membership within it.

    b. Discussion of relationships between Members with Non-Members.

2. There is a 100% no tolerance policy for violation of external confidentiality.

3. Our Family upholds the privacy of its Members wherein it vows to protect its Members from judgment and public insult.

4. Our Family values the public anonymity of its Members; therefore, external confidentiality is an essential tenet of membership.

5. Breach of external confidentiality will result in a Consequence either: at the discretion of the Branch Head in minor cases OR at the discretion of the Our Family Head in major infractions.

(B) Internal Confidentiality:

1. As with surveillance, all matters and interactions between Members are of interest to all Members within your Branch.

2. There is limited internal confidentiality within Our Family.

    a. The methodical framework of Our Family dictates the levels of accountability and disclosure.

        i. Current Standing for Iris Gladwell: Branch Level

Sexual Safety, Contraception, and Exclusivity:

1. All Members must undergo a full STI panel annually. Results must be submitted directly to the Branch Head.

2. Reproductive health:

   a. All individuals in Our Family acquire membership with the understanding that they will not, at any point during active membership, plan to reproduce or to conceive.

   b. Our Family understands that the choice to reproduce is a deeply personal one; if a Member makes the choice to reproduce, this must be communicated directly to the Branch Head.

      i. The status of membership in this situation will be evaluated on a case-by-case basis.

      ii. Membership may be suspended or terminated.

   c. It is the responsibility of all female Members to acquire approved birth control. This is limited to one of the following:

      i. A birth control pill

      ii. A birth control patch

      iii. An IUD

      iv. Other, considered on a case-by-case basis only

3. Under no circumstances will a person who has not secured approved contraception be allowed to acquire membership in Our Family.

4. Condom use is encouraged. Condoms are available and freely provided at all Mixers and formal events; however, their use is optional and at the discretion of the participating individuals involved.

5. Members commit to maintaining sexual exclusivity within Our Family **only**. Our Family understands that its Members have healthy sexual appetites. While placing limits on play may seem counterintuitive, the sexual safety of Our Members is a primary tenet of Our philosophy.

   a. Members agree that all sexual exploits will occur exclusively with other Members of Our Family.

      i. Play is **not** limited to your designated Branch; Inter-Branch play is permitted and encouraged.

      ii. See Our Leaflet for a catalog of Members and their contact information.

  b. Play with Non-Members is **prohibited**.

      i. Violations of this rule will result in at least a Consequence and at most expulsion.

      ii. Exceptions exist within OFRT only.

It all falls into place. *I* fall into place. With each word, the pieces of my most intimate self are forged together in a way that feels like Our Family was constructed solely for me. This is my place. It's dark and unconventional, but feels so right. So *me*. A wave of gratitude washes over me. How lucky I am to be invited into this incredible group - to find my place among the Members of Our Family. My eyes well up, the promise of hot, grateful tears threatening to spill out of me. I can't stop reading; it's obsessive. I force myself to take several deep breaths before continuing on. Parker kisses my neck, and it helps to ground me.

Next, I click on the check mark icon at the bottom of the screen. Responsibilities. Here we go.

Section One - NDA
AT YOUR EARLIEST CONVENIENCE, please read
IN ITS ENTIRETY the following non-disclosure agreement.

Not this dreadful thing again. To my relief, I see that this section is already complete, with an upload of the paper copy Parker had me fill out already.

Upon scrutiny of the Non-Disclosure Agreement IN ITS ENTIRETY, please sign below:

[SIGNATURE ACCEPTED]
IRIS GLADWELL

NDA RECORDED & ACCEPTED

Section Two - Sexual Health and Contraception
AT YOUR EARLIEST CONVENIENCE, please submit the results
of a FULL STI panel. Results must be dated within the last three months.

<CLICK TO UPLOAD DOCUMENT>

As a reminder, it is the responsibility of all females within Our Family to obtain an approved method of birth control.

AT YOUR EARLIEST CONVENIENCE, please submit a copy of your birth control prescription below, along with photos of your prescription with expiry dates visible.

<CLICK TO UPLOAD DOCUMENT>

Hardcore. But, understandable. Can't have a bunch of swinger babies baking in the oven - that would be a huge killjoy. I make a mental note to ask the pharmacist to print me a copy of my prescription when I go in next week to pick up my pill refill. I consider the fact that I'm one of the fortunate few who doesn't get my period when I'm on the pill. I smirk, foreseeing my ability to attend all of Our Family's events without Aunt Flo souring the mood.

Section Three - Responsibilities
Agreement of Responsibilities: AT YOUR EARLIEST CONVENIENCE
and upon full understanding of the rules, policies, and responsibilities
of membership, please sign below:

I, IRIS GLADWELL, pledge myself to uphold my Responsibilities as they are outlined in the Rulebook for Branch 29 (Harold) of Our Family. I acknowledge the rules and agree to abide by them, at all costs.

_____

IRIS GLADWELL

I can't sign this one - the box is blacked out. A tinge of disappointment wisps around me. I feel as ready as I'll ever be to sign my life away to this organization.

Section Four - Consent
Acknowledgment of Consent: AT YOUR EARLIEST CONVENIENCE,
review the following Consent Form and its conditions.
Make amendments and adjustments to your own personal
preferences, as desired.

I click and open the Consent Form. It's much shorter than the ramblings of the NDA, but still comprehensive. They aren't cutting any corners. The first section outlines my sexual preferences and orientations, and I find it strangely liberating to check the box beside *bisexual*. There. I'm out. For my people to see.

The next section is... unexpected. *Our Family is proud to supply its Members with various garments as they are required for participation in Mixer activities. Please provide your body measurements, so we may provide you with a personalized wardrobe of items.* Somehow, asking for my size and measurements feels strikingly more intrusive than consenting to anal fisting. It just so happens I conveniently do have my measurements, though, having taken them just a few months ago when I needed to buy a dress for a wedding where I was Ben's plus one. I open the note in my phone where I have them stored, then copy and paste them into the form. A personalized wardrobe, huh? Sounds excessive, but then again, I most definitely won't complain about having a couple of new lingerie items to add to my modest stash.

The final section is an exhaustive list of kinks, fetishes, and preferences. My insides throb as my eyes devour the endless inventory of possibilities. Parker rubs his fingers along my thigh, and I smile at him, smugly checking off item after item. The pride swells inside me as I consent to nearly the entire list.

Upon full understanding and completion of the Consent Form, please sign below.

I, IRIS GLADWELL, give my full consent to participate in the activities of Our Family, as they are outlined in the Rulebook for Branch 29 (Harold). I acknowledge the rules regarding my consent, and understand that I can withdraw and amend my consent at any time. I further acknowledge the limits on my consent, as outlined in the Consent Form herein. I hereby provide my consent to Our Family.

_____

IRIS GLADWELL

I eagerly swipe my finger across the signature box. While there may be nothing sexy about NDAs and RX uploads, the Consent Form gets me hot. Just considering the many pleasurable ventures that await, joining Our Family can't come fast enough. I run my hand along Parker's thigh, mirroring his touch. I can't help but notice the sizable bulge that has formed at his center. I guess I'm not the only one turned on by lewd paperwork.

The third icon, a gear, opens my Settings & Personal Information. I try to tap on it, but, like the signature box for Responsibilities, it's blacked out. It seems strange I can't access my own information, but, at the same time, I understand I'm not yet an official Member. I assume and accept that some content is understandably off limits.

The next icon is a calendar. I click on it and open the tab.

Calendar: No past or future events to display

Dead end. I shrug. The next icon is an envelope, which brings me to the Communications area of the app. There is one notification awaiting me there: a greeting from the woman named Desi.

Dearest Iris,

Welcome to Our Family. We are delighted you have been selected to join us in Our lifestyle. We hope upon acceptance of your invitation that we may soon entertain the pleasure of your company. We request that you carefully read the documents herein, as they outline important rules as well as your Responsibilities. Please don't hesitate to reach out to me should you have any questions that Parker is unable to answer. We eagerly anticipate your response.

Truly Yours,
Desi Harold
Our Family - Head of Branch 29

Another greeting worded differently but saying the same thing. No word from Mallory, who Parker had mentioned I would likely have a message from. The thought of receiving a notification and the subsequent urge to check this app later sends butterflies through my core. I'm pathetically giddy.

One icon left: a camera for Recordings. I gulp. These must be the recordings of Our Family events. *Access to Recordings begins following participation in your first Mixer*, I remember reading. I tap the icon, but, as expected, this, too, is blacked out. I suppose I'll need to accept membership before I can indulgently peruse the graphic content hidden here.

Having explored the app in its entirety (as accessible by me), I drop my phone in my lap. Parker kisses my cheek and waits patiently for me to digest. I take a minute to lay back and sink into the cushions behind me. Parker heads into the kitchen and grabs us both large glasses of cold water. I gulp mine back heartily. Running rampant with thoughts over what I just read, my head swirls and I feel a headache coming on. I close my eyes and mentally revisit it. It's overwhelming, to say the least, but also wildly validating.

I'm not alone. This organization might be the place where I really belong.

"Wow," I mutter. "I'm kind of in shock."

"In a good way, I hope."

"Yeah. Honestly... I know this is going to sound corny as shit, but. Our Family sounds like everything I have always wanted, but didn't think I could ever have. I didn't think an organization like this actually exists. I really *do* feel honored. The relationship I have with you is a dream, to me, really it is. And membership in this thing would take it to the next level. I always hoped there were others out there like me. Like us." I exclaim. I let out a burst of nervous laughter.

"I knew it. I knew you'd be perfect. You're so fucking perfect. God, I love you," Parker proclaims.

He climbs on top of me, and we both sink deeply into the plush of the couch. I cast my eyes upward, feeling small under his straddle. I lift my chin slightly, edging my lips closer to his. At what seems the pace of a snail, Parker inches closer until, at long last, our lips graze and meld into a soft kiss.

"I love you," I whisper.

Twenty-Eight

"So, now is the time when I answer all of your burning questions about Our Family," Parker states, solid and sure of himself. "I'm an open book. And if there's anything I can't answer, Desi will be able to."

"And Desi is the Head of the Branch. The one who runs the events and organizes Mixers?" I ask. Parker smiles, nodding.

"You're a quick study," he chuckles.

"And there are... sixteen people in Our Branch?"

"Fifteen. Sixteen, if you join. I was the only one without a long-term partner. But now that I found you, everyone in Our Branch is partnered up."

"How can that be? You can be in the Branch without a partner? I thought it said in the rules that Members exist in partnerships?"

"You're right. Our Branches are composed of partnerships. This isn't the same thing as couples. Some of the partnerships in the Branches are not couples. Everyone is recruited individually, and some at different times. So, until a long-term partnership is established, you are paired with a short-term partner. When I didn't have a long-term partner, I was paired with a short-term one. That's where Georgina comes in."

"Your co-worker."

"Yes. *Co-worker.* I was partnered with Georgina until I met my match. Until you." He chuckles and rubs his fingers against his chin. "I was recruited by another male in a different Branch, and Georgina was recruited by another woman. We were placed in Desi's Branch temporarily until we each found our long-term partners. Georgina is still on the hunt, so she has moved into another Branch with a different short-term partner. I stayed in Desi's Branch." I gawk at Parker, confusion clouding my expression. His eyes trace me, slowly taking note of every detail in my body's language. "It sounds a lot more complicated than it is. But recruitment isn't something you have to worry about. You and I are partnered together and we're good to go."

"But what does that mean? Recruited? You keep saying I was recruited. You were recruited. Everyone was recruited!" I throw my hands up like

Oprah awarding everyone a new TV. I laugh like a hyena. "How does a recruitment process like that work?"

"The recruitment process is very thorough," Parker explains. He rubs the back of his head as if to loosen the thoughts within it. "I can't really get into all of it right now, but I can say that extensive research goes into finding new Members. Once found, new Members undergo an intensive vetting procedure. For you," he pauses, still rubbing the back of his scalp, "I was responsible for that. I don't know how to say this without sounding... calculated." Parker fumbles. For the first time, he seems insecure. He sighs. "We didn't meet by chance, Iris." I stare at him, my lips parted and thirsty for answers. "It was all planned. This sounds heartless, but I swear to you it's not. You were, essentially, my assignment. But I *never* viewed you as that. To me, you've always been this beautiful, wild, captivating soul. I fell in love with you almost immediately, Iris. I know it sounds twisted, but I'm grateful to Our Family for having a hand in it, because otherwise, I don't know if I ever would've met you. You, Iris, the woman I love!"

I let his words sink in. I've been inundated with so much information that the shock value is slowly decreasing with every new piece. Knowing that I was Parker's assignment doesn't make me feel betrayed - that's too strong a word. But it does make me feel deceived. I run our history through my head. Me, meeting Parker; me, meeting Nina and G; me, joining this organization - it was all... orchestrated?

Parker hurries to fill the silence. "Please don't hate me. I'm sorry I couldn't tell you." He becomes emotional, his voice booming, while I sit speechless before him. "It's all part of the process. The same thing happened to me. To all of us. We are all recruited and go through the same thing," Parker offers. "And how I feel about you, Iris, that's authentic and real. That wasn't part of the plan, but it's been the greatest outcome. Please tell me you're okay."

"It's just a lot to take in." I say it, then immediately laugh. I can never turn off my dirty brain. Parker sputters and howls and the silence between us disappears. "Tell me how you became a Member."

"Well, that's a great story," Parker snickers in his throat. "Are you sure you're ready for this? I have thrown a lot at you."

"I can take it," I chuckle. Can I?

I can.

"Okay." He takes a deep breath and reaches for my hands. He intertwines our fingers and wiggles them, playing with them together as he speaks. "I was recruited by another Member. A buddy I knew from college. We were both studying business, so we took a lot of classes together and really got to know each other. We partied a lot," he giggles in his reverie. I can't tell if it's in nervousness or fondness. "As college guys do, we joked a lot about sex and what we were into. We shared a lot of common... interests." He's glowing, smiling ear-to-ear, boasting with joy and pride. It's infectious, and I hang on each word.

"So, how did he recruit you?" I prod.

"He'd been in Our Family for almost two years. I had no idea, but he had been vetting me for membership for a solid six months. I found it so easy to open up to him. He became my closest friend," Parker shares. "We were at one of his buddy's houses one night. There were a lot of very attractive people there!" he exclaims. I'm consumed with fascination. "It was a crazy night. Everyone just sort of hooked up with everyone. We were all fucking like a living, breathing, hedonistic creature. The atmosphere felt like magic. It was so easy; everything just flowed. It was so organic and, honestly, fucking amazing." My eyes tunnel into Parker's. I'm completely enthralled. "That was the first part of my test. We had several other wild nights like that. Those were some of my best memories of college." Parker chuckles again. "Then, I was in."

"That sounds incredible," I say breathlessly. I clear my throat. "Wow."

"Yeah. Our Family changed my life. And now that I've met you, I feel complete."

"Parker!" I smack him. I'm completely smitten with him. It's disgustingly cringe.

"I mean, I always dreamed of finding someone who would be my partner in Our Family. There have been plenty of females for me to interact with, but I didn't have my person. I belonged, but not fully. Then, I was assigned you," he continues. I beam.

"What was my test, then?" I ask, not sure which was the pivotal event granting my membership. Parker laughs.

"You don't know?" he teases, amused once more by my ignorance.

"I don't..." I trail off as a wave of shame hits me. I feel utterly stupid for not deciphering this part of the puzzle.

Parker takes a deep breath, lets it out, then speaks softly. "Your test was interacting with Nina and G."

"Of course." It clicks. Duh.

"And you passed with flying colors!"

"Wait," I ponder. "Wait. Are Nina and G in Our Family, too?" I shudder.

"Ha! Smart girl," Parker applauds. "They are indeed! They belong to a different Branch, but both are Members."

"Well, that explains last night at the gallery. When I saw you and G together."

Parker grins, nodding. "Yes. We were just grabbing drinks. Chatting about our relationship." He nudges me playfully.

"Our relationship," I echo, trying to make sense of how our independent relationship stands in relation to Our Family.

"That's right. We aren't just Members of Our Family. We are a couple, madly in love with each other, with a bright future ahead! We will have a beautiful life. Being a part of Our Family simply enriches that." Parker explains.

It's profoundly liberating to be able to discuss topics like this with someone I love without having to face judgment or feel ashamed of my truth. I grin, my body on the brink of bursting with lust. I push into Parker. My body melds into his. As he wraps his muscular arms around me, I retreat into my thoughts, grappling with the shocking realizations about my new reality.

I've always believed monogamy is dead. It's an archaic institution, built to control and cage us. Humans are social animals. We aren't meant to spend every day, for years on end, or in some cases the rest of our lives, surrounded by the same people. What stifling monotony. To expect us to spend our every day in companionship of the same person is absolute ludicrous. I crave more. I crave freedom. Why does society restrict us, setting boundaries on our behalf? My private life is exactly that - private. Why shouldn't I be allowed to share company, intimate or not, with whomever I please? Why should I allow the confines of modern definitions of relationships to have power over me?

I am an adult. I am mature. I have power and independence. I determine the rules that govern my private life. No one can cage me... unless of course I want them to.

Parker understands me. Our Family understands me; they accept me - embrace me. They encourage me to reach the fullest potential of all that I am. And I am wild, different, and wanton. For once, I can surround myself with a group of people who identify as the same.

I am done with the judgment and condescension from those who don't understand me. Outsiders will never understand me. I exist as more than an individual, or as half of a couple. I can be one part of a beautiful, glorious creation that's greater than myself.

They say variety is the spice of life, and I'm ready to up the heat.

That's not to say that there isn't enough between me and Parker to satiate my hunger. Parker and I are the base - the solid foundation off of which we can grow and enhance our lives. And the strength of that foundation lies in our trust, connection, and communication. Without those essential elements, our arrangement - both within our relationship and Our Family - would crumble.

We are solid. Parker is it for me. I have found in him my perfect partner. I love him with every part of my being. I want us to spend all our days together, lost in love and joy. I don't want us to grow resentful, tired, and sick of each other. Our sex is sacred, special, and unique to only us. I know him, all of him. Envy is an emotion of weakness. I am more than happy to share. Our love for each other and our choice to play with others can coexist in the same space. In fact, supporting Parker in being sexually expressive and exploring other encounters is one of the ways I, in turn, express my love for him. No two bodies are the same. Male or female, we all have diverse differences in our form. Why jail Parker into only ever being able to explore my body? Sex isn't love. Sex can be a form of love, but it is also an expression of self. And in some ways, watching Parker with other women is expressive in showing me his love. I acknowledge my shortcomings. Not everything is appealing to me. Parker and I are different people with different interests. There are experiences that I want that Parker can't give me. There are experiences Parker wants that I can't give him. I love him, and I want him to have those experiences. Our Family enables that.

I can't believe how fortunate I am to have this man.

"I accept the invitation," I whisper into Parker's chest. "I can't wait to experience this with you."

"You won't regret it," he promises.

I sincerely doubt I will.

Twenty-Nine

Parker whips out his phone and sends a message to Desi letting her know that I have accepted the invitation to join Our Family. They message back and forth, and the entire exchange has Parker grinning widely. God, I love his smile.

"Great. Desi is going to get the ball rolling. Check your Communications in a bit. I expect you'll have a new message in there soon." He tucks his phone into his pant pocket and refocuses his attention on me. "I suppose you've earned a little treat, since you were so good in accepting the invitation," Parker teases. My body immediately responds, my heart gaining speed and my skin prickling with heat.

"What kind of treat?" I ask, in any tone but an innocent one.

He immediately falls to his knees in front of me. I barely have time to take an expectant breath before he leans into me and pulls my jeans (and panties) from my waist, down my thighs, and over my ankles. He kisses the insides of my legs, then pulls me toward him. I yelp as I slide onto my back.

"Look at you. So wet already."

Parker takes a long lick of my pussy, his tongue wide and thirsty. Learning about Our Family has been an unexpected foreplay, and my lower lips are drenched from it. He laps up my fluids, sucking and flicking his tongue against my slick folds. I reach for him and grab a tuft of his beautiful hair in my hand. Parker's fingers squelch as they wiggle into my opening, filling me up slowly.

"So fucking wet, my easy little slut."

I whimper. My mind turns to mush as my primal need for Parker's touch consumes me. I squirm as his fingers slide in and out of me, fucking me gently, then without mercy. He inserts his entire fist into my hole and I wail, breathless. The fullness is overwhelming. His mouth worships my bud, expertly caressing my most sensitive region. It builds, my release looming. I push his face into my pussy, forcing it closer, suffocating him in my femininity. Clenching fistfuls of his hair in my hands, I quiver as he gasps for air between my legs. He quickens his pace and plunges his hand in and out of me. Then his thumb twists into my back hole, and the

207

sensation is too much to bear. My orgasm radiates through me. It makes my ears hot and my body heavy. I shudder and shake, the exhilaration of my climax overtaking every particle of my existence. Parker emerges from my center and plunges his fingers into my mouth. I suck on them, savoring the incredible taste of my own cum.

"Let's see what you can do for me." Parker stands, and I struggle to force my body upright. I fall into him and weakly unclasp his belt buckle.

"Don't be so fucking lazy," he says as he uses the loosened end of his belt to whack me in the cheek. He pulls out his cock and orders me to suck it.

I open widely and allow it to slide deeply into my throat. But... something about it feels different this time. He pushes hard into me, heaving and thrusting deeper than he ever has. His voice gradually becomes louder and fiercer until he is full-blown yelling, commanding me in a harsh sneer. It's the most intense interaction we've ever had. I can barely breathe; his shaft is shoved so deep in my throat. Still, he pushes, more, harder, deeper, and it feels like he's never going to let me come up for air. I gag, and he slaps me with his belt again. It stings so good.

"You can take it, I know you can!" he exclaims, almost maniacal. He groans. "You are such a good little slut! Choke on it! Choke on it, you whore! Fuck yes!"

At long last, he pulls out, and I spit and cough onto the carpet beneath me. He pumps his fist along his length and spews his load onto my back. I have never experienced Parker at that level - at that intensity. It's shocking. But welcome. Challenging. Wonderful. So fucking hot that I think I might pass out from the euphoria of it.

"That was perfect," he praises, petting my hair. "How was it for you?" he asks, a light air of hesitancy in his voice.

"Wow. So good," I sigh. "Parker, that was different. In a good way," I chuckle.

"You liked it?" he asks, hopeful.

"Yes, yes, I really did!" I exclaim. "You didn't hold back. I love that."

"Don't ever forget to raise your arm. If you want me to stop," he says, reminding me of one of our non-verbal signals.

"I didn't want you to stop. Listen, Parker. I want you to know that I accept you. All of you. I never want you to be anything but yourself." Tears threaten the corners of Parker's beautiful blue eyes. "You said it yourself - we aren't like other people. And I love that. I love that about us. We are different. Unique. I love that we don't follow the rules of society or the norms that every other ordinary human does. I never thought I'd meet someone who shares my same values. Someone fucking deviant, like me."

"I fucking love you," Parker declares, pulling me into him and giving me a passionate kiss.

Pulling away, he looks me straight in the eyes. I stare back at him, the black of his pupils looking larger than ever. He bores in, fixated, unblinking. He takes a deep breath.

"We are entering into a contract - with each other... and with others. You know I love to watch you. And, of course, you love to be watched. The way you get off on knowing I'm in the background, keeping a close eye on everything you do, Jesus, Iris, it drives me fucking mad. I can't get enough." I blink, looking down at my feet. He grabs my chin and readjusts my gaze. His fingers pinch. "You like to be humiliated and have your limits pushed. I did that, just now. And you loved it. We can have everything we want. Together," he states with absolute certainty.

I might explode. He's right - he's right about all of it. I immediately think of our arrangement with Nina and G. Parker was there, spectating our every interaction, watching us from the dark corners of the world. Parker was there at the bar, watching me flirt with them during our first meeting. When we were at the wine bar and at G's, it was more difficult, but I was sure to surreptitiously place my phone in just the right spot, call him, and he would mute his end. That way, he could hear every glorious sound we made.

He has a way with me. His words, his touch. He can convince me of anything. Parker knows me better than anyone. I have never been as vulnerable and authentic as I am with him. I have never trusted anyone as wholeheartedly as I trust Parker. It's like he can peer inside my soul, into the deepest parts of me, and nourish those pieces that had been emaciated, starving, and desperate for their fill. He can piece together those ravaged bits, arranging them in such a way that the purest, most genuine, sincerest form of who I am can shine.

Parker is everything to me.

He reaches down to where his jeans are strewn across the floor. In their back pocket, he retrieves his phone, which is buzzing and lighting up with a new notification. Parker mischievously grins, then bites his lip. I wait patiently, anticipating good news.

"It's Desi. This is great! Check your phone," he instructs, pulling his jeans back on.

I reach for my phone on the coffee table and pick it up. To my delight, I have a notification hovering on my home screen.

ONE NEW NOTIFICATION
OF
NEW MESSAGE

I excitedly click on it. The app opens, and face ID allows access to my unread message.

Dearest Iris,

It is with Our anticipation and excitement that we invite you to join us for your Confirmation this evening! Event details can be found in your Calendar.

We have heard a lot about you, Iris, and greatly look forward to making your acquaintance! See you tonight!

Truly Yours,
Mallory Chambers
Our Family, Branch 29 Communications Officer

"Tonight?" I gasp.

"Tonight," Parker echoes, matter-of-fact. He grabs my arm and yanks me to standing. "No time to waste. Let's get you ready." He swoons like a fangirl.

I hop in the shower to ready myself for the evening ahead. I'm completely uncertain about what to expect, but to be safe, I shave my armpits, legs, and tidy up down below. I throw my face under the hot stream of the shower and scrub it with exfoliant. Refreshed, I shut off the water and quickly dry my body using a gray towel that was once plush, but now has the texture of sandpaper. Yet, somehow, the abrasiveness of it is oddly satisfying.

It reminds me of rope.

Parker and I spend the next hour ripping my modest closet apart looking for options suiting a young woman who is about to be confirmed as an official Member of a secretive swinger's organization.

I'm not sure I have anything of that caliber.

Nevertheless, I play dress-up, and Parker casts judgment on my three top contenders. With Alexa playing *Nectar Radio* in the background, Parker pours me a glass of wine, and I model each outfit to his satisfaction. I twirl and pose, putting on a proper runway show. It's fun and lighthearted; the perfect break from the crippling anticipation that will undoubtedly plague me soon.

First, I try a navy A-line dress with a simple sweetheart neckline. The loose skirt dances down my legs almost to the floor. It has a high-thigh slit that usually goes unnoticed, hidden in the loose layers. I smile, wondering if Parker's keen eyes for observation make note of it.

Of course they do.

Next up is a high-neck, black sheath dress with a champagne-colored top decorated in elaborate black lace. It hugs my curves just right, allowing mobility but still flattering my shape. Its straps crisscross along the back and leave me (pleasantly) feeling a little exposed.

My final option is a maroon-colored V-neck, with wide shoulders and ruching around the waist. This one gives me amazing cleavage and is a little more formal than the others. It's a beautiful dress, but I hate it. I wore it to Zach's wedding, so it always reminds me of my shortcomings. I suppose I'm not that great of an actress, because Parker says that my wrinkled nose gives away my disdain for it. Sorry, not sorry.

The navy dress comes out on top, but Parker gives me strict instructions to wear the champagne and black lace dress another time. He informs me he has a healthy stash of navy suits in his closet, so matching will be an easy feat.

Parker leaves me to get ready while he makes a quick trip back to his place to change. In his absence, my anxiety taunts me.

What am I getting myself into?

Thirty

First impressions are a real thing. I'm not vain, but something in me makes me want to impress this group of strangers more than I've ever wanted to impress anyone in my life. I slip into one of my favorite thongs - a black, lacy G-string - and pair it with a simple, seamless black bra. Next, I apply some makeup. I kept it simple, with winged black eyeliner and dark mascara. I pat a light dusting of powder all over my face, then pick out a muted red lipstick to apply after my dress is on. I let my hair down and then spritz it all over with a sea salt spray. I finger my strands, and between the humidity of the bathroom and the chemicals c/o Bed Head, they form gentle, beachy waves.

Save for my dress, I'm ready to go. It surprisingly took me almost no time to get ready, so I decide to settle onto the couch and read while I wait for Parker to return. I happily get lost in the pages, thinking of nothing but the possibilities of what happened to Judy during her three-month disappearance from her small, seaside town.

Some time later, Parker knocks on the door. I scramble to pull on my dress and struggle to get the zipper all the way up. I hold it to my chest and answer the front door.

"Hey!" I greet, letting him in. He looks incredible, dressed in a sleek navy suit and simple plaid necktie. Also freshly showered, he smells woodsy and gloriously manly. I breathe him in.

"Hi, beautiful," he hums. "Wow. You look absolutely stunning."

"Thank you," I reply, blushing brightly. "You don't look too shabby yourself," I smile, my nerves suddenly hitting me. He pulls me in for a gentle embrace, and I hopelessly try not to melt in his grasp.

"Will you help me with this?" I spin to reveal my exposed back. The zipper hovers just above my cheeks, and Parker's fingertips brush against my warm skin. They linger for a moment, slipping under the lace of my thong, and my body tingles. I feel Parker's breath against my shoulder, and I fight the urge to push myself backwards into his body.

"Nice choice," he mumbles, throaty, snapping my thong against my skin. I jump, surprised. And aroused.

He slowly pulls the zipper up, reluctant.

I wander into my bedroom for one last peek in the full-length mirror. I brush on a simple line of red lipstick, and I'm ready to go.

And then, it washes over me. The realization.

An epiphany.

Everything about this is exactly right.

Everything.

Parker and I belong together. We are a rare breed. The bond we share transcends what a relationship is defined as in mainstream society. And in this moment, the freedom of it settles inside me. Parker accepts me as I am. And I feel pride in knowing that Parker trusts me with his honest, true, vulnerable self, too. I can carry that around with me now, knowing it belongs to me, in the same way mine belongs to him.

"I love you," I say softly. "We are so lucky. To have what we have. The trust. Our bond."

"I'm so glad you trust me."

"Always," I reply. Because I do.

Our bond is deeply intimate and stronger than any bond of marriage or legal condition. It's a true, authentic, and raw representation of our innermost selves.

Parker steps back, taking my hands in his.

"Are you ready?"

I gulp. "I am."

• • • •

ON THE WAY TO MY IMPENDING Confirmation, Parker eases my nerves by doing his best to fill me in on what I'm about to walk into. I'll meet all the Members in Our Branch, including Desi, her husband Marc, Mallory (who had sent me the Confirmation information), her partner Davis, and many others whose names I have already forgotten and likely won't remember even after meeting them. My mind is swirling. Parker is calm and collected, yet there's an edge to our conversation. An unspoken expectation. I'm desperate to make him proud; I don't want to disappoint him, or those who are accepting me into their circle.

Most of all, I don't want to disappoint myself.

Parker promises tonight will strictly be an introduction and not a traditional Mixer. More of a meet-and-greet than anything. It'll set the stage for future interactions.

We drive for some time. Parker switches on the satellite radio, flipping through several instrumental options before settling on one aptly titled *beautiful music*. The sound of the orchestra softly diffuses throughout the quiet corners of the vehicle, in turn calming my nerves. I'm smiling like an idiot, eager to meet the *others*, and even more so to become an official Member of a group where I belong. My excitement feels shameful, which, as my sexual kryptonite, turns me on the more I try to stop it from doing so.

Driving for almost forty long minutes on the freeway, at last we come to our turn off. Parker exits, takes two additional turns, and then a left onto an unlit, unpaved road. The gravel beneath crunches under the truck's tires. I can't help but clench my jaw in response, my teeth involuntarily clicking together.

"Yikes!" I squeal, taken aback.

"Yeah, the road is pretty rough getting there."

"Where exactly is *there*?"

"Just ahead. Marc and Desi's Estate."

"Estate?" I gasp.

It's not an understatement. Parker keeps course, driving toward a sprawling property lit by overhanging vintage street lamps. It's elegant and grand, with a main house composed of several wings extending on either side. There are also at least half a dozen stand-alone buildings to the right, which look like a series of mini homes all in a neat little line.

"Wow," I breathe.

"Pretty impressive, I know."

"I feel out of my league!" I uncomfortably giggle.

"That's exactly the thing," Parker begins. "This *is* your league, Iris!"

Parker navigates his truck in a semi-circle, maneuvering it around a landscaped island precisely pruned and elegant, noticeable to me even in the oncoming darkness. Parker cuts the engine, hops out of his seat, walks around the front of his truck, and chivalrously opens my door for me.

Offering me a hand, I exit. We make our way from the left of the property and climb countless stairs up to the front doorway. I cling to his arm, feeling like a celebrity about to make her first public appearance since becoming famous. My cheeks are the same red as my lipstick and ache from the wide grin I've been trying so hard to suppress. My heart is in my throat.

The front of the building houses double-tall French doors as black as a midnight sky. Speckled around the entrance are windows of various sizes. They're foggy and opaque, with a leaf pattern frosted onto them. As we inch closer, soft light pours from within, but I can't shake the distinct eerie feel of this grand entrance. Parker knocks heartily to announce our arrival. My nerves twist like knives in my stomach.

Shadows dance across the windows as our host approaches.

It's time.

Thirty-One

"Welcome! Welcome, Iris! So wonderful to meet you at last! Good to see you, Parker!" We're greeted by a tall, olive-skinned woman wearing a gorgeous dark green dress. She floats across the shiny terracotta tiles of the spotless floor. She has a bright smile and gleaming, nude-colored lips. "We are so excited to meet you!" She leans across the threshold and kisses me on both cheeks. Her dark ringlets brush against my skin. I blush. More. Again. Still. "Come in, come in!" She opens the door widely and ushers us inside.

"Desi, you look stunning, as always," Parker compliments, his voice calm and light. Still holding my hand, he gives Desi a half-hug and quick peck on the cheek. "It's my pleasure to introduce the beautiful Iris!" he proudly announces. He drops my hand and steps away. If there's a spotlight, I imagine it's shining brightly on me.

"Hello," I squeak.

"Iris! Welcome to Our Family. I'm Desi. I'm so pleased to meet you!" Desi exclaims, enthusiasm and confidence seeping from her every word.

"Thank you for having me, Desi. I'm honored. You have a beautiful home," I mutter, my voice feeling lost in the enormity of this place. And this situation.

"We are honored to host you. Come, come, allow me to announce you," Desi states, inviting me to follow her. I do as instructed, marching behind this magnificent creature.

We wander down a long hallway, past countless other rooms with countless other halls. The deeper we go into the home, the more I wonder if I'll be able to find my way out of this stunning labyrinth. At last, we turn a corner, descend a narrow staircase, and enter into an expansive, grand room. With white marble tiles decorating the floors and walls, it reminds me of a ballroom in a royal castle. Who am I kidding - this place *is* a royal castle. There are no windows, but it's lit beautifully, with several massive chandeliers glowing softly above. Ambient music echoes off the walls to cut through the stifling silence that would otherwise plague such a massive space. The size of the room makes the population of it less intimidating.

I count around a dozen others, each standing at different cocktail-height tables distributed around the front center of the room. As we stroll toward the others, conversations die, bodies straighten, and attentions are redirected to us. It's flattering, having this impact simply by existing. I look at Parker, our hands weaved together. He beams.

Desi floats to one of the tables and lifts up two glasses of champagne. She delivers one to me and one to Parker, then returns to the table for one for herself. The others wait patiently, their attention on Desi.

"Good evening, everyone," she greets the others. The room stills. She returns to where Parker and I stand, bringing along with her one of the men, who I assume is her husband, Marc. He stands loyally by her side. He's not as tall as Desi, but still one of the tallest in the room. His shoulders are broad, and he has groomed salt-and-pepper facial hair and dark eyes. He wears a stark black suit with a thin tie that matches the same rich green of Desi's gown. Adorable.

"Thank you all for coming this evening. Please join me in welcoming Our newest Member, Iris!" Desi exclaims, her voice loud and certain. It echoes off the walls and reverberates inside my ears. The group breaks into soft claps, except for one enthusiastic Member who whoops loudly. My cheeks turn a darker shade of pink as we make eye contact. He's bitterly handsome.

"Iris," Desi turns to me. "We are so happy to have you here! We are looking forward to getting to know you, and having you get to know us!" I'm biting my lips now, my nerves rising to the surface. "Welcome. To Iris!" Desi raises her glass. The room follows, and together we take a swig of crisp champagne. It burns and bubbles in my throat, a little too reminiscent of last night at the art gallery. I politely put it down on the table with no intention of picking it up again.

Quiet conversations resume, and I look to Parker for guidance.

"Now I'll introduce you to everyone," Parker whispers. "Ready?"

I look down at my abandoned champagne flute and regretfully reach for another sip. The liquid cuts against my throat. "Now I am," I cough.

Making my rounds, I talk to each of the Members of Branch 29.

I meet the bubbly Mallory and her partner, Davis, who are high school sweethearts. They are lovely. Davis is an accountant, and although Mallory doesn't have a paying job, she tells me she's in charge of scheduling, paperwork, and other management duties within Our Branch. She playfully warns me that I will be hearing from her a lot! I smile and giggle, captured by her friendly, energetic personality. Davis is much less outgoing than Mallory, but still easy to talk to. He's lean and tall, with blonde hair and striking green eyes. He wears a navy suit similar to Parker's, although Parker looks superior, in my humble opinion. Mallory, conversely, is short, possibly the shortest in the room, at a *travel-sized 5'2"!* she jokes. She's curvy and voluptuous, with the perfect hour-glass shape. Her brown hair is long, straight, and almost grazes her waist. With brown eyes that match mine, she listens intently to everything I say. I know immediately that Mallory and I will be fast friends. As I take them in, it seems Davis and Mallory are an unlikely couple. They aren't married, but have been together now for almost 20 years. They credit their longevity to Our Family, speaking highly of how it enriches their relationship and enables them to be their most primitive selves.

I meet Marie and Evan, who remind me most of Parker and myself. Evan is a construction manager with a love of adventure. Marie is a wildlife photographer, and the two of them together just fit. Those two perfect puzzle pieces. Marie has an edge to her; she's outspoken and bold. Evan thrives on it. Marie is a strawberry blonde, and the tips of her hair dance on her shoulders that have been left naked by her stunning strapless black dress. Evan is a full-blown red-head, with ginger locks tucked behind his ears, and the two of us find solidarity in our identical hair color. These two are relatively new Members, they tell me, having been married for five years but only active in Our Family for half of that.

I meet Scarlett and Aki, who are the newest Members of Branch 29. Aki has been a Member for almost six months, while Scarlett joined only two months ago. These two are not a couple, but exist in a partnership Our Family has crafted for them. I pick their brains, hungry to know their experience as newbies trying to fit in. They speak highly of the group and promise me that, although it feels strange at first, have faith that I've made the right decision to join. They assure me that it only gets better. Aki has a soft, hypnotizing Japanese accent that blankets me in immediate comfort. He wears a broad smile with perfect teeth. Scarlett is much quieter than her partner, with a mysterious edge to her. She intrigues me. Her long, black hair pours over her shoulders and all the way down to her inconceivably thin waist. Her skin is pale as a ghost. I can't help but feel like there's more to her, something left unsaid.

I meet Sunny and Wyatt, who bring life to the group. These two are obscenely outgoing, loud, and clearly extroverts. Wyatt (the whooper) has light brown hair, blue eyes, and a muscular frame. He removes his black suit jacket, and the sharp outlines of his chest and arm muscles are distinctly visible under the white of his dress shirt. He's remarkably handsome, charming, and very easy on the eyes. Sunny was born in India, she tells me, but moved to the States when she was two. Her mocha skin glows under the light of the chandeliers, augmented in its richness against the champagne-colored dress that plunges deeply into her cleavage. She is one of the most stunning people I have ever set eyes on. She and Wyatt own a party planning business together, specializing in weddings and, true to Wyatt's heritage, a variety of mitzvahs. Even in our brief introduction, I feel drunk on their confidence.

I meet Bea and Riley, who are undeniably the most awkward of the bunch. Riley is quiet and reserved, with dark hair that messily crowds his face. Between his mop of hair and bushy eyebrows, it's truly a crime to hide the bright blue eyes lurking underneath. He listens intently as Bea runs the conversation, her full lips rapidly moving with each word. Bea's hair is spunky and bright, with tones of blue, pink, and blonde. She's refreshingly unconventional, although difficult to keep a conversation flowing with. She tells me she's a hairdresser and that Riley's an engineer, and that they have been part of Our Family for two years. She promises me that she's an excellent judge of character and predicts that I will fit right in.

I meet Julia and Thom, who are thick as thieves with Desi and Marc. The four of them have been friends for years and rarely do anything without each other; they claim to be foursome more than anything. They are honored, they tell me, to be Founding Members of Desi and Marc's Branch. I nod politely, having no idea whatsoever of the meaning of that claim. Thom is clean-shaven, with dirty blonde hair scattered with hidden bits of gray. He has sharp blue eyes that slice through me, making me feel vulnerable and exposed, somehow. He's in good shape and, like Wyatt, has removed his suit jacket to reveal a toned chest beneath. Thom takes good care of himself. He's a physical therapist and co-owner of a karate studio with a childhood friend. Julia matches Thom in her figure - she's athletic with the body of a runner. The muscles of her toned leg peek out from her shimmering silver dress, and I'm reminded of the slit in my own. I wonder if anyone has noticed it? Inspired by Julia's confidence, I wiggle a bit, shuffling my skirt and quickly exposing my slit, then just as quickly re-tucking my leg beneath. Julia is as interesting as she is beautiful, with blonde hair wrapped into a relaxed bun, a few unruly strands hanging around her face and framing her brown eyes. She makes a living as a psychologist who works with at-risk youth.

I am in the company of some incredible and incredibly successful humans.

At last, Desi introduces me to Marc. He is well-spoken and carefully maintains eye contact, with his dark browns staring deep into my eyes. Desi does a wonderful job of moving our conversation along. Marc is more of an observer, much like Parker, and this immediately draws me to him. Having met everyone else, Marc fills in a lot of the blanks. He has a mysterious intensity about him, and speaks abundantly of the discretion involved in being a Member. He reiterates it about a hundred times, pushing to instill in me a sense of absolute secrecy. He warns that my commitment to Our Family is demanding, deeply intensive at times, and should not be taken lightly.

With the initial meetings out of the way, I relax and, glancing at Parker, can see he was too.

Yet there's a different type of tension, predominant and thick, running through the room. It's hopeless to deny the sexual energy; it is, after all, the reason we are all gathered here together. Attraction permeates into every crevice of the room.

Desi ushers the men apart and gathers the women together for a more intimate chat.

We share everything. It's so easy between us. We openly discuss our deepest kinks and fetishes, and there's nothing uncomfortable about it. It's the acceptance - the way everything that I *am* is embraced by those who are just like me. My kinks, quirks, and queerness are welcomed. Our interactions indulge all my deepest fantasies and validate all my strangest thoughts. It feels like I have known these women forever, and they relate to my every word. Having these discussions with others like me is profoundly liberating. They aren't ashamed of their truth, or deceitful of who they really are and what they like. I'm further comforted in learning that I'm not the only bisexual one in the group: Desi readily reveals that Marc identifies as bi as well, and Bea and Sunny say that of course they are, too.

It's as though that piece inside of me that was always scrutinized by society and its conventions is replaced by a nurturing knowledge that I belong here, in this group. In Our Family. I fall in love with these women, for their validation of me, and, in turn, mine of them. We are all peas of the same pod. I feel my soul fill up. I have found my place.

I belong in this group of libidinous freaks.

I am one of them.

"Iris, we are so happy to have you here!" Marie exclaims. "Welcome to Our Family!" She pulls me in, hugging me tightly. She kisses me on the cheek, and it leaves me feeling warm and tingly. The other women follow, each taking their turn showing me an affectionate hug and cheek kiss, as if I'm in a receiving line. They shower me with nurturing words, and I smile, my face reddening still, as I whisper *thank you* over and over and dig deep to keep the tears of joy at bay. Seeing themselves in me, they empathize, admitting that they had all been brought to tears before their own Confirmations. I am so grateful to these women - for their understanding and for their acceptance.

I excuse myself; I need a moment to get it together. Mallory takes my hand and guides me to the bathroom. She offers to stay, but I graciously decline. The bathroom is, of course, huge and impressive. White tile marbled with gold streaks and stark black cabinets make a bold statement. There's a humongous glass-walled walk-in shower with ten different nozzles, hoses, and various jets, as well as ample space to fit at least half a dozen people. I plop myself on one of the vintage upholstered chairs lining the wall and take several deep breaths. I feel high, almost, like I've injected a pure dose of lust into my veins.

And I'm crying. The tears spill out of me like a pot boiling over. I take a deep breath, desperate to steady my racing heart. I'm sure it's going to explode right out of my chest. My mind swirls. As if going to a ginormous mansion in the middle of nowhere and meeting a new group of practically perfect people with exactly the same worldviews as me isn't enough, let's add in the fact that we will fucking each other's brains out sooner or later.

The tears pour down my cheeks. They aren't of sadness, or fear, but distinct overwhelm. I am overwhelmed as fuck.

But it's okay; it will all be okay. I force myself to ride the wave, despite its intensity, because I know it's guiding me to a gorgeous new horizon. I cry and cry and cry. I don't know how long I cry for, but the tears don't stop.

Until finally, they do. I dab my eyes with a tissue, fix my blotchy eyeliner with a cotton swab, and ready myself to rejoin the group. I am really, truly, happy. This is an exciting time. Overwhelmingly exciting. Incredible things are yet to come.

Despite my puffy eyes, I admit it to myself: I'm strangely at home in this strange place.

I wander back to the ballroom, proud of myself for finding the way without the help of a detailed map. Ha! Proof I *do* belong right here. Parker checks in with me following my unplanned absence, and assure him that I am very much alright. I honestly feel better than ever now that I've purged my emotions and digested all the love and acceptance surrounding me. Parker whispers all the right things in my ear, kisses me passionately with his lips firmly pressed against mine, and I feel new again.

In my absence, the front cocktail tables have been transformed and now boast an impressive charcuterie spread. My grumbling stomach is terribly grateful to have something to satiate it. Most everyone has already helped themselves, so I join in, savoring the flavors of fine cheeses and fresh strawberries.

Bea jokes that she's a Greek slave as she feeds Marie, her beautiful muse, grapes off the vine. We all laugh, our bond strengthening in each shared moment. Bea turns to me, giving me a turn to be worshiped. Her fingers graze my arm as she walks the grapes up to my mouth. Her touch burns with promise. I lean my head back and scold her for her unacceptably slow pace. In all its fun, the air in the room thickens with heat. The other women look at me expectantly.

I can't let them down.

I raise my hand and slap Bea. Right across the face. The shock of it incites gasps from the group. Bea exhales and drops the grapes onto the floor beneath us. The men look over, hearing the sudden wave of gasps. Bea gapes at me, her mouth hanging open in awe. I raise my eyebrows and challenge her to make her move. She leaps onto me, pushing her succulent lips into mine. Our kiss is fiery and warm, and it builds and grows as she presses her body into mine. Her breasts melt gloriously into my chest. I whimper and pull her close. The group stares on, with murmurs of approval and other smutty commentary audible amongst them. Bea pulls away. Her eyes remain glued to mine.

"Pass me a grape," she heralds to Marie. Marie acquiesces.

Bea pops the grape between her lips, then leans into me again, passing it from her mouth to mine. I take it greedily and bite down. My teeth puncture its skin, and the sweet juices of the grape flow over my tongue.

"Well done, my servant," I congratulate Bea.

Our scene over, we all break into laughter, giddy and hopelessly turned on.

Desi takes the floor, claiming my and Bea's performance is the perfect interlude to her speech.

"Please join me, Iris," Desi requests. I gallop over to her, exhilaration jolting through my body. "At last, the moment we've all gathered to celebrate. Iris. It's been a true pleasure getting to know you this evening. We are all very eager to learn about you more *intimately*, I'm sure, especially after that impressive performance." The crowd cheers. Still, the humiliation swirls in my stomach and piques in a significant wetness between my thighs. I look away, but Parker lifts my chin up with his hand. He's beaming, a broad smile painted on his face. "It's time for the official moment!" Desi turns behind her and picks up an iPad. She passes it to me, sliding it from her delicate hands into mine. My face lights up in the brightness of the screen, and my eyes scan the words before me.

What is this?

RECORD FOR MEMBER NO. 000045981

PERSONAL INFORMATION:

- FULL NAME: IRIS BRIENNE GLADWELL
- DATE OF BIRTH: NOVEMBER 16, 1990, 21:18 PST
- PLACE OF BIRTH: ORANGE COUNTY, CA
- PHONE NUMBER: 949-555-5342
- ADDRESS: #5 - 112 GRIANTIDO AVE, VISTA LOMA, CA
- EMPLOYMENT: DR. VAL'S PETVET / PETCATION - VETERINARY TECHNICIAN (APPROX. 8 YEARS)

FAMILY INFORMATION:

- MOTHER: DARLA MCKENZIE GLADWELL (MAIDEN NAME: JONES)
- FATHER: BRIAN ANDERS GLADWELL (DECEASED JANUARY 4, 2001)
- SIBLING(S): ZACHARY AUGUST GLADWELL; TWIN; BORN SIX MINUTES EARLIER

EDUCATION:

- HIGH SCHOOL DIPLOMA: Y
- COLLEGE NAME/ PROGRAM / STATUS: WINDSOR COMMUNITY COLLEGE / VETERINARY TECHNICIAN / GRADUATE

HEALTH & WELLNESS

- OVERALL HEALTH: GOOD
- SEXUAL HEALTH: GOOD
- CONTRACEPTION: Y *DOCUMENTATION OUTSTANDING*
- ESTIMATED CUMULATIVE SEXUAL PARTNERS: 100+

OUR FAMILY PARTNERS OF INTEREST:

- PARKER JAMES DOUGLAS - BRANCH 29 - RECRUITMENT SUPERVISOR
- GUZEER ADIM PARVEZ - BRANCH 15 - TEST ADMINISTRATOR
- NINA SARAH EVERSTON - BRANCH 15 - TEST ADMINISTRATOR

MEMBERSHIP INFORMATION

- MEMBERSHIP ACTIVATION: JUNE 17, 2023
- MEMBERSHIP EXPIRY: JUNE 17, 2024
- MEMBERSHIP STANDING: **POOR**
- CONSEQUENCES RECEIVED: NONE
- CONSEQUENCES OUTSTANDING: NONE

IDENTIFYING DOCUMENTS:

- DRIVER'S LICENSE = UPLOAD COMPLETE
- PASSPORT = UPLOAD COMPLETE
- SOCIAL SECURITY = UPLOAD COMPLETE
- IDENTITY VERIFIED: Y

BANKING INFORMATION:

- BANKING INSTITUTION: BANK OF AMERICA
- ACCOUNT NO.: 289943232306
- CREDIT: GOOD
- BALANCE: $3823.48

MEMBERSHIP DUES - 2023: **OUTSTANDING**

APP ACCESS:

- DEVICE: IPHONE 11
- FACE-ID: Y

My mouth gapes open as my stomach hits the perfectly polished floor. Goosebumps crawl along my skin from head to toe, and the blood drains completely from my face. How the fuck is all of my information in here? Shock radiates through me, my skin bubbling with heat.

I feel... violated.

Why is it turning me on?

Everything about me is in here. Disturbingly so.

"On behalf of Our Family, I ask that you verify your information so that we may process your outstanding dues, rectify your membership standing, and officially welcome you as one of Our own!" Desi's voice throbs in my ear drums.

"I..." My voice is missing, gone somewhere in the depths of my sanity.

"Everything is in order, Iris. It was the same for me. For all of us. Once you sign to verify everything, you're in," Parker assures me.

I gulp, clamping my mouth shut. I run it through my brain, my eyes focused on the words. It makes sense that they would need access to this information... for the safety of everyone involved. I am who I say I am, and everyone else here has had their same information divulged.

It makes sense.

I pull my stomach up off the floor and swipe my finger across the flawless surface of the screen.

It's official.

"Wonderful! It's my pleasure to proudly Confirm you, Iris Gladwell, as an official Member of Our Family, Branch 29!" Desi announces. "Congratulations on your Confirmation!" Applause breaks out, with several whoops and cat calls, coming predictably from Wyatt.

"Thank you, thank you so much," I say, my voice back now, and to my surprise, light and joyful.

"We are so pleased that we have found you! Welcome to Our Family!" Desi repeats. I have heard those same words, over and over, all night long, and have never grown tired of them. "Please join me in one final toast to Our new, Confirmed Member!" Thom scrambles about to deliver a fresh flute of champagne to everyone without a glass. "To Our Family, and to Iris!" Desi cheers.

"To Our Family, and to Iris!" the crowd repeats, raising their glasses and downing their champagne.

I smile, glowing, and chug back the tart, bubbly liquid.

Thirty-Two

A whirlwind. Things have been a complete whirlwind.

Between briefly meeting the Members of Branch 29, learning the rules of Our Family, and settling into the unconventional relationship dynamic between me and Parker, my brain has been inundated with information - and my body with anticipation.

But I am truthfully enjoying every overwhelming moment of it.

There's an inexplicable intimacy in knowing this side of Parker. The part of him hidden from the world around us. It doesn't take long for me to process the strange, unwelcome, and surprising feeling of deception that first overcame me when Parker revealed his truth. *We didn't meet by chance, Iris. It was all planned.* Somehow, it's made the thrill of joining Our Family even more palpable. I was wanted - hunted, even - to be a part of this organization. For this, I am deeply grateful.

Likewise, Parker himself is grateful. He's an open book, sharing with me his experiences and expertise. While I am not only willing, but honored, to join Our Family, many others, Parker reveals, have not felt the same. He tells me stories of recruitments gone wrong, of potential Members expressing utter disgust, of long-term Members terminating their membership. With each tale of rejection, my commitment roots deeper. To those who found Our Family to be abhorrent, I find it unquestionably desirable.

I can't wait to show my commitment.

Parker and I go over the finer details of my membership. Discretion, as Marc reminded me of profusely at my Confirmation, is one of the most serious aspects of membership in Our Family. Fuck that up, and it's big trouble. Exclusivity is another, and I'm heartbroken wrestling with the hard truth surrounding Simone. I realize I won't be able to follow through on much of anything with her besides a very platonic, friend-zone lunch. My interactions with Vienna, too, will leave a lot to be desired. It leaves a sour taste in my mouth.

One of the hardest parts about relationships for me is the feeling of being trapped. Caged. Forced into monotony. And while Our Family requires that commitment to exclusivity, there is a vast pool of Members for me to interact with. Still, I'll miss Simone and Vienna. But I trust that what Our Family offers will be more than sufficient to fulfill my unique needs and desires.

Parker and I fall back into our partnership effortlessly. For the first week after learning about Our Family, we are in a daze, so in love and infatuated with the promise of our future. There's no further communication from Desi or Mallory, or anyone from Our Family for that matter. It almost feels like a dream, a lofty fantasy I created only in my mind.

Mom and Willard are happily settling in in their new home in Hawaii, and, as horribly guilty as I feel to admit this, it's a huge weight lifted. I no longer have to commit to seeing her every week and subsequently enduring her endless commentary on how I should live my life. We Facetime, although it's only for a sliver of time out of my week.

My mom calls me early on Monday, and we have a brief chat mostly about her and how she's been so very busy getting the new home all sorted out and decorated and oh there are just so many rooms to consider and also it's so close to the beach, it really needs that tropical *feel* but there's also Zach and Molly and their brood to consider and making sure it's safe and accessible for the grandkids, and should they put in bunk beds? and so on. She's psychotically happy. I admit that I'm happy for her. Willard too, I suppose. But the shameful truth is that I am most happy for myself.

Things are going incredibly well between Ben and Kai. We meet up for dinner on Wednesday at Giuseppe's, the three of us. Kai wears olive green slacks and a sharp white button-down. His shiny, thick mane of dark hair is combed back, and hiding behind tortoise-shell round glasses, he has some of the most stunning green eyes I've ever seen. He is devastatingly handsome. As I get to know him, I learn he is level-headed and honest, with just a sprinkling of goofiness. Kai is, without a doubt, a ten-out-of-ten. The two of them together are a unique match; the exact balance of same and different. After indulging in a bottle of Giuseppe's finest, I conclude that Kai is it for Ben. His missing piece.

Work is slowing down. Finally. In addition to Robbie, we hire a new seasoned tech named Michael, who has a strong work ethic and excellent interpersonal skills. He is wonderful with the patients and exceptionally charming. He has an air about him that's fresh and cheerful, with a generally optimistic temperament. Michael is everything we needed after weeks and weeks of feeling burnt out.

Everything is falling into place just right.

Which makes me worried. Incredibly worried.

When things are as good as they are, I can't help but fear that it's just a matter of time before something goes wrong.

Very wrong.

Thirty-Three

"**Y**ou're too busy," I grumble, seething with whine. I know I sound like a broken record. It's the biggest complaint I have in our relationship. Parker is too busy. His schedule is full to the brim. Our time together is very meticulously scheduled for Tuesday nights, Friday nights, and Saturday nights only. I get a bit of Sunday with him, too, and then the cycle repeats. Occasionally he's out of town for business trips, too. Parker is notoriously overcommitted.

"I have a lot of responsibilities, Iris."

"I have a lot of needs, Parker."

"Insatiable." He flicks his thumb against the bottom of my lip.

It's a Tuesday. It's always a fucking Tuesday. We're back at Pearl Wines and Eatery, and the nostalgia of this place is getting the best of me. We had our first date here, and now we are here, again, for our first date of a different kind - as Members of Our Family. Frequented by many others in Our Family, Pearl is a staple in *the community*. My eyes dart around, curiously making guesses as to who of the many patrons filling the restaurant are Members, and who are merely ordinary humans on ordinary dates. A great, sensual game of Guess Who.

"That's the beauty of it," Parker whispers in my ear. I gaze at him quizzically. "Let's talk about this tonight."

The wait of another cryptic puzzle tortures me. If I didn't like it so much, I would elbow Parker in the gut.

I nurse a glass of white wine and munch on a caprese skewer. A ripe tomato bursts in my mouth. The juices spill down my throat, causing me to cough, and Parker digs into me, teasing how I surely have had some experience with liquids shooting down my throat.

Humiliation. Gets me every time.

We can't get out of here fast enough.

We pile into Parker's truck, and I straddle him in the backseat. I whip off my pants and unbuckle his jeans with dexterity worthy of a Guinness World Record. I mount him, his length sliding easily into my sopping folds. I immediately moan. I'll never tire of the incredible feeling of Parker as he fills me. I rock my body. Sliding against him, Parker's cock glides inside my opening. The angle is perfect, with his length tapping right into my G-spot. It takes no time at all for me to come, and I crumble onto him as the wave of my release stretches into a minute, at least. Parker rips my blouse off and cups my breasts in his hands, massaging them as I recover.

"Fuck," is all I can muster.

I lean forward, pushing my clit against his body, and thrust my hips again. Parker grasps my neck and wraps his fingers around it. He squeezes and I hold my breath. I shake and quiver against him, my orgasm hitting me like a wall once more.

"Don't stop. Don't you fucking stop," he wails breathlessly into my neck.

I push through the overstimulation and rock onto him still. My body aches, the intensity of my climaxes straining the muscles inside me. Parker slaps my ass, again and again, and I writhe in sweet agony. At last he comes, breathing heavily under our spell.

I still don't know if the truck's windows are tinted.

• • • •

BACK AT MY APARTMENT, I pour two glasses of ice water, and we chug them down. I perch on the corner of the couch, and Parker slides in beside me.

"Have you looked at Our Leaflet yet?" Parker asks, fidgeting with his phone in his fingers.

"Our Leaflet?"

"The directory of all the Members in Our Family. It'll be your new best friend," he laughs. "You should be able to access it in the app."

How the fuck have I not been obsessively scouring this thing?

"Uh," I reach into my back pocket and procure my phone. My throat feels dry. I open the app and search through the many tabs. "Where is it? I don't see it here."

"Should be under Communications. Beside the inbox tab."

Despite my desperate scrolling and tapping, Our Leaflet is nowhere to be found. "Ugh!" I grumble. "I don't see it. I just have my messages from Mallory and Desi in here."

"Oh, that's right. You probably don't have access to it yet." I can't help but feel like Parker baited me on purpose, only to provoke my excitement and subsequent embarrassment in the disappointment of having my prize withheld. I sigh. "But it should be available to you after your first Mixer."

"And it's a list of everyone in Our Family?" I squeak.

"For the most part. The reason I bring it up is because... I know you hate me for being so busy. It's a great way to connect with other Members in the lifestyle, outside of formal events. You can edit your own profile in there, too. Add your availability, that sort of thing."

"Availability, huh?" My eyes grow wide.

"Then you can search and filter based on that. Boom. Someone to help you out on a lonely Thursday night while I'm otherwise engaged."

"So, it's basically a fuck book?" I blurt.

"In so many words."

My insides clench. Holy shit. Holy fucking shit. I will literally have access to a list of people willing to hook up any day of the week.

Pinch me.

"You can also filter based on sexual preference," Parker adds. "Helpful for when, you know, you feel like eating pussy."

I let out an awkward gasp laugh. This has to be a dream. Not only is the love of my life telling me I can have sex with other people, but he's giving me the resources to do so.

And they say romance is dead.

"Mixers are generally held at the end of the month. So, we've got a while before your first one. Whatever are you going to do while you wait?" he teases. I gulp. "I spoke to Marc. He and Desi have agreed to mix with us this weekend, if you're up for it."

"I am very up for it," I belt out. Probably too quickly and too enthusiastically.

"I thought you would be." Parker chuckles at my keenness. "They've agreed to host us this Friday night. It'll be a good opportunity for you to explore the Estate a little more, too. Get comfortable with the setting. Marc is very experienced. He'll take good care of you."

I think I'm going to combust.

Thirty-Four

P arker has been a Member of Branch 29 for just over a year. During that time, he has gained a thorough understanding of everyone's unique tastes and preferences, and, to my benefit, has intently passed that knowledge onto me. I like to think it gives me an edge, otherwise I'd very much be going into this whole thing completely blind.

Desi, Parker tells me, is very into BDSM. She's a switch, who primarily likes to be dominated, but occasionally takes the reins and enjoys dominating her partner. She likes spanking, restraints, and leather toys. Parker and Desi typically engage in rough play, he tells me, and, much like me, Desi has a kink for humiliation.

Parker informs me that with Marc, I will be playing with myself a lot. Fingers, dildos, vibrators, butt plugs - any and every toy I can wield with my own hands will please Marc. Marc's kink for voyeurism is key, and, if I really want to impress him, I should handcuff him while I touch myself. The sweet torture of being unable to touch his cock while I fuck myself with my various implements will surely be his undoing.

Eager to please, I heed Parker's advice.

I hope he's not leading me astray.

• • • •

IN THE DAYS LEADING up to our private exchange with Desi and Marc, I take initiative and re-read the entire Rulebook. I make note of the outstanding items requiring my attention, and I put in a call to my gynecologist for a copy of the results from my latest STI panel, which was only a few months ago. Right before I met Parker, actually. I also make a trip to the CVS for copies of my birth control prescription, and upload the pertinent documentation in the app. With the paperwork out of the way, I rest easy, assured that it's smooth sailing from here.

• • • •

ON FRIDAY NIGHT, I'M a ball of nerves, anxious to impress the Head of Our Branch and her loyal husband. Parker assures me that private exchanges are much less formal than Branch Mixers, and more so resemble a casual dinner date. On our way over to the Harold Estate, we stop at a small, locally-owned Chinese restaurant to pick up some eats. The smell of orange chicken and chow mein invades the air and makes my stomach grumble. It's a gamble picking up from somewhere we haven't tried before. I hope with all of me that the food isn't a bust; I'm desperate to make a good impression.

I know almost nothing about Marc, other than what Parker has planted in my brain. Desi and I, on the other hand, get along fairly well, and talked quite a lot at my Confirmation. But Marc is solemn, mysterious, and much less outgoing (and therefore seems less friendly) than Desi. Simply put, Marc intimidates me. He challenges me. I want to please him. Parker assures me that Marc is just like us, depraved and sexual. My insides clench in the truth of it.

As we approach the Harold Estate, the grandeur of the property wows me all over again. In my black jeans and loose, sheer blouse, I feel insultingly underdressed.

Informal my ass.

As per Parker's guidance, I kept my underthings casual, too, with a simple black bandeau bra and black boy shorts layered under my clothing. My heart starts jumping in my chest as I sit, frozen, feeling like a fool for not choosing something fancier. Dressier. Parker, although casual, looks smart in a pair of dark jeans and a green and blue plaid button-down. He laces his fingers in mine. His touch distracts me from my worry.

Desi answers the door in a beautiful dress with a deep v neckline. It's casual enough, with vertical white and olive-green stripes. It flatters her figure beautifully. Her hair is tied half-up, with her signature shiny brown ringlets bouncing on her shoulders. There is something so bright and cheerful about Desi; she lights up every room she's in. She takes my breath away.

She waves us in, welcoming us with a quick peck on each of our cheeks. The sensation of her kiss stays on my skin and I blush. We travel down the hall and to the left, where we enter an oversized living area. The atmosphere is mysterious with hushed ambient music and dim lighting. Marc is standing at a wet bar, dressed in casual slacks and a golf shirt that matches the olive of Desi's dress. These two are always adorably matching. He pours himself and Parker a scotch, then offers me and Desi a glass of wine. I keenly accept.

Desi and Marc have an air of elegance about them, and Parker cautions me that they are always the best-dressed in the room. (I suppose it comes with being filthy rich.) Parker dumps the bags containing our Chinese feast on the bartop, where it gets cold as we get lost in conversation.

We start chatting as a foursome, but soon Marc invites me to take a seat beside him on their velvet couch. I comply, my nerves still churning in my center. We talk casually, and he asks me how I'm feeling about joining Our Family. I immediately turn red, my skin sticky with warmth, as I answer with such enthusiastic joy that I'm sure I sound fantastical and insane. I must've said something right, though, because Marc's shell starts to melt away and he moves closer to me, tucking an unruly strand of hair behind my ear. His thumb lingers on my chin. I part my mouth just so and whimper.

"You're a good girl, Iris."

"I try to be," I say, leaning into it. "I am so grateful to Our Family. And to you," I add.

He likes that.

Marc leans forward and kisses me, our lips just barely grazing. It's fleeting, almost like a ghost of a kiss that I'm not sure ever really happened. My heart races and my nipples tingle. I glance down in Marc's lap and see the happy outline of his cock, growing hard, like my nipples, beneath the fabric of his pants. I try to hide my grin, my cheeks aching in effort.

"What do you say we dig into this delicious feast you've brought for us?" Marc announces into the room.

I look over to Parker, who has Desi trapped against the wall. It gives me an immediate rush. Between my legs.

To the relief of both my nerves and my stomach, the food is delicious, even at room temperature. As we nibble on fried rice and Beijing beef, the air heats up with sexual promise. Parker is right - the sounds of satisfaction that fill the air during a good meal are very arousing indeed.

The conversation flows like we are the oldest of friends. Parker leads with his mad charm. He kisses my nose and runs his fingertips along the back of my jeans, and somehow it feels taboo.

Marc is mostly quiet, his voyeuristic tendencies blatantly obvious. It's overwhelming to feel both his and Parker's eyes on me while I chew my food. Overwhelming, but also very welcome.

It's fun to watch Parker flirt with Desi, her perfect teeth white and bright as Parker cracks stupid jokes. He rubs her arm and goosebumps prickle across her skin. Their chemistry is undeniable. I'm captivated by their connection, and watch intently as Desi nibbles on Parker's ear. His hands on her, her mouth on him - it's a thrill unlike any other.

Maybe there is some validity to voyeurism.

After dinner, my momentary calm evades me and my anxiety spikes. Parker gives me a long, lingering kiss, then turns to Desi. It's time to go our separate ways. They disappear upstairs to one of the countless guest rooms on the second floor. I imagine Parker leaning Desi over a spanking bench and wailing on her perfect skin with a *SLUT* paddle. As her cheeks speckle with red, so do mine.

Marc escorts me in the opposite direction, through the various hallways of the mansion over to the ballroom where my Confirmation was held. We exit through a side door and I follow him, my arm draped over his, down a path lit overhead by vintage lamplights. The air outside is refreshing and calm. I sniff it in. A combination of fresh flowers and summer heat invades my nostrils. A gentle breeze wisps through my hair and tickles my nose. Finally, we arrive at a line of guesthouses. That's what Marc calls them, anyway. They look to me like a series of row homes, all identically sizable, that have been sliced and given space to breathe between them. There are at least ten, all in a neat line, all replicas in their external appearance. We stop at a sign reading, *Guesthouse #4*.

"This will be your home while you're here," Marc explains, leading me to the front door. From inside his pant pocket, he pulls out a golden key engraved with the familiar tree silhouette on one side, and the #4 in bold on the other. "Your interactions during the Mixers will be held in this guesthouse. Go on in. Take a look around."

I step across the threshold and into another world. Decorated in black, red, and hues of purple, the guesthouse reeks of sensuality. The seductive atmosphere sucks us in, with dim lighting and dark, explicit artwork adorning the walls. Molly would most definitely not approve. There's a large L-shaped couch just inside the door and, beside it, a generous kitchen with black cabinetry. The distinct smell of peppermint and pine is coming from a candle that stands beside the sink. The flame flickers, diffusing the intoxicating scent into the air.

Marc is behind me now, his hands on my hips, his lips against my shoulder. He watches as I take it all in. My new home.

I sink into him, my body relaxing as I find comfort in his touch. Against the small of my back, I feel the firmness of his cock and hum in satisfaction. I turn to kiss him. Our lips join for the second time. I linger, wanting more, but Marc keeps it agonizingly brief.

"Let me show you upstairs."

Marc's breath is shallow. I know the wait is killing him, too. But, fuck, does he have good self-control.

Marc guides the way around the corner and up the stairs. A loft-like, open room awaits us. The walls are decorated with a large wardrobe on one side and several shelving units on the other. It's exciting - my eyes exploring another unknown. A four-poster bed draped with black and crimson linens sits in the center of the room. Behind the bed is a large, floor-to-ceiling window.

Marc watches me expectantly.

I first approach the wardrobe and peer inside. It's filled with countless exquisite, themed costumes. My fingers explore the various textures and fabrics. There are the usual suspects: frilly French maid, sexy cop, hot nurse, and naughty schoolgirl. But, to my delight, there's also an abundance of more niche wear: garments carved out of leather, vinyl, and latex; studded straps and buckles; D-rings and cuffs. I work too hard to keep my jaw from falling open. Marc's eyes follow my every move.

At the shelving units now, I pull out the bins contained within them. Each bin is full to the brim with its own assortment of treasures, ranging from every vibrator and massager you could dream of to anal toys of all kinks. There are floggers, whips, and crops; handcuffs, rope, and belts; ball gags, nipple clamps, and cock rings; collars, leashes, and masks. Implements galore. On the top of the shelving unit, displayed on a plush, black towel, is a healthy assortment of various sexual lubricants.

I soak in the possibilities: things I've done, things I haven't, and things I've always been curious about.

"There's more over here," Marc breathes. He opens a door that lies hidden by the opened curtains of the window. Plagued with curiosity, I peek inside, expecting a closet. But it's not. It's a second room, full of large fetish furniture pieces. My eyes flutter from one corner to the next. There's a Saint Andrew's cross, metal spreader bars, sex swings, a spanking bench, a bondage chair, and even a metal cage.

"Inclusive," I compliment, impressed with the collection. "But not exhaustive."

"Oh, no?"

"No."

"May I ask what's missing?" Marc's voice echoes among us. He sounds slightly offended. I like it.

"A stripper pole," I deadpan.

Marc laughs and falls onto the bed. He pats the crimson sheets to call me over, and I eagerly take my place next to him. He leans into me, whispering sweet nothings into my ear as we lay side-by-side. Talking is, I'm learning, a big part of foreplay for him. He praises me, telling me how good I am and what a wonderful partner I am to Parker. He tells me that I'm so sweet and innocent, that I do everything with my full heart. I blush at his kindness, but dismiss it, telling him thank you, but really, I'm still finding my way and just doing my best. Marc plays on this, challenging me to do my best with him.

His eyes seep into mine, and I'm certain I'm going to burst into flames under the heat between us.

I push into him, softly at first, kissing him and gently biting his bottom lip. He skims his fingertips up and down my arms, then down to my hips and along my bottom. His touch is fire, sending waves of want through my core. I hum. Our kiss deepens, and at last Marc is giving me more. More tongue, more movement, more intensity. I shift my body and reach for his waist. I play with my fingertips along the skin of his stomach and back and feel the warmth of his flesh tingle through them. I pull at his shirt, wiggling it up to remove it, and he stares at me, our lips broken, his eyes piercing into mine. The spotlight is on me. I bite my lip and sneak a glance down at Marc's pants then back up again. I focus on the green specks in his pupils as I remove my shirt. I unbutton each clasp slowly, ever so meticulously, while maintaining eye contact. I shrug the blouse off of my shoulders, exposing my black bandeau.

"You are so beautiful, Iris," Marc whispers.

"Thank you," I breathe. "I hope I please you."

"Good girl," he replies.

I sweep my body off the bed and remove my jeans. I wander over to the bins and sift through them. I gather up a few items and innocently ask Marc which of them are the toys that the good girls use. He smiles widely, his erection profoundly visible beneath his slacks.

"The purple one."

I select the medium-sized, bright purple vibrator with a bumpy shaft, and return the others to their bin. I also sneak a pair of handcuffs, but covertly slip them under the pillow undetected. I climb back onto the bed. Marc is on his side, resting his head on his hand. I sit up tall, turn my head to the side, and run the vibrator around the corners of my mouth.

"Do good girls do this?" I ask, my tongue playing at the tip of the toy. Marc chuckles and nods. He shifts uncomfortably, the confines of his pants no doubt paining him.

I move the shaft into my mouth while maintaining eye contact. I push it into my throat and force myself to gag. He loves it. He moves his hand down to his waist, unbuttons his pants, and shimmies them off. To my delight, his boxers depart with them. It takes everything in me not to look down at his naked cock. I want it. I want to see it, to grab it, to thrust it in my mouth. But I don't. I don't look, I don't indulge my primitive impulses. With my eyes still searing into Marc's, I move the vibrator down to my chest. I lower my bandeau and my breasts bounce free, exposing my soft nipples. I run the toy along them, hardening them with little effort. I moan in pleasure, close my eyes, and throw my head back.

"Very good," Marc breathes. He has acquired a bottle of lube from the shelf and squirts it onto his hand. The slick sounds of his hand pumping along his shaft fill my ears.

I have to look.

Here he is: exposed to me at last. I look in his eyes, then below his waist, then back in his eyes, and he smiles in the corner of his mouth. I drop the toy and pull the bandeau over my head. Raising myself to my knees, I slip off my underwear and hover, fully naked, for Marc to admire.

"Fuck, you're so beautiful. Fuck, Iris," he moans as he moves his cock in his hands.

"No, no," I chastise, pulling Marc's hands up. I lean into him and kiss him gently, as is our norm. With his hands now above his head, I reach for the handcuffs. I quickly lock one wrist in, but I'm not fast enough to do the other.

"What are you doing?" Marc barks. The air shifts. All the enjoyment of the scene drains from his voice.

"I- I- I was going to handcuff you," I explain. A wave of shame overcomes me and my throat tightens. "I wanted you to watch me without being able to touch yourself," I offer further. My heart falls into my toes and my face turns red. I wish I would drop dead right this instant.

"Oh, you silly girl," Marc speaks, shaking his head. "So naive as to think that you can control me like that." His tone shifts from soft to harsh. "Handcuff me? No. You have a lot to learn. Such a shame, our first interaction together and you make a fool of yourself like this. Tsk tsk tsk," Marc tuts. I shrink and pull away from him. A pool of wetness gathers between my thighs. I want to die. I also want Marc to fuck me as hard as he can.

Marc grabs my arm and pulls me toward him. "Remove this now," he demands.

"Marc, I-" I choke. I feel the heat of tears threatening behind my eyes. I swallow and sniff them back. I do as instructed, undoing the handcuff that I had thrown onto his left hand.

The glorious torture of my shame and its undeniable arousal swirls in the pit of my stomach.

"I thought you were a good girl. Well, what should I do with you now?"

"Please," I beg, leaning into the scene, "I want to please you. That's all I want." My desperation infects the air.

Marc runs his hand along my jaw and gently pushes his thumb into my chin, just as he had done earlier before dinner. It sends my heart into a frenzy, making my chest thud so hard I'm sure my skin is hopping.

I part my lips. "Please," I whisper, "let me please you."

Marc gruelingly studies me. Time stretches as he calculates his next move. The wait forces the wetness at my core to surge.

At last, he leans forward and kisses me, the softness in him returning. "I admire your commitment," he praises, kissing me deeper this time. I hum and open my mouth wider, inviting his tongue in. He pushes it into mine, finally, and together our tongues mingle. Our kiss becomes messier and deeper.

Suddenly, Marc throws me onto my back. He straddles me, his cock just inches from my mouth. I smile and ready myself to devour it. But, instead, he grabs my hands and throws them into the handcuffs. He thrusts my wrists overhead and wraps them beneath a pillow. I suck in a gulp of air. I like being restrained; it's thrilling to let go of that control.

Marc is unpredictable. He first goes down on me. His tongue moves expertly around my clit as he consumes me at my most vulnerable center. His mouth is unrelenting in its focus. Meanwhile, he manages to maneuver the purple vibrator rhythmically in and out of me. I writhe under him, the indulgence getting the best of me. He laps up the wetness blanketing my folds and sucks on my lower lips. I moan in deep pleasure as my entire body squirms. He positions his free hand up to my mouth and I lick at his fingers, gently biting on them to muffle my yelps of enjoyment. I come once, then again, and again, greedy in my gratification.

Marc rolls me onto my stomach and pulls me to my knees. He teases his cock at my opening, wetting it in my slippery juices. He slides it back and forth over and over, and that alone makes me feel like I'm going to come again.

Then, he thrusts inside of me. Bracing himself on my hips, he moves in deeper. His firm cock slams against my inner walls. I shiver, my body weak after the countless waves of pleasure that have passed over me already. Marc rocks his hips slowly, moving with such precision, it's as though he's trying to feel every inch of me. It's intoxicating, and I can't keep quiet. He quickens his pace, the tip of his cock hitting me in just the right place. I wail.

"Now that's a good girl, Iris," he praises breathlessly.

"Yes," I pant. "Fuck, yes."

Marc pulls himself fully out of me and a whine in the dreadful sensation of emptiness.

"I'm going to fuck your ass now," he tells me. "You'll like that, won't you?"

"Yes, please," I beg. Because I will like that, very much.

Marc slathers my hole with lube. The anticipation of his length filling my ass just about puts me over the edge. He pounds inside of my pussy once more, wetting his cock with my abundant juices. Then, he pushes my knees apart to lower my ass just slightly, and spreads my cheeks apart. He gently nudges his hips forward into me. I feel every inch of him as he slides into my ass, and I moan in ecstasy. Goosebumps prickle on the surface of my skin. I shudder and gulp as he painstakingly moves his entire length to fill my hole.

Anal is my absolute favorite.

"Fuck, oh fuck," Marc utters in pleasure.

His hips rock back and forth, gaining speed, and I feel the mound of his sack smack my slit with each thrust. We breathe together, our sounds primitive and hedonistic. I yelp into the darkness as a wave of gratification hits me, and I come harder than I have this entire evening. My body shudders and shakes, spewing liquid from deep inside me.

"Oh, fuck!" Marc screams.

My insides clench as I squirt, and it sends Marc to the edge and beyond. He groans as he leans deeply into me, howling in pleasure. At last, his own delectable climax finds him.

"Wow," he breathes into my ear. "Now that's a good girl."

"That was incredible. Thank you," I pant.

"Thank you, Iris."

Marc pulls himself out of me and releases my wrists from the handcuffs. I'm relaxed, my body floppy, still relishing in my sweet release. And his. I lay on the bed, feeling the evidence of my first encounter with Marc pool out of me and onto the sheets below.

Marc lays with me for some time. We join hands as if to hold onto the euphoria of our shared intimacy. We start to drift, our eyelids feeling heavy from both the alcohol and the post-sex contentedness. I roll into him, kiss his chest, and trail pecks up past his speckled beard and onto his lips. He makes little, sweet hums, and I feel proud of them. We kiss, but before it transforms into something more passionate, Marc pulls away and departs to the bathroom downstairs for a quick shower. I'm tempted to join him, but decide against it.

I rifle through the wardrobe and find a cozy, plush housecoat the same color as the bedsheets. I shrug it on, the softness of the fabric an immediate comfort to my flushed skin. I strip the bed, find a supply of clean sheets in a bin beneath it, and layer on the silky soft crimson sheets.

I settle onto the couch downstairs and flip through one of the magazines decorating the coffee table. There's a pile of them, from lingerie catalogs to fetish features. I drink in the graphic nudity, and daydream of Parker and his time with Desi. I picture her in one of the many latex costumes featured in the magazine, and Parker with a crop in his hand.

Marc appears some time later, smelling delightfully clean. It makes me want to get him dirty all over again. He sits beside me and runs his fingertips along my thigh. We kiss again, but he pulls away. This infuriating game of cat and mouse.

Thirty-Five

The morning arrives early. Marc and I are up before five, despite our exhausted bodies. Marc is endlessly interesting, and I spend the first hour of my waking minutes listening to his voice. He tells me about his recruitment and subsequent test, how he met Desi, and his experience in Our Family. I'm surprised to learn that Marc and Desi didn't get married until a year ago. Not a traditionalist in any sense, it took a lot of convincing for Desi to come around to the idea. Marc confirms that he is indeed bisexual, and I feel validated in sharing the same truth about myself. Our Family, he tells me, is the perfect place to fulfill our unique needs and desires, especially as a queer person. He brings up Our Leaflet and encourages my use of it. I eagerly await access.

Having showered after Marc the night before, I spend just a few minutes freshening up in the bathroom. I choose a fresh pair of panties and layer my jeans back on, then pull on the classic white tee over the nude bra that I had packed in my tote and brought with me. I return the housecoat to the closet, and run my fingers along the edges of the clothing housed inside the wardrobes once more. It's eerie, I think as I finger a leather corset, that everything in here fits me. I struggle to fathom the expense of all the costumes and fetish wear... it's dizzying to consider the bill. I make a mental note to ask Parker about it. There's no way my meager $1,500 in membership dues even begins to cover it. And I doubt Desi and Marc spend their own personal fortune to supply me (and, I assume, the other Members) with a full wardrobe.

Marc escorts me back to the main house. He guides me into a large room just down from the one we mingled in last night. He calls it the *breakfast room*, and explains that this is where we will always meet the morning following Our Mixers. The sun spills through the four, fan-shaped windows lining the far wall. A long, oak table stretches the length of the room, with enough space to fit at least twenty people. It's already set with a selection of foods, ranging from muffins and fruit to breakfast pastries, eggs, and sausages. Marc politely excuses himself and retreats to his room, where he intends on changing out of his linen housecoat and into fresh clothes. I spot a carafe of orange juice on the table and pour myself a glass. It tastes fresh and delicious, although a bit tart. Coffee. I want coffee. I scour the table, but see none. I wince, aware that my caffeine withdrawal headache is imminent.

I approach the window and notice an orchard of orange trees in the distance, and wonder if the juice came from those trees? As I hover there, I watch the birds on their early-morning journeys, hunting for bugs and seeds. Their sounds are loud and happy, traveling through the walls and echoing around me in the empty room.

"Good morning." It's Parker. I grin a stupid, childish grin. The sound of his voice nestles in my ears.

I spin to see him. He's probably been standing there, watching me, for minutes now. He leans against the doorway, smug and confident. The smirk painted on his face makes me want to slap him, then push him against the wall and fuck him. He waltzes over to me, my skin pink under his gaze, and brushes the back of his fingers along my cheeks and jawline. Eyes wide, I study him, tracing the outlines of his body. I close my eyes and bask in the sweetness of his touch. And there, at my core, it flutters.

"Hi."

"Have fun?" he asks. If he didn't have me under such a spell, I'd give him hell for embarrassing me by telling me Marc likes to be restrained. What a prick.

But I don't. I melt, my body turning to putty, my eyes flickering, my heart dancing. I breathe in his distinct, woodsy scent and hum. "Mm hmm." He pets my head.

"Good morning!" Desi's voice rings around us. She's positively glowing. "Hi, Iris! How was your night?" she asks, pulling me in for a hug. Her body leans into mine, and she lingers. Then she kisses both my cheeks and looks at me expectantly. My face turns pink with pleasure.

"It was... great. Really, great." I sound like an idiot. I can barely talk. Between last night with Marc and this moment with Parker, my brain is malfunctioning.

"I'm so glad. I hope Marc was good to you!"

"He was wonderful."

"Thank you for the five-star review," Marc says from the doorway.

Desi waltzes over to him and leans in for a kiss. They fall into a passionate daze, their kiss deepening and their bodies interlocking. They fit together like those two perfect pieces.

Parker pulls my gaze from them and lifts my chin to meet his eyes. He gives me a light peck. I push into him, but he pulls away. It's a familiar dance, not unlike the once I experienced with Marc the night before. I'm already weary of it.

Desi surfaces for air and takes a deep breath. She walks over to me and invites me to take a seat at the table. She settles in the chair next to mine, and we chat, smiling and giggling like teenagers. Desi is so easygoing and sweet, it's impossible to feel uncomfortable around her. While you might expect sitting beside the woman whose husband you just fucked to be wildly awkward, she makes it easy. Fun, even. She asks about what Marc and I got up to, and I immediately open up. I share our night, retelling my episode of embarrassment, the anal grand finale, and everything in between.

"Thank God for Our Family, I swear. I do not enjoy anal!" she laughs. "I am so grateful to leave that up to you and the others!"

I chuckle, amused, but also surprised. I'm shocked that, of all people in Our Family, the Head of Our Branch doesn't enjoy anal. I have a hard time understanding how anyone wouldn't enjoy it, though. I suppose it is something that is acquired. I'm glad I was brave enough to explore it when I was young and experimental.

I think back. I was 21 when I met the man who introduced me to the wonderful world of anal play. Cole. Cole and I had the potential to be great. We met at the bookstore in true fairytale fashion, and I wondered if he was going to be it for me.

He wasn't. But he was good, very good, for the hyper-active sex drive of my early twenties. We fucked endlessly, everywhere, and all the time. We couldn't get enough of each other. Cole first brought up the idea of trying anal when he was balls-deep inside me, and I couldn't reply because I was wearing a ball gag. I grunted and drooled while he fingered my back hole. I felt so helpless, so paralyzed, so incredibly turned on. He mentioned it again afterward, and, with me curled in his arms, together we hunted the forbidden pages of the internet for my first anal toys.

The kit arrived a few days later and came with five different sizes of butt plugs. We started with the smallest one and increased the size over many weeks. When I got home from work, Cole ordered me to insert one. It became my routine - the thing I most looked forward to in the day. I slathered the plug in lube and bent over my bathroom sink, playing out a scene in my head. I'd imagine Cole there, humiliating me and calling me a *prude* as he eased the plug into my hole. We eventually worked up to the largest plug in the set, and Cole was pleased with my commitment. He would fuck me while I wore the plug, and the sensation of being so full felt euphorically disgraceful. Cole would call me names as he pounded into me, the fullness of my front and back sending me over the edge and into the abyss. I loved every second of it. Eventually, Cole decided I was ready. He pushed my face down into the pillow as I arched my back with my knees under me. He slathered his length in anal lube and eased into me. His cock pushed into my hole, opening me up and filling me in a way that felt unthinkable and deplorable. He invaded me, sliding into my ass over and over again. It was nothing like the butt plugs, which would stay in place. Cole's movement added another dimension of pleasure. It launched me into ecstasy. He bucked his hips and spread my ass cheeks apart with the firm grip of his hands. I felt ashamed for finding such pleasure in it, which only doubled my enjoyment. I wailed, my eyes filling with tears. The twisted gratification of anal was my undoing. I begged him, *please, please, fuck me harder*. It flowed out of me like an instinct, something feral and raw. My first time having anal sex with Cole was unlike any sexual experience I had ever had before.

It changed me.

Sometime during my reverie, Marc procures a large pitcher of coffee and has supplied me with a generous mug of it. It tastes incredible. The caffeine immediately works its way into my veins. The steam hits my nostrils, the glorious perfume restoring my consciousness.

Back to the unbelievable reality of my present.

Thirty-Six

T he glow radiating off my body as we leave Desi and Marc's is sublime. I look at Parker – the contentment in his smile, the warmth on his skin, the relief in his body. He's satiated.

For now.

We thank our gracious hosts for a wonderful night, and Parker drives us back to the city.

"So, what did you think?" he asks. He runs his fingers along my thigh as he maneuvers off the gravel and back onto the main road.

"It was so different than I expected."

"Different?"

"Yes. I mean, I didn't expect to have my own fucking house with a stocked closet and toy room!" I exclaim. Parker meets me with a hearty laugh. "It seems excessive. I mean, where does the money come from? I hate to ask, but Desi and Marc aren't shelling it out themselves, are they?"

"Oh, God, no," Parker chuckles. "Our Family pays for everything. Your annual dues help cover some of the expense, of course."

"And where does that money come from?" I hope it's not drug money. Or gang money. Or any other ethically questionable money for that matter.

"Our Family is a very well-established organization. There's a lot of wealth there. From various sources." It's not really an answer. I let it go.

"Do you have a wardrobe like that? I didn't see anything for Marc in the guesthouse."

"All the women are assigned a guesthouse, where their items are stored for the duration of their membership. The men do have a modest collection, which is housed in trunks of our own. Each evening after partners are selected, the staff delivers the trunks to their appropriate guesthouses. Marc probably didn't have anything in your guesthouse because, well, it's his property."

But it's not the Harold's property at all. Parker reveals to me that it belongs, in fact, to Our Family. As Head of Branch 29, Desi and Marc inhabit the Estate and manage the Branch and its events from there.

This information makes me doubt the financial legitimacy of Our Family even more. But a big part of me wants to forget it, lock those doubts away in the back of my brain, and indulge in all Our Family has to offer regardless. Because I like to indulge. Endlessly.

We arrive back at my apartment, and Parker jokes that all this talk about finances is turning him on. I tease him, whispering words like assets, capital gains, and equity into the crook of his neck. He tosses me back onto the couch, spreads my legs, and nestles his body in between them. He lays his head on my chest and quiets. The room shifts, the heat between us replaced by a soothing warmth. I wrap my arms around him and pet the back of his head. My fingers knead into his scalp. His hair is soft and messy and smells of his typical woodsy aroma. In deep breaths, I take him in, his head rising and falling on my chest, the weight of him on me, the comfort of his body against mine as we share the silence. I could spend every weekend of the rest of my life like this. Me and Parker together, our shared breath, our bodies blended, our hearts one.

This is what love looks like.

Thirty-Seven

Mixing with Desi and Marc does take the edge off. I feel better prepared for what to expect at the Branch Mixer, but it does nothing to satiate my sexual cravings. Unfortunately, I still lack access to Our Leaflet, which makes the next two weeks agonizingly long. I fill the time with Monday book club (which is still very painful with Gemma running it, but I force myself to go anyway because books are life), with babysitting Sir Snowball (for a couple of days while Vienna is traveling for another conference), and with extra hours at work (which is great, actually. I become really bonded with Turkey, an elderly Newfoundland pooch with the sweetest personality).

My vibrators help me out a lot, too.

Getting over that mid-week hump is always the hardest.

On Wednesday, my watch buzzes with a notification from Our Family. What timing.

I pull out my phone from the pocket of my scrubs and hover my finger over the screen. I want to open it. I feel desperate to open it. But I know I can't. Not here. Not at work. Fuck me. My eyes stare at the Our Family tree emblem. It taunts me. It's only ten-thirty in the morning, and I'll have to go about my entire day as if there isn't a message from my secret swinger's club waiting for me, testing me. I sigh heavily, my fingers tapping anxiously against the glass. I have to wait.

I have to.

I try to busy myself with paperwork and even take several of the pooches from PetCation out for walks. Twice. We make a special trip to the river, where Turkey sniffs and splashes at the water's edge. It's a brief reprieve from my debilitating anxiety. But things are slow at the clinic, we don't have many appointments, and with three of us working, there just isn't enough to keep us all occupied. Every moment I'm not doing something, I'm obsessing over that red notification icon nagging at me on my home screen. It takes everything in me not to open it. *Everything*. But I can't. I don't want to fuck up my membership when I haven't even been able to enjoy the spoils of it yet.

At long last, 5 p.m. comes. Of course, Stefanie asks for a hand administering some meds to one of our cats just as I'm about to leave, so it's not until 5:20 p.m. that I'm able to bolt out of there.

Finally. On my way home.

My pace nears a jog when Parker calls me. He laughs in my ear, making a joke about what could possibly be so urgent as to warrant my expediency. Prick. He knows exactly what.

"Call me back after you've opened it."

I huff and murmur in compliance, quickening my pace still.

Once home, I fall onto the couch with a racing heart. At last, I tap the screen and open the Our Family app. The face ID allows me access, and I immediately click on the Communications icon.

Hi Iris!

Hope you've had a good couple of weeks and have had some time to digest everything we've thrown at you! Know that we are all here to support each other, so please reach out to me or any one of us for anything. We've got you!

It's my privilege to provide you with the first communication since your membership was Confirmed. We hope you're excited!

Attached, you will find the invitations to Our next two Mixers. Please open and read in a discreet, private space. You'll also find these events posted in the Calendar for you.

Thank you, and I'm looking forward to seeing you soon!

With love,
Mallory xox

PS: Before Our event this weekend, please sign off on your Responsibilities. It's the only outstanding item on your file. Thanks so much for your promptness in this!

I'm a fucking idiot. I've had weeks now to do the paperwork, and paperwork is my specialty. I thought I completed everything already, weeks ago. I feel utterly stupid for having left my file unfinished. I quickly switch to the Responsibilities section of the app and swipe my finger to sign the empty box. There, done. So simple. A big part of me feels like I deserve a *Consequence* for being so tardy on this. I narrow my eyes.

Clicking back on the message from Mallory, I tap on the attachment. Two documents appear, both identical in appearance and different only in the dating. They are both decorated in the signature style unique to official communications from Our Family: bold, black lettering on a white background bordered with vines and golden leaves snaking around the edges.

<u>B29 Mixer Event - July</u>
Please join us for Our July Mixer,
Saturday, July 29 - Sunday, July 30
6 p.m. - 11 a.m.
At the Harold Estate
We look forward to the time with you.

Truly Yours,
Desi Harold
Our Family - Head of Branch 29

<u>B29 Mixer Event - August</u>
Please join us for Our August Mixer,
Saturday, August 26 - Sunday, August 27
6 p.m. - 11 a.m.
At the Harold Estate
We look forward to the time with you.

Truly Yours,
Desi Harold
Our Family - Head of Branch 29

This is real. The pounding in my chest migrates all the way up into my ears. My nose burns with warmth, my eyes widen, and I can't wipe the stupid smirk from my face. I'm relieved that Parker isn't by my side, for surely he would seize the opportunity to tease the fuck out of me. Wow, this is happening. This is actually happening. I take a moment to compose myself after my fingers fumbled once already trying to call Parker back.

"Hi, beautiful," he answers. His voice is smooth like wine.

"H-hhey," I reply. Apparently I'm still so worked up that I can't put my words together.

"Excited?"

"Very. I-I can't wait," I stammer.

"Your first time," Parker laughs. "So fresh and unknowing." He's taunting me.

"So ignorant." I play along, both amused and ashamed by the ironic truth of it. Because I am ignorant. I know the venue. I know the hosts, pretty intimately. Ha. But everything else is a giant question mark.

I can't fucking wait.

With my fingers tingling and my mind spinning, I read the invitations again. Saturday to Sunday, an overnight stay at Desi and Marc's magnificent Estate. 6 p.m. - 11 a.m.: similar to the *test run* mixer that Parker and I had with them already. My thoughts shift as I think about the other Members in Our Branch. They seem like ghosts now, existing only in my memory. I swipe through the app, looking for clues of their existence. Back in the Rulebook, I find their names listed and read through them again: Desi & Marc, Julia & Thom, Scarlett & Aki, Mallory & Davis, Marie & Evan, Bea & Riley, Sunny & Wyatt, Iris & Parker. Seeing my own name on there is surreal. I consider the possibilities - my potential Pairings. My mind runs wild with lewd, graphic imagery. The mere thought of the Mixer is putting me in a frenzy. My lips go dry, and my pussy, damp.

How I'm going to get through the next two days, I have no fucking idea.

Thirty-Eight

But I do get through them. Those two days. Shout out to my black vibrator for working overtime.

Friday comes at last. Starving by the time Parker gets off work sometime past 7 p.m., he drives through McDonald's to pick us up some eats. Aptly joking it's our *Last Supper*, we gorge ourselves on Big Macs, salty fries, and a Sprite for me, Coke for him. We feel equally disgusting and disgusted with ourselves after indulging, but at the same time it does take the edge off my stress, and I feel satiated for the time being. I decide the occasional emotional binge on fast food is perfectly acceptable.

With still many hours to ruminate over tomorrow's happenings, Parker senses a distraction is in order. We hop into his truck and he shifts into gear. I ask where we are going, but Parker declines to answer. So mysterious all the time. I massage his thigh to loosen his jaw, but he stays tight-lipped.

Eventually, we end up at a shopping plaza about twenty minutes away. He maneuvers his truck around the parking lot, almost as though he's deliberately trying to cause confusion as to our destination. At last, he parks in front of a Trader Joe's. My eyes dart around, searching for clues. I catch sight of Pinot's Palette and hope with everything in me that Parker isn't taking me for a paint and sip. I have zero artistic ability.

With our fingers weaved together, Parker leads me down several stores, past Pinot's, and to the last section of the building.

There it is: Moonlight Lanes. We are going bowling.

Oh, fuck, no.

Bowling weirds me out. As an average human who doesn't pursue bowling as a passionate hobby in my spare time, I don't own bowling shoes, or my own bowling ball, which means renting a pair of shoes that God knows how many other people have put their feet in, and using communal bowling balls that I'm certain are almost never disinfected. Additionally, bowling halls have a distinct smell about them that is overtly unpleasant, bordering on repugnant.

Maybe it would've been better had Parker taken me painting.

I wince. I do *not* want to go bowling. Nope. No.

Parker threatens that he's not above throwing me over his shoulder and carrying me inside if he has to. I cross my arms and invite him to make good on his promise. He tosses me up effortlessly and hauls me in. There's no end to the number of ways this man turns me on.

Despite the objectionable choice in activity, Parker does an exceptional job of distracting my attention away from the upcoming Mixer. And although my lips are curled in a sour expression for the bulk of our two-game stint, we laugh once or twice and I'll admit to having an infinitesimal shred of fun.

Is it all part of his game? Is Parker simply watching me squirm, aggravating me, and mocking me intentionally?

Of course he is. What an ass.

I suppose I should've seen it coming. Parker always makes sport of my discomfort and then rubs my nose in it. And... I will never deny that him doing so arouses me beyond belief.

Fueled by my shame, I trust that our time bowling is merely serving as foreplay for an especially steamy bedroom rendezvous later this evening.

It fucking better.

Thirty-Nine

Abstinence. Celibacy. Chastity. Ridiculous constructions of sexual censorship. I love to fuck. I love to *be* fucked. The reason sex is so pleasurable is *because* it's so fucking pleasurable. Whether giving or receiving, both are loaded with overwhelming, intense feelings of primal gratification.

It. Feels. So. Fucking. Amazing.

Which is why I'm contemplating murdering Parker right now. I'm not taking any of his bullshit about how anticipation is a huge part of the pleasure. Of course it is, I know all about edging, thank you very much. The point is, fucking is a release. (Duh. Orgasms. Literally a release.) Scientifically speaking, sex releases endorphins, oxytocin, and dopamine. All of which lower stress and trigger happiness.

So fuck me already.

But Parker refuses. I warn that I am perfectly capable of coming with or without him, but he threatens me further, telling me of an unofficial *rule* wherein all Members refrain from all sexual activity within 24 hours of all Mixers. *I get it*, the point is to heighten the pleasure. I don't like it, but I suppose I have no choice but to go along with it.

Parker leaves me alone, returning to his own place for the night, and I spend a sleepless night contemplating the validity of this 24-hour rule. More than once, I take out, and subsequently put away, my magic wand vibrator.

· · · ·

SATURDAY MORNING HITS like a brick wall. My body floods with energy, crazed and anxious, despite my exhausted state. I have the desperate urge to prove myself. I clean my apartment top to bottom, vacuum the carpet, wash the laundry, and check my phone at least twenty times an hour for any communication from Our Family. Parker doesn't even send a *Good morning* text, only deepening my madness.

Finally, around noon, I get a message from Mallory.

Hi Iris,

Thank you so much for submitting your outstanding documentation. Your file has been officially approved! We are so proud to call you one of Our own! Looking forward to seeing you tonight.

Much love,
Mallory xox

I breathe for the first time today. Okay. Great. Whew! Relief! It isn't a dream. This is real.

One worry down, countless running amok.

Six more hours to go.

Despite my apartment being spotless, my brain is cluttered as fuck. I haul ass to the library, desperate for escape in another world.

One quick pit stop for coffee.

Every time I see Simone now, it's bittersweet. She's outgoing and friendly and much too generous, especially given that I'm a giant fickle asshole whose only consistency with her has been inconsistency. Hot, cold, warm, warmer, then ice cold again. I've sent her so many mixed messages, I don't know how she still manages to smile and treat me with respect. Despite my remorse, I know it's laced with selfishness. I'm choosing Our Family over Simone in my own self-interest. Simone deserves better than that - she's much too good a human for me.

She places my usual brew on the counter in front of me, and I wait a beat before grabbing it, so as to avoid our hands touching. I hate that this is what has become of me.

I hate it, but, fuck, do I love what Our Family offers me.

I need the library.

Fantasy isn't typically my genre, but given that I'm pretty much living in an alternate reality, I decide to entertain the possibilities of it. My fingers run along the bookshelves, the feel of each spine grounding me. Getting into the heat of summer now, the sun is pouring in through the windows, providing a beautiful natural light that's perfect for reading. Staying true to my vow to never judge a book by its cover, I close my eyes, wander the length of the F-J aisle, and select a book blindly. I pull the black spine toward me. Taking care not to read the title, I bring it over to a table near the window, and settle into place. I take a sip of my sinfully sweet coffee and dive in.

It's wonderfully escapist. Following a family of fairies with a history of dark secrets, the pacing and vivid description keep my attention for over an hour. My coffee is a distant memory, and still I continue to read on.

My wrist buzzes with an incoming call from Parker. It jolts me back to the present. I can't be one of those people who answers their phone in a library, so I reluctantly ignore the call and text him instead.

> ME
> At the library, what's up?

PARKER
Just finishing up with some work stuff. You ready for tonight?
I'm planning on heading to you shortly.

> ME
> Ah! I cannot wait!
> Mind picking me up from the library?

PARKER
You bet. Msg you when I'm there.
xxx

> ME
> xxx

Holy shit. It's getting closer by the second.

I can't go back to my book now. I head over to the mystery section and find the read for Monday's book club. As I'm making my way over to self-checkout, I see a familiar face.

It's Maisie.

"Iris! Hi!" she calls at a library-appropriate volume.

"Hi, Maisie! How are you doing? It's so good to see you."

"You as well. You look... different. Like, good, different. How are things going?"

"Ha," I chuckle awkwardly. I'm flattered, but it catches me off guard. "Thanks. I, uh. I'm good. Things are good! Still not able to make it to Fridays. But Mondays have been mostly okay." I mumble. Why am I like this? Idiot.

"That's good to hear."

"Yep."

Our exchange feels strange. Very strange. Maisie stares at me, her eyes wide, her smile expectant. There's a shift between us that I can't place.

"Well, I should get going. Enjoy the rest of your weekend!" she chimes. Her voice is soft and sweet. There's something irresistible about her.

"You, too!" I call after her, then return to the self-checkout scanner.

Just in time, too. Parker messages me that he's five-minutes out. I type in my card number, scan the books (yes, I'm hooked enough to finish the fairy one), and hurry outside to meet him.

• • • •

BACK AT MY APARTMENT, I will time to slow down. The long hours of the day are suddenly replaced by the shortness of those we have to get ready. I'm rushed. There's no time to be mad at Parker for holding out on me anymore. My only focus is to make myself presentable and somehow get my nerves to calm the fuck down.

I frantically finger through my closet, assessing the suitability of my wardrobe. I pull out the lacy black and champagne dress that Parker suggested I wear to our next event. I examine it, and I'm pleasantly reminded of how gorgeous Sunny looked in her champagne dress at my Confirmation. My stomach swirls, the realness of tonight hitting me as I'm transported back... back to that night and the friendly, beautiful faces that greeted me, the sense of belonging I felt, the heat and sensuality of the room around us.

Slap me before I faint.

Parker enters my bedroom looking dapper in a sleek, black suit.

"Help me with my tie, would you?" It's sharp, narrow, and the same irresistible shade as his eyes.

"You look damn good." I lick my lips.

"You look like you're not changed yet."

"Observant of you."

"Tardy of you."

I'm so wound up, our banter sends heat surging across the surface of my skin. I blush. My nipples harden under my black tee. "What are you going to do about it?" I say, provoking him.

He rubs the stubble around his chin and pushes his black-rimmed glasses up his nose. I love when he wears his glasses. Suave and sophisticated. So fucking hot.

"Well, unfortunately for you, I can't do much about it right now. But I can promise you that being late to your first Mixer will likely earn you some smack from the other Members. And your Pairing might use it to your disadvantage," he threatens.

"Oh, is that so?"

"That's so."

"Well, the least you can do is help me get ready."

"Actually, yes I can. In fact, I have something for you. A little surprise from Our Family." He disappears. I peek out of the bedroom door in an attempt to catch a glimpse.

"Tsk tsk tsk," Parker clicks his tongue. He returns to me with a simple black envelope in his hand. "You're going to have to work on your patience. You really are incorrigible." He clears his throat and straightens up. I giggle. Pfft, the pot calling the kettle black. He grins, showing his teeth, trying hard not to laugh, too. "Iris, this is all very official, you know," he chides.

"Of course, yes, of course. Apologies for my *incorrigibility*, sir."

He shakes his head. "Iris, I'd like to present you with this." He passes me the envelope. "On behalf of Our Family, we offer you this, in honor of your first Mixer."

My eyes widen. I take the black envelope from him. It's sealed with the signature golden tree emblem. I rip across it to reveal a white note card from Desi.

Dearest Iris,

Congratulations once more on your Confirmation. We are proud to welcome you as a Member of Our Family, Branch 29.

As we eagerly await your participation in tonight's Mixer, we present you with this gift, a gesture of good faith on Our behalf. We know you'll wear it well.

As a reminder, tonight's Mixer will seal your Confirmation, making you an official Member of Our Branch.

We look forward to it.

Truly yours,
Desi Harold
Our Family, Head of Branch 29

Parker watches me. "You ready?" he asks. I nod.

He disappears once again and returns with a heavy garment bag.

I couldn't wipe the stupid smirk from my face if I wanted to. Holding the hanger high up in the air with one hand, Parker uses his other to pull down the zipper of the garment bag, revealing the surprise within.

Revealing is right.

My mouth gapes open as I study the lacy black material with my fingers. I pull it from the bag and try to make sense of what I've been presented with. A flood of heat rushes through me, my blood pumping with a combination of fear and excitement. Is this lingerie? Or a dress?

"Try it on," Parker urges. "Should be the perfect fit. I can't wait to see it on you."

I slip off my tee. Beneath it, I'm wearing a basic blue bra, yet Parker leans back into the plush of the bed, his thumb rubbing his chin as he admires me. I love how he is equally attracted to me regardless of how simply or elegantly I'm dressed. I shimmy out of my jeans, my blue panties with a white, lace trim becoming visible. I bat my eyes at Parker. He looks overly concentrated on studying my body.

"I'll never tire of admiring you," he breathes.

I'll never tire of it either.

I slip off my panties, letting them drop in a free fall to the floor. I kick them off and they land at Parker's feet. To replace them, I slip into the supplied black G-string. It slides right into place, wrapping my hips and sliding comfortably between my ass cheeks. The throbbing between my thighs returns, and I immediately know the thong is already saturated in my wetness. I walk over to the statuesque Parker and turn my back to him. Bending my knees, I allow my ass to ever so lightly graze his thighs, and I politely ask him to unclasp my bra. He gently runs his fingers up my spine, and I shiver as small bumps of stimulation break out over my skin. He continues to tease me, barely touching my shoulders and skimming my hips around the strap of my G-string. I lean into him more, sitting my bare ass on the hardness of the erection straining beneath his pants. I wiggle to find just the right position. Parker begins to groan, and I find my rhythm as I bend forward and slowly rock against him. The clump of fabric separating us makes it feel forbidden, but I continue, my wetness only growing. A heat blasts through me as pleasure seeps into my veins.

Parker shoves me off.

"So *incorrigible*!" he snaps, yanking my bra undone.

With a coy grin on my face, I slip the fabric of the black dress over my head and pull it into place. It's quite the puzzle, with so many straps all crisscrossing here and there. The front is sheer, with mesh and lace details covering a high neck and fitted bodice. Two black straps travel over my shoulders and join an elaborate design of several more straps decorating my back. At my waist, a heavy satin fabric splits into two, creating a skirt that is divided by large gaps at my hips. The skirt travels down my legs and falls to my feet. It's distinctly sultry with a Grecian vibe.

I feel incredible in it.

Unable to hide his approval, Parker smiles widely. "You look... just... wow."

I spin, the panels of fabric floating around me as I do. I trot over to my closet mirror and admire myself. It's the perfect fit. Parker's eyes follow, his gaze never leaving me.

I bite my lip.

• • • •

JUST A FEW MINUTES behind schedule, we are in Parker's truck and en route to the Harold Estate. Now that I'm dressed for the occasion, my nerves have slowed. The worry is fading, the anticipation is less intense.

Parker reminds me of what to expect, his voice is nurturing and warm, like being wrapped in a blanket right out of the dryer. He makes it all sound normal, relaxed, and fun.

As we travel down the gravel road, I focus on my breath, turning inside myself for calm. I close my eyes, and when I open them, we're there.

The Harold Estate: as impressive as ever. I'm flooded with the recollection of having been here just weeks prior for our private exchange, and before that for my Confirmation. I remind myself that I've been here before, I've met these people before, and this, *this*, is where I belong.

Parker opens the door of his truck, offers a hand, and helps me down. "Let's go have some fun!"

Smiling, I grab hold of his arm and we make our ascent up the steps to the massive doors of Desi and Marc's mansion.

Unlike when we came for my Confirmation, or even our exchange after that, Desi doesn't answer the door. Instead, we are greeted by a young, twenty-something with short black hair, dark eyes, a chiseled body, and tight, black mesh briefs. I try not to let my mouth hang open.

"Good evening, Iris. Parker. Welcome," he says. His voice is light and his smile is bewitching.

"Good evening, Kyle."

"Hello," I mutter, still shocked to be greeted by a man in nothing but sheer underwear.

"Come in. Sylvie will take any layers you wish to shed, coats and all that... and your devices, just down the hall. Then you may join the party in the ballroom."

We step inside and Parker leads me down the hall. Thankfully, after our encounter with Kyle, I'm better prepared for meeting Sylvie. We turn into a room on our left, but once more, my expectations are upended. At almost six feet tall, Sylvie is a blonde-haired drag queen with neon pink and blue eye makeup, fuchsia-colored lips, and an elegant black pleather jumpsuit speckled with rhinestones.

"Good evening, my honeys!" she says with southern accent charm. "Parker, so good to see you," she says, offering her hand out to him. He kisses the back, the true gentleman he is.

"Sylvie, may I say you are looking spectacular tonight," Parker compliments.

"Well, of course you can, honey!" Sylvie giggles and pretends to fluff the ends of her puffy blonde wig. "And might I say that it's about time I get to meet you, Iris! I've heard so much about you. You are just the talk of the town!"

I'm sure I blush brighter than the color of her lipstick. I freeze. Paralyzed. Speechless.

"We are very fortunate to have her as one of Our own," Parker swoops in. Thank God.

"Alright, well don't let me keep you from the fun! I'll take your overnight bags and devices, please! Give 'em up!"

Parker drops our bags beside her and surrenders his phone into Sylvie's finely manicured hand. Then he unbuckles his watch and she swipes it from him, too. I do the same, saying goodbye to my phone and watch. It's liberating to have a night without them nagging at me.

"You two are clear to go. Now, get out of here. Over to the main room with you!" Sylvie shoos.

Parker wraps his hand in mine, and we make the walk to the ballroom together.

Forty

As we step into the ballroom, I find comfort in the familiar. There are several cocktail tables in the same place as during my Confirmation, but this time, they're draped in black cloth with an assortment of candles at the center. An aroma of spicy warmth perfumes around us. It's potent and undeniably sexy. The chandeliers above have been dimmed to their lowest, and ambient music fills the gaps in conversation. It appears as though everyone is already here, their champagne flutes half-empty and their shoulders relaxed. We make our entrance with ease.

There are two others I don't recognize - a male and a female server, both wearing the same outfits as Kyle and Sylvie. Kyle's twin rushes over to offer us a glass of bubbly, and we each take one gratefully. I have to remind myself mid-sip to take it slow, instead of instinctively gulping down the crisp liquid to calm my nerves. Parker doesn't leave my side. It feels right.

Marc is the first to approach us. In a light gray suit and black shirt, he looks modern and handsome. He clinks his glass against each of ours.

"Welcome to the party," he greets. "So good to see you, Iris. You look stunning. That dress. Wow."

"Thank you. It's great to be here," I reply, relieved that my stint as a mute has come to an end.

"Great to see you, Parker."

"As always, Marc," Parker smiles. "How are things?"

The two of them break into a conversation about the stock market and other financial topics I have no interest in, so, instead of feigning such, I gather my courage and approach Aki, Marie, Sunny, and Wyatt. They shower me in hugs, express their excitement over my membership, and, most importantly, speak to me with respect and a sense of belonging. How I can experience this sort of respectful, polite, and authentic exchange with people who fuck each other's spouses monthly gives me a sense of hope and confidence I had only ever dreamed of.

Soon, I feel a hand graze the small of my back. I turn to meet Desi's eyes, and she pulls me in for a hug and kiss on the cheek.

"Iris! You made it. So glad to have you," she says, beaming. Desi is quite possibly the most beautiful human I've ever met. Her olive skin glows under the soft lighting of the room. Dressed in a ball gown made of delicate, wispy white fabric with a sprinkle of rhinestones along the bottom, she dazzles.

"I'm honored to be here," I reply.

"Having a good time? Everyone is behaving, I hope."

"Yes, of course! All of you are so nice. So welcoming."

"Wonderful! Let's get this night going then, shall we?" Desi sweeps me along with her, over to Parker, who is in a very intense conversation with Riley about cryptocurrency. Several minutes pass before the two of them feel they've at last exhausted the topic, and Parker joins me and Desi as we make our way to the front of the room. Marc is there waiting for us. With a full glass of champagne in hand, Desi delicately clinks a knife to gather the attention of the room. Conversations quickly die down, and all eyes turn to face us.

"Welcome, everyone! Welcome to Our July Mixer!" Desi announces. "Don't mind if I say that each and every one of you look utterly fantastic tonight!" The crowd stirs and Wyatt's loud, *whoop, whoop!* blasts through the room, garnishing scattered laughter. "Tonight is an exceptionally special night, as we have Our new Member, dear Iris, here with us for her first Mixer. Let's show her a good time, shall we?" My heart jumps, my cheeks burning as the gaze of many sears into me. As claps ring through the air, Marc passes Desi a large, golden goblet. "It's time for Our Selections. As always, ladies first." Desi turns to me. "Alright, Iris, are you ready?"

I nod. Anticipation is coursing through my veins; my heart is pounding in my ears. I reach my hand inside the goblet and feel the glossy heaviness of the objects within. I pull out a polished, purple stone with carved details. It's only after inspecting it that I realize the rock is in the shape of a leaf.

"Wonderful. Amethyst for Iris. Marie, care to go next?"

Each of the ladies takes their turn selecting a stone. All are the same, leaf-like shape, but differ in color. Marie selects topaz; Sunny, emerald; Mallory, sapphire; Scarlett, obsidian; Bea, amber; Julia, ruby; and finally, Desi is left with a quartz stone.

Next, the gentlemen are presented with a second, identical golden goblet containing the same, identical stones. It's becoming real now, watching as the men pick stones, knowing one will match mine. I hold my breath. Marc picks first: obsidian. Marc and Scarlett. Evan is next. He chooses ruby and is partnered with Julia. I can't breathe. A reprieve comes when Riley selects Bea's amber stone, and laughter rolls through the room. He promptly returns it to the goblet, his ears pink with embarrassment. The next moment, he pulls out the amethyst stone. Me. Riley selects me. He lifts his stone in my direction, as if toasting to Our Pairing, and smiles a beautiful, playful smile. His bright, blue eyes are radiant and captivating. My stomach flutters.

Parker leans in and whispers in my ear. "You two will have fun. He's not as shy as he seems."

I swoon, feeling my nipples harden under the lace of my dress. I'm sure everyone can see them. The humiliation of it is invigorating.

Parker chooses next, partnering with Marie. Her lush lips shine in the candlelight as she gives Parker a satisfied grin. He winks at her.

"Have you been paired with Marie before?" I inquire curiously. They have chemistry, so my assumption is yes; but, then again, there isn't a corner of the room that doesn't reek of seduction.

"Yes, many times," Parker admits freely.

His honesty is fresh. I feel a rush of satisfaction from it. The truth is, I want this for him just as much as I want it for me.

With the official Pairings out of the way, the group of us continue to mingle. I find myself better able to relax and engage in conversation now with that big unknown revealed. Out of the corner of my eye, I see a selection of keys on a table off to the side - the keys to the guesthouses. I lean in to peek, noticing my key, #4, is there waiting for me, attached to a chain with a medallion marked with Our Family's emblem.

Mallory and Wyatt are the first to take their leave. They announce their departure, wishing us all a pleasant evening. Bea and Aki are the next to retire to their private guesthouse. Suddenly the reality of what's to come hits.

I can't wait.

Riley is quiet and reserved for the most part, but I can't help but feel there's more to him, as Parker alluded. He approaches me at last, and we chat with relative ease. Our conversation mostly revolves around the basics of getting to know each other: where we grew up, our jobs, and how we inevitably made it to this point. Riley has a shockingly deep voice, and the iciness of his blue eyes pierces me deeply. I flirt, letting my extroverted tendencies take over and guide me through our interaction. I catch Parker's eyes more than once, his look of approval encouraging.

I decide it's time.

Grabbing the blue tie flopping around his neck, I guide Riley behind me. He follows like an obedient puppy; it floods my veins with endorphins. I pick up the chain with the key to my guesthouse, glance back at Parker, and blow him a kiss.

"I'm ready if you are," I tell Riley, more confidently than I really am.

"Absolutely."

Riley grabs my hand in his and our skin touches for the first time.

Forty-One

"**L**adies first." Riley smiles, unlocking and opening the door to *Guesthouse #4*. My house.

I step inside. Everything is just as before, right down to the candle burning on the kitchen counter. The predictability, the consistency, is a delightful surprise.

"Welcome home," I chuckle.

I toss the key onto the coffee table, next to the fetish magazines, and Riley closes the door behind him. With the heat buzzing in the space between us, I approach Riley and stand before him. His blue eyes are bright and intense. They put me under a spell.

"Can I touch you?" he asks. So gentlemanly of him.

"Yes," I sing.

"Can I kiss you?"

"Yes."

"Well then." Riley surveys me. "Can I fuck you?"

"Yes," I mutter, breathless.

"In that case, you're in for quite the treat, Iris." He walks in circles around me. I'm his prey, being hunted. "I can't wait to play with you."

And our game begins.

The entire world swirls in euphoria. My body is light and heavy all at once; a hefty weightlessness. Riley's circles become smaller, his body drawing nearer and nearer. At last, he leans toward me, close to my cheek, his chin hovering over my skin, teasing our touch. "You're quite something," he whispers. The warmth of his breath heats my skin on fire. "I want to lick you. All over."

He bites my earlobe, at last ending the torture of our separation. I squeal. His tongue then moves down my jawline to my chin. Sprinkling a mixture of kisses and licks under my lips, my breath becomes ragged and wanton. Frenzied, I pull him into me for our first kiss. It's blissfully deep. Our hands explore each other's bodies; I run my fingers along the back of Riley's pants, then along the front, cupping his package in my grasp. Hard and full, his cock intrigues me. His hands brush gently along my back, and

I feel the light scratch of fingernails against my skin. He breaks our kiss and licks my neck, then makes his way down to my breasts. Through the sheer fabric of my dress, he licks my nipples, teasing them with his capable tongue. I moan and soak in the pleasure of it. He pushes the drapery of my skirt out of the way and eagerly explores the soft skin of my ass. His touch continues to be light, which feels almost cruel. I'm desperate for him. At last his hands probe the apex of my thighs. He slides his fingers along the saturated fabric of my G-string, groaning in satisfaction at the evidence of my arousal. I run my hands through Riley's thick, dark mane of hair. His tongue continues its journey south, to my belly button, then down to the top of my G-string.

"This thing is in my way. Take it off."

"You're wearing much more clothing than I am," I retort. Riley raises his eyebrows in response to my sass.

"Well, I suppose you ought to do something about that, then."

Accepting the challenge, I whip off Riley's belt. I loosen his tie and pull it off in one swift movement. His shirt goes next, then his pants. At last, his black boxers drop to the ground. I grin in approval, Riley's engorged cock standing before me, begging to be touched.

I can't resist.

But Riley can. He steps away, giving a *tsk tsk* of objection. "Take it off," he insists, motioning at my dress.

I step out of my G-string, but my skirt drapes over my hips, hiding my secrets. Riley shakes his head, unsatisfied. I turn my back to him, revealing the myriad of straps covering my back.

"You'll have to help me pull this over my head," I inform him.

He's happy to.

The first thing I feel is his erection, sliding over my skirt and finding its place between the cheeks of my ass. He rocks his hips ever so slightly, creating a stimulation so minute, it's almost overwhelming.

Riley likes torture just as much as I do.

I moan and push my hips back so we move in unison. Just as we get in a rhythm, Riley pulls away. He lifts my skirt up and licks my ass, his tongue moving along my cheeks and then into the crevice. I yelp and lean into the enjoyment of it. He teases me with nothing more than a taste, though.

Riley runs his fingertips along the straps of my dress and lines them with kisses. I breathe deeply. Together, we lift the dress up and over my head, revealing my naked body.

Then, it all shifts. With our most vulnerable selves exposed, neither of us can take the wait any longer. Riley bites the tender skin between my neck and shoulder, and I whine in unexpected ecstasy. I turn and leap into him. Our lips meet once more and his kiss overtakes me. I fall down into a hole of pleasure where every look, touch, kiss, and movement is otherworldly in its enjoyment. We tumble onto the couch and Riley plunges his full length deep into my slit. Between the sensation of his fingers rubbing at my delicate nub and his rhythmic thrusts, I have no chance of withholding my indulgence. We kiss still, Riley pushing both his lips and his hips deep into me. I holler beneath him, my climax hitting in an immediate, euphoric wave.

"How was that?" Riley asks, a hint of pride in his throat.

"Not good enough. I'm sure you can do better," I mock. It's fuel to the fire.

Riley pushes me back, a playful and determined smirk on his face. He runs his cock along the crease of my ass. Covered in my cum, it slides easily back and forth. His hands play with my breasts while he nibbles my neck. My breath is ragged, still reeling from my release.

His luscious lips devour my pussy, sucking and worshiping my delicate folds. I yelp as he forces his entire fist inside of me, taking no time to work his fingers in bit by bit. It feels shamefully good. My body quivers as I hold my breath, on the cusp once more. Riley senses it and pulls away.

Such cruel, delightful torment.

"Follow me upstairs."

Riley's beautiful, firm ass guides the way around the corner and up the stairs. The room is exactly as before - spotless, dim, and dripping with sensuality.

Riley pushes me against the wall. He kisses me ferociously, his lips devouring mine. I scratch my nails down his chest all the way to the base of his member. He grunts in response. Crouching on my knees, I continue the trail down, lightly teasing his balls and moving along the inside of his legs.

I wrap my lips around his sack and suck. As I move my tongue, eliciting pleased sounds from Riley, I decide he's in for a treat.

The perineum is a highly pleasurable region of the body so often neglected. I can't let it go unattended. I slip my fingers into my folds, wetting them. Then, taking his cock in my hands, I pump my fists and lift his length to expose the tender skin beneath. I slip between his legs, bend my head back, and greedily worship his taint with my tongue. Riley trembles, crumbling under my touch. His body welcomes me. I find power in it.

While I enjoy sex just as much as the buildup to it, for Riley, the foreplay is everything. I suck his cock, opening my mouth widely for it to enter. I run my erect nipples over the head of it, sure to vary my pace to heighten the pleasure. Unable to take any more, Riley pushes me forward onto the silky sheets of the bed and I crouch with my knees under my body. He dives his face into me, invading my slit with his mouth and his tongue. He licks me, fists me, and eats my ass. It's so exhilarating that I come again, and again, and again, my body quivering in sublime, overstimulated agony.

Riley's a giver, I'm learning.

At last I mount him, slowly lowering myself as I allow his length to fill me up. I take it slow and rock my hips gently. Riley raises his hips to push deeper into me. Halting my movement, I watch him squirm with desire beneath me. It's empowering. He becomes more desperate for release with each tiny twitch of my hips. His eyes sear into mine. I lick my lips and scratch my nails along his chest once more. Riley pushes himself onto his forearms and I grab his mess of hair, pulling him in for a frenzied kiss. We thrust together, entwined in our joint pleasure.

Riley wails and bites my lip, hard, as he reaches his climax. His body shakes as his warm fluid oozes into me.

"Fuck, that was good." The contentment in his voice makes me proud. Riley falls back onto the bed, and I find my place beside him.

Riley kisses me once more, but this time, instead of passion, a tender adoration blooms between us.

I am where I belong.

Forty-Two

With Mixers held only once per month, we can't waste any of our precious moments together. Riley and I sleep four hours at most, and spend the rest of the time admiring each other's bodies. We talk a lot, albeit mostly about our sexual experience, preferences, and the like. Parker was right - Riley is surprising. Appearances are wildly deceiving.

I take a hot shower and slip into a casual belted dress and flat shoes before we head to breakfast. Riley informs me that the group meets at 8 a.m. sharp the following morning for a shared meal. I feel giddy at the thought of seeing Parker and learning about his night. I hope it was just as satisfying as mine (and mine was pretty fucking satisfying). Riley and I had a lot of fun.

Yet still, in my depths, Parker has never left me.

Riley and I are the second Pairing to appear in the breakfast room of the main house. Bea and Aki are munching on fresh fruit when we make our entrance.

"Well, aren't you just glowing!" Bea announces as she approaches for an affectionate hug. "Have fun?" she asks, her nose wrinkled and her face expectant. "You better have done her good," she adds, raising her finger and flashing a playful, threatening smirk at Riley.

"Mm hmm," is all Riley can muster as his typical quietness takes back over.

"We had a great time," I assure Bea. "How about you two?" I ask, eager to hear of their exploits.

"Aki always takes great care of me," Bea admits. She squeezes Aki's shoulders affectionately.

The room begins to fill with other couples joining after their private evenings together: Davis and Desi, Thom and Sunny, Evan and Julia. Wyatt makes quite a show of his entrance. His voice booms loudly as he declares victory over having had the best night of us all. Mallory's cheeks turn a flattering shade of pink as she heartily agrees with him. Mingling with the other couples, I'm eager to learn about their time together. But I can't help but feel an emptiness in the room. Parker and Marie remain absent.

Scarlett shares smiles and tidbits about her time with Marc. Bea can't keep herself from joining in our conversation, claiming that Marc is one of her favorite Pairings. We sip fresh orange juice (mixed with champagne, of course) and taste bits of bread and fresh fruit as we reminisce. Marc saves the morning once again with an oversized pot of fresh coffee that I am the first to indulge in. Mallory joins us, then Desi, and soon all the women are gathered in a cluster. It's only when I feel the soft, strawberry ringlets of Marie's hair graze my shoulder that I realize I've been nearly holding my breath. My eyes deviate from the girls as I search for Parker.

There he is. Standing against the door. Alone. Raising his mimosa in my direction. My mouth breaks into a wide grin. I race over, jumping on top of him, as though we are two lovers separated by war and reuniting for the first time in years. His arms wrap around my thighs. We share a deep, passionate kiss that's disgustingly full of love. The movement of his lips, the dance of his tongue - it all reaffirms my belief that no one ever in the history of the universe can kiss me better than Parker can. He lowers me back to earth, but our lips remain sealed, locked in an intimate bond that belongs only to us. I run my fingers along his scalp and make a mess of his already disheveled hair.

"Fuck, I missed you," he breathes into my mouth.

"You taste so good. I missed you!" That hint of desperation in my voice is there - something I've learned to accept as a byproduct of true love. It's repulsive, I know, but it's there.

Desi calls the room to order. We each take a seat, everyone instinctively returning to their partner's sides, instead of sitting with their Pairings from the night prior. We are served a decadent breakfast with fresh pastries, fruits, and eggs of all kinds. Kyle and Sylvie seem a distant memory now as two fully-clothed men offer us made-to-order pancakes and French toast. Laughter and warmth fill the room. I watch, soaking in the energy.

"Awfully quiet, Iris," Parker observes. Of course he notices. He notices everything about me.

"It's interesting. Just listening and watching everyone after last night."

"Mm hmm," Parker hums. "And what do you hear and see?"

"It's just... I don't know how to really put it into words. Everyone is so... normal." Parker laughs.

"Did you expect us to be aliens?" he teases. I elbow him in the ribs.

"You know what I mean! It's just... the way everyone is interacting. It's so normal. There's no discomfort, no awkwardness. I mean, we all fucked each other's partners last night. And, yet, here we are."

"It *is* normal. For us."

"I love that."

"I love you."

"May I have your attention, everyone," Desi chimes, clinking a spoon against her teacup. "Thank you for attending Our July Mixer. It's been a pleasure, as always. A few announcements before we reluctantly invite you to make your leave. Firstly, a reminder that the playbacks of last evening's interactions will be available Wednesday, for your enjoyment." Wyatt whoops loudly and the room laughs at his endless enthusiasm. "Yes, Wyatt, very exciting," Desi indulges him. "Secondly, Iris, congratulations on surviving your first official Mixer. You are now one of us. We are so happy to have found you!" Applause, whispers of congratulations, and more of Wyatt's yells fill the air. I smile broadly and mouth *thank you* to everyone for their kindness. "Third, although it is still very much summer, please everyone save the date for Our Family's largest fall event. Our Annual Masquerade Ball will be held on Saturday, October 21, to Sunday, October 22. It is essential that no absences are recorded for this date, as it is one of Our Family's two official Inter-Branch events. We expect you all to be there in your finest. Lastly, Our next Mixer will be at the end of August, and we look forward to seeing you all there. Thank you so much, everyone!"

The room thins out quickly after Desi's announcements. I throw back the last of my third cup of coffee, and Parker and I begin to say our goodbyes.

That's when Sunny and Wyatt approach us. With broad grins and bright teeth, they romance us with the proposition of a private exchange next week. My cheeks grow hot as they invite us to their home, promising it will be very casual. They are both breathtakingly beautiful, and I'm flattered by their proposal. Thursday is the best day for them, they say, but Wednesday would work, too. Parker reluctantly declines, citing his ever-busy schedule, but encourages me to play without him. I study him, confused.

Sunny brushes her fingertips down my arm. "I'd love for the three of us to play together," she suggests. Her voice is light and warm.

I think I'm going to faint. I gulp, my skin reddening under her touch.

"You up for it?" Wyatt chimes in.

"I am very up for it," I blurt.

I am. Very. If I don't die of humiliating arousal first.

Forty-Three

Wednesday brings with it a new depth of my membership within Our Family: Recordings. In the flurry of skin and hands and lips and tongue with Riley, the fact that all interactions are recorded completely slipped my mind. I forgot entirely. When the notification that the Recordings are now available pops up on my phone, my stomach drops. I have no idea what to expect.

The entire day at the clinic, I can barely focus on the inputting of insurance and statements in our billing system. The day drags, and when, finally, it ends, I race home. I barely get inside the door of my apartment before I open the app. But then I stop. A pang of insecurity plagues me. I've never watched myself before. I hope with all that I am that I don't look a fool. The entire Branch has access to this. The shame turns my cheeks pink and floods my pussy with warmth. I revel in it.

Right on cue, Parker messages me.

PARKER
Quite the show you put on with R. Impressed.

Fuck. Fuck fuck fuck. My insecurities burn in a passionate mix of shame and pride. Parker has already watched it - watched me.

PARKER
I knew you'd fit right in.
I love you
xxx

Between the anticipation and the dread, I feel like I'm going to throw up. Enough delay. I click on Recordings, select last Saturday's event date, and scroll. There's footage of everything: the cocktail reception, inside each guesthouse, and even the morning-after breakfast. I find *Guesthouse #4: Iris & Riley*, and almost click on it. But above it is *Guesthouse #1: Marie & Parker*. I can't decide which to watch first. Biting my fingernails, I toss my phone and house key on the kitchen counter. I rifle through the cupboards to source a bottle of Cab Sav and pop it open. Pacing, I make the totally-not-insecure choice to watch the Recording of me and Riley first.

There are two playback options: time lapse or full footage. Unable to maintain any patience, I choose the highlights reel.

The euphoria of that night comes racing back as I watch our bodies intertwined. It's exhilarating - to see us, two adults outside of our own, private relationships, making an intimate physical connection. Reliving that night sends prickles down my spine. We look incredible together, and experiencing our interaction again in this way makes me hot. I fight the urge to grab a vibrator to accompany me on this trip down memory lane.

It's time to see what Parker got up to.

It turns out Marie is fairly vanilla. Or, perhaps, she and Parker made the intentional choice to keep it tame, for my consideration? The Recording of them together, making out on the couch, then fucking with Marie leaned over the side of the bed is, in all honesty, disappointing. There's no *heat*. It all seems very bland. I finish the footage feeling guilty, somehow, for the intensity that Riley and I experienced. It rolls through my veins in a passionate fervor.

I call Parker, but, seeing as it's Wednesday and he is never available to me on Wednesdays, I'm not surprised when it goes to voicemail. I text him instead.

> ME
> Impressed? Wait until you see what
> I have planned for Friday.
> xxx

I'm drawn to the other Recordings like a moth to the flame. It's an addiction. I watch the cocktail footage in its entirety, paying close attention to the confidence and warmth radiating from everyone in the room. At first, my hesitancy is noticeable; I'm surprised to see how insecure I look, shooting glances at Parker for reassurance. But soon enough I find my place, and with each passing moment I blend more and more into the crowd. We become one large entity, an integrated group all tangled together in a beautiful mess of lust and sexuality.

Having already viewed the footage for *Guesthouse #1: Marie & Parker*, I select *Guesthouse #2: Scarlett & Marc*. The Recording shows... nothing. For the entire duration of the evening, there isn't a single person in that guesthouse. Considering the event was at Marc's Estate, I guess that he and Scarlett stayed in the main house? But then again, that doesn't make sense - or follow the rules for Mixers. Shrugging it off, I move onto *Guesthouse #3: Bea & Aki*. They are an interesting Pairing. Both seemingly reserved in the large group, they surprise me with their intensity. Bea takes advantage of the various costumes supplied in the wardrobes and plays dress up. She dons a seductive nurse-themed teddy, and Aki, dressed in a sheer white jumpsuit with open mesh shorts, appears to be her trainee. She binds him with rope to the columns of the four-poster bed and uses various implements to spank him. I watch, wide-eyed, reliving their connection, the arousal of their interaction provoking my own.

I steal away for a moment and strip out of my navy scrubs. I peel off my bra and panties and settle into the plush of my bedsheets. What's the point of watching these Recordings if I can't enjoy myself while I do so? My slit already damp, I gently slide my fingers along my opening. I reach into my bedside table and select a large dildo to keep me company. After another swig of wine, I prop up my phone and select the next Recording: *Guesthouse #5: Julia & Evan*.

It's a good one.

Guesthouse #2 was empty because, to my shock and delight, Scarlett and Marc were with Julia and Evan in their guesthouse. I watch the footage while stroking my folds, more intrigued than I'd care to admit. The screen splits in two. Julia and Scarlett are naked downstairs, while Marc and Evan are upstairs. Unexpectedly, Marc tosses Evan back onto the bed and leans into him. He showers him with kisses, beginning at his mouth and ending, after many detours back to his mouth, at the base of Evan's cock. My wetness growing, I reach for the dildo. As Marc takes Evan into his mouth, I plunge the toy into mine. I watch on as Evan writhes under Marc's mouth. Downstairs, the ladies sit on opposite ends of the couch, chatting. They soon wander upstairs, and just in time for the show. The screen becomes full again as Marc lathers himself generously in lubricant and teases Evan's rear opening. With Evan draped forward over the edge of the bed, Julia and Scarlett settle on either side of him. Julia brushes her lips against Evan's ear, and Scarlett plays with Evan's red locks, twirling her fingers around his curls. Evan yelps as Marc enters him at last. Julia grabs his ass and spreads his cheeks apart. Marc rocks his hips, slowly and rhythmically, gliding deeper inside Evan's ass. Marc braces himself against Evan's hips as he quickens his pace. Scarlett rises and licks Marc's lips, then leans back onto the bed and begins fingering herself. Her dark hair surrounds her face, making it impossible to decipher what she's thinking. Evan pushes up onto his elbows and moans in enjoyment, his own cock hard under him. Julia passionately kisses him and grabs his length in her fist. He wails in pleasure as Marc thrusts deep into his hole.

Watching Marc and Evan connect in this raw, sensuous way is undeniably exhilarating. Their sexual queerness validates my own.

The Recording continues, and it's not long before Marc nears his climax. He pulls his lengthy cock out from Evan's ass, pumps his fist along the shaft, and shoots white cream all over Evan's back. He groans heartily. Julia immediately licks the warm goo, then pushes Evan onto his back. Without missing a beat, she mounts him. Bouncing wildly and bucking her hips, she rides him without mercy. Evan is the object of the night - being used and fucked as desired. Scarlett, who up to this point has been very much putting on her own show, stands up and departs the room. She and Marc disappear into the bathroom, where the screen splits again and documents their intimate shower rendezvous. Evan shrieks out under Julia, her body pushing him to the limit. I fuck myself with my toy, sliding it inside of me and pressing against my G-spot. I wail and moan with Evan and Julia and Marc and Scarlett, the five of us indulging together in the deep pleasures that Our Family has to offer.

The smutty content in these Recordings does something to me. It does something beyond validating me; it makes my desire for pure, raw sex seem completely ordinary. It normalizes my hunger for the physicality of that intimate connection. It's as though a secretive box that was hidden deep inside of me, locked and chained, has been unbound and pried open. The release is transcendent, shifting my whole sense of self in the greater world around me.

Our Family is more than simply a lifestyle organization. It's a community of belonging and inclusion, of being understood and of understanding, of being accepted and accepting.

Our Family is where I belong.

I've found my place.

> ME
> Holy shit.
> Holy fucking shit.
> Just... Wow. Wow.
> Thank you for this. Thank you for
> bringing me into this.
> I love you so fucking much.

I throw in a crying face emoji and heart-eyed emoji, because I can't decide which of those two emotions is my most prominent right now. I want to cry in my overwhelm, but I also feel so joyfully drunk on my own elation.

Parker texts back immediately.

PARKER
You're the one.
xxx

Forty-Four

In the heat of my revelation, I have the private exchange with Sunny and Wyatt. The timing couldn't be better. With the rush of confidence and passion still fresh, I can't wait to play.

They live far. I pull up directions on Google maps, but there's no way I can walk over an hour each way to their address, especially since I don't plan to stay the night. We all work in the morning. I concede and order an Uber. In my black lace and champagne dress (an intentional nod to the one Sunny wore during my Confirmation), I wait outside my apartment for Ahmed in his black Prius.

Parker messages me, wishing me luck with Wyatt, who he has heard is just as enthusiastic in the bedroom as outside of it. He encourages me to enjoy my time with Sunny, too. *Don't be shy*, he orders.

When am I ever?

Tucked safely inside my ride, I open the Our Family app and send Sunny a message to let her know I'm on my way. *We can't wait to have you,* she replies.

I swoon.

Ahmed pulls up in front of a modest white house with a well-kept garden and large front windows. It's remarkably normal. I take three deep breaths before I exit the car and follow the oversized red brick steps to the front door. Wyatt pulls it open before I even get there.

"Iris! Sunny! She's here!" he yells. I'm sure the entire neighborhood is aware of my arrival now. "Come in, come in!" he urges, his arms wiggling like an octopus's tentacles, hurrying me inside.

Barely through the door, and he has me pinned against the wall. He shoves me backward and whispers in my ear.

"Iris. Sunny and I really want to record this. Post it for the group to enjoy. You in?" His voice is hot and wet. It turns my brain to mush.

"Oh, Wyatt, give the woman a minute to get inside!" Sunny calls. She walks toward us, wiping her hands on a tea towel. "Sheesh. No patience, this one," she says to me. "Iris, so good of you to come. We are looking forward to hosting you."

"Thank you for having me," I squeak, the heat from Wyatt still thick on my skin.

"I believe what my *enthusiastic* spouse here is trying to say is that we would be delighted if you'd consent to recording our exchange." She leans into me and whispers in my ear, "Wyatt is just a tad narcissistic and has a thing for watching himself." She giggles.

"To be honest, I totally forgot that the Mixers were recorded. It was kind of a shock when I opened them and watched them. I... liked it," I admit. "Parker and I had an exchange with Desi and Marc before the Mixer, but I guess that one didn't get recorded."

"Did they ask you if they could? With much more tact than Wyatt could ever muster, of course."

"No, they never mentioned it. It was my first exchange since joining Our Family."

"Didn't want to hit you with it too hot, I guess," Wyatt chimes in.

I laugh in his face. If he only knew how fucking hot it really was. "Well, yes. Yes, I do consent to having our exchange recorded," I decide. Also, so Parker can watch it. I want him to see our show.

"Fuck yes!" Wyatt booms, raising his hand and offering us each high fives. Amused, I shake my head.

"You look lovely, by the way," Sunny compliments.

My eyes admire her. She's wearing a beautiful coral blouse and tight teal pencil skirt. "As do you!"

"And I'm hot, I know," Wyatt adds. Sunny rolls her eyes and scoffs.

We make our way into their kitchen, which is white and bright. Along the back wall is a series of floor-to-ceiling windows that reveal an incredible ocean view. My mouth drops open. The green and blue of the waves swell in the distance, filling my eyes with wonder.

"Wow. What a view!"

"Thanks. Can I offer you a drink? Wine? Something harder?" Sunny's voice is deeply comforting. I already feel at ease around her.

"I'd love a glass of wine. Whatever you have, I'm not picky."

The decadent smell of red wine fills the kitchen. Wyatt approaches me with a glass, but offers it only in exchange for a kiss. I lean into him and give him a quick peck.

"Prude," he jokes, handing the glass over. I give him a sassy grin.

"Wyatt!" Sunny snaps.

I take an indulgent sip of wine and let the thick elixir travel down my throat. It settles into my stomach and pushes my nerves down with it.

Wyatt pours himself an old fashioned, while Sunny nurses a glass of wine with me. She invites me onto their back porch and we sit, side-by-side, in their wooden deck chairs and listen to the push and pull of the ocean. It's meditative - the sound of the water, the warmth of the wine, freshness of the salty air. I lean back and close my eyes, lost in it.

That's when I feel the closeness of Sunny next to me. Her mocha skin, creamy and sinfully soft. Our arms graze against each other. The spark of her touch sends a surge of warmth through my body. I keep my eyes closed but part my lips, just so, and Sunny plants her mouth on mine. Her lips are decadent, plump, and warm. Our kiss is slow and deep, laced with fondness. Her body shifts and she moves on top of me. I spread my legs to welcome hers, and she plants her thigh against my center. Her hair falls into me, tickling my cheeks, and I unintentionally giggle.

"Ladies!" Wyatt snaps. "Let's take this party inside."

Lips and cheeks still warm, we follow Wyatt's suggestion and make our way into the house. My insides throb.

"Upstairs. The loft."

Sunny wraps her arm around mine and we skip upstairs. Wyatt trails behind, and I half expect him to jump us at any second.

He doesn't. Instead, he takes slow sips of his drink while Sunny and I get comfortable on their black, leather couch. He paces, looking painfully uncomfortable, as though holding back is going to surely make him explode.

Sunny tucks my hair behind my ear and runs her fingers along my fringe. I close my eyes and focus on the gentle softness of her fingertips as they swipe across my skin. I lean into her and our lips join once more. She breathes deeply and our kiss blooms. As her tongue swirls against mine, I feel our hearts thudding in our chests. I pull her close, reaching for the bottom of her blouse and urging her to pull it off. She lifts her arms and we wiggle it off together, exposing her naked chest. My hands caress her round, plump breasts, and I moan as we lose ourselves in a kiss once more. I feel greedy, hungry to explore every inch of her skin. I lick her lips and gnaw on her neck, then push her backwards so I can admire her body. Sunny yelps as she falls against the unforgiving leather of the couch, and I wrap my fingers around her neck.

"Stay here," I order.

Sunny nods, and I take her nipples into my mouth. They are impossibly tender, but soon become hard and stiff under the torturous stimulation of my tongue. I flick and nibble, relishing in Sunny's soft squeals of pleasure.

"Eat her out," Wyatt booms, his voice loud and commanding.

Who am I to defy the wishes of my host?

I look over to him, forgetting before he spoke up that he was even there. He's stripped himself naked, his erect cock in his hand, standing across from us, watching on. I smile in the corner of my mouth.

I push the silky fabric of Sunny's skirt up, expecting to expose a lacy pair of panties. To my delight, just as she wasn't wearing a bra, she's neglected to put on underwear. I breathe in the erotic scent of her pussy. It's intoxicating, sweet, and feminine. I dive into her, pushing my nose, mouth, and tongue into her folds all in one nimble movement. The sound of her yelps tunnel into my ears.

"Fuck, yeah!" Wyatt groans. "Fist her," he blurts, directing our interaction.

I wiggle my face against Sunny's center and slowly insert my fingers. First one, then another, then another. I patiently work my way up to all five, then plunge my fist into her crevice.

"Fuck!" Sunny wails. She lets out the most erotic whimper I'm certain I've ever heard. It sinks into my eardrums.

Possessed by her scent and sounds, I worship her clit, caressing her nub with my tongue. Lick, flick, suck. Lick, flick, suck. I find my rhythm as I continue to thrust my fist inside of her. She wiggles and shakes; her climax is close. I pull out my hand and lick off her juices, moaning in the sweet, forbidden taste of them. I plunge my hand back into her, then out, then in, over and over as I stroke her bud with the tip of my tongue. She writhes under me, and I wiggle at her G-spot. Pushing against it, I tap my fingers. Sunny comes undone. Her orgasm spreads through her entire body, a blast of heat surging over her skin. Her muscles palpitate against my fingers, and I gasp at the pleasure of feeling her come.

"Fuck, yes!" Sunny screams into the air around us.

"God, you feel so fucking good," I breathe into her. "Mm..." I moan.

"That was amazing, Iris, truly," Sunny pants.

"That was fucking hot," Wyatt chimes in. "Now come over here and blow me."

"Wyatt!"

"What? My turn!" he insists.

I shrug my shoulders and crawl over to him. I open my mouth wide and he delves into it. I immediately choke, gagging under his furious thrusts.

"Goddammit, Wyatt. Be gentle with our guest. Especially if you ever want her to come back!" Sunny threatens.

"Fuck, she's good," he mumbles, ignoring her advice and continuing to fuck my face with vigor. I hold my breath, and lean into his rhythm. "Look up at me. Up here, Iris," he pants. "Like that. Fuck, just like that."

I look into him, his gaze blue and intense, and try to keep my eyes open. But each time his cock hits the back of my throat, I instinctively close them. He pulls out and smacks me across the face, backhanding me. I gasp.

"Look at me, I fucking said," Wyatt repeats. He takes my chin in his fingers and squeezes my cheeks. "I want you to look at me. You can do that, can't you?" I nod, weak. And aroused as fuck. "Good. Now look at me while I fuck your mouth. Got it?"

I open up and stick out my tongue. I focus on the dark blue speck in Wyatt's left eye, and zero in on it while he harshly pummels his cock into my throat. Sunny appears beside me, and starts whispering in my ear.

"You're so good, Iris. Look at you, taking Wyatt's big, hard cock all the way, deep inside your throat. Mm. Just taste it. Let it fill your mouth. That's good, like that. Good, Iris, good."

Sunny's hands find me, and suddenly her touch is all over my body. My chest, my ass, my chin, my neck.

"Wyatt, she's still wearing her clothes. I think we should make her take them off, don't you?"

"Fuck, she feels so good, though," he complains.

"Come on, baby. I know she feels good. Let's see how beautiful she looks naked."

"Fuck." He leans in deep, forcing his cock to push against the back of my throat. I hold my breath. "Fuck, fine. Ugh!" he grunts as he pulls out of my mouth at last.

I cough and spit a wad of saliva onto the tile below us. My insides are throbbing, my heart pounding. Our game is pushing me to the brink.

"Take off your clothes for us, won't you, Iris?" Sunny sings. She melts me with her charm.

"Of course," I answer, still catching my breath. I shimmy my dress up to my thighs and, feeling bold, stop. "Actually, I could really use your help, Sunny." I spin around. "My zipper, here. I can't get it on my own."

Sunny's hands find me again. Her fingertips trace the edges of my dress, playing at the length of my zipper. I feel her press hard into me, her nipples against the skin of my back. She runs her hands along my front, teasing her touch on my breasts and down to the exposed skin of my thighs.

Wyatt intervenes, impatient. He pushes Sunny off me, yanks down my zipper, and pulls my dress up over my head. "Let me look at you."

I spin in a slow circle, the dribbles of arousal marching down my inner thighs.

"I'm going to fuck the shit out of you." Wyatt throws me onto the couch, my cheeks pushed down against the seat and my ass up in the air. He plunges his cock deep inside of me. "Oh my God. You're so fucking wet. Sunny! Holy shit! Fuck!" He pounds into me. "She's so fucking wet. Get under there. Lick it up," he instructs.

"Mm... So wet. Iris. Look at you." Sunny positions herself under me as Wyatt furiously thrusts his hips. She runs her tongue up and down my inner thighs, tasting my intimate fluids as they leak down my legs. "You taste incredible," she hums.

Sunny's tongue on me, Wyatt's length deep inside my hole, and smell of sex wafting in the air - it's a glorious cocktail I'm drunk on. I bounce against Wyatt, feeling my release marching inevitably closer. He smacks my ass, declares he is *The King,* and plunges into me deeper. His thumb finds my back hole, and he pushes it inside. I wail.

"Next time, I'll fuck you here," he promises.

I'm breathless.

"I want you to come," Sunny whispers in my ear. She rubs her hand against my clit and bites the edge of my ear. "Come for us. We want you to."

"Let me feel you, Iris. Come for The King!"

Sunny's hand frantically shakes under me, forcing my release in a matter of seconds. It overwhelms my entire body and I quiver, shaking and wiggling as the power of it hits me. My heart feels like it's going to explode.

"Good, Iris, good," Sunny praises. "You're doing so good."

I feel small and big at the same time. Wyatt is still heaving into me, but, undone by my own release, I'm weak and heavy.

"Sunny, get me a plug," Wyatt commands. "I want to see her ass full. You'd like that, wouldn't you, Iris?" he asks me. "You like to feel that fullness, don't you?"

Breathless, I answer with a pathetic, "I fucking love it."

"The biggest one we have. Iris is a proper slut, aren't you?" My pussy floods with warmth. "I said, aren't you?" he repeats.

"I'm a fucking slut," I answer, finding shameful pleasure in uttering the words.

"Yeah, you are. Let's fill that ass up."

Sunny spreads my cheeks apart while Wyatt squirts lube into my crack. He rubs it in furiously, then shoves a huge plug into my hole. I wail, the size of it stretching and challenging me.

"You can take it, Iris. You're so good," Sunny encourages. "Almost in. Come on, you can take it."

"Fucking take it in. Oh, God! Yes, fucking fill that ass up! Mm!"

"How's that feel?" Sunny asks. "It's a big one. But we know you can take it in. Just like that."

"So good," I gulp.

I think I'm going to faint. Our scene engulfs me in an overpowering euphoria. My heart is racing, my mind is swirling. It feels sinfully incredible to play this game with Sunny and Wyatt. I hate myself for loving it, but I do. I fucking love it.

Sunny kisses me, her tongue in my mouth, and I'm acutely aware that every single one of my holes is full in this moment.

Wyatt wiggles the plug in my ass as he continues to thrust into my slit. My body on fire and my senses overwhelmed, I come in a wave, weak and dazed, the air hot, my head spinning.

Wyatt pulls out of me and pumps his fist along his length, spewing his cum onto my back and over the plug. He pronounces himself *The King* once more, then kisses Sunny deeply, moaning in lust.

"Let me grab a couple of towels." Sunny disappears down the hall and returns with two perfectly white, plush towels. She gently dabs my back, the softness of the towel a welcome sensation after Wyatt's harsh smacks. "How was that for you?" she asks. "Wyatt can be... a bit much." Wyatt scoffs. We chuckle.

"It was great. Really. I enjoyed that a lot." Too enthusiastic? Oh, well.

"Of course it was great. Sunny and I are The King and Queen!"

Sunny rolls her eyes. "I'm going to pull out the plug now. You ready?"

I relax my muscles and nod. She gently tugs, and the plug slowly pops out of my opening. She discreetly wraps it in the towel and puts it aside. Wyatt has laid the other towel along the length of the couch, and the three of us plop onto it. The air is quiet, our bodies now still in their satisfaction.

Being the gracious hosts they are, Sunny and Wyatt welcome me for dinner. Sunny and I finish the bottle of wine and take in the spectacular ocean views while Wyatt grills steak and potatoes beside us. The entire experience is surreal to me: the view, the food, the sex. It all seems too good to be true.

Sometime around nine, I order an Uber and head home. Despite getting my fill with Sunny and Wyatt, coming home to my empty apartment is profoundly sad. I want nothing more than to hop into bed beside Parker and retell my experience, wrapped in his arms with his smell consuming me. But it's Thursday and very firmly not *my* night with him.

What is he doing without me?

Forty-Five

How did I survive, I wonder, for the first six years of my life before I learned to read? Books are such an important part of my life. From the magic of the stories to the way they are crafted, I'm certain I would die without them.

I devour the book Maisie had recommended to me in one haunting, thrilling, and deeply lascivious session. The perfect mix of erotic and mysterious, I love every word of it. It's been a bit since our paths have crossed, so I plan to go on Monday, straight after work, and hope to catch Maisie before she leaves for the day.

I'm relieved to see Parker tonight and spend a proper weekend together as a couple. We haven't had that in some time.

Inside Urban Grind, Simone has my coffee all ready for me, and I gratefully lean behind the counter and give her a hug. It feels risky, but I convince myself it's friendly.

Just friends.

"Thank you! You don't know how much I need this today. Well, every day," I admit.

"I got you, girl!" Simone winks. "Anything else today? It's Friday, why not treat yourself to a chocolate croissant as your prize for getting through the week?"

Such an enabler.

Fifteen dollars later, I'm settled in my spot by the river. Just about to open my book, I hear an incessant buzzing that keeps me from focusing. I had forgotten to put on my watch, and I realize the buzzing is coming from my neglected phone. I pull it out and see it's a call from my mom. Strange. It's not even 5 a.m. for them in Hawaii. Suddenly, my stomach drops.

"Iris! Honey! I'm throwing my things in a suitcase as fast as I can! Willie is getting the car ready, and I should be at the airport within the hour," she babbles in a frenzied, panicked state.

"What? What's going on?"

"Didn't Zach call you? Molly is in labor! Oh! My sweet baby granddaughter will be here soon! I'll stay with you, of course, I can't impose on them in their home with the new baby and all. I'm such a good grandmother, giving them their space as a family, respecting boundaries and all that *new age* stuff that I keep hearing about, don't you agree? Well, I'm just about ready here, I'll be there as fast as I can! I expect I'll see you at the hospital? I'll head straight there when I land. Oh, goodness! Such an exciting time! Oh! Zach's on the other line. Got to go, honey, see you soon! Love you!"

Did she say stay with *me*? Oh, no. Fuck, no.

I unlock my phone and see five missed texts from Zach.

ZACH
Heading to the hospital. Molly's parents are
watching the kids. Having some contractions,
this might be it

Then

Waiting in triage

Then

Doc says Molly's 6 c.m. already, calling mom

Then

Mom says she's flying out here, even when I tried to
convince her not to. She insists on staying with you,
I'll try to talk her out of it. We have plenty of space
for her to stay.

Then

8 c.m.!

Then, as I'm mulling over my response, another text.

Mom won't hear it, I'll try to convince her once she's here.

What chaos this day is turning into. I call Zach.

"Zach! Oh my God, this is insanity," I blurt.

"I can't believe it's happening right now. I thought I'd be more prepared with baby number three. But she's a week early. Lily and Nora were both late. I guess I just had it in my head that Felicity would be, too." He sounds like a zombie, in a complete numb daze.

"Is Molly okay?"

"She's doing great, actually. We are in our room now, she has an epidural going. Oh, Iris, can you believe it?"

"I'm really happy for you both."

"Thank you. Thank you. We are sort of shocked right now! But couldn't be happier."

"I'm at work today, so call the clinic when you are ready to receive visitors. I'll do my best to jet out of work early and come meet her."

"Thanks. Okay, I will."

"Love you, Zach."

"Love you. Talk soon."

I chug back my coffee, gobble down my croissant, and return to Simone for round two. She's happy to see me.

I'm gonna need a miracle to survive what's coming my way.

• • • •

SEEING AS I HAVE A uterus that has never been, and will never be, home to an unborn child, I completely underestimate the process of childbirth. My mom gets to the airport, takes a flight from an island in the Pacific to Southern California, and subsequently travels in a cab from said airport to the hospital, and Molly is still laboring.

It might be the first time I've ever felt true sympathy for her. The thought of those pains searing through my back, stomach, and tender insides makes me feel like I'm going to pass out. Poor Molly. And even more so with my mom by her side, no doubt narrating her every thought the entire time.

Maria is over the moon when I share the news, abundantly happy to disclose that she has extensive knowledge in managing three little ones from seeing her sister and two brothers raise their own large broods. It's at this moment my sympathy for Molly is doubled; why is the matter of raising children something everyone so publicly has to have, and loudly share, an opinion about?

With my morning ritual corrupted by my mom's panic, I opt to take Turkey and a few of the other pooches at PetCation out for a stroll as soon as I arrive at work. The walk does me good. I send Parker a text to let him know what's going on, and bitterly inform him that our weekend plans are most likely kiboshed by my mom's impromptu hotel stay in my tiny apartment.

With a clearer head, I give Turkey an extra scratch behind his ears and head back to the clinic. The day is in full swing. Maria and Michael are occupied at the front desk with a series of patient comings and goings, so I join Dr. Val in the back, surprised to see he's in today.

"Good to see you, Iris," he says as he scratches the gray stubble along his chin.

"You as well, Dr. Val. What can I do to help?" I ask, a little desperate for a distraction.

"We have a number of routine checkups today. I'll need rooms A-D cleaned and prepped, and if you could please give a call into Dr. Caroline confirming her arrival this afternoon. I would sincerely appreciate it."

"My pleasure," I nod, grateful for a running list of things to do.

"Oh, and Iris? In between that, do a routine disinfect of the cat kennels, would you?"

"Absolutely."

Stefanie is also in today, and the four of us techs are a dream team. Focused and productive, we slay the day. Off at five and still no word from Zach, I head back to my apartment. Time to clean the shit out of it before my mom comes to criticize my various *distasteful* life choices.

Halfway through vacuuming, my watch buzzes with a call from Parker. I eagerly yank my phone from its home in my tote bag and answer.

"Hi!" I sing.

"Hello, beautiful. You at the hospital?"

"No, I'm at home. Still no word from Zach. Mom's flight got in, though. I think she's at the hospital," I say tartly.

"Wow. Flying in for that. Dedication."

I roll my eyes. "She's so over-the-top. So, yeah. I guess this weekend I'll be holed up with my family. Which really sucks because I miss you so fucking much. Like, so fucking much. It hurts, actually." I rub my chest, feeling my heart beat under my skin. It's real - the ache.

"I miss you, too. I was really looking forward to hearing about your exploits yesterday."

Yesterday? That feels like a million years ago now. I take a breath as the memory of Wyatt pounding into me and the sweet taste of Sunny in my mouth comes back to me.

"It was a great time," I admit. "And they recorded it. So. You'll be able to watch it."

"Mm," Parker hums.

"You know, I don't see why you can't come over at least until I get the call from my brother. And to be honest, I'm not sure I'll survive if I don't see you all weekend."

Parker chuckles. "I'm not sure if I'd survive, either."

Forty-Six

A quarter past seven and still no word from Zach. I finish getting my apartment as clean as can be, which I know will still disappoint my mom in a million ways, but I come to terms with it. Parker calls me from the gate and I gallop down the stairs to let him in.

I'll never tire of the rush I get when I see him. All dark wash jeans, plain white tee, hair tousled just right. He's wearing his glasses, which I'm sure he put on just for me. The black of the frame makes the blue of his eyes dreamier than ever. I swoon.

"There you are," I breathe, reaching through the holes in the gate so our fingers touch. It sends a shock through my system. I might faint. "I was starting to question my sanity," I whisper. "I was thinking maybe I had just made you up."

"I was thinking the same about you. But here we are. Very real, it seems."

I pull the gate open and leap into him. Will those butterflies ever go away? I certainly hope not. We kiss, our lips joining in a way that it seems they were made to, every day, for the rest of forever. Parker hauls me into him, lifting me up. I wrap my legs and arms around him and fall into him. I run my fingers through his hair, grasping it in chunks, and scratching his scalp with my nails. His hands knead into my ass.

"I fucking love you," I breathe into him.

"I fucking love you," he echoes. "And I fucking love fucking you."

We need to get upstairs. Now.

I leap off of him and we run up to my apartment. Barely inside the threshold, as seems our ritual, we are on each other again. I run my hands against the thin fabric of Parker's tee and feel the lines of his chest under it. Our tongues dance together, swirling and twisting in a hypnotizing kiss. I reach for the firm cheek of his ass and squeeze it. I whimper as he grasps my throat in his hand, immobilizing me and flooding the apex of my thighs. We shuffle over to the couch and fall onto it in a heap.

Parker strips his clothes in record speed and, just as enthusiastically, makes quick work of mine. He pries my legs apart and thrusts into me, his mouth on my chest, his tongue on my nipples. He wraps his hand around my neck again. My arousal builds in the most agonizing way. I moan and wiggle, Parker's touch suspending me at the edge. He pulls himself out of me and licks my nub. I yelp, the pleasure surging through me with unimaginable intensity. Parker guides me around to the back of the couch and I bend over it. Cupping my breasts in his hands, he pounds into me again, sliding with ease into my slick slit. He bites the side of my neck and pinches my nipples in his fingers. I'm at the precipice, my climax taunting me in its closeness. I shut my eyes and drag my fingernails across Parker's naked ass. I whimper as I'm thrust into oblivion, my orgasm firing through me, the euphoria of it seeping from my pores. Parker grunts into me as he reaches his release, too, and we come together, our muscles sore and soft and infinitely satisfied.

Then there's a knock at the door. Several knocks, in fact. A soft, short knock, followed by several increasingly urgent knocks. And they don't stop.

"Fuck. Oh, my God. Oh, my God, I bet it's my mom. Shit!"

In frantic bewilderment, we layer our clothes back on. I push my finger to my mouth and signal for Parker to stay quiet. The problem isn't him, though. I fall back into the coffee table as I'm trying to pull my pants up and let out a loud grunt.

"Iris! Iris, honey! Are you in there? Let me in! Your poor mother, out here, after traveling all day, up at four in the morning, hours at the airport! What's the hold up? Let me in. Iris?"

I open the door to my mother's frenzied grimace.

"Ah! There you are. Finally, please, let me in. It's been a day, you can't imagine how exhausted I am. Thankfully Willie sweet-talked one of the pilots at the airport and was able to get me onto a flight at the last second, but the turbulence! Oh, my, well, it was just awful. Absolutely horrid. And of course I was stuck beside the dullest passenger on the plane I'm sure. She wouldn't utter a word to me, not for the entire flight! Five and a half hours of stark silence between us, it was *so* uncomfortable. I'm sure you can imagine. Then, when we land in L.A., of course it's nearing rush hour, so I'm stuck in traffic for over two hours to get down here. What torture that was, I really don't understand how anyone can ever commute such a distance, I'm telling you. At least the taxi driver was pleasant enough and made the journey a little more enjoyable. Anyway, I finally make it here at last, and of course I have the driver drop me off at the hospital, because I *need* to be there for Zach, and Molly, too, of course. But I get there, and they won't let me in! Can you believe that? The audacity! I'm the grandmother! I was ready to make a scene, I tell you. Zach came down and suggested I go see the girls, which I suppose was rather rude but I was glad to see my two granddaughters. Nora is getting so big! I can't believe how much she's grown in just the last few months! My heart! And Lily! Well, she's just turning into the most perfect little pumpkin. Of course Mary and James were there, though, watching the girls, so I couldn't very well stay and impose. So, James nicely offered to drive me to your apartment and, boom! Well, here I am!"

After months of distance from my mother, I had forgotten how incredibly overwhelming her energy is. She struts in, her pink suitcase trailing behind her, and falls into the softness of my couch. She doesn't notice Parker standing with me, or the smell of sex in the room. (Thank God). I breathe a moment and survey her. Her light brown hair is astray, her mouth is pursed in an unpleasant pout, her legs are crossed, her sweater is buttoned crooked. I reach inside myself for some compassion for her. If I could do it for Molly, I can do it for my mom.

"That is quite the day for sure, mom. Here. I made the bed fresh for you. Would you like to have a lay down? I'll stay by the phone and let you know as soon as I hear from Zach." In a trance, she stays silent. I gently touch her shoulder and she looks up at me. "Come lay down, mom." I guide her into my room, close the shutters, and tuck her into bed. She immediately shuts her eyes. To my astonishment, she doesn't utter another word.

"That was... a lot."

"Yeah, she is. She doesn't give up that easily," I laugh. "She must really be exhausted. She usually has a lot of fight in her."

"Do you want me to stay with you? Maybe until you hear from your brother? Or should I give you and your mom some space?"

I stare into Parker and lick my lips. "Parker, no world exists where I don't want you by my side for everything. Please, stay."

"As you wish."

"Very *Princess Bride* of you," I laugh, my cheeks red with lust.

We snuggle up on the couch, order takeout, and turn on an old black-and-white.

Forty-Seven

Felicity Jane Gladwell: born 20:52, Friday, August 4, 2023. 7lbs, 3oz, 21" long. Red hair, brown eyes. Her mother's mouth, her father's nose. Welcome, baby Felicity.

There's something intoxicating about the impossibly soft skin, distinct baby scent, and quiet calmness of a newborn. As I hold baby Felicity in my arms, wrapped in a pink-and-blue receiving blanket, all my worries melt away. There's just now. The present. Her tiny inhales and exhales, the little twitches of her mouth. She's so small and precious and completely magical.

"She's beautiful. Congratulations, you two."

"Thank you, Iris," Molly beams, looking still infuriatingly perfect, despite over fourteen hours in labor.

"She looks like dad, don't you think?" I suggest to Zach. He nods, a tear escaping his eye. "He'd be so proud of you. Look at this perfect family you've created. Look at this perfect baby you made!" My eyes burn. I sniff it back.

"You don't know how much that means to me," he gulps, letting out little sobs.

Parker looks on at us, caught between the inside and outside. He wraps his arm around my hip and kisses my cheek.

"If you ask me, I think she looks an awful lot like her Auntie," he whispers into my ear.

Moments later, mom scoops the sleeping bundle from my arms. She sings *Twinkle Twinkle Little Star* and bounces her around, petting the soft cheeks of Felicity's fresh skin. Despite all the drama with my mom, I will never deny that she is the absolute best with babies.

Molly's parents, Mary and James, are bringing the girls to the hospital in the afternoon, and Nora and Lily will meet their new baby sister. Mom can't wait to snap a family picture of Zach's brood all together, which she says will be the new background image on her iPhone.

"Such an exciting time!" my mom says on repeat.

Zach assures mom that he has plenty of space at their house for her, and thankfully she makes the reasonable decision to stay with them. While

I loved sleeping with Parker last night, I didn't like the neck pain I woke up to from being contorted on the couch. I could cry I'm so relieved.

Having our fill of traditionalism, Parker and I make a quick exit.

We still have today. Tonight. Together.

Parker is generous in playing taxi and shuttles me around while I pick up some pink and white flowers for the once-again parents. We stop off at my apartment and I eagerly load up my mom's suitcase into the back of Parker's truck. With joy, we relocate the luggage and the flowers to their new home at Zach and Molly's.

The unbelievable chaos of the last 24 hours is at last behind us. Now, it's just us again.

Me. Parker. Us.

Forty-Eight

Wild sex is one thing, but it's the little sprinklings of adoration that solidify the love Parker has for me. Like how he just knew that Urban Grind was the first place we needed to go after visiting the hospital. Or how he sneakily picked up a little bouquet of lilies from the flower shop while I was distracted asking the shopkeeper which bouquet was appropriate for the third-time parents of a perfect family that has it all. Or how he shoved a little note into the pocket of my jeans before he left on Sunday morning, knowing I wouldn't find it until I did laundry that evening.

Iris,
There are countless things I love about you.
But I'm a numbers guy, so I'll count. Let's start with 10.

1. The way your bangs are always a mess.
2. The look you get in your eyes when you see me.
3. How your mouth gapes open when you come.
4. Your love for animals.
5. The feel of your heart beating in your chest after we fuck.
6. The fact that you're an active member of a weekly book club. My beautiful dork.
7. How hard you love.
8. The noises you make when you eat. Food. Dick. Pussy.
9. The pride you have in who you are.
10. The smell of your skin.

I love you.
x Parker

My heart explodes into a million pieces. My eyes burn with salty wetness as they study the words again and again. I half hate him for leaving this note for me to find in his absence. He knew full well it would make me miss him even more than I already do. It's a knife straight into the most tender part of my heart. My throat tightens and I start to cry. There's no stopping it. Like the roar of a waterfall, the tears come. Loud, sharp sobs echo off the walls. My ears go numb. My brain is a blanket of blackness, heavy and clouded.

Parker is the love of my life. I'm so in love with him, it hurts.

The tears march down my cheeks and fall onto the pile of clothes in my lap. They erupt like lava, spewing from the depths of my insides. I welcome them and allow myself to feel all of it: my love for Parker, my gratitude for him, the acute loneliness that plagues me when we're apart.

In the emotional chaos of it, I make a choice: I'm all in. Parker is the one for me. Our Family is my future. I am going to live a life true to who I am.

It begins now.

Forty-Nine

F elicity is perfect, fitting in just where she belongs. Zach and Molly can proudly proclaim that they have the perfect little family. And I'm not salty about it. Because what Parker and I have is perfect to me.

And I belong in a different type of family.

Through my emotional meltdown, I have navigated the waters of my insecurity surrounding Parker's schedule and come to terms with it. What I have with Parker is special. Sacred. I soak in our moments together, basking in its unequivocal perfection. As for when we're apart, well... I have fortunately found myself as a Member in an organization that specializes in filling that void.

As anticipated following my first Mixer, Our Leaflet has officially been unlocked for me. In the rush that was gaining access to the Recordings, participating in my exchange with Sunny and Wyatt, and the subsequent the birth of my third niece, my time and attention has been otherwise engaged.

I make a date with myself to browse through Our Leaflet tonight.

I feel incredible this morning. All my worries and uncertainties have been shed away. Sometimes, the best healing is done in a river of salty tears. I look ahead, eager to dedicate myself to Our Family and make the most of my membership. I can't wait to explore Our Leaflet. Even before I've had my caffeine fix, I'm a shaky ball of energy. I skip across the street and over to Urban Grind earlier than usual, catching my coffee crew off guard.

"I've never seen you so bouncy pre-Americano," Simone jokes. "What's the deal?" She raises her eyebrow, studying the glow of my skin and my stupid smirk.

"Oh, you know!" I shout. *True love. Non-monogamy. Just living the dream!* "Monday. A new week! Fresh start!"

"Uh, huh," Simone rolls her eyes.

Fifteen minutes earlier than usual, I'm settled at the river, coffee in one hand, book in the other. I take a sweet sip of my drink and smile. It's going to be a great day.

• • • •

DR. VAL IS IN A MOOD. I'm not sure what I did, but he is not pleased with me today. He's come in for only an hour this morning, but for the entire time he's here, he's either avoiding me, giving me disapproving looks, or speaking to me with harsh disappointment in his voice. In all the years I've worked for him, he's never treated me this way. I try not to take it personally; perhaps he's having a bad moment, or a bad day. But it *does* feel personal.

"Does Dr. Val seem off today, or is it just me?" I ask Maria, seeking validation.

"He's been fine with me. Why, what did he say?" Maria wiggles in close to me, her body language begging for workplace drama.

"Nothing specifically," I admit. "It's just... I don't know. He's been kind of short with me. He brushed me off like I didn't know what I was doing when I was inputting data into the system in the back. It was just really weird. And he just looks mad at me. Like, his stare. He's intense and seems angry. Did I make a mistake somewhere? In the scheduling, or paperwork?"

"I don't think so. Not that I've caught. Maybe he's going through stuff with the wife. You know, we've never seen her. She's never come in here. Maybe he's going through a divorce? Or something with his extended family?" And so goes the rumor mill.

Despite the many plausible reasons for his mood, I can't shake it. It stays with me for the rest of the day, even after he leaves and Dr. Vincent takes over the duties of the clinic. Desperate to repent, I stay late, clean the cat kennels, and take Turkey for an extended walk.

My mom leaves a lengthy voicemail on my phone inviting me to Zach's tomorrow night for dinner. She insists she's making a quite the spread and it's only the second day that Felicity will be home so it will be such a special time for us all to be reunited as we welcome the new addition to the family and there's nothing more important than family and how fortunate Willie was able to fly in last night and he's just over the moon to meet his new granddaughter and oh she's just so glad she can cook a homemade meal for us all to enjoy together and wow how lucky we all are and she can't wait to see me then.

Of course tomorrow is Tuesday. It's always a Tuesday. I send Parker a quick text asking if he would accompany me to family dinner. Even though I have to make an appearance at this reunion charade, at least Parker and I will have later in the evening together. Just us two.

I pick up a rice bowl on the way home and scarf it down in a hurry. I check my watch: 7:02 p.m. If I'm going to make it to book club, I have to leave now. I'll have missed Maisie; our discussion of the lurid book will have to wait until another time. I hesitate for a moment, contemplating skipping out on book club, but end up throwing on my converse and dashing out the door. I need the distraction. The walk to the library isn't the nicest - I have to pass several busy intersections that bring with them a lot of noise, traffic, and waiting. I also pass the skateboarding park, which is obnoxiously loud. I pop in my earbuds and choose an energetic EDM station on Spotify. I zone out and focus on putting one foot in front of the other.

I get to the library just on time. Gemma is settling into her chair alongside Nancy and Olga. A couple of new faces are visible, too. A welcome change. I pull my book out of my tote bag, ready to dive in.

It probably helps that this week's book was a good one, with lots of suspense, red herrings, and more than a handful of probable suspects, but our book club meeting is surprisingly great. We have a compelling group discussion on the motivations of the various characters, as well as an in-depth analysis of the victim's character development as told through a series of flashbacks. Our meeting stretches beyond the designated hour, and I find myself still with more to say and an ear for more to absorb. Driven by a strict routine, Olga leaves at exactly 8:30 p.m., but the rest of us remain and give our opinions on why the setting was significant to the story. I'm nerding out so hard, but it's intellectual porn to me. I can't get enough of discussing this book. Gemma suggests we read another by the same author in a couple of weeks, and as a group we unanimously agree.

I don't get home until close to 10 p.m., but I feel wired from all the brain stim. I pull out my phone to see a reply from Parker, agreeing to subject himself to dinner with my family in exchange for hot sex. (My terms, not his.) I reply to my mom's thirteen messages and confirm that yes, I will be there tomorrow, and yes, Parker will be with me. The last message I have is from Ben.

BEN
Iris, my Queen
I'm honored to extend to you this invitation
to accompany me to Shahara's wedding next week
Please be my plus one!
Kai can't make it wahhhhhhhhh
Traverse Golf Course, 4 p.m. next Saturday the 19th

I start to type out a reply, then stop myself. I open my calendar and check my schedule for next weekend. Nothing. Empty. I should be good to go, but I decide to open my Our Family Calendar first just to double check the August Mixer dates.

My phone rings.

"Hi, mom," I answer.

"Hi, sweetie! Oh, I'm so glad you answered! I've called you at least half a dozen times today. And I sent you a ton of messages, too."

"I know, but I was working, then had book club at the library."

"Yes, of course, but I'm sure you've looked at your phone at least once today to see I've been trying to get a hold of you!"

"I did, mom, and I texted you back just now. I'll be there tomorrow. Parker can come, too."

"Wonderful! Oh, that's just so great. You know, today was the first day that Cici has been home, and I have to tell you that Molly is just the most natural mother! They've fallen into a routine already, nursing, tummy time, napping. And the girls are just head-over-heels in love with their new little sister! It's such a joy to see! And they keep asking for you, Auntie Iris. Tomorrow will be so great, all of us together!"

"Yeah, looking forward to it, mom. See you tomorrow."

"Alright, see you tomorrow. Oh! And if you wouldn't mind, could you pick up some dinner rolls and a bottle of that bubbly juice, what is it, Martinelli's? For the girls. We're going to do a little toast to celebrate their growing family! Oh, it's just so wonderful!"

"No problem. I'll grab that before I head over. See you tomorrow."

"I'll let you know if there's anything else I need. Okay, tomorrow, then. I love you, Iris!"

"Love you, too, mom. Bye."

"Bye, honey!"

As I hang up, I hear a rustling noise at the front door. I walk over to it, surprised to see a familiar black envelope has been pushed under the door. I pick it up, my heart jumping in my chest. I fall onto the couch and rip across the Our Family golden tree emblem.

Iris Gladwell - Notice of Consequence

Offense #1
Date of Offense: Thursday, August 3, 2023
Time of Offense: Approx. 7 p.m.
Violation Category: External Confidentiality Breach
Description: The Our Family app was opened in a public space (inside of an Uber vehicle) and a message was both sent and received through the app within this public space.
Degree: Minor
Consequence: Access to the OF app is a privilege; remove this privilege for a time period of (4) days; access suspended Monday, August 7, through Thursday, August 10, inclusive
Approved by: Desi Harold, Parker Douglas

My heart falls into my feet. I'm an idiot. Fucking stupid. I opened the app to message Sunny that I was on my way. In the Uber. Like a dumb dumb. I can't believe I was so careless. Not even a month in and I'm already receiving my first Consequence? My disappointment in myself drops into my stomach and churns. I read the note card again. My access to the app is suspended for four days, which means not only can I not check the Calendar and get back to Ben about the wedding next weekend, but I also cannot search through Our Leaflet. The feeling of defeat builds, burning in the back of my throat.

What a day this has turned into.

Fifty

The following is no better. Maybe I'm in my head about it too much, but being cut off from Our Family rolls through me like poison. My desperation to do better, be better, and earn my place back in the good graces of Our Family festers inside me. Even Parker seems distant.

I message Ben back and confirm I will be his plus one next weekend, regardless of what I have scheduled. It means missing out on precious time with Parker, but Ben is my greatest friend. And our time together is limited even more so than mine with Parker. Besides, I'll still have Saturday night after the wedding - and nothing fuels my sex drive like experiencing a night worshiping the confines of monogamy.

Dr. Caroline is in today, and my focus is on scheduling for September and October. I make it over to see Turkey for a quick cuddle, too. Stefanie comments on our budding relationship, and my immediate response is to take a break from our daily visits. His proper pet parents are coming back from their month-long trip to Greece at the end of next week, and I am, admittedly, growing attached. I'm not sure I can handle the heartbreak.

I change into a casual, floral summer dress as soon as I get home and layer a pretty yellow and white apron over it. I cut up some fruit I picked up at the grocery store on the way home and plop it into a large pitcher. I'm attempting to make a homemade sangria. I flick at my phone screen, closing the various pop ups and swearing more than once as I struggle to get a solid screen cap of the recipe. The sweet, summery smell of oranges and apples soon fills the kitchen. I pop open the bottle of red I'm doctoring and let it sit.

Parker messages that he's at the gate, and I dash down to let him in. I can't wait to see him. Those beautiful blues. His hair all a mess. The outlines of his chest under his shirt. But even more than that, I can't wait to hear his voice. The comfort of it. The warmth. The edge of mockery for my stupid mistake. I'm so hungry for it, I might burst.

I hop down the stairs, but he's not there. I open the gate and check on either side of the building. Where is he? I turn back towards the gate and there he is: standing tall, just within it, those blue eyes and gray suit jacket tearing me apart. I leap onto him, my tummy doing somersaults and my head exploding with lust. I wrap my legs around his waist and my arms around his neck.

"I fucking missed you so much," I breathe into his skin. He smells incredible, an intoxicating blend of cedar and mint. I feel drunk on it.

"I missed you," he says pointedly. "But, you're in trouble." Parker drops me down in front of him. My stomach flips.

"I-I-I know," I stutter shamefully. "I'm so sorry. I feel like an idiot for fucking that up. Already."

"We are so disappointed in you, Iris."

We. It stings. It stings like salt on an open wound.

"We expect better from you." There's that edge to his voice. That dark, deepness that he brings out when we play. I lean into it, blending reality and our game together. He twists a lock of my hair around his finger and watches me beneath the edge of his nose. I look up to him, big-eyed and desperate.

"I know. I'm so sorry. I know I deserve my Consequence," I pause. I readjust my gaze to my feet. "I also deserve a punishment. I'm sorry for my mistake, I know I shouldn't have done that, and I am ready to face the repercussions."

He likes that.

"Upstairs, now."

I do as told and trot back up the stairs and into my apartment. Parker follows close behind, his smell still lingering in my nostrils.

I stand in the doorway. He approaches me and pushes me with a single finger backwards into the room. He directs me into the kitchen, then walks around to the other side of the counter.

"What are you making?" he asks, as if the sexual tension between us isn't the most important thing in the universe right now.

"Uh," I look at him quizzically. "I was making sangria. To take over to Zach's."

"Finish it."

Parker watches me intently while I struggle to manifest my inner chef and chop up an apple without losing a finger in the process. I manage, but not without feeling like a complete moron. My brain isn't thinking about slicing apples. It's thinking about naked Parker, and his tongue on my pussy.

"We have to get going. Finish up."

Get going? What about the super-hot sex we've been having in my head?

We load the sangria, dinner rolls, and a bottle of apple cran Martinelli's into Parker's truck. Still, nothing. No kissing, no touching.

"What the fuck is going on?" I blurt out.

"What do you mean?"

"What do I mean? I *mean* we haven't seen each other in days, and somehow you have the audacity to hold out on me like this?"

"Yep."

"Yep?" I practically screech.

"Your punishment. But don't worry, it hurts me just as much as you. I do feel somewhat responsible for not *drilling* the rules into you a little *harder*." He smirks. I try to ignore the flood of want between my legs. "Next time I fuck you, you can tell me a running list of the places that are appropriate for you to open the app."

I scoff.

Parker wins this one.

· · · ·

WE PULL UP TO ZACH'S house, and my mom just about bursts into tears at the lot of us all being together again, reunited by sweet baby Felicity. Parker helps me carry our contributions to dinner inside, and I immediately pour us each a glass of the fruits of my literal labor. It's not the worst. It takes the edge off, which is all I really care about right now.

Zach and Molly live in the nicest part of the Vista Loma, with just one house situated on a plot of land where four houses are everywhere else. They have an obscenely large backyard with a pool (gated off for the safety of the littles, of course), a wooden play structure with swings and slides, and a fruit tree orchard. Inside, they have five bedrooms upstairs, several bathrooms, and a playroom bursting with all the stuffed toys, Duplo bricks, Magna-Tiles, dolls, and cars that a child could dream of. Their main floor is open with impossibly high ceilings. An ornate dark wood kitchen and generous dining area flow freely toward the floor-to-ceiling windows overlooking the backyard. There's yet another bedroom-and-bathroom combo downstairs. And the girls have a second playroom next to the living room, because of course they do. Their home is the picture of the suburban American dream.

Despite the long labor, Molly is radiant in her new-mom glow. She's nursing Cici, who already looks so much bigger than she did at the hospital just a few days ago. As I look down at her against the pale skin of Molly's chest, her hair is undeniably red. I smile, my mind flashing with images of Dad and his charming, contagious grin.

Zach looks exhausted but full of joy, with Lily climbing on his back while Nora snuggles in his lap. She's nibbling a pre-dinner cookie that Willard snuck over to her, no doubt trying to win her favor.

While my initial instinct is to find my place beside Remi out on the back porch, I couldn't live with the guilt of leaving Parker to fend for himself inside. I reach down and give the pooch several enthusiastic scratches before returning indoors. I help my mom in the kitchen, which mainly consists of her barking orders and me trying with everything in me not to fuck them up. I'm not much of a cook, and the last thing I need is my mom reminding me of yet another of my shortcomings. Parker steps up and offers to help wash and peel potatoes or mix the salad, and despite my mom's instinct to decline his help, she is still exhausted from the events of the past days and allows him to lend a hand. He takes my side and together, we prepare dinner as a team.

Molly disappears with Felicity, putting her to bed for the night, and Zach wrangles the girls over to take their seats at the table. Willard and I take our places, too, and Parker assists my mom in bringing out the dishes and setting them on Zach's expansive, reclaimed wood dining room table.

It's an absolute feast, with fresh Caesar salad, roasted whole chicken, mashed potatoes, gravy, peas and carrots, and even ambrosia. Lily lights up at the sight of "murshmurloo slad!" and Zach scoops a generous portion onto her plate. Willard once again leads the family in grace, and I'm reminded of Lily's comedic outburst last time we were all together. I chuckle in my throat.

Parker charms the crap out of mom and Willard, and I'm beyond grateful for it. He keeps the focus off of me and manages to answer all of their annoying little questions and quips with a smile painted on his face. I run my fingers along his inner thigh to express my appreciation, but he shoves my hand away.

Parker is very intent on punishing me.

Molly sits with us briefly, but excuses herself to pump, and Zach suggests it's time to put Lily and Nora to bed. I give each of the girls a big hug and kiss and tell them to have sweet dreams. Turning to Zach, I give him a proud smile. I squeeze him tight, pulling his body into mine, feeling that special bond between the two of us that connects our souls in an inexplicable way.

"You did good," I whisper in his ear. "Making these babies. Building this life for yourself. And Molly."

"Thanks, Iris," Zach mutters, emotion in his voice.

"I mean it. I'm really proud of you."

"You should be proud of yourself, too," Zach snaps back. "You're really hard on yourself, you know? You have a lot to be proud of. Look at your life. It's beautiful."

I'm sure I'm going to cry.

My mom beats me to it. She's howling, making a whole show of her tears, sobbing loudly as Willard rubs her back. He looks profoundly displeased, and I can't help but like him a little more for it.

"Don't be a stranger, okay?" Zach says, breaking our embrace. "You're welcome here anytime." Mom squeals into the air. "Maybe wait until after she goes back to Hawaii, though," Zach laughs, and I get a serious case of the giggles.

Zach, Ben, Parker. I have the most amazing men in my life.

Fifty-One

The first thing I do when I wake up on Friday is open the Our Family app. Four days has never felt so long. My access is now restored, and I immediately check the Calendar for next weekend. Thankfully, my memory served, and the August Mixer isn't until the following weekend, which means I can freely accompany Ben to the wedding without a scheduling conflict. I notice a red dot over my messages, so I click there next and open them one by one.

> Dearest Iris,
>
> Welcome back. We've missed you. Please take the time to ensure all missed communications are read and all outstanding items are attended to. It's my responsibility to ensure the rules of Our Family are upheld at all costs; therefore, we hope that your first violation is also your last.
>
> Truly yours,
> Desi Harold
> Our Family, Head of Branch 29

It stings. Desi's disappointment emanates from the message and my guilt is doubled. I try to shake it off, fully aware I can't undo the past, and my only control is over my choices moving forward. The next message is from Mallory, sent on Monday.

> Good morning, Iris!
>
> Hope your week is off to a good start! It's my pleasure to send you the invitation to Our September Mixer. Save the date! In October, we will be participating in an Inter-Branch Mixer with several other Branches for Our Family's Annual Masquerade Ball. Keep an eye out for that invite coming soon. As a reminder, Our August Mixer will be held in a couple of weeks, on August 26.
>
> We are very much looking forward to seeing you at all of Our upcoming events!
>
> Much love,
> Mallory xx
> PS: I've added these dates to your Calendar as well.

<u>**B29 Mixer Event - September**</u>
Please join us for Our September Mixer,
Saturday, September 23 - Sunday, September 24
6 p.m. - 11 a.m.
At the Harold Estate
We look forward to the time with you.

Truly yours,
Desi Harold
Our Family, Head of Branch 29

A stupid grin immediately spreads across my face. The thought of meeting even more like-minded Members and mixing with other Branches is wildly exciting. And a Masquerade - I do love dressing up.

There's also a message from Sunny informing me that our Recording is up, and the sting of being deprived of inclusion in Our Family for the last four days is swept away in a wave of heat. My ears burn as I consider my time with Sunny and Wyatt, seemingly ages ago, and I blush in the knowledge that Our entire Branch can experience it. It feels outrageously promiscuous, but I can't help the rush I get from it. We did put on quite the show.

I immediately click on Recordings and, to my surprise, have to scroll past several others to find ours. Sunny, Wyatt, and I are not the only ones since July's event who have mixed and simultaneously recorded the interaction for Our collective enjoyment. There are three other Recordings. I have to watch them all – the curiosity of who and where is almost too much to take. But my watch buzzes with a secondary alarm to inform me I need to get a move on. I reluctantly close the app, acutely aware that there is still so much I don't know.

In the shower, I can't help but fantasize about who mixed with who. My mind wanders, creating Pairings and scenes I can only hope aren't a stretch from the truth. I imagine Bea and Riley pairing with Mallory and Davis, their bodies a blur of heat and stimulation. Bea pushes Davis down onto the cold stone of the floor beneath them with her foot, and he crouches at her mercy. She demands he prove himself worthy of her time and attention and thrusts her big toe into his mouth. Davis rises to the occasion, his erection growing as he worships each of Bea's perfectly manicured toes. Meanwhile, Mallory is spreadeagled on a plush, pink rug with Riley's face between her legs. She wiggles and shakes as Riley plunges his fingers into her pussy and swirls his tongue along her nub.

With my eyes closed, I stroke at my own folds, the scene playing in my mind. My skin breaks out in goosebumps as the heat of my body mixes with the water streaming from the showerhead above me. Lightheaded, I lean into the pleasure. I pant loudly, feeling the buildup at my center. I wail out, my fingers moving faster and faster. I mount the large dildo I have suction cupped to my shower wall and bounce on it. It fills and empties me at a rhythmic pace. My fingers continue to work against my clit, while my mind focuses on my imagined scene. I picture the euphoric faces of Bea, Davis, Mallory, and Riley, and my ears fill with their distinct, carnal sounds of pleasure. Riley wraps his hand around Mallory's throat as she nears her climax. At last, Bea has allowed Davis to stand, and he thrusts greedily into her folds. I scream out, my insides throbbing as I come, the surge of warmth and pleasure overcoming us all.

At this rate, I'm going to be rushed getting to work. I try to focus on shampooing my hair and shaving my legs, but my thoughts keep regressing.

I really am insatiable.

At last, I emerge from the shower, my skin warm inside and out. I throw on my scrubs, choosing a summery, bright floral top and plain black bottoms. In an effort to keep from getting completely lost in my own thoughts, I consider the day ahead. Fridays are typically pretty light on appointments. Dr. Val usually ensures we have lots of openings as there tends to be an influx of pre-weekend emergencies.

Simone, as wonderfully predictable as ever, has my drink ready promptly at 7:30 a.m., but given my indulgent shower, I'm a little later than usual. I still manage to snag a few minutes at the river and dive right into a new, smutty read. It gets spicy just as my watch buzzes, killing the mood for the second time this morning.

Dr. Amar is running the show today, and he's in a surprisingly good mood. I think back to Dr. Val on Monday, and wonder if I've jumped into some alternate universe where the two docs have switched temperaments. Dr. Amar keeps us busy despite the general lack of appointments, and Stefanie steps in to defend Maria when a client screams at her about pet insurance coverage and *what a scam this place is.*

I don't take Turkey for a walk. It makes me deeply sad. My heart shatters in two as I grapple with the remorse of getting too close to him and the deep regret of staying too far away.

The moment I set foot inside my apartment after work, I open the Our Family app. There's a new message from Desi waiting for me.

Dearest Iris,

I apologize for my error in excluding important information in Our last communication. After a Consequence has been issued and subsequently executed, the violating individual must submit a Violation Acknowledgment Form. Please complete and submit the VAF as soon as possible. Thank you.

Truly yours,
Desi Harold
Our Family - Head of Branch 29

They are really raking me over the coals on this. I've learned my lesson in abundance, but if they need me to sign a form to make it official, I'm more than happy to. Whatever it takes to make the bitter taste fade. I click on the linked form in Desi's message, scroll to the bottom, and swipe my finger across my phone to sign and date it. Done. I am absolved.

With that behind me, I eagerly click back into the Recordings portion of the app. Which to watch first? I decide to indulge in mine.

I'll never get used to watching myself. It's almost an out of body experience, seeing the look in my eyes, hearing the sounds I make, feeling the rush of endorphins all over again. Wyatt is intense, Sunny is gentle, and I fit somewhere in between the two of them. I wonder, as I watch myself eating Sunny's pussy, if Parker has seen the footage? I bite my lip. I really, really hope he has.

The next Recording is also of Sunny and Wyatt, but they are with two other individuals I don't recognize. They must be other Members from within Our Family, I assume, because of the exclusivity clause in the Rulebook. Seeing two fresh faces makes the entire thing seem so much more real - like it extends beyond my realm of comprehension.

Our Leaflet. How could I let it slip my mind? I still have that to explore. Is that where Sunny and Wyatt sourced the partners for their exchange?

Questions flood my brain. Having put off looking at Our Leaflet for long enough, I close the video and switch back to Communications.

There it is. Just as Parker had said, beside the inbox tab, there's a little leaf icon. I tap my finger on it, and a new folder pops up.

Welcome to Our Leaflet - Our Family's Member Directory
Manage Profile
Browse
Search
Options

Most of my information is already filled out in my profile, including my name (Iris G.), age (32), gender identity (F), and sexual preferences (M & F). I have to custom upload my own photo, which I select from an existing one in my photo library - a selfie I took by the river a few weeks ago. There's a form that allows me to input my *Exchange Availability*, and I grow giddy as I fill in the schedule for when I'm free to hookup.

The most excitement, though, comes from browsing Our Leaflet itself. There are hundreds of Members - more than I ever dreamed possible. The list is seemingly endless. I flick my finger and continue to scroll down, down, down. Not everyone has an official profile set up, I notice. The bold names have accounts with additional information, whereas those not bold, don't. I scroll all the way down to the P's and find *Parker D.* To my surprise, he doesn't have a profile set up. Parker's been a Member for almost a decade now; I'm shocked he doesn't make use of this resource. At the same time, though, he barely has time for me, work, and Branch 29. I guess it checks out.

In the interest of confidentiality (I read in my head in a posh, strict voice), there are no last names, just initials. There are two other Irises - Iris T. and Iris M. Parker is the only Parker, Desi is the only Desi, although there is one other Desiree. Desi does have a profile, as does Marc, Mallory, Davis, Sunny, Wyatt, Thom, Julia, and Scarlett.

I try out the advanced search feature and look for a match that lines up according to my own availability. I'm shocked when a running list of names pops up. There are probably close to fifty people, if not more, who are equally in need of sexual fulfillment on a lonely Wednesday or Thursday evening. My mouth gapes open as I scroll through the results, taking in the possibilities.

A text flies in from Parker, snapping me back into the present.

PARKER
Heading to you in 15.
Suggestions on what I should pick up for eats?

I quickly type back.

ME
It's definitely a pizza kind of night.
Veggie with pineapple - don't argue.
Pineapples are totally allowed on pizza.
Especially upside down...!

Parker's pity laugh rings in my ears. I put my phone away (despite the nagging temptation to spend hours entertaining the possibilities within Our Leaflet) and get changed out of my scrubs. I dig through my lingerie, select something special for tonight, and place it delicately on the top of my clean laundry pile. In my bedside drawer, I find exactly what I have in mind.

Tonight is going to be fun.

Fifty-Two

The smell of fresh pizza - tomato sauce, roasted veggies, and melted cheese - wafts through my apartment. I'm ravenous, and not just for the food. I pounce on Parker and give him a deep, intense kiss. He grabs my ass in his hands and moans into me.

"Fucking finally," I mutter into him. I respect Our Family and my Consequence, but it seemed double, given I was disallowed access from the app as well as denied affection from the man of my dreams. "I was beginning to think we'd never kiss again."

"I would sooner die," Parker declares, devouring my mouth with his tongue.

The pizza sits on my kitchen counter, cooling with each passing second, while the temperature between me and Parker rises. I whine against him, my desperation for his touch finally abetted. We push into each other, and Parker runs his fingertips along my cheek and down my neck. With a firm grip around my throat, he shoves me back against the wall. Pinning me in place, I pant as a rush of wetness surges between my legs. I want him. Oh, fuck, do I want him.

Parker holds my neck firmly in place with his hand outstretched. He takes a step back and studies me, his eyes taking me in from head to toe. I hold my breath to stay still, but inside, I'm screaming. I want my hands on him, his hands on me. I want to kiss his skin, feel his body, suck his cock. I want him on me, in me, beside me. I want Parker, all of him, us together, always.

Torture is his specialty. As though he can read my mind, he holds me there, testing my resolve to remain still. Every second chips away at it, the bright, severe blueness of Parker's eyes shattering me into pieces. I reach for him, but he pushes me back, tightening his grip around my throat. I cough, my air restricted.

"So impatient."

I close my eyes. When I reopen them, my body is calm and my breathing slow, steady. Pleased, Parker's arm falls to his side. The space between us feels like a chasm, huge and unrelenting.

The wait is pure agony.

At last, Parker closes it and pulls me in for a big bear hug. His arms swallow me up and I melt into him. The air of sensuality shifts. The passion is replaced with warmth, the seduction with adoration. It's pure love.

I breathe him in, his scent snaking into my nostrils and curling around my brain. I dig my face into his chest and listen to his heartbeat. It thuds beneath his skin and sings in my ear. I smile and squeeze him closer.

"I love you, Iris."

"I love you, Parker."

We eventually attend to the pizza, gorging ourselves on the comfort of it. My mind flickers to the surprise I have planned for Parker in the bedroom, but I decide it can wait until later. Instead, we spend most of the night just *being* together. It feels intimate in a different way, and I savor it.

I don't realize how exhausted I am until I feel myself falling asleep on Parker's chest, his heartbeat lulling me off to la la land. Sensing my drowsiness, Parker guides me into my bedroom and we tuck in, our legs and arms laced together, our noses touching. I'm asleep seconds later.

• • • •

WAKING UP NEXT TO PARKER is my number two most favorite feeling in the world. (Number one is falling asleep next to him.) I want to throw up at my sentimentality, but Parker has entrenched himself deep in my soul. He's found his home there, and it's hopeless to fight it. I'm pathetically lovesick.

Today might be the best day we've ever spent together. The entire day feels like a delusion. Nothing more than my overactive imagination hard at work. But it's real - all of it. All of the sex, the skin, the arousal, the love. We spend the entire day in my apartment. We fuck in every corner and on every surface. We talk about nothing and everything. We exist as each of us and as one. It's disgustingly perfect.

• • • •

ON SUNDAY, I GRAB THE supplies I prepared on Friday night. Time for us to get kinky. It takes some work to slip on the panties I selected - with five straps wrapping around my hips and meeting at a center O-ring in both the front and back, they easily tangle in my hands. I'm not sure I've worn crotchless panties for Parker before. I lick my lips. Successfully pulling them on, I admire myself in my closet mirror. Perfect. I'll need his help with the rest.

"Get in here," I call to him. He appears in the doorway and leans against it, studying me. He pushes his glasses up his nose and wolf-whistles.

"Hot damn."

"There are rules," I start.

"I'm *very* good at rules," Parker replies.

"Take this." I toss a heavy bag over to him. He nearly drops it. Reaching inside, he reveals a thick bundle of bondage rope. His eyes light up.

"Hello, old friend," Parker says. His fingers stroke against the fibers of the rope. He begins to pull it out, wrapping it around his fists and fingers. My eyes widen, already coming undone at the seductive sight of Parker wielding the rope in his hands.

I clear my throat. "I have a video of a chest harness I want to try. It's here, on my phone. But!" I shout, as he starts to approach, "you don't get to touch me. Well, I mean, you have to touch me to tie it, but NO copping a feel." It's a warning for him as much as it is for me. If he does touch me, I'm not sure I have the wherewithal to stop him.

"Alright," Parker bites his bottom lip. "I'll try to behave."

I have to stop myself from panting already.

I stand before him, a mannequin in need of erotic dressing. With the help of YouTube and his natural rope-wielding talents, Parker wraps my chest. Made of natural hemp, the rope's abrasive texture scrapes against my skin. The sting travels through me and teases my center. My eyes watch Parker in his craft in the mirrors of my closet doors. His eyes are focused and intense. I breathe deeply to keep my arousal at bay as he tightens the rope around me and twists it between my breasts. My tender, sensitive skin responds to his every movement, and when his fingers graze the edge of my neck, I feel like I'm going to pass out. I blink rapidly and my eyes catch the outline of Parker's cock as it strains against the fabric of his pants. I close my eyes and imagine him plunging into me while the rope rubs into my skin. I almost come from the vision alone.

Parker ties off the end of the rope before I faint. Or orgasm. Or both. He stands beside me, and we admire his work in the mirror. Between the chest harness showcasing my ample breasts and the crotchless panties that are doing nothing to contain the drips of pleasure emerging from my pussy, I look incredible.

"How does it feel?" Parker asks, running his fingertips against the harsh material of the rope.

"Fucking amazing."

I pull Parker into me and leave a wet mark against his left thigh. The passion between us is thick and heavy.

"Wait!" I yell, more to myself than to him. "One more thing." From my bedside drawer, I pull out a thick leather strap with a D-ring at the center and a metal buckle at the back. "Help me put it around my neck?" Parker smiles broadly and wraps it below my jawline.

"Don't mind if I grab an extra piece of rope for this, do you?" he tells more than asks.

Using an impressive tie, Parker attaches a short rope to the D-ring around my neck. He yanks on it to pull me into him. I yelp, and my body falls into him. Foreplay is definitely my hottest aphrodisiac.

"You look so fuckable." Parker moans into my mouth.

He yanks the rope down, and I fall to my knees. He unbuckles his belt and I reach into his pants to release his aching cock. Swollen and erect, it bounces free. I open my mouth and take it in, the sweet taste of it overwhelming my senses. Parker gently thrusts as I lick his length, finding my rhythm. He chokes up on the rope and pulls me into him, forcing himself deeper into my throat. I loosen my jaw to let him in; he grunts and moans. My special talents are forever pleasing to him. He pulls and releases the rope, directing me for his pleasure, while the leather of the collar rubs into my skin. Softer than the rope, it still digs in, only heightening the agonizing buildup.

Parker pulls on my rope leash and leads me up to him. We kiss deeply, our mouths fitting together like two interlocking pieces. It whisks me away into ecstasy. I pant into him, then he turns me around to enter me from behind. He swipes his fingertips along the myriad of straps on my panties and ties the rope attached to my collar to the O-ring at their center. The sweet truth of being bound in so many different ways makes my vision cloudy. At last, Parker plunges his cock into my crevice, filling me with his manhood. I wail as he grasps the rope tied around my body and uses it to brace himself as he rocks his hips. His length slides into my folds, then out again. In and out, in and out. The rope sears into my skin, setting me on fire. It's tight. Brutally so. I pant and yelp in the sweet agony of mixed pleasure and pain. I'm possessed by it, my release looming.

"Come for me," Parker whispers in my ear. The heavenly burn of the rope, the glorious sensation of Parker inside my pussy, the sweetness of his voice provoking my undoing - it's a provocative potion that thrusts me over the edge.

My climax hits in a burst of euphoria, the bliss spreading through my body and weakening my every joint. I crumble under the power of it. Parker smacks my ass with his bare hand, and the aftershocks paralyze me.

"Fuck," I whine, almost breathless. My body tingles.

Parker heaves still, the muscles of my insides massaging his cock. He comes a moment later, and his body joins mine in its ethereal release.

• • • •

WHEN PARKER PEELS THE rope off me some time later, pieces of it have embedded themselves in my skin. Red and raw from the pressure, my body is marked with evidence of our scene. I admire myself in the mirror and run my fingertips along the inflamed trail.

"Oh, fuck, are you okay?" Parker gasps. "That looks painful. Shit. Did I tie it too tight? Why didn't you tell me? We have safe words. Make sure you use them!" he panics.

"It was tight, but I liked it," I admit, ashamed of my newfound kink for pain. It makes my ears burn. "These marks are kind of hot," I laugh.

"You insatiable slut," Parker chuckles, shaking his head.

"Mm hmm. *Your* insatiable slut," I correct him.

He likes that.

Parker tosses me onto the bed and face-dives into me. His tongue and mouth and lips worship the apex of my thighs. My pussy, my clit, my ass - Parker devours all of me. My body twitches and writhes under his unwavering dedication to my pleasure. I scream, heat radiating from every pore in my skin. I come easily, over and over.

• • • •

SUNDAY NIGHTS ARE ADMITTEDLY the hardest. The reality of our separation is still fresh, and I find the void in my heart the most unbearable right after Parker leaves.

I tap my fingers.

What to do, what to do...

Fifty-Three

Blythe E. is blonde, voluptuous, and stunning. She's the first match that pops up in Our Leaflet for a last-minute Sunday night encounter, so I send her a hopeful message.

She replies almost instantly.

Blythe invites me to her home, but, citing my limited method of transportation, I ask if she can come to me instead. She happily accepts.

I let her in the front gate, my eyes overwhelmed with her real-life beauty. Her near-white hair cascades down her back, the tips of it lingering near her plump, round ass. She's wearing a short, black skirt, black crop top, and impossibly high black stilettos. The attraction is immediate.

We fall onto my couch, and I get lost in the curves of her lips. I wrap her hair around my wrist and sink into our kiss. She smells like Flowerbomb, and I drink in her scent. My hands explore her body, moving from her shoulders to her waist, then down to her knees. Her skin is soft and warm, and my fingertips buzz against it. I find my way to her thighs and pry them open. I wet my fingers against her exposed opening and stroke them along her creases. She moans and pants, and I find pride in each sound I usher out of her. I push my fingers deeper and she yelps. Drunk on her noises, I quicken my pace. Her body intuitively responds, and she begins to wiggle and rock in rhythm.

"Fuck my fingers," I breathe into her ear, and she pants into my chest.

I bite her neck. Thrusting my fingers into her, she rocks on them and I tap at her G-spot.

Bingo.

She screams out into the air between us. Her orgasm hits, the pleasure spreading through her body. Her muscles squeeze and twitch against my fingers. The sensation makes me want to explode.

"You feel so fucking amazing," I breathe into her.

"You're pretty fucking good," she mutters, breathless.

I pull my fingers from her and lick them. The sweetness of her cum is delectable.

"Let's do this again soon," Blythe says.

Let's.

Fifty-Four

Our Leaflet is life-changing.
    Sunday: Blythe.
Monday: My other love. Book club.
Tuesday: Parker.
Wednesday: Tamsin.
Thursday: Andrea.
Friday: Parker.
Saturday: Ben. It's Shahara's wedding day.

Shahara is Ben's oldest friend. They met in kindergarten and have been a part of each other's lives ever since. I've met her on multiple occasions, and I'm honored to be a guest at her wedding. A pediatric therapist, Shahara has a compassionate heart and endless patience. She's found her forever in Josh. This will be the first time I meet him, but Ben assures me he's worthy of her heart.

Today, we gather to join them in eternal monogamy. I vow to put on a face of support, despite my deep-rooted disapproval.

Ben is a vision in a classic black tux and edgy, pink-and-purple shoes. I pull my conservative little black dress from its dungeon in the back of my closet and pair it with some red pumps that Ben always bugs me should get more wear.

Together, we take our seats on the expansive green of the Traverse Golf Course. There are probably over two-hundred chairs lined in front of an elaborately-decorated wooden archway. Pink and white flowers, lush greenery, and woven rope knots are the feature, along with hints of gold here and there.

The rope. I feel the phantom of it burn as the fabric of my dress brushes the indented marks of last weekend's memory. I hum, my mind wandering back to Parker.

Ben taps me on the shoulder, and I shoot back to the present. We look behind us, and Josh begins his walk down the aisle. His smile is infectious, and against my better judgment, my face breaks out in a wide grin. Ben sniffs.

Josh takes his spot beside the officiant. He towers over everyone, tall and thin with groomed black hair. And that smile. He's positively beaming. Not a shred of nervousness on him, he waits with patience and pride.

The music starts. Elvis Presley's voice fills the air.

Take my hand
Take my whole life, too

It echoes across the green, and the crowd stands in honor of the bride. Just like out of a fairytale, everything blurs as Shahara enters our view. In a stunning white-and-pink wedding dress with layers of lace and tulle, Shahara looks like the epitome of a bride. Her mother and father are on either side of her, dwarfed by her glow, as Shahara floats toward her husband-to-be. Tears prickle in the corner of Josh's eyes, the shine of them visible even from my seat ten rows removed.

Shahara and Josh pose for the photographer before the ceremony begins, and the crowd breaks out in oohs and aahs over Shahara's indiscriminate beauty and what a perfect couple she and Josh make. My gaze shifts from the bride and groom to Ben, who is holding back his own tears.

"You're such a softy," I tease him, smacking his arm with the thick ceremony program forced upon me by Aunt Enid.

"Shut up, you cold bitch," he retorts.

"She does look incredible," I admit.

"She does!" Ben wails, then breaks into embarrassing sobs.

I pull a wad of tissues I had stowed in my black handbag in anticipation of this moment and place them in his hand, assuring him that yes, Shahara is beautiful, yes, love is wonderful, and yes, one day his time will come.

"Maybe that will be you and Kai in a few years," I offer, hoping to lift him up.

"Iris, you don't know how deep my love runs for that man," he chokes.

A loud hush comes over the crowd and the officiant begins the ceremony.

• • • •

CLOSE TO AN HOUR LATER, the fun begins.

It turns out that Josh is a professional event planner, and he sure knows how to throw a party. No expense was spared on the reception, from food and drink to music and entertainment. There's a magic show for the kids, a VR gaming area enclosed for the tweens and teens, and an impressive fire dance show to close the night out for the adults. I drink more than I should, but who am I to reject an open bar from its advances?

Ben and I take the dance floor together, laughing like we did in our youthful club days, and we even get the guts to subject the poor guests of the wedding to our horrid rendition of *Single Ladies*. Tequila helps me slay the vocals, and Ben does Beyoncé proud in his on-point dance performance.

Midnight comes in the blink of an eye, time lost in the pure, unadulterated joy of the best wedding I've ever been to.

Parker graciously agrees to pick me and Ben up, and we fall into his truck, our ears ringing and our voices hoarse.

• • • •

I WAKE UP THE NEXT morning with one of the worst hangovers in recent memory. My head is throbbing, my stomach is in my throat, and the room is still spinning.

"Morning, party girl."

I roll over to see Parker. A sight for sore eyes. I want to kiss him, but I feel vomit creeping up my throat. I run to the bathroom and barf my guts out. Yellow and pink and white gobs of last night's festivities spill into the toilet. I groan. Today is going to suck.

Parker rubs my back and holds my hair out of the way while round two hits me, and I throw up even more than I did the first time. The smell burns in my nostrils. It makes me gag, and I barf again. Against my will, I start to cry, the overall feeling of shittiness taking over without my consent. I sob into the toilet, my head on my arms. What a pathetic vision am I. Parker offers me a glass of cold water and I chug it down greedily, only to expel it a moment later. With my insides sufficiently emptied into the bathroom toilet, Parker tucks me back into bed and gives me a kiss on the forehead. I squirm under the sheets, my body hot then cold.

Some time later, like an angel, Parker appears above me, sweet nectar of the Gods in hand: a tall cup of my usual brew from Urban Grind. I cry again, but this time, they're tears of gratitude.

"Thank you," I sob.

"You're welcome. I also have Tylenol for you. Should help with the headache."

"If only," I whine. I push myself up to sitting and take the first, delectable sip of my coffee. "Mm. Amazing. Oh, God, I love you. Thank you for getting me this. And for holding my hair in the bathroom. And for picking me up last night. And for sitting here, still, despite the mess I am today."

Parker exhales and smiles. He bends to give me a kiss on the forehead. Pushing my bangs out of the way, he pecks my skin, making me feel all warm and fluttery. I'm so fucking lucky to have him.

I finish my coffee and thankfully keep it down. For now.

I make my way over to the couch, where I curl up and read. Parker tucks me in a little cocoon and offers to pick up some takeout, but my stomach swirls in repulsion of the idea. He pulls out his laptop and taps away on it, sending emails and doing various other very important financial things. My eyes catch his, and the magnetism between us sets my soul on fire.

I'm so smitten, it makes me throw up.

Again.

Fifty-Five

The August Mixer arrives at last. Even though my first Mixer was just a month ago, it seems ages have passed since. So much has happened. And changed. Mostly good.

Actually, mostly great.

The anticipation of seeing everyone again suddenly shakes my nerves. I pull almost everything out of my closet, try on one thing after another, choose something to wear, second guess it, and continue to change my mind about a hundred times before throw on a pair of black dress pants and a strappy black top. It doesn't feel right. I change again. It's only when Parker arrives in a panicky rush urging that *we really have to get going* that I concede. I end up wearing a black pencil skirt and emerald sequin crop that I surely would've changed out of if I had five extra minutes.

Parker, as put-together as ever, looks smart in a gray suit and yellow dress shirt. He opens his glove box inside the truck and pulls out an assortment of ties, selecting one that most closely resembles the green of my top.

"Oh, you know, just have my secret stash of ties in my glove box," I tease him.

"Well, we have to match. One up Marc and Desi."

I laugh. "We don't match at all!" Parker is bright and summery, and I look like I'm going to a Christmas party. "And that tie is going to wreck your entire look." I take it from him and hand him a sensible gold tie instead. "There. Just the right amount of dazzle to go with the yellow of your shirt." He looks at me with raised eyebrows, and I add, "I may have spent too much time with Ben critiquing the attire at Shahara's wedding last week." It's painfully true that I'd have zero fashion sense without Ben.

By the time we make it to the Harold Estate, the Mixer is in full swing. Just as before, Kyle greets us at the door, and Sylvie takes our overnight belongings and devices. Everyone is in the ballroom except for Scarlett and Aki, who Desi informs us will regretfully be absent from this month's Mixer. Parker and I make our rounds, saying hello and chatting with everyone, and I spend a large portion of my time getting to know Julia and Davis. Julia has a heart of gold, and I admire her not only for that, but for her solid trust and devotion to Our Family. Davis, although quiet, is incredibly easy to relate to, and the three of us have a wonderful conversation about our choice of lifestyle. I tell them about the wedding I went to last weekend, and it's deeply validating to have them agree with my perspective on monogamy. Davis and Mallory are not married, and Davis shares a similar view to mine on the traditional definitions of marriage. To my surprise, Julia argues that breaking those stereotypical definitions can actually help us liberate ourselves and redefine the relationships we have. I nod, listening intently to the rhythm of her voice. Julia gives me a new perspective on marriage. She explains what marriage means to her and Thom, who have been simultaneously married and non-monogamous for twelve years now.

"Communication really is the key," she asserts.

Desi pulls me aside just before the Pairing Selection and has a word with me about my violation.

"I hated doing that to you," Desi admits. "You're brand new, and we've all made stupid mistakes. But the seriousness of breaching confidentiality can't be understated. The higher-ups are really coming down on us about it. I hope you understand. It wasn't personal."

"Oh, no, of course not! I would never think that!"

"We all love you, Iris, we really do. Just please, be more careful. We'd hate to lose you over something silly like this. Our Family means the world to each of us. We are counting on you to uphold its values," Desi states, her voice a mix of warm and cold. I stare into her brown eyes, getting lost in them.

"Absolutely," I gulp. "I apologize, really I do. I feel like such an idiot for my mistake. I am so grateful to be a part of Our Family. I don't want to do anything to jeopardize that."

Julia leads the ladies in their Selection of stones this month. The air grows thick with anticipation as the men take their turns, pairing up one-by-one. Julia and Parker are matched up first, both choosing the amber stone. Next is Sunny and Marc with sapphire, then Marie and Riley with emerald. Bea and Davis both select quartz, and I'm finally paired when

Thom selects my matching obsidian stone. The final matches are Mallory and Evan with amethyst and Desi and Wyatt with ruby.

Conversations rise and fall as the room thins out. I know very little about Thom; we haven't talked much at all, and Parker has rarely mentioned him in our discussions of the kinks and quirks of the various Members in Branch 29. I'm intrigued by him, though - his hair wild and eyes narrow. He keeps his cards close to his chest, and I'm curious to see them.

I help myself to a fresh glass of champagne and approach him. "Hi."

"Hi."

"So."

"So."

"Shall we head to the guesthouse?"

"Let's."

With a nod at Parker, I turn and collect the key to Guesthouse #4. In gentlemanly fashion, Thom offers me his arm and I take it, wrapping my hand along the muscles of his bicep. I squeeze gently. He's in excellent shape with impeccable endurance (I hope).

I unlock the door and we step inside. The familiar fragrances diffuse throughout, but I notice the lighting has changed a bit. Instead of simply being dimmed, the lights now have a slight purple hue to them.

"Tell me what you like. I'm a great listener," I say, my voice laced with promise. I settle onto the couch and he joins me, taking his place beside me.

"Right to it, huh?" Thom chuckles. It sends a shock of shame through me. I'm too eager, too desperate. My cheeks burn with redness. I look away, to the floor, my humiliation only fueling my desire to please him. It's blissfully vicious.

"I want to get to know you better," I mumble. "So I can make sure you enjoy Our Pairing." I'm sure I sound pathetic.

Thom turns to me and takes my face in his hands. Our eyes sear into each other. "I've heard great things about you. I can assure you that I will enjoy Our Pairing. You don't need to worry about that!" He exhales in an almost-laugh, and again, it cuts me somehow. His hands fall into his lap and he looks away, breaking our stare. My eyes stay on him, desperate for attention. "I've seen your Recordings. You're a firecracker. Indulgent, but also incredibly giving. I'm impressed by you. Most Members, when they're brand new, take a while to warm up. But you? Whew! Ready to go right out the gate."

I should be flattered, but I'm not. I'm deeply ashamed - of my sexual appetite, of my hunger for physical connection. I'm especially ashamed of my love for the shame. My heart thumps in my chest and my lips grow dry. All I want is to prove to Thom that I'm good, that I can be good for him. My eyes search his face for some semblance of approval. Meanwhile, I can't ignore the throbbing between my legs - and the generous bulge between his.

"So. I guess I'm in for it! Let's see if you can live up to your reputation." His words are full of expectation. They fuel me. I can't let him down.

I grab the lapel of his blue jacket and yank him into me. I put my mouth on his, our lips meeting and molding into a soft, flirtatious kiss. It reeks of more to come. I pull myself onto Thom, straddling him and slowly lowering myself onto his lap. He moans as my center rests on his, and I carefully, painstakingly slowly, sway back and forth. Thom grunts as I tease through the layers of fabric, his swollen mound begging for my touch. Our kiss deepens and so do our bodies. The pressure between us builds.

Thom's hands find my hips and he pushes me down onto him. He groans and thrusts upwards, aching for more. I yank on my top, pulling it down towards my waist, and allow my breasts free. They pop out of the tight material of my crop top and bounce into Thom's face. I reach behind his head and grab a handful of his hair, then force his face into my chest. I suffocate him in my cleavage, pushing the tender skin of my chest into his cheeks. I smack him with them, my nipples hardening with each whack against his face. I moan as Thom takes my breasts into his mouth. His tongue wiggles and flicks against my nipples. He sucks and nibbles on them. I whine in the sweet agony of it.

I tug on Thom's hair once more, forcing his head back and chin up. I lick his neck, from collarbone to chin, and bite his bottom lip. Decadent. My fingers find the buttons on his dress shirt and I undo them. Pulling it open, his broad, muscular chest sends a pang of wetness between my legs. His body is solid and firm. I bite his nipple and he slaps me. My cheek burns from the surprise of it. My insides clench.

"Fuck, no," he snaps. I pout, my eyes wide. "No teeth."

Noted.

I unlatch Thom's pants and pull them off, a distinct wet spot visible where I was crouched on top of him. I wince, imagining Parker shaming me for being *so easy*. Thom lifts his hips and slides his pants and underwear off. At last, his swollen cock is free for me to attend to. I kiss the head first, then slowly lick his entire shaft from base to tip. I gain momentum and take Thom's cock into my mouth. He groans, a satisfied sound of *finally!* coming from deep in the back of his throat (similar to where I have his cock in mine). He pushes into me, bracing himself with hands on the back of my head. I hold my breath and take him all in. When he releases his hold on me, I bring my hand up and pump my fist along his length while I bob my head. I occasionally add in some sucking of his balls, eliciting a hearty groan from him.

Thom stands up and thrusts his hips into my mouth. He fucks my face, holding my hair in a ball behind my head as his cock slides in and out of my mouth.

No teeth.

"Fuck. Mm! Fuck, yes!"

He pulls his cock from my mouth and shoots his cum over my chest. I pant, trying to find my breath.

With a satisfied exhale, Thom falls back onto the couch and pets my cheek.

"You're fucking good."

I smile at him. "Thank you."

"Seriously. Might be the best blow job I've ever had," Thom asserts. I blush, my cheeks redder than they were when he slapped me. "Give me an hour. Then you're going to do that again. Please."

Thom is a taker, I learn. We make our way upstairs, and he sprawls himself onto the soft sheets of the bed. He insists I try on a series of outfits from inside the wardrobe. I play dress up while he critiques and comments, waiting to regain his stamina. In line with his indulgences thus far, a sultry French maid costume comes out on top. I change into the frilly, barely-there apron. The chest is a series of cut-outs, leaving my breasts fully exposed, and the back gapes open to show off my white G-string. It leaves very little to imagination, and Thom loves my body in it.

I lean over him in a 69 position and take his cock in my mouth once more. He slides his fingers past the straps of my thong and pushes them into my pussy. His touch ricochets through me.

"You're so fucking wet. You like sucking my dick, huh? Makes you soaking wet!" he groans and grunts.

I wiggle in my shame, my incessant need for sex, always wet and wanton. I lick Thom's balls again and take them into my mouth. They roll across my tongue as I pump my fist along his shaft. Feeling brave, I run my lips along his perineum, hoping to double his pleasure.

"Fuck, no!" he screams at me, throwing me off of him and grabbing my face in his wet hand. He squeezes my cheeks between his fingers. They reek of my scent. "Don't you ever fucking touch me there. Understand?" I weakly nod. His temper is like fire, wild and unpredictable. It's thrilling, but very real. I hate that I love it. It drives me into a frenzy. Still, I remind myself of the safe words, just in case I need to use them. "Now keep your mouth on my cock, where it belongs."

The throbbing between my legs intensifies, aching now without Thom's touch to satiate it. I have to prove myself worthy of it again, so I focus on doing what I do best, and I give Thom another earth-shattering blow job.

Thom throws me a bit of stimulation here and there - a nipple tug, an ass slap, the occasional kiss. But the bulk of our evening stars my mouth and his cock. And I'd be lying if I say I don't love it. Because I do. The pleasure that my mouth brings Thom gives me a rush of my own.

"You're so fucking good," he says over and over. I beam with pride.

• • • •

THE FOLLOWING MORNING, Thom can't shut up about it. In the breakfast room, he confers with the men, asking Marc, Riley, Wyatt, and especially Parker why they haven't screamed from the rooftops about how incredible my blow jobs are. So incredible, he declares, that we must have a private exchange in the next couple of weeks. My entire body speckles in red and my cheeks flush. I'm certain I'll burst into flames over the humiliating pride I feel.

Parker and I agree to schedule something with Julia and him soon.

Desi stands and clinks the side of her mimosa glass to draw the attention of the room. Everyone falls silent, ears intent on hearing the monthly announcements.

"Thank you, everyone, for a memorable August Mixer. I always love seeing the satisfied faces the morning after," Desi chuckles. Claps and Wyatt's whoops fill the air, as usual. "Our next Mixer will be in September, on Saturday the 23, to Sunday the 24. We look forward to seeing you all there. The following October Mixer will be Our second Inter-Branch Mixer of the year. I'll pass it off to Mallory to fill you in on that in just a moment. But, first, I'd like to take a moment to recognize each and every one of you for your outstanding commitment to Our Family. Your dedication is not overlooked. We appreciate each of you as Members. Thank you for being part of Our Family!" Desi raises her glass. We all cheer and take a hearty swig of our various breakfast beverages. "Alright, now onto Mallory." Desi sits and Mallory pops up in her place.

"Members of Branch 29! It's my pleasure to officially announce the date for Our Family's Annual Masquerade Ball!" Mallory's voice is jittery and quick. "I'll be sending each of you the official invitation in the app, but let me fill you in on the details. This year's Masquerade Ball will be held with two other Branches - Branch 04 and Branch 15. There will be a total of fifty-four of us there, as long as all Members are able to attend! This event will be held at the Dominguez Estate, so make sure you check your Communications for the address. And, of course, we can't forget the date! Mark your calendars for October 21, to October 22.

"I know we have several new Members who haven't had the pleasure of attending an Inter-Branch Mixer yet. And let me just tell you, you're in for tricks *and* treats!" Mallory giggles. Adorably dorky as always. "In honor of the spookiest time of year, the theme for this event is, obviously, a Masquerade. Theming is an absolute requirement, so be sure to dress to impress! For any of you who need a hand with putting together a costume, I'm happy to share Walter's contact information. Walter is Our Family's resident theming expert, and I can promise he'll set you up with the best! As always, feel free to reach out to me with any questions!"

The room buzzes with excitement and energy. The idea of mixing with other Branches makes my heart jump erratically. Parker assures me that the Masquerade Ball will be an event to remember. *Heavily hedonistic*, are the words he uses, in fact. It's incredible, being surrounded by people who freely fuck each other without a shred of jealousy, resentment, or hurt.

Acceptance.

This is what belonging feels like. I truly can't believe I am a part of this.

As we get ready to say goodbye to the group and head out the door, Thom leans in close and whispers, "I'll be dreaming of your mouth."

Parker smirks, knowing.

Fifty-Six

With all of Thom's talk of my incredible mouth and deep-throating skills, Parker can't wait to get me home and show me how proud he is of me. Expecting to give him the same treatment I did Thom, I'm surprised when Parker denies me of it. He instead lays me on my stomach and ties my arms and legs to the corners of the bed. *More rope.* He praises me, insisting Our Family is thrilled to have me as one of their own. He bites my neck and breathes into my skin. His tongue finds my earlobe and he plays with it, sending shivers down my spine. He fucks my ass with a large, black dildo and makes me come so hard that I squirt all over the bedsheets. My body quivers and shakes, on the edge of passing out.

Two months in Our Family under my belt. Literally. And my life is forever changed. I have blossomed into my best self and found my place in the dark corners outside of mainstream society. My skin tingles at the thought that the best is yet to come.

Parker and I spend the month of September in an inebriated bliss. We fall into a predictable routine, and our time together grows into the most meaningful part of my week. We spend our weekends between the sheets, in the shower, and on the balcony. We experiment and push each other, and in doing so grow closer than ever. Parker has seeped into every fiber of my being and invaded my every thought. The two of us have become intertwined in the most intimate way possible. Parker isn't my better half - he's a deeply entrenched part of me.

I take full advantage of Our Leaflet to get my fill during times of Parker's absence, and it does wonders for curbing my appetite. I meet with Blythe twice more this month, and we really begin to connect. She's a lesbian, and I learn that there are many same-sex Branches within Our Family. She speaks highly of the acceptance she's gained and the community she's grown since becoming a Member. She also speaks highly of my dedication to her pleasure.

We indulge Julia and Thom, having them over to my apartment for an informal, private exchange. Julia and Parker play in my room, while I blow Thom in the living room. My jaw aches with pride by the end of it.

I can admit that, for the first time in my life, my sexual needs are being met.

I'm in love. I'm sexually satisfied. Everything is perfect.

Even at work, things are on the up-and-up. My personal life bleeds into my work one; I'm engaged, optimistic, and in overall good spirits. The only negative thing I come to terms with is the departure of Turkey, who does, inevitably, get picked up by his mommy and daddy in the first week of the month. On the upside, though, they schedule him in for another stay at PetCation next month. With a two-week cruise on the books, I can look forward to many more walks with Turkey by my side. I vow not to push him away next time. Getting close to him doesn't necessarily equate to a painful separation from him. Our Family has taught me this in abundance.

On Monday night, a notification from Our Family pops up on my screen. My phone practically buzzes against my body, begging for me to open it. But I've learned my lesson; I'll be patient.

Gemma wraps up our book discussion, and I bolt out of the library.

As soon as I'm home, I open the app. I have two messages. The first is from Mallory.

Hi Iris!

Hope you're enjoying the last few weeks of summer before fall officially sets in! I've attached the reminder for Our September Mixer, as well as the invitations for the upcoming Inter-Branch Mixer for Our Family's Annual Masquerade Ball and Our November Mixer.

Please open and read in a discreet, private space. You'll also find these events posted in the Calendar for you.

Thank you, and I'm looking forward to seeing you soon!

With love,
Mallory xox

B29 Mixer Event - September
Please join us for Our September Mixer,
Saturday, September 23 - Sunday, September 24
6 p.m. - 11 a.m.
At the Harold Estate

We look forward to the time with you.

Truly Yours,
Desi Harold
Our Family, Head of Branch 29

Inter-Branch Mixer - Our Family's Annual Masquerade Ball
It's Our pleasure to invite you,
Iris Gladwell,
To Our Family's Annual Masquerade Ball.
Please join us
Saturday, October 21 - Sunday, October 22
6 p.m. - 11 a.m.
At the Dominguez Estate
Dress your best - themed attire required.
We look forward to the time with you.

Truly Yours,
Felicia Dominguez
Our Family, Head of Branch 15

B29 Mixer Event - November
Please join us for Our November Mixer,
Saturday, November 18 - Sunday, November 19
6 p.m. - 11 a.m.
At the Harold Estate
We look forward to the time with you.

Truly Yours,
Desi Harold
Our Family, Head of Branch 29

Wow, dates for the November Mixer already. I realize from looking at the invitation, that my birthday is on a Thursday this year. Disappointment floods through me. Will I need to get down on my knees and beg Parker to spend it with me? I'm not beneath doing so.

The second message is from someone I don't know - someone contacting me through Our Leaflet.

Message from: Fel W.
Iris G.,
I see you're available Wednesday night. I'd love to
have you accompany me to dinner. Hope to hear
back from you.
Fel W.

Up to this point, every interaction I've had through Our Leaflet has been with someone I've sought out. My heart tingles to receive my first message from someone seeking *me* out. I'm flattered.

Message to: Fel W.
I'd be delighted. I'm free after 7 p.m.
Let me know when and where.
Looking forward to meeting you,
Iris xx

After sending my reply, I realize that I have no idea if Fel is a male or female. I'm tempted to click on the name and view their profile, but I decide against it. Surprises are rare in life, so I choose to let Fel's identity be one.

Fifty-Seven

As I wait for my Uber to arrive and whisk me away to my dinner date, I wonder: who is Fel W.?

I can't wait to find out.

The blue Nissan Versa pulls up in front of an expansive apartment complex. I thank my driver, hop out, and approach the front gate. I find *Fel W.* on the buzzer, and press the corresponding button. It lights up, and a moment later, the gate buzzes.

I'm in.

I travel down a pathway and follow the signage on the buildings to find unit #116. I knock.

A beautiful man with enormous dark eyes and a patchy, black goatee answers. "Iris?" he says. His voice is smooth and deep. I nod, speechless. "Come in." I nod again, glad that I left his identity a surprise.

Fel is goddamn fine. His skin is dark and smooth, and he has an easy six inches on me. IN HEIGHT. As for the other thing... I'm sure there are inches and inches there, too. My eyes dart down at his slacks, but they give nothing away. Yet. His black button-down, though, strains against his broad chest. My fingers twitch, wanting desperately to undo the delicate, round buttons.

Fel gives me a polite kiss on the cheek and asks me to wait just inside his apartment. I step across the threshold. It's dark but smells clean - the distinct scents of citrus and lavender fill the air, like he just scrubbed the bathroom and generously squirted room spray. I look around me. The living room is wide and flanked by a fireplace on the side closest to me and an open kitchen on the other. The cabinets are white, but add no light to the space. It's distinctly dungeon-like in here.

I like it.

Fel retreats down the hallway and returns a moment later with a black leather jacket.

"Hungry, I hope," he says.

"Very!" I answer enthusiastically.

"A good friend of mine owns an amazing seafood restaurant on the coast. Shall we?" Fel offers his arm to me - the perfect gentleman - and I wrap my hand around it. Off we go.

. . . .

FEL DRIVES A TOP-OF-the-line, luxurious black Audi. It maneuvers like a dream, gliding sleekly along the freeway and city side streets. It's easily the nicest car I've ever been in. The new car smell is still very prevalent, and Fel reveals that he's had it for just a couple of months. We make small talk, and it feels more like a real date than any other interaction I've had. Somehow, I'm more uncomfortable talking about what we do for a living than I would if he just fucked me in the dark glow of his fireplace.

He's a lawyer. Estate law, he tells me. His clothing, his car, his career all reek of wealth. The shoddiness of his apartment seems extremely out of place.

Fel pulls his car in front of a sprawling building with the name *Harbor Palace* glowing in yellow above it. Being the gentleman that he is, Fel opens the door for me and offers his arm once again. I take it, and we walk across a long bridge that brings us to the open patio of the restaurant. The hostess recognizes Fel immediately, and we follow the click-clack of her high heels and the brightness of her platinum blonde hair over to a table at the edge of the patio. I lean over the welded railing and realize that we are suspended above the ocean. The soft patter of waves dances against the rocks below, and I even spot a couple of crabs scuttling between hiding places. Fel pulls my seat out for me and I slide into place. He sits across from me, and the hostess offers to bring us a bottle of wine. Fel looks to me. I choose red.

A moment later, a man identical to Fel appears at our table with the bottle of wine. I do a double take. And then another. What the hell?

"Fel, nice to see you, man!" he says. Fel rises and leans in for a bro hug. My eyes dart between them, my brain swirling with confusion.

"Richie, this is Iris," Fel says, politely gesturing towards me. "Iris, this is my brother, Richie. My twin brother."

I jump to standing and shake Richie's hand. "Great to meet you," I muster.

"Wonderful to meet you, Iris." Richie loiters for a moment, smiling at me. Then he pours our wine, tells us today's specials, and, after he leaves, the awkward moment seems like something I made out to be worse than it was.

Seated again, I take a hearty sip of wine. The burn as it slides down my throat is a welcome sensation.

"I'm a twin, too," I offer, then take another swig of wine.

"Are you really?"

"I am. Not identical, though. Fraternal. Me and my brother, Zach."

"That's so bizarre. What a coincidence!" Fel exclaims.

"So, it's your brother who owns this restaurant?" I hazard a guess.

"He does. Has the best oysters you'll ever taste," he promises.

I raise my eyebrows and give him a coy smile. "Well, then. We'll have to give those a try, won't we?"

The food is good and the company is pleasant, but there's a distinct lack of *something* between me and Fel. Most - actually, all - interactions I've had with Members through Our Leaflet have been entirely sexual in nature. This is the first time I've had a date-like interaction. And it feels... strange. I tell myself that challenging my expectations of what Our Family is supposed to be is good, but, for some reason, things with Fel seem off.

Maybe if we could wrap this thing up and head back to his apartment, my opinion would change. Maybe he gives the best head in the universe. Maybe his muscles are most useful when it comes to suspending me against his body and fucking me unrelentingly. Maybe there's more to Fel than I'm giving him credit for.

I politely decline dessert and focus on the possibility of what's to come.

Fel drives us back to his apartment in the same polite nature that comes to him naturally. Somewhere between the conversation of the real estate market and impending recession we've been hearing about for at least half a decade, I decide that if there's a chance of anything happening between us, I'll need to make the first move.

We pull up to a stoplight. I lean over to Fel and kiss him on the cheek, then ever so slowly slide my hand along his thigh.

He freezes. His body grows stiff. He stills. I use my other hand to pull his chin towards mine and kiss his delectable lips. He doesn't kiss me back.

It feels wrong. So wrong. I retreat back into my seat and wish I could disappear.

That was possibly the most awkward thing I've ever experienced.

The mood dies. Fel goes mute. I wish I was a bug getting squished on the immaculate windshield of his new car.

Finally, we arrive at his apartment and he pulls into the garage.

"Wait here," he says. It's a relief to have his voice break the painful silence.

Fel exits and comes around to the passenger side to open my door. He offers his hand, and I reluctantly take it.

"Fel, I'm sorry," I offer. "I just, well, I guess, I mean, I'm a pretty new Member. I've never had an interaction quite like this one. I'm sorry I overstepped and breached your comfort level." I mean it. It's obvious I made Fel deeply uncomfortable, and I feel bad about it. This is whole other type of shame - not the kind that arouses me, but the kind that makes me feel deeply guilty.

"Iris, you don't know me. I don't know you. That was the point of this dinner. I wanted to get to know you, and to have you get to know me." I nod, relief sweeping over me at the sweet sound of Fel's voice. "I apologize for not being more upfront with you about that. I know a lot of the interactions are hookups. I'm not like that, though. I'm looking for something more meaningful, I guess."

It's at this moment that I realize that Our Family consists of all types of humans, seeking all types of connections.

And that, I think to myself, is a beautiful thing.

Fifty-Eight

After my interaction with Fel, I have a fresh perspective on the differing Members in Our Family and the various kinds of experiences they are looking to have. It's about the sex, yes, but also about the connection. As I arrive at the Harold Estate for the September Mixer, I keep this in mind.

Tonight, I pair with Aki, and he's the most nurturing person I've met in Our Family. His voice dances in my ears and settles in my heart. His gentleness is like a warm hug, soothing and comfortable. The timing of our match couldn't be better; we form a genuine, warm connection. The attraction is there, but also the comfort. And, Aki has a kink for Shibari. I think about the sting of the rope, the burning sensation as it rubbed against my skin, when Parker tied me in a chest harness last month. My skin tingles in memory, the ghost of its marks still embedded there. With my heart thudding as I reminisce, I enthusiastically let Aki know that he can restrain and tie me in whatever manner he desires.

"Your skin is so beautiful," Aki sings. "So soft and smooth. The rope will pull and rub against it. Will you enjoy that?" he asks.

I gulp. "Yes, I definitely will."

Insisting we take it slow, Aki begins by binding my arms together in a wrist restraint tie. A rope expert, he ties it quickly and with ease. As promised, the rope grinds into my skin. I love it. Aki pulls on the restraint, closing the space between us. Our lips come together, and we kiss. It's soft and light and gentle. Behind me, the roughness of more rope teases against the naked flesh of my back.

"I want to blindfold you. Then I'm going to do a chest tie, if you'll allow me."

"Yes, please," I whimper.

I close my eyes, and Aki slides a soft, black blindfold over them. I take a deep breath. He finds my chest and rests his hand over my jumping heart.

"I'm going to take good care of you," he promises.

Every sensation is doubled in magnitude as my obstructed vision only heightens my sensitivity. To touch. To smell. To taste. To sound. It's exhilarating. Aki's fingers gently stroke my wrists as he massages the imprints on my skin left behind by the rope he has slowly untied. I drop my arms by my side, but, even with my hands free, I feel trapped.

Aki runs the rope along my shoulders and around my neck, slithering it against me like an erotic snake. He moves around my body soundlessly. The only thing I hear is my own ragged breath amongst the twisting and zigzagging of the rope. A stab of wetness pulses between my legs.

Suddenly, Aki strikes me with an end of the rope, snapping the fringed edges against the tender skin of my nipples. I yelp and nearly leap off the ground.

"How does that feel?"

I gulp. "Good."

"Good?"

"Yes."

"Remember our safe words. Please tell me if there's anything I do that you do not enjoy." A true gentleman.

I nod.

Aki exhales loudly and continues his craft. He tests my tolerance, slowly increasing the intensity of his touch - and the rope's tightness. He yanks the rough texture of the rope across my nipples. The pain surges across my skin and I shudder. The next second, the rope is in my mouth, pulled tight across my cheeks and tied behind my head. I want to gasp, to call out, but I can't. My body is paralyzed. Aki bites my lower lip, which is jutted out under the rope, and the dull scrape of his teeth against my tender flesh makes me feel like I'm going to combust. Then his mouth is on my nipples. Oversensitivity rattles through me, and I flinch and try to pull away. But Aki's teeth dig into my skin once more, pulling on my delicate nipple and snapping me toward him. The pain of it is invigorating, and I pant and squirm until finally Aki releases me. The rope in my mouth slides down my chin and across my throat. The taste of the fibers stick against my tongue as I struggle to find my breath.

Now the rope is twisting along my back, and Aki is tying it around my shoulders and neck. He moves fast, then slow, brutally slow, then yanks the knots into place. I'm completely at his mercy, eager to surrender to his every command. I dance for him as he wraps my chest in an intricate weaving of knots and ties, twisting like this and turning like that. I can't see; I can't breathe. Goosebumps sear across my skin as Aki moves his fingers between my thighs and touches the drenched fabric between them. He pulls my thong down and I step out of it. I'm so disoriented that I feel like I'm going to topple over, but Aki holds me firmly. I feel safe in spite of my senses kicking into overdrive.

My arms are bound against my body and Aki pulls on a series of knots at my sternum. He pulls me down, and, without my sight, I'm sure I'm going to fall forever into a black hole of endlessness. But the floor is right there, and my body lands gently on a plush rug below us. I'm on my back, immobilized, and my heart is thudding so loudly in my ears that I can't hear a thing.

But feel? I feel everything. I feel Aki's lips on my chin. I feel his fingers slide into my creases. I feel them wiggle and twist inside of me. I feel his cock leaking fluids against my thigh. I feel his tongue on my nipples. I feel all of it. I've never had my senses so overloaded in my life. The arousal is so thick and so intense that the inside of my thighs is completely, humiliatingly flooded.

Aki straddles me and yanks on the knots against my chest. He pulls me into him, and his cock slides effortlessly into place inside of me. I yelp. The burn of the rope against my skin hurts so good as Aki rocks his hips, moving his length in and out of me. He pulls me close, lowers me away, thrusts in, slides out, and in a matter of seconds, I come. My orgasm hits me like never before. It's heavy and explosive, laced with both pain and pleasure. My body shakes uncontrollably as I ride the wave of my release, and Aki hums and groans as my insides squeeze around him.

He wraps his arms around me, holding me in a tight and nurturing embrace. He kisses my cheek, then my mouth, and lowers me back onto the floor. He rolls me over and pulls the rope on my back to guide me and gently drape me over the bed. I fall into the comfort of the sheets, the softness of them an overwhelming contrast to the chafe of the rope. Aki grasps the rope against my spine and plunges inside of me again. I bounce on his cock, my crevice wrapped around his shaft. He maneuvers the rope to move me in rhythm, and I soon unravel again. My insides pull Aki in. The two of us pant and groan, our shared release hitting in a burst of unimaginable pleasure.

Aki slides the blindfold off and pulls me to standing. I look into his eyes, deep and dark and warm.

"Thank you, Iris. That was wonderful. Did you enjoy yourself?"

"I sure fucking did," I answer, sounding much too pathetic, but too relaxed to care.

Aki carefully unties the knots and untwists the rope. With my vision back, I watch him, deeply intrigued by the focus in his eyes as his hands move the rope with swift precision. His fixation is hypnotizing. As the rope releases me from its hold, my skin breathes again. The air swirls around the marks carved into my body. Aki runs his fingertips along the divots, studying them with his eyes and his touch. The familiar heat returns as my skin prickles and my insides throb. He presses the heel of his hands into the marks now, following their pathway along my arms and around my back. Even though I'm not tied up anymore, I feel completely at his mercy. I can't move - Aki's touch controls me.

I'm on the bed again, the raw skin of my chest and stomach luxuriating in the forgiving fabric of the sheets. Aki lowers himself on top of me and melts his body onto my back. The heat and weight of him on me somehow comforts me from the outside, in. He stands back up and his hands are on me again, moving in slow, certain circles. A flush of warmth surges at my center, and I instinctively moan.

Then he's gone. My body aches in absence of his touch. The room is brutally quiet.

CRACK!

My entire body shocks to life as the leather of a flogger smacks against my back. I wail and wail as the startling force of it comes down onto me again and again. I turn inside myself and count.

CRACK!

CRACK!

CRACK!

It comes down on me six times. I think it's over - hope it's over - when the sting of Aki's hand smacks into the tender skin of my behind. My body is on the verge of convulsing. I squeeze in anticipation of another blow, but none comes.

Aki plunges his fingers into my slit. He pulls my hips upward and I'm on my knees. His fingers dive into me and he strokes at the delicate tissue of my insides. I respond to him instantly, writhing and whining and panting a symphony of primal sounds. Effortlessly, he pushes me to the precipice and over, my body coming undone at his fingertips.

I've become his puppet.

And what a skilled puppet master he is.

Fifty-Nine

I've come to love the mornings following Our Mixers. The energy circulating in the air is infectious. It bleeds into me and cloaks my body with endorphins. I have great respect for every single Member of Our Branch, and I admire each of them in distinct, beautiful ways.

And there's always that moment: when Parker's eyes sink into mine. I feel it, there, in my soul. Despite the brevity of our split, the spark of our reunion is a rush like no other. It's as though two parts of one are sewn back together after years of agonizing separation.

The two pieces are a perfect fit.

We settle into our seats and the indulgences continue with a hearty breakfast. I greedily devour the pastries and fresh fruit and a made-to-order omelet with ripe tomatoes, melted cheese, and panfried mushrooms. I drink more coffee than I should, given the buzz I have simply from the company surrounding me, but I gratefully accept *one last cup* before Desi makes the monthly announcements and we each take our leave.

"Thank you, everyone, for attending Our September Mixer!" Desi calls. In predictable fashion, Wyatt whoops and the rest of us clap. "It's been a delightful exchange this month, if I do say so myself!" Desi's blushing, and it's the first time I've seen her flustered. I think back to the Pairings, and remember she spent the night with Evan. Everyone shoots glances between Desi and Evan. Evan's face has turned a shade redder than his hair. We all chuckle, and Marie smirks, knowingly. Desi clears her throat. "As you're all aware, October is around the corner, and with it brings Our Family's Annual Masquerade Ball. I know there are a few of you who haven't attended an Inter-Branch event yet, so it's my responsibility to make it abundantly clear to all Members of this Branch that attendance is compulsory, as is themed attire. I can promise you all that *this* will be an event to remember."

"Fuck, yeah!" Wyatt hollers.

"The date for the Masquerade once again is October 21, to October 22, and this event will be hosted at the Estate of Branch 15. And looking further ahead, we also have the dates for Our November Mixer scheduled. I'll pass it off to Mallory now to fill everyone in on the details."

Mallory jumps up and tucks her thick, dark hair behind her ears. She looks giddy as always, eager to share the news of what's to come. "Thank you, Desi! I want to really hone in on what Desi just reminded us of with the Masquerade. It's imperative that you all dress up! If you feel like you need a hand with this, once again I am happy to pass along Walter's information. I rely on Walter's help every year for this event, and he's never let me down! Also, as Desi mentioned, this event will be held at the Dominguez Estate, so keep an eye out for directions. I'll push them out on the app the day of the event. Onto November, now. Our November Mixer will be held on November 18, to November 19. We have a little something *new* brewing for this one, so be sure you can make it! Thanks, everyone!"

In a flurry of gratitude and kisses, the couples depart one by one.

The second last to leave, Parker and I say goodbye, together, hearts as one.

Sixty

The days become shorter, the weather becomes cooler, and in a blink, October arrives. Parker and I have settled into our new dynamic, and it truly has brought enrichment to our relationship. To our lives. Our relationship is now stronger than ever. Nothing can rock our boat. We are solid, deeply in love, and happier than in my wildest dreams. My membership in Our Family has surpassed my every expectation.

My entire existence has evolved.

With my first Mixer a distant memory and several others behind us now, Parker and I have fallen into a routine that is predictable and comfortable. Our monthly rendezvous adds a sprinkling of spice, fun, and variety that we both crave and generously indulge in. The Mixers teach me a lot - about myself, what I'm capable of, my limits, my preferences. They give me an outlet to fulfill my most hedonistic needs. And the best part is that they do the same for Parker, and we both support each other in that.

Everything is going perfect.

And I don't doubt it. I don't doubt its perfection, and it's the very first time in all my life that I have felt that way. Old me, desperate to find my place of belonging, would've immediately sensed a dark sky and gathering of heavy clouds on the horizon. But new me feels light, joyful, and truly happy. It's a welcome, albeit surprising, change.

My personal life is perfect.

My work life is not.

Ever since I did whatever I did to upset Dr. Val, things at work haven't felt the same. Maybe it is all in my head, maybe I'm psyching myself out, but I definitely don't feel the same amount of satisfaction in my work as I had before. Someone is always checking what I've already done, and I'm questioning myself every time, second-guessing my competence. The passion I had for my job is hitting a rough patch. I hope it will pass. But it's hard, in the meantime.

Staring into space in the break room, I sigh dramatically. I need something to distract me. I unconsciously begin picking at the skin beside my thumb and yank a thick piece off. Blood spews out and I race to find a tissue in the bathroom. I wrap it snuggly around my wound. It's my lunch break, but I don't have an appetite. I mindlessly flip through the trashy celebrity magazines sprawled out on the table in front of me.

And that's when I see it.

The Secretive, Controversial Marriage of Joan Oakley and Sam Thomas - Revealed for the First Time

Intrigued, I flip through the pages until I find it. The article explores the *deeply unique - and contentious - choice that celebrity chef, Sam Thomas, and his model wife, Joan Oakley, have made to foster an open marriage.* I find myself completely sucked in. My eyes devour the words as I compulsively flip from one page to the next.

It's absolute ludicrous. The way the author portrays open relationships is so far off the mark that the article is nothing but an over-embellished fabrication. Judgment is weaved so deeply into the writing that I can't believe it's not a joke. Yet, I read on, my eyes grazing the pages and getting stuck on key phrases, such as *what is marriage for, if not to dedicate oneself to a single other?* and *these unconventional choices threaten the sanctity of marriage,* and *childlike and greedy, with a blatant disrespect of emotional wellbeing and significant risk to mental health. Adultery* is the cherry on top. I find myself laughing at the ridiculous implications of the article, entertained too much by its outrageous conclusions on non-monogamy.

I pause for a moment, letting my superior knowledge on the subject matter soak in. In some strange way, it gives me power knowing that author *nobody* Amy Burke has no idea what she is writing about. She has it all wrong. And that's when I realize - it's for our benefit. It's for the benefit of me, Parker, and everyone else who makes the choice to participate in a non-monogamous lifestyle. It's for the benefit of Our Family. It's for the benefit of all lifestyle organizations that exist outside traditional constructs. As long as the public believes this bullshit about infidelity and the brazen disrespect on the institution of marriage, Our Family can be kept safe and secret. I shut the magazine, snap a photo of the cover, and text it to Parker. I'm sure he'll be just as entertained as I am.

I toss the tissue wrapped around my formerly bleeding thumb into the trash and go wash my hands in the bathroom sink. My break is over.

I'm just about to head back into the clinic when my phone vibrates in my hand.

Incoming Call from
Mom - mobile

I check my watch. I need to get back to work, but I can use this as an excuse to keep our call short. I swipe to answer.

"Hi mom."

"Oh! Hi honey! I'm so glad you answered! I wasn't sure if I'd get you since you're working today." Wordy as usual.

"I'm just finishing up my break. I only have a minute or two."

"Oh, great. Okay, well, I won't keep you long."

"Thanks. What's up?"

"Oh, well, you know, the usual. Things are... good..." she drones. "Good, good, yep. Good."

She has something to tell me. I can feel it. Oh, God. Oh, my God. Please don't let her be enga-

"Willie has asked me to marry him!" she squeals. I push the phone away from my ear, hoping to avoid permanent hearing damage. "Can you believe it? I said yes, of course! Oh, sweetie, he's just the absolute best! He treats me like a dream. I am so spoiled, living here in this amazing ocean-front villa in Hawaii! Fresh fruit picked from our own trees for breakfast every day! Walks along the beach with my perfect man! I couldn't be happier!" Her voice is shrill and manic.

"Wow. Congratulations, mom. And Willard," I add, still holding my phone a few inches from my ear.

"Thank you, honey! We are so happy to have found each other. You know, I was telling Willie the other morning over coffee that at our age, we are so lucky to have had the good fortune to meet each other. So many seniors live out the rest of their days lonely and, well, you know, alone," she clucks, proud of her superiority over all those other sad, single, lonely folk. "Willie and I bring out the best in each other, and we are going to do so for the rest of our lives!" she declares, as if making an inspirational speech in front of a large crowd.

"That's really great, mom. I'm so happy for you both," I feign enthusiasm.

"I know, sweetie. We are so happy! I am so relieved to have told you! Here I was, stressing over the *endless* list of friends and family to contact. I was so worried about you hearing the news from a third party! I wanted to be sure you heard it right from the source."

Is she a newscaster now?

"Yes, so glad we were able to touch base. But I do need to get going." Now. Please. Make this stop.

"Of course, honey, of course. You get out there and save those puppies and cats and birds and squirrels or whatever!" She maniacally cackles. "Oh, and call your brother. He said he hasn't heard from you since Cici was born! Ah, a wedding. A great opportunity for the family to be reunited in the spirit of love!"

"Yep, okay. Sounds good mom. Congratulations again."

"I love you! I'll call you later with more details! I'm sure you want to know how he asked me, all the plans moving forward. You know, spill the tea, as the kids say!"

Cringe.

"I love you, too, mom. Talk to you later, bye."

I still have three hours left in my shift and my head won't stop ringing from my mom's high-pitched, frenzied voice. I dig through the contents of my locker and thankfully unearth a bottle of Tylenol with a few tablets left. I throw back two, chugging them down with a tepid glass of tap water, and take another deep breath before returning to work even more emotionally exhausted than I was before my break.

The rest of the day drags, even with the rush of clients coming and going all afternoon. I clean and disinfect the intake rooms and assist Dr. Val with the scheduled checkup appointments. There's just over an hour left in my workday when he insists on my help administering the topical anesthetic on a Pomeranian's gums before he has his tooth pulled. The dog is feisty and energetic, but I take on the challenge with enthusiasm, pathetically desperate to prove my skills. I take a deep breath and focus my mind. I scratch under the pup's chin and charm him into submission.

Dr. Val smiles, impressed. "Well done."

I beam.

· · · ·

MONDAY IS BOOK CLUB night, and I'm intent on heading there early to finally chat with Maisie about the erotic horror book I finished some time ago. I'm annoyed with myself for being so tardy with checking in with her, but my attentions have been elsewhere. And I can't deny that I've very much enjoyed *elsewhere*.

Done work just before five, I head straight to the library so I can hopefully catch her before her shift ends.

She's not there.

The thing with Maisie is, we aren't really friends. At the same time, we're more than acquaintances. From the many months we've spent discussing books together over the last year, I've learned how her brain works, how she thinks. I've learned her thought processes as we dive deep into the mysteries of twisty minds and strange characters. What you read reveals a lot about you, and your opinion on it reveals even more. I feel like we know each other in this *other* way, but it's gray, not really defined.

I can't believe how stupid I feel about it. A big part of me wants to ask her the next time I see her for her phone number, so we can text about our thoughts on what we're reading. I think we have similar tastes. But somehow a piece of me thinks that would be crossing some undefined line. I'm not sure *why* I feel weird about it. I'm terrible with friendships. But dork me would love love love to have a book friend.

I decide that it would be relatively harmless to ask another one of the librarians when she'll be in next.

Susan is standing behind a computer, scanning in returned books and placing them neatly on the re-shelving cart. In her mid-fifties, she has long gray-blonde hair and square glasses perched on her nose. She's not known for her friendliness, so I approach her cautiously.

"Hi, sorry to bother you," I begin. Her eyes dart up at me, but her head stays tilted down, facing the computer screen. "I have just a quick question. The librarian who does Friday book club, Maisie, do you know when she'll be in next?" I try to keep it short and sweet.

Susan exhales loudly and types away on her computer. I awkwardly wait. She still says nothing, and I contemplate running out of the library as fast as I can and never showing my face here again. The silence cuts like a knife.

"Looks like she's out on leave," Susan says at last.

"Oh. On leave? Do you know when she'll be back?"

Susan exhales again, annoyed. "It's not listed here."

"Oh. Okay. Thanks for checking."

"Here." Susan scribbles on scrap paper with one of the tiny library pencils. "This is her work email. You can try sending her a message and maybe she'll reply to you when she gets back."

"Great, thank you so much!" I exclaim.

"Mm hmm." Susan gives me a small smile.

I fold the paper in my hand and exit the library's main doors. I find a spot at one of the tables in the reading courtyard and settle into my seat. The chairs are wrought iron and not comfortable by any stretch, but I don't plan on staying long. I pull out my phone, pleased to see several messages from Parker.

> PARKER
> What a disgrace to the sanctity of marriage.
> A truly disgusting arrangement.

He's replied to the article I sent him. I giggle.

> PARKER
> I guess we have a lot of work to do in proving them wrong.
> Miss you xxx

My heart flutters. Sarcastic and suggestive in the same breath. My soulmate.

I open my email and type a message.

Hi Maisie,

This is Iris, from book club at the library. I'm sorry we haven't crossed paths in a few weeks! I've been meaning to catch you and give you my thoughts on that book you recommended to me a while back. I absolutely loved it! You have great taste! Let me know when you'll be around, and I'll try to swing by to discuss it with you.

Thanks, hope all is well.

Iris Gladwell
PS: got your email address from Susan at the library. Hope that's okay.

I click *send* before I have time to overthink it.

Sixty-One

Tuesdays remain my favorite day of the week. I'm up early today, and I deeply breathe in the cool air sneaking through my cracked window. The refreshing scent of nature envelops me. I shiver, the surface of my skin prickling with goosebumps. I pull the bedsheets up over my body and run my hands over my chest. I take several deep breaths, indulging in my own touch against my supple, bare skin.

Insatiable.

I roll out of bed and have a luxuriously hot shower. Scrubbing my skin thoroughly, I give my hair a good wash and shave my legs. Feeling fresh and clean, I hop into a pair of autumn-themed scrubs, with cats and dogs leaping and playing in piles of fallen leaves.

Urban Grind is busier than usual, and Simone is nowhere to be found. It's Lane and Omar today, along with a fresh-faced black-haired woman who I'm sure graduated from high school yesterday, she looks so impossibly young. They must be training her, which would explain the backlog. I catch Lane's eye and he gives me a nod, but I hold my place in line, ninth or tenth before it's my turn for coffee.

"Good morning," I greet Lane when I finally reach the register.

"Morning, Iris. This is Paris."

Paris raises her delicate hand. "Hi! First day. Sorry for the delay!" She's perky and outgoing. She'll be a great fit.

"No problem at all."

"The usual?" Lane confirms.

"Yep. Always."

Lane walks Paris through my custom order, I pay, then wait off to the side. Omar is the only one making drinks, but he does so with style. Like Tom Cruise in *Cocktail*, he makes it a show, tossing coffee cups here and there, twirling syrup bottles in the air. Everyone is having a great morning, it seems.

With my drink finally in hand, I check my watch and am met with my five-minutes-until-work alarm. No time to read by the river this morning, but I let it go.

At the clinic, the mood shifts. Maria is sobbing behind the reception desk, her face red and her lap piled with wet tissues.

"Oh, my God, Maria, are you okay?" I gasp. I've never seen her cry before.

"No!" she squeaks.

I run over to her and rub her back. "What happened? What's going on?"

"My husband. I just found out he's cheating on me!" she screams, making an awful guttural sound in the back of her throat.

"Oh, Maria, I'm so sorry!"

Her head pops up and she looks me square in the face. "And you know what? I found out last week that I'm pregnant. I'm fucking pregnant with his child and Antonio is out there sticking is dick in someone else!" She wails, overcome with grief.

"Oh, my God! You're pregnant? Congratulations, Maria, that's wonderful news."

"It's horrible news!" she falls back onto the desk. "How could he do this to me? To us?" Her voice cracks and her sobs echo between the walls of the empty clinic. I lean into her, squeezing her body in mine.

"I'm so sorry," I whisper. "I'm so sorry."

"I don't know what to do! I can't stay with him! And now I'm going to have his baby! And what of Angelo and Mateo? Their father is a cheater! He's destroyed this beautiful, growing family! How could he!"

Maria's pain spreads from her body to mine. I feel it in my chest, heavy and grim. My watch buzzes again, and it's time to open the clinic.

"You should go home. Don't worry about work, I'll talk to Dr. Amar. I'm so sorry, Maria. Go take care of yourself. Have a bath, drink some tea. Do you want me to call your sister? Have her come get you?"

"No, I'll get home just fine. Thank you, Iris. I'm sorry!" She sobs into my neck.

"You have nothing to be sorry for. I've got this."

I throw an entire box of used tissues into the garbage, wipe down the front desk with disinfectant, and open the clinic seven minutes late. I apologize profusely to the two customers waiting outside, but, thankfully, they are understanding and in good spirits.

Robbie agrees to come in an hour early, so he's here by nine, and together we manage the day without too much difficulty. Dr. Amar isn't particularly pleased with the situation, but understanding enough, I suppose. Dr. Val pops in toward the end of the day, and it seems like, at last, the strain between us has been remedied.

As I gather my things at the end of the day, I think of Maria and her predicament. It's hard for me to grasp the concept of cheating, given my unconventional lifestyle choices. And when it comes to having children, I also struggle to understand those relationship dynamics. I would like to think that non-monogamy and having children are not mutually exclusive, but given my lack of knowledge and interest in the politics of reproduction, I can't really form an opinion on it. Part of me thinks that Maria and her husband could still have a healthy, happy family if they were open to sexual interactions with others. Antonio could whet his sexual appetite while still maintaining the family unit that is so important to Maria. Why do love and sexual exclusivity have to go hand-in-hand? They don't, if you ask me.

But a relationship tainted by betrayal, regardless of what that betrayal is, stings. Maria's pain is very real to her, and my heart aches for her. She has a beautiful heart, and seeing her weak and broken is incredibly sobering. But she's strong, smart, and resilient. I know she'll come out of this hardship okay.

I give Parker a call, and he answers on the third ring.

"Hi, beautiful."

"Hey. I'm just leaving work now. How long will you be? I was thinking of grabbing Chinese before I head home."

"Uh," he pauses. "I probably won't be there until closer to seven-thirty. I have to stop off at home before I head to you."

"Oh. Uh, okay."

"I'll pick something up on the way. You want Chinese, you said?"

"Sure, that sounds good." I'm starving now, though. I don't know how I'll make it another hour and a half before Parker gets here.

"Great. I'm excited to get caught up on our *content*," he says with seduction and mystery in his tone.

"Mm. Me, too." I admit.

"See you soon. I love you."

"Love you."

Parker and I have gotten into the routine of viewing the Recordings from Our events together. It's such a turn on. We've unlocked a new level of eroticism in experiencing them together - watching each other with different partners. It's about the sex, yes, but more so, it's about validating who we are at our cores. It's about accepting each other, embracing each other fully, and encouraging each other to live our most honest life.

It's true and raw and beautiful. I wouldn't trade it for anything.

So, when Parker mentions that he has his ten-year recognition coming up this weekend, I glow with pride in kind. Ten years is a huge milestone. Ten years of commitment to Our Family and its ideals is a great honor.

"How does it feel?" I ask, my mouth full of chow mein and orange chicken.

"Surreal, honestly," Parker admits. "It seems like it's been forever and no time at all."

"Where is it? At the Harold Estate?"

"No, it's..." he pauses.

"What?" I ask, confused by his thoughtful stare.

"It's just that... I'm sorry, Iris. I can't bring a guest."

A guest? "I'm not a guest. I'm your partner." My voice is harsh and unrelenting.

"I know, but the rules are clear on this. You're still very green. I'm much more senior than you. In time, you'll learn more. But this event isn't it."

I'm awestruck. The blood drains from my face. Parker may as well have told me he needs to cut my hand off. It hurts, the exclusion. Together, Parker and I are a team. I certainly want to be there to support him at an event of this significance. It feels wrong to tell me so candidly that I can't.

I fight it. I fight it with everything I am. My voice rings between us, fiery and loud.

Parker stays calm. He placates me in a soft, gentle tone. "You need to know that I understand. I understand you wanting to be a part of this, to know more. It's complicated, because of our gap. I have ten years of involvement bearing down on me. You're still so fresh. I wish it didn't have to be like this, I really do. But I promise, I *promise*, there will come the time when you'll be able to attend these events alongside me."

That's not good enough.

I immediately reach out to Mallory about it, and she forwards my message to Desi. While Desi acknowledges my concern, she confirms that I am unable to attend given the *sensitivity of the events* surrounding the ten-year recognition.

For the first time since I joined Our Family, I doubt it.

The secrecy of it doesn't sit well. I understand that discretion is at the forefront of the existence of Our Family, but I'm hungry to devour everything about it. And, up to this point, I felt like I pretty much had. Knowing that there are parts of Our Family that I don't know about makes me as excited as it does uneasy.

Why don't I get to know?

Sixty-Two

What a turn the week has taken.

I try not to take the news about Parker's ten-year to heart. I mean, I do take it to heart, but I'm actively working to distract myself from the pain of it. And there's no better place to do that than at the library.

I haven't heard back from Maisie. I didn't really expect to, if I'm being honest. I search up the author of the book she recommended to me and find that she has several other published works. I spend Wednesday evening scouring the shelves, selecting a couple new books, and add one by the horror erotica author to my pile. I finish next week's book club read and dive into a new one. It doesn't hook me right away, but I decide to stick it out.

I head home with my new pile of books sometime around eight. I open my patio slider to let the cool evening air in. I settle into the cushions of the couch, pull up a fuzzy blanket around me, and reopen my book.

I don't get far. My wrist buzzes with a notification from Our Family.

My heart skips as I open it.

Message from: Matthew I.
Hi, Iris. My name is Matthew. I'm looking for some
company tonight. If you're interested, message me
back. Hope to hear from you.

This is the second time someone has sought me out through Our Leaflet. My cheeks redden and I struggle to hide my giddy grin. I type a response.

Message to: Matthew I.
Hi, Matthew. I'd love to keep you company.

An immediate reply pops up.

Message from: Matthew I.
Wonderful. My address is 617 West Cove Street.
Apartment 2.
9 p.m. work for you?

Message to: Matthew I.
9 p.m. is great. See you soon.

Message from: Matthew I.
PS: Wear your hair down. Please.

The address Matthew gives me pops up as just a few blocks away. Relieved I don't have to pay for an Uber, I skip across the street in my black Mary-Jane shoes and make my way according to the nice Google maps lady. As per Matthew's request, I've let my hair down.

Matthew greets me with a broad smile and strong handshake. He has huge eyes that look almost too big for his head. He's also incredibly skinny, making me feel gargantuan with my shapely curves. But it's just sex, so I smile back, give him a kiss on the cheek, and follow him into his apartment.

It's small, but clean, with a white kitchen and spotless surfaces. I put my bag down on the table near the front door, and Matthew welcomes me into his living room. We talk for a bit, getting to know each other. He seems a little on edge, but I chalk it up to nerves.

"How long have you been a Member?" I ask him.

"A couple of years, now," he smiles. "But you're pretty new, aren't you?"

"I am. I joined in June."

Matthew nods. "What Branch are you?"

"Branch 29. Desi Harold?"

"I'm Branch 15. Dominguez."

"Dominguez?" I mull the name over in my head. I know it. How do I know it?

"That's right." Matthew stares at me suspiciously.

"The Masquerade!" I call out, excited at having solved the puzzle. "We are mixing with Dominguez for the Masquerade. I think. Is that right? I think it is..." I pull out my phone and check the invitation for the Masquerade. "Yep. Here it is! Dominguez and Rachels." I show my phone to Matthew. "What are the Inter-Branch Mixers like?" I ask him. "This will be my first one."

Matthew laughs in his throat. "You're in for a treat!"

I stare at him, eyes wide, hungry for more.

"They're not like the Monthly Mixers. At least, not for us. Every Branch is probably a little different. But, in my experience, Inter-Branch Mixers are more... indulgent."

I nod, aware that that information tells me exactly nothing. "Well, I'm looking forward to it. I'm glad we met - it's always nice to see a familiar face, especially at an event as big as the Masquerade is going to be. Over fifty attendees!"

Tired of the conversation, Matthew seeks to silence me with a kiss. It's sloppy and awkward at first, but I lean into it. I fall onto my back and Matthew straddles me. He pushes his center into mine. His tongue slips into my mouth, and I meet it with my own, our kiss growing and changing. He bites my lip and kisses my throat, then moves his tongue against the neck of my red blouse.

"This color looks fantastic on you," he compliments. "I especially love your red hair," he breathes. He grabs a tuft of it in his fist and pulls on it, cricking my neck to the side. He moves back up to face me, and gives me a quick peck. "Can I chew on it?" he asks.

"My hair?" I ask, my voice shrill with bewilderment.

"Yes. It smells incredible," he says as he sniffs at the ends of it.

"Sure," I muster. I've had men and women alike ask me a lot of strange things in my life, but never have I had someone ask me if they could chew on my hair. It's abundantly clear to me that I am not really attracted to Matthew. And we don't seem to be compatible in our interests, either. But if chewing on my hair will get him off, maybe I'll find my own arousal in it, too.

Matthew kisses me again, breathing a heavy sigh into my mouth. He breaks our kiss and licks my forehead, taking my bangs into his mouth and gnawing on them. He moans in arousal, his bulge pushing firmly into my thigh. I wiggle under him, struggling to find a comfortable position. He flips me onto my front, and I quickly remove the pillow I was just laying on before it suffocates me. Meanwhile, Matthew is planted on my ass, his bulge pushing into it as he makes out with my hair. He sniffs it, licks it, takes it into his mouth. Clumps of it made wet by his saliva fall onto my neck, and I almost recoil. But Matthew is hard as fuck, enjoying the smell and touch and taste of my hair more than anyone ever has. I shift, deciding that, even though I'm not going to get off during our interaction, the least I can do is ensure that Matthew has fun.

"Can I come in your hair?" Matthew whispers into my ear, his breath hot and wanton.

"Please, come in my hair, Matthew. I want you to." I'm impressed by how convincing I sound. How desperate. "Please," I beg.

Matthew hops off of me and I hear the clang of his belt as he undresses.

"Do you want me to sit in front of you? I'll turn around so you can grab my hair," I offer.

"Oh, fuck, yes," he moans.

I get up, turn around, and crouch on my knees in front of him. I shake my head. My hair dances down my back, and I hear Matthew quiver.

"Do you like that?" I ask him. "Do you like it when I shake my hair for you?"

"Yes. Yes, I fucking like it," he grunts.

I wiggle it some more, and then he grabs a fistful and pulls me into him. I yelp. His grip tightens as I feel his cum shooting onto my scalp and falling into my hair. Matthew grunts and moans, then falls onto the couch beside us. I turn to him.

"Your cum feels so good in my hair." I run my hands down it, working his warm goo into the strands. "Thank you for doing that."

Looking rabid, Matthew grabs my hair again and pulls me into him for a harsh kiss.

"Fuck, Iris. That was incredible," he exhales loudly.

Another satisfied customer.

• • • •

AS I WALK HOME FROM Matthew's with fresh cum caked in my hair, I go over our interaction in my head. While my role was mostly as a prop, I can't say that our time together was completely unfulfilling for me. Just as not every social interaction I've ever had with a human has been the most thrilling in my life, not every sexual interaction will be. And I can accept that. The knowledge that I gave Matthew something he wanted, that I was able to fulfill his niche sexual desire, gives me power. Every experience I have with each different partner is unique, and it challenges me to do things differently that I typically do, and to, of course, try new things. It's not just about me, either. Pleasure exists on a delicate spectrum, and I love to give to others. I decide my interaction with Matthew is exactly that - giving him pleasure, which in turn, fuels my own. I'm proud of myself. Even if I didn't get my own orgasm out of it.

Home again, I spend a lengthy shower washing the remains of my interaction with Matthew out of my hair. The more I think about it, the more my pride swells.

It somehow also cleanses away the doubt I had about Our Family earlier. I was being immature and sensitive. I've come to understand not being invited - I'm practically brand new to Our Family. It's bittersweet being unable to be by his side, though. I'm proud of Parker. I'm proud of his commitment to Our family. I'm proud of what he's accomplished in his membership, even though I certainly don't know the half of it. But I'm most proud of Parker for being himself. In my mind, there's no greater accomplishment than being authentically, genuinely, who you are. For this, I admire him profoundly and wish I could be there to congratulate him on his impressive achievement.

Instead, I'll be at home, thinking of him, alone, while I play with one of my many vibrators.

Sixty-Three

F riday. TGIF. I arrive home after work to a pretty little package in front
of my door. A small white box about the size of a book is wrapped up
with a crimson red ribbon. Attached is a brown tag etched with black
cursive writing.

> *My darling Iris,*
> *Yours - no matter what*

My heart leaps in my chest. I bite my lip and eagerly scoop up the box.
Unlocking the front door, I drop my keys and my tote bag down on the
floor and slam the door loudly behind me. I yank the ribbon off the box.
The soft velvet material catches along the edge of the box and snags. I finally
push it aside and open it up. At last. My gift is hiding beneath a blanket of
red tissue paper. I slide it off to reveal a red collar fashioned from the same
velvet as the ribbon. Attached to a shiny silver D-ring is a long, black leash.
There's also something fluffy hidden at the bottom, which I immediately
recognize as a novelty butt plug. I pull it out and run my fingers through
the soft faux fur of a tail. My insides clench and I grow wet with excitement.
Role play isn't something Parker and I do regularly, although we both enjoy
it. Finally, at the bottom of the box is a fuzzy, orange headband affixed with
fox ears.

I glance at the time: 6:52 p.m. Shit. Only a few minutes to get myself
ready. I can't be late. Or else.

I pounce into the bathroom and wash my hands thoroughly. I strip off
my scrubs and toss them into the overflowing basket beside my dresser. I
really do need to tackle the hoards of laundry. Beneath my sink, I scour the
clutter for a bottle of anal lube. I wash the steel of the butt plug carefully
in warm water, scrubbing it with soap and bubbles, paying extra attention
to not get the orange and white of the tail damp. I dry it delicately, then
squirt a gob of lube into my hand. I lather the plug in it, turning myself on
more with every movement. I use the excess on myself, running my fingers
around my rear opening and trying excessively hard to focus on getting
ready and not on how much I want to play with myself. Bending over, I

slide the plug inside of me, gulping as it settles into place. Fuck. I am so fucked. This feels so good already and Parker isn't even here yet. I look at my watch again, the pressure of time weighing heavily on me. I wash my hands, scrubbing hard to get off the excess lube, and then grab the collar. It has several latches, making it easy to find the perfect fit around my neck. I feel breathless as the soft velvet rubs snuggly against my throat. I slide the ears onto my head and take a quick glance in the mirror, turning and posing as I admire myself from head... to tail.

I run to the front door and unlatch the deadbolt. I decide to curl up on the bed and wait for Parker to arrive. Laying on my side, I check the time: 6:59 p.m. Any second now. Taking deep breaths, I start counting. I get to 27 when the door clicks open. I rustle around, turning so my back is facing the doorway. When Parker walks in, the first thing he'll see is my tail. Knowing he'll see me before I'll see him sends a thrill electrocuting through me. He could stand there, loitering in the doorway for minutes without my knowledge, rubbing his thumb to his upper lip while he judges my appearance. He could walk up to the bed, just a foot away from me, and stare, his eyes fixed on my curves, then my tail, then the quickness of my breath. The thoughts alone cause my heart to race and my pussy to become slick with juices. I'm ashamed of how aroused I am at simply the thought alone of Parker watching me. I become so lost in the fantasy that I almost forget that Parker really is here, likely somewhere in this room.

My head yanks backward as a soft, black fabric is forced into my mouth and tied aggressively behind my head. I am caught so off guard that I feel instinctive tears prickle at the corners of my eyes. I fall onto my elbows to brace myself. I grunt, making sounds of surprise and anguish. I look up, my vision backwards and dizzy, but I am able to meet Parker's fierce eyes. He softly touches his finger to lips, letting out a near-silent *shh*.

I fall onto my back now with my tail peeking between my legs. Parker pulls my hands up and my elbows fall out from under me. He grabs the leash, holding it with tension.

"Foxes can't talk, you know," he declares, pacing the edges of the bed, his eyes piercing into mine. "Mm..." he lets out a satisfied hum. "You look fantastic, Iris." He loosens the leash a bit.

"On all fours. Now. I want to inspect my little pet." He whips the leash and it smacks into my nipples. I have no choice but to let out an accidental gasp.

"Shh..." Parker whispers softly.

I turn and push myself up onto all fours with my knees and hands under me. Parker leans onto the bed and reaches over to run his hand up and down my right thigh. I feel myself stiffen and clench. My breath quickens, but I focus hard on trying to slow it down. The soft skin of the back of his hand glides up to my ass, and I gulp. Suddenly, Parker spanks me forcefully, and I yelp in response. I'm doing a terrible job of being silent.

"Naughty, naughty," Parker teases. "You're being too noisy."

He continues petting me, both his hands now gliding along my legs and ass. He gropes my left cheek with one hand and gently tugs my tail with the other. I feel like I'm coming apart. My body is weak. I'm so wet that I can feel my fluids beginning to leak, droplets marching down my thighs. Every tug of my tail makes me clench. Fuck fuck fuck. It feels too good.

"How do you like your tail?" Parker asks, knowing full well I cannot answer. "It suits you, my pet."

Parker tenses the leash now, forcing me to arch my back as my neck stretches. He grabs the base of the tail and begins to turn it, the plug swirling inside me as he does so. He moves it at an angle, forcing the tip of the plug to slide along my inner walls. The pleasure is extreme. I shut my eyes and growl a deep, primitive moan.

Parker immediately stops.

"Well, this doesn't seem to be working. You're still making too much noise, my naughty fox." He moves over to my head and unties the satin gag that's now sopping wet with my saliva. He walks over to the bedside table and opens the drawer. "Let's try this instead." He pulls off a thick piece of restraint tape that he then smacks over my mouth. "This should work a little better, hm?" He pinches my nose, and my entire body quivers. I am at his mercy. His sweet, salacious mercy.

At last he releases his hold on my nose and yanks on the leash. I'm lost in pure ecstasy, my mind and body floating in some other heightened plane.

"Down here, my pet," Parker says as he leads me off the bed. He pushes me back onto my heels. I crouch, anxiously anticipating his next move. My eyes are wide with wanton desire. My fox ears are crooked - I can tell by the feel of the headband against my head. As if reading my mind, Parker reaches to adjust them. He tightens his grip on my leash and pulls me into his waist.

My cheek pushes into his crotch. The fabric of his jeans is sandwiched between my soft skin and his hard cock. He pulls my leash back and forth, and I comply, rubbing my face into him. Then he holds the back of my head and thrusts into my face, once again forcing me to hold my breath. I feel the warmth of his cock begging for the caress of my tongue. With his free hand, I feel Parker reach behind me and grab hold of the base of my tail, wiggling it and working it around inside me. I'm teetering on the edge. I want to let go, to give into the deep pleasure blooming within me. I shake my hips and quiver again.

Suddenly the leash is over my head and behind me, and my body is forced to follow. I lay on the carpet on my back. I take a deep breath, grateful for a gulp of air. Parker ties the leash to the foot of the bed and pinches my nipples. I can't help but yelp. My nipples are perky and desperate for his touch. He moves his mouth over me from nipple to belly button, working his tongue in a torturous pattern of licks and nibbles. His hands torment me, grazing my clit and gently tugging my tail, but never giving me more than a tantalizing taste.

At last, Parker plunges his fingers deep inside my pussy, stretching my opening wide. His thumb works to stimulate my clit, and my eyes roll back. His fingers dance in circles, and my hips find the rhythm. I moan, making feral sounds in my throat, my gratification excruciatingly near. Parker yanks on my tail, and I'm pushed right over into oblivion. I shriek in my blissful release. My insides squeeze, my body quivers, and my skin prickles with sweat and satisfaction. My orgasm is all-encompassing - otherworldly, even. This one absolutely ranks in my top five best orgasms of all time. Ever.

"Fuck, yes," Parker mutters breathlessly. I'm shaking, the aftershocks of my climax injecting me with an unimaginable ecstasy. "Fuck! Yes!" he grunts. The pride he gets from making me come that hard makes me hot all over again. It makes me crave more. And more. Parker licks his fingers, slurping up my cum. "God, you taste fucking amazing. Now that's my good pet."

I throw my head back, still reeling from my release. I feel Parker climb on top of me, and he rips the tape off my mouth. It burns so good as the adhesive pulls on my stimulated skin. I suck in a deep breath.

"Fuck!" I yell, both in response to my orgasm and the pain of the tape. "Fuck, that was so good. You're so fucking good, Parker."

He beams as he inhales. He begins to untie my leash from the bedpost. "Now it's your turn to thank me. Show me how grateful you are to have me, my sweet little fox."

I nod.

Parker stands up to remove his shirt and pants. I push myself onto all fours and wiggle my ass to swing my tail from side to side. Even in that small movement, the plug feels amazing. I raise my gaze up and admire Parker before me, where he stands fully naked. I'll never tire of admiring his body. His muscles are defined but not overly so. His skin is soft and touchable. His cock is thick and ready for me. I pounce on it, teasing the tip with my tongue and his sack with my fingertips. I grab the cheek of his ass in one hand and squeeze it unyieldingly, my nails digging into his flesh. He flinches, and I revel in the power I have over him in this fleeting moment.

"Ouch!" he yelps. "Watch your claws!" he warns. I smile up at him with mystery in my eyes.

I continue to tease him, tickling his sack with my tongue and fingertips, watching him grow increasingly frustrated with my pace. I pump my fist along his shaft a few times and kiss the tip with each slow movement. I continue to knead my nails, scratching them up and down his leg and threatening to do the same to his ass.

Parker begins pushing his hips toward my mouth in his impatience, pleading for me to take him in. Still basking in the bliss of my own release, it's difficult to resist. He's already leaking fluids from the tip of his cock, and they taste deliciously sweet on my tongue. I open my mouth widely and slowly move his length inside. Relaxing my throat, he slips in deeply. Sounds of his satisfaction echo in my ears. I pull him out, slow.

The craving for more fogs the air around us.

Parker can't take it another second. He yanks on my leash and plunges his length into the back of my throat. I gag and cough. A smile catches in my throat. This man is so impatient, but fuck does he feel incredible in my mouth. I bob my head and allow Parker to set the pace. I move my hands behind him to cup his ass. With each deep thrust of Parker's hips, I knead my nails into his tender cheeks. He grunts and moans. Intoxicated by his noises, my own wetness grows once again.

Between my legs, my tail swings with each of Parker's thrusts. The fur brushes and tickles the insides of my thighs, teasing the memory of my mind-blowing orgasm. The contrast between the softness of my tail and the harshness of Parker's thrusts sets fire to a primitive part of me.

Suddenly, Parker releases his hold on the leash and tosses it aside. He guides my body around, and I turn away from him. Parker mounts me from behind and rams his entire length deep inside my crevice. He slides easily into my sopping mound and I whimper, my body sensitive and overly responsive to him. As Parker thrusts forward into me, his body slams into my tail. It's a sensation unlike any other. I tremble and come immediately, crumbling forward in euphoric anguish.

"I'm not done with you yet, my pet," Parker grunts into my ear. He grabs onto my hips and quickens his pace. My impulse is to pull away - the stimulation is almost too much to bear.

"Fuck, fuck," I exhale under my breath.

"I'm so close," Parker promises.

He pulls me up onto my knees and massages my breasts in his warm hands. He teases my nipples, pinching and yanking on them. I come again, and a moment later, with one final thrust, so does he.

We fall onto the floor, our breaths ragged and our bodies covered in a slick layer of sweat.

"That was fucking amazing."

"You are fucking amazing," Parker responds.

Best sex I've ever had.

And I've had a lot of sex.

Sixty-Four

I wake up in the morning still warm from the sex Parker and I had the night before. Our connection is like a drug, seeping into my blood and making me high. Sometimes, I literally pinch myself to prove that I'm not dreaming. It doesn't feel real. It's too good to be true.

Then I realize that it's Saturday, and a large portion of our time together is about to be stolen away from us. Parker has to leave for his ten-year recognition at eleven; we have less than an hour left before this moment is a distant memory. I push myself into him, drinking in his scent. He kisses my forehead and taps my nose with his thumb.

"Boop."

I laugh, his playfulness making light of the impending darkness.

"My mom got engaged." I meant to tell Parker on Tuesday, but things got tense. Much more at ease now, I open up again.

"She did? Wow, congratulations to her. And... Willard, is it?"

I nod. "Yeah. Thanks. She's super excited."

"I don't sense the same excitement in you." Parker shifts his body and turns so our eyes meet. "You okay with it?"

"I am. I don't know why I'm weird about it. Willard is *fine*, I guess. He and mom seem decently happy."

"But?"

I ruminate on it for a moment. "But... he's not dad. I know she's not trying to replace him. She's just finding happiness. I guess I need to be okay with that."

"When's the wedding?"

"I think April. Sometime in the spring. Cici will be old enough to travel without too much trouble."

"So, they're having it in Hawaii?"

"I think so. Willard has a mansion out there, from the sounds of it. Mom said that she had *so many people asking about the details of the engagement* that she emailed me a whole novel recounting it." Parker raises his eyebrows. "He has a fucking sailboat. I think their wedding will be pretty over-the-top."

"But your mom will be happy?"

"I think she will," I admit.

"You know, I've never been to Hawaii." Parker settles his face into my neck. He feels warm and insanely comforting.

"Me either. It'll be a first for us both, I guess."

"Ah, the wonder of matrimony!" Parker declares sarcastically. It hangs in the air between us, taking everything in me not to explode in a tirade of marriage-bashing. Parker's provoking me, like he always enjoys doing, but I'm not giving into the game this time.

We have just enough time for crepes at River's Edge. The early-morning crowd has thinned out, and Parker and I sit at our usual booth overlooking the water near the back of the restaurant. I order a pot of coffee; Parker has a screwdriver. The service is quick and we devour our meal just as fast. My stomach was grumbling.

Parker bids me a bittersweet goodbye; he has to get ready for his ten-year recognition. We stall, our fingers grasping at the tips, as Parker backs away toward his truck. I jut out my lower lip in a dramatic pout-infused protest.

"I wish I could go with you," I exclaim in one last, desperate attempt. Parker looks at me with pity. I can't fight it - it makes my skin hot. "I know I can't, though. I'm proud of you. Just know that." I smile at him one last time.

"I love you. I know you support me. That means everything, Iris. It really does."

Why, then, can't I come?

Sixty-Five

In my weak state following Parker's departure, I decide to call Zach. We arrange to meet up at the park this afternoon, in the hour-and-a-half window the girls have before their nap time.

I hate to admit it, but my mom was right. I needed to talk to Zach.

Of course, I can't confide in him about anything. Not really. But Zach understands me. Maybe it's a genetic twin thing, or maybe it's the fact that we went through the same childhood together at the same time. My money's on the latter. Regardless, though, I know he'll have words of wisdom when it comes to understanding and accepting all the things I cannot control.

Promptly at 2:30 p.m., I spot Zach and the girls digging in the sandbox. Remi is with them, sitting patiently next to the stroller with his leash tied to the frame. Molly is home with baby Cici, who, I realize, is already over two months old. A sudden pang of guilt hits me. It's been a full two months since I've seen my brother and his family. I need to do better. I need to be a better sister to him and a better auntie to my three nieces.

Lily catches my eye and takes off, losing her shoes in the grass as she crosses over to me. She attacks my leg, wrapping her whole body around it in a hug.

"Auntie Iris!" she yells. "Come play!"

"Hi, Lily! Oh yes, I will, of course. Just give me a bit to have a chat with your dad, okay?"

A second later, Lily is off, climbing the structure and shooting down the slides.

Nora stays put, toddling around in the sandbox, very intent on building a moat around her sandcastle.

I approach Zach with a large coffee for each of us.

"It's a peace offering," I say, handing Zach his.

"Iris, so good to see you," he replies. He pulls me in for a snug hug. My defenses immediately disintegrate. "I've missed you."

"I've missed you so much, Zach," I blurt out, trying hard not to cry already. "I'm sorry I've been a stranger. A lot has happened." It's true, but no

393

excuse. "And I've missed you, Mr. Rembrandt!" I say, scratching the pup's ears. His soft fur is an instant comfort. "So, what of mom and Willard?" I exclaim. "They're getting married?" Saying it out loud doesn't make it any more real.

"Yep, so they are. Mom asked the girls if they would be her flower girls. They don't know what it means other than wearing a puffy dress," he laughs. "Cici will still be so small, so Molly might have to help her walk down the aisle." Zach laughs. "It's really happening soon. Just a few months."

"April, right?"

"March. March first. I'm assuming you're bringing Parker with you?" I'm sure he doesn't mean for it to be condescending, but it comes across that way.

"I am. Zach," I say longingly, "Parker is my person. I'm so in love with him. It's kind of insane, actually, how much I care about him. I'm enamored by him. He's the most interesting person I've ever met."

"That's really great, Iris. I'm so glad for that for you. You know, you are pretty amazing. It's about time someone appreciates you for you. Who you really are."

Nora comes up to Zach and asks him to help her build "the most biggest castle of biggest castle big ever!" I take the moment to breathe in Zach's words. It feels good to be *seen*.

"So, tell me about what you have been up to. Besides raising a small army of children and conquering the business world," I laugh.

"Lots to fill you in on, actually." He smiles suspiciously. After filling up two buckets of damp sand to create an epic sandcastle for Nora, he returns to sit beside me on the bench. We each take a big swig of our coffees. "The girls don't know yet," he begins in a whisper, "but we are expecting."

"What?" I gasp. I almost spit out my coffee. Well, I do, sort of. A couple of dribbles surge out of my mouth.

"Molly's only a few weeks along. We got pregnant pretty much immediately after we had Cici. We called last week to share the news with mom," he explains. "Can you believe it? Baby number four!"

"Wow. Wow. Congratulations! Wow, that's so exciting!" I hug Zach tightly once more. He's beaming. I'm clenching.

"We still can't believe it. We're so thrilled. It doesn't seem real. Not yet, anyway. It's still really, really early, but I hope this is an easy pregnancy for Molly. Nora's was the hardest."

"I'm so glad for you both." Jesus fucking Christ. Four children. My vagina aches at the mere thought.

"Thanks. It feels surreal, this early. But it's a really great surprise. And work is good. They're really generous with paternity leave. I'm still working four-day weeks most of the time, and I'll be able to take the time off when the next baby comes. And a few months from now there will be promotions and cost-of-living increases. We should be in good shape." I nod, taking in the successes of my twin brother. "And Molly recently hired a couple of interns to do some of the managing at the gallery so she can focus more on creating. With almost four kids," he laughs, "she doesn't have much time to paint. So that's helping to free up some for her. How's work going for you?"

My brain is swirling with everything Zach's thrown at me. I take a few decadent sips of my coffee before I respond.

"You know, work has been good. Busy, but good. We've had some turnover so still trying to come back from that. At least my days of overtime are pretty much over. Things are coming together."

"That's great."

"Antee Ireez, play wish me!" Nora trills, pulling me by the hand to ascend the stairs leading to the slide. I follow her, and some twenty minutes later, I feel liberated by the magic of play.

Nearing nap time, Zach loads the girls up in their double stroller and heads back to the car. He thanks me for meeting them, but I assure him that I needed this just as much as they did. He gives me the details on the flight they booked for mom's wedding, and I promise him that I'll look into booking ours in the next couple of weeks.

With three children, another on the way, a successful career, a beautiful wife with a booming business, and an adorable dog, Zach has the perfect life.

For him.

Our lives are vastly different. Similar in their fulfillment, but tremendously different in their construction. While Zach is busy managing business accounts and changing diapers, I'm fucking strangers. Somehow I think I have it better.

What started as a private game between me and Parker has transformed our lives. We are proud to have found our place in a lifestyle where we share the same, unconventional values with others just like us. It's a true honor.

And now, Parker has made it ten years. I'm at home, without him, while he celebrates with the fortunate *others* who have the privilege of treasuring this moment with him. From the communication Desi and I have had about it, she knows I'm not happy. Which is why I'm nervous when I receive a message from her. I tap on it and hold my breath.

Dearest Iris,

On behalf of Our Family, I'm honored to recognize you in your steadfast dedication thus far. Our Family understands your desire to be supportive of your partner; therefore, it's my privilege to inform you of an upcoming opportunity that we believe will be of interest to you.

Iris, in spite of your minor infraction, you've grown to prove yourself a faithful, devoted, and trustworthy Member of Our Family. You've made a significant impact within Our Branch, word of which has traveled throughout the organization as a whole. We see huge potential in you, Iris.

We are exceptionally impressed with you.

It is with great honor that we extend to you the opportunity to hold an Office within Branch 29.

Congratulations, you've earned it.

Please inform us of your decision to accept or reject this additional responsibility, and we will move forward in whichever manner you choose.

We trust in you, Iris.

Truly Yours,
Desi Harold
Our Family - Head of Branch 29

My mouth gapes open. I'm shocked.

I have a lot of fight in me, but when it came to Parker's ten-year, I conceded. Even though I still hold resentment around it, I knew they weren't going to bend the rules and allow me to attend, regardless of how much I challenged it. But being offered additional responsibility with the stink I made around it? That, I was not expecting.

It pains me to admit the truth: the undercurrent of all my upset has been rooted in envy. I've been sick with it. The gross, staggering awareness that other Members have deeper roots in Our Family than I do has made me disgustingly envious. I'm desperate; I crave the connection, the understanding. The inclusion. Our Family has enriched my life. I've finally found where I belong. Even with how new I am, I know I'm ready to pledge myself fully to Our Family.

Of course, I have no idea what this looks like. As a newbie, I haven't been privy to the knowledge that others have already unlocked upon their significant milestones. *I'm too green.* For me, everything is clouded, obscured behind a dark veil. Even Desi's message offering me additional responsibility is severely ambiguous.

But the torture of exclusion has piqued with Parker's ten-year. (I won't even ruminate on all of Parker's secret meetings and calls.)

I want to know all of it. I want to give myself to all of it.

Parker told me when I first joined Our Family that each milestone of membership grants additional privilege. If I accept this Office, I know I won't gain the level of involvement that Parker has, but it's a start. I know it has to be earned. I respect that it has to be earned. I will put in the work. They just have to trust me to.

It's my time. I am ready.

Desi,

First and foremost, thank you for your kind words. It's a true privilege to call myself a Member of Our Family. I am delighted to be offered additional responsibility and gratefully appreciate the opportunity. I gladly accept.

Thank you for believing in me.
Iris x

I fall into bed with a stupid, giddy grin on my face.

Sixty-Six

I half-expect to hear from Parker after his ten-year; I'd hoped we'd still get to spend some of Sunday together. But since my message from Desi, my phone has remained still and silent. I decide to check in with Ben. I know it's a long shot, but I miss him.

ME
Brunch today?

He types back immediately.

BEN
Can't today... meeting Kai's family! GULP! Wish me luck!
Girl, we NEED a date soon!
Thursday???? Dinner???

ME
O.M.G.! That's HUGE!!
You're easy to love, I'm sure they'll adore you!!!
Yes, dinner Thursday

BEN
It's a date!!
(If I survive this family gathering. Eek!)

With no plans for the day ahead, I decide to just let it take me where it will. I have a shower, throw on a decisively fall outfit (orange flannel, black jeans), and head to Urban Grind.

Paris is still training, but the line is nothing like it was last week. I search for Simone, but don't see her. I haven't seen her in a bit, I realize.

"Good morning, Iris!" Paris sings. "The usual?" she asks, her curls bouncing on her shoulders.

"Hi, Paris! Yes, please!"

"Be right out for you," Omar calls from behind the chrome of the coffee machine.

"Hey, I wanted to ask. Has Simone been around lately?" I haven't seen her, but then again maybe our schedules just aren't lining up. Paris looks at me quizzically, almost as if she's never heard of Simone, and she's someone I simply made up. Her wrinkled face makes me question my sanity for a split second. She turns to Omar.

"Omar?" she calls. "Iris is asking about Simone?"

"Simone? Yeah, she sort of dropped out on us at the last minute. Here one day, gone the next. It wasn't like her. Felt kind of weird." Omar explains.

"She's gone?" I ask, aghast. There's a hint of panic in my voice that surprises me.

"Yeah, I guess. Maybe Lane knows more? He'll be in tomorrow. You can ask him then if you want." Omar passes me my drink.

"Oh. Okay, thanks. Alright, see you guys tomorrow!"

As I open the door to step out into the pale sunlight of the day, I can't shake the feeling that something is wrong.

Very wrong.

Simone wouldn't just disappear like that. Would she? Until I can ask Lane about her tomorrow, my mind will torture me over a million imagined scenarios, all in varying degrees of horror.

While I certainly can't focus on reading a book right now, I decide that taking a walk along the river might help ease my mind. There are lots of people out today, all with the same idea to make the most of a leisurely, autumnal Sunday. The sun is casting small slivers of light through the mostly cloudy sky, and there's a distinct cool breeze that playfully wisps my fringe and the ends of my hair. I pop in my earbuds to drone out the sounds of conversation and children yelling, and choose a peppy playlist on Spotify. I walk the full mile and a half along the river pathway, then turn around and make my way back. I focus on the sweetness of my coffee and the tinge of coolness at the tip of my nose. I consider what to do with the rest of my day, and come to the undeniable conclusion that there's only one thing that will really take my mind off everything else.

• • • •

BACK HOME, I OPEN THE Our Family app and tap in my search criteria into Our Leaflet. I feel hopelessly pathetic looking for another lonely soul in the middle of the day on a Sunday, but when over twenty matches pop up, the comfort of validation takes the sting away.

Autumn A. is my first match listed, and I immediately know she's the one. I type her a quick message.

> Message to: Autumn A.
> Hi! Up for keeping me company today? xx Iris

Nearly an hour passes before she responds.

> Message from: Autumn A.
> Hello hello! Thanks for reaching out. Sorry,
> can't today, otherwise engaged. Another time.
> x A.

The disappointment pangs, and I don't have it in me to look at other matches. Rejection, regardless of how innocent, sucks. I'll have to get through the day alone today, I guess.

I check the time: almost two. I can totally justify a glass of wine right now. I wander into the kitchen and unscrew the cap to an ultra-cheap bottle of red that a pet parent gifted to me in honor of her dog's fifth birthday. I pour myself a large glass and take a hearty sip. It's pretty awful, but it was free. I squeeze my eyes shut and take another gulp. I settle onto my bed and I pull open my laptop to search for some free porn. Within seconds, thousands of lewd videos are at my fingertips. Ah, the wonders of the internet.

I slowly sip my almost-not-drinkable wine and click from one video to the next, getting more aroused by the second. The wine has certainly calmed my nerves, but the videos are winding me up in a big way. I find one that I deem worthy of my full attention, and set my glass down. I rifle through my bedside drawer and gather a few supplies, then settle back into my warm spot against the headboard.

I press play. The scene is between a blonde and a brunette, both naked already, laying together on a leather couch. They passionately kiss, running their hands through their hair, along their cheeks, and against their shoulders. The blonde wraps her hand around the brunette's throat, and the brunette gives out a weak moan. They kiss more, and as the scene unfolds, I realize that these two women have a real connection. Either they are incredible actors (unlikely), or they are real-life friends connecting in a genuine way. Regardless, the video is exactly what I'm looking for. I peel off my shirt and watch on.

The blonde removes her hand, revealing a ring of reddened skin around the brunette's throat. They share a passionate kiss, making such delectable sounds that I immediately become wet. It's as though these two are finally giving into their mutual attraction after denying themselves of it for years. Their connection is an undeniable aphrodisiac. The blonde moves her mouth in a series of licks and pecks, all the way from the brunette's lips down to her supple breasts. She sucks on her nipples, kneading them in her mouth. The brunette's eyes are overcome with enjoyment as she wiggles, and the blonde relishes in her response. I turn my attention to my own breasts, and grasp them in my hands. The blonde kisses the brunette's mouth once again, then her neck, then her nipples, and I pinch my own between my fingers. The brunette pulls the blonde up to her and they share another intimate kiss, their bodies pressed firmly into each other. The blonde gently pushes the brunette away, laying her on her back, and kisses her from lips to nipple once more. Then she massages her hands against the brunette's hips, spreading her fingers wide to take in the sensation of her bare skin. The brunette is panting in her arousal, but there's a hint of nervousness in her body. The blonde kisses her belly button, then trails lower to her sensitive nub.

"Is this okay?" she whispers, and the brunette enthusiastically nods and moans.

The blonde worships her bud, licking and kissing and gently caressing it with her mouth. The brunette watches her, then tosses her head back, then looks down at her again. She is authentically enjoying herself, and I can't stop myself from participating alongside her.

I slide my jeans off, kicking them and my panties aside. I reach for my clit vibrator. As I watch the blonde's tongue move against the brunette's delicate pearl, I push my vibrator against mine. Switching it on, its immediate, unrelenting pulses shock my system. I lean back and spread my legs wide. My body quakes as I hold it in place. The vibrations are electrifying. I writhe and moan, wondering how the fuck the brunette is keeping so quiet because all I hear are my own sounds reverberating off the walls. I switch between my fingers and the vibrator, trying to mirror the blonde as she slowly brings her hands to the brunette's glistening folds. The blonde's pace quickens now, urging the brunette to succumb to her pleasure. The brunette won't have it though, and she pulls the blonde back to her mouth. They kiss again.

I watch on, and the brunette reaches for a purple dildo from the table beside them. It eerily reminds me of my own, which is waiting patiently to my left. On their knees now, they kiss again, and the brunette slowly moves the toy between them.

"I want to put this inside of you," the brunette says. The blonde nods, her eyes wide with expectation.

Their mouths are on each other again. The blonde's hands play with the brunette's nipples once more, and the brunette gently slides the toy into the blonde's opening. The blonde gasps, and her sounds send a surge of wetness at my own core. I grab my toy and push it into me, too, moving it in rhythm with the brunette. It slides in and out of me with ease; I'm drenched. The brunette's pace is slow, but the feeling is incredible.

The blonde wails as the brunette swipes her tongue against her clit. Pumping the toy into her, she twists and flicks her tongue, and the blonde nears her undoing. She pants, and I echo her intoxicating sounds. I reach for my clit vibrator and hold it to the spot. My release, too, is imminent. I listen to the blonde, awaiting her own climax, but I can't hold out a second longer. I thrust the toy into my G-spot as the vibrator works its magic on my nub. My orgasm unfolds in a glorious wave of euphoria. My body quakes and I yelp, the immediate sensitivity of my clit forcing me to remove the vibrator. My inner walls contract against the toy, and I fall back into the pillows, breathing heavy.

Lost in my own bliss, I turn off the video and think of Parker.

I wish he was here to see this.

I miss him. Fuck, I miss him so much.

I stare at the bumps and dips of the knockdown ceiling above me and think of him, picturing the curves of his body and the softness of his lips.

I know we never share Sunday afternoons together, but it seems infuriatingly childish that he insists on spending his Sunday evenings at his house. What is it, a school night? I want to roll my eyes, but doing so seems impossible in this moment - the aftershocks of my orgasm are still coursing through my veins. They make my body feel like jelly. I hum, thinking of the blonde, the brunette, and Parker.

My watch vibrates with a notification from Our Family. It takes a moment to regain my strength, but eventually I reach for my phone. Smiling, I excitedly open the app. It's a message from Mallory.

Hello my lovely Members of Branch 29!

I'm pleased to provide you with a reminder of the upcoming Inter-Branch Mixer: Our Masquerade Ball! This year, we are honored to be sharing this event with Branch 15 - Dominguez and Branch 04 - Rachels.

Attached, you'll find the invitation for Our Family's Annual Masquerade Ball. As a reminder, this event will NOT be held at the Harold Estate. On the day of the event, directions to the Dominguez Estate will be provided here in the app. I've also included the contact information for Our costuming expert, Mr. Walter Jacobson. We encourage you to reach out to him for assistance in acquiring your costume, as themed attire is required for this event! Dress to impress!

Thank you! Looking forward to seeing you all again soon.

Truly yours,
Mallory

Inter-Branch Mixer - Our Family's Annual Masquerade Ball
It's Our pleasure to invite you,
Iris Gladwell,
To Our Family's Annual Masquerade Ball.
Please join us
Saturday, October 21 - Sunday, October 22
6 p.m. - 11 a.m.
At the Dominguez Estate.
Dress your best - themed attire required.

We look forward to the time with you.

Truly Yours,
Felicia Dominguez
Our Family, Head of Branch 15

Contact Information
Walter Jacobson
Costuming Extraordinaire
Contact discreetly through the app - <u>Send a message to Walter</u>

At Our last Mixer, I listened intently as the ladies discussed the upcoming Masquerade. I'm not alone in my Masquerade virginity - this will be the first for both Scarlett and Aki as well. I decide to reach out to Scarlett to see if she wants to come with me to meet Walter and have him dress us up. Opening the messages tab of the app, I click on Scarlett's image. Her black hair is down as it always is, and she's lightly biting her lip. Scarlett is a mystery to me. She oozes sexuality, and I can't help but feel mesmerized by her.

> Message to: Scarlett S.
> Hi Scarlett,
> Wondering if you'd be interested in finding
> time to visit this Walter character together?
> I was thinking of reaching out to him
> to see if he's available to dress me up
> sometime this week. Let me know if you
> have some time to come with.
> xx Iris

Theme parties are always a blast, but the Masquerade is going to be extravagant beyond anything I've ever attended. My mind blooms with imagined costumes - exquisite gowns, lacy masks, intricately embroidered bodices, beaded corsets, feathered headpieces. What a grand event it will be.

I close my eyes to envision my perfect costume - and Parker peeling it off.

Sixty-Seven

Walter really is an expert. Or a magician. He gets right inside my head and pulls the vision I have for my Masquerade costume right from it. Scarlett and I visit him on Thursday, and several hours later, we emerge from a grungy-looking building feeling like stars of our own extravagant period film.

I hadn't intended for the costuming to take so long, but the layers of fabric and lavish accessories required special care. I unintentionally double-booked plans with Ben and Kai - we were supposed to have dinner at 7:30 p.m. I make up an excuse about work holding me up, and instead meet them for a dessert date an hour late.

They know something is up.

My skin is flushed. My hair is disheveled. My shirt is backwards. That's the dead giveaway. Also, the stupid grin from ear-to-ear.

"Girl, you are a mess!" Ben announces. "Look. At. You. Okay, spill the tea! I want to know all about the mind-blowing sex you're having with Parker."

"We both want to know!" Kai chimes in, playfully pushing Ben aside as he leans close to me.

I giggle and look away mysteriously.

"Unless it's *not* Parker!" Ben suggests. "Did he... did he loosen the leash and let you dabble elsewhere? You lusty slut!" He cackles. Kai looks positively mystified.

I feel my stomach fall into my feet. I gulp, realizing that I have to choose my next words very carefully. I've never been guarded with Ben before. He knows everything about me. We've always had an open, liberal relationship. It feels like a betrayal to lie by omission. But to disclose any of my recent truths to him means treading on thin ice. Virtually my entire private life is now highly confidential. It feels like an impossible task to choose between honesty with my best friend and belonging in the one place I really do. But the risk is too great. I can't afford to lose everything I've gained through Our Family because of a stupid slip up. The rules are blatantly clear: I can't allude to Our Family, or mention its existence, or identify anyone belonging to it.

"It *is* Parker," I insist. "It's also not Parker," I admit. I form an honest lie that I hope will satiate Ben and be safe with Our Family.

"Iris!"

"What? Do you want to hear this or not?"

"I want to! I have no idea what's going on but I want to hear it!" Kai's eyes widen as he awaits an explanation.

I look at Ben. "Have you told him?" I gesture to Kai. "About me?"

"Not my story to tell."

"Well, then, I have a lot to fill you in on." I grab Kai's hands and he giggles. "So. As you know, I'm in a relationship with Parker. And I have been for several months now." Kai nods politely. "But..." I tease, "I'm attracted to women, too. Pink, purple, and blue proud! And, historically, I'm not exactly good at exclusive relationships. Both because I'm attracted to men and women, and also because I, well, I love to fuck. A lot." Kai gasps. "My relationships are always short-lived because I need more freedom than most people in relationships see as appropriate. But, guys! Parker is different. He's so different. He understands me. He loves me for me and it's... it's a feeling that transcends any other form of love because it's so validating." That's the truth.

"Yeah, yeah, we get it. Parker loves you," Ben says. "So, get on with the details. Who are you fucking?"

"Well, Parker, obviously."

"And it's good?"

"It's amazing."

"And...?"

"And he's just like me. He likes the freedom, too. We have a certain... understanding, I guess. We agreed on an open relationship," I confess. It's not a lie. Our relationship is open. Even more so than Ben or Kai could ever imagine.

"Living the Iris dream," Ben sighs. "I'm really glad for you. Monogamy would never suit you." He winks at me and I blow him a kiss.

"Don't you ever get jealous?" Kai asks. He looks utterly appalled. It takes me by surprise. I try not to laugh in his face.

"No."

"You... don't?" Kai insists. I never thought a gay man could be such a traditionalist.

"No."

Kai sits back in his chair, arms crossed. His lips are curled in disgust.

"Don't worry, baby, I don't need an open relationship to feel fulFILLed by you." Ben giggles.

"I see what you did there!" I shout. Ben and I laugh boorishly, and I give him a high five. Kai turns several shades of pink.

"Parker's just always so busy," I tell Kai. I decide to take another angle on it, hoping to reason my way into his understanding. "An open relationship allows me to still have my physical needs met while he's otherwise engaged. And just because I'm with a man doesn't mean I can shut off my attraction to women. This way, I can... have my cake and eat it, too." Ben and I howl with laughter.

"How do you know he's not just hooking up with other women while he says he's busy?"

"Because an open relationship is built on trust. And we have incredible communication. If he's hooking up with other people, he tells me. And I'm okay with it." But the moment I say it, I question if it's true. I know on my end, it is. I always give Parker a rundown on my week, including who I've interacted with. But, come to think of it, I'm not sure he's ever had an interaction outside of the Mixers. Because he hasn't told me of any. He's usually busy with work. I assume. Or with other responsibilities within Our Family. Which, I am realizing more and more every day, I know nothing about. I don't know what those *responsibilities* are, what they entail, or who he collaborates with. He hasn't told me. And when I've asked, Parker cites his seniority in Our Family and how I'm simply too new.

But they're piling up. The questions. The secrets. The sting from being excluded from his ten-year recognition is still very fresh.

I give Kai a weak smile and we let the topic go. But my mind is swirling. Those seedlings of doubt are sprouting. Only Parker can weed them out.

"So, tell me about what you two have been up to! How's the sex?" I sing, pushing the spotlight back on Ben and Kai.

"I mean, look at us. How could we possibly have anything but magical, unicorns-jumping-over-rainbows sex?" Ben exclaims, his skin bright and beaming. He bumps his shoulder into Kai and Kai smiles, nodding, his face pink once more.

We order a double chocolate chip brownie with chocolate fudge ice cream. As we indulge, I study the connection Ben and Kai share. I admire them - they are as lovesick as you can get. Kai has already proudly introduced Ben to his family, and they are very supportive of their relationship. Ben, on the other hand, is dating a nice Catholic woman named Kay, according to his mother. My heart aches for him. The pain of being misunderstood is one thing, but having your family dismiss and reject the essence of who you are is entirely another. Drawing on strength from Kai, though, I've never seen Ben this resilient and confident. Not usually one for PDA, he and Kai share several lingering kisses, and Ben even licks a spot of chocolate off of Kai's cheek. It's disgustingly cute. I can't get enough of these two.

Ben asks me if I've met Parker's family yet. I stutter in my reply, nearly paralyzed by the truth that no, I haven't. It's another thing about Parker that eludes me. It's not like he hasn't mentioned them - he's told me plenty about them, his childhood, and his relationship with them now. But I haven't met them. He's met my mom, of course. She's a force in my life I can't tame regardless of how hard I try.

Our conversation plows ahead, and they invite me to Kai's school fundraiser at the end of the month. I politely decline, citing that Parker has some work event. Ben raises his eyebrows and gives me a quizzical look. He's skeptical as to why Parker, the financier, would have a work event on a Saturday night right before Halloween. It probably would've been safer to say Molly had some art thing, but I'm not that quick on my feet when I've been run over by a bus of doubts.

Just one interaction with someone outside of Our Family and I'm struggling to keep my lines from getting crossed.

Ben would all but die at the idea of a Masquerade. I'm sure the incredible costume I just picked out would give him a heart attack. It takes willpower that I don't know I have to keep from telling him. What a loss -

all that fabric, the dazzle, the poof that Ben will never know blanketed my body.

He can't know about the Masquerade. He can't know about any of it. I must stay firm in this. I owe it to Our Family, but most of all, I owe it to myself.

Sixty-Eight

I t's finally here - the event of the season: The Masquerade.

"I must admit, I feel sorry for the other attendees," Parker coos dramatically.

"And why is that?"

"Isn't it obvious?" I shake my head. "You will outshine them all. The stunning Iris in her gorgeous gold gown."

"Uh huh. I don't know about that. Pretty much everyone else knows how to dress for this thing. I'm just counting on Walter to have not led me astray."

"Well, as someone who has attended nine of these masquerades, I can assure you that Walter is the foremost expert in this area and has indeed, if anything, gone above the call of duty."

"Nine? Holy shit." If I didn't feel like a noob before, I sure do now.

"Nine. Inter-Branch Mixers are very different though. All the themed Mixers are different from monthly ones. I hope you're ready to have your mind blown." I stare at Parker like a deer in headlights. He chuckles. "Just relax and have fun. Lean into it. It's going to be a great time. I can't wait to see you shine."

Laid on my bed is a mess of fine fabrics and ribbons. My costume alone consists of eight distinct pieces: corset, petticoat, stockings, shoes, gloves, mask, shawl, and the dress itself. I'm as excited to put it on as I'm sure I'll be to pull it off at the end of the party.

Parker helps me with my corset, fingers expertly lacing it up with care. I'm transported back in time. The corset hugs my curves and accentuates my figure. It feels erotic, and Parker can't help himself. He brushes his fingertips against my bulging breasts, creating a bulge of his own underneath his trousers.

"Lady Iris," he hums, "the things you do to me. Such a temptress."

"Good sir," I play along, putting on my best British accent, "do control yourself. It's quite unseemly for a gentleman to behave in such ways."

"I find it nearly impossible to resist such beauty."

"I implore you," I whisper, breathing quietly into Parker's lips.

His mouth joins mine and we kiss. It feels forbidden for us to be engaging in such *vulgar acts* before the Masquerade. But Parker is as irresistible to me as I am to him. I want to devour him. My tongue delves into his mouth. He tastes positively delicious, a mixture of mint and warmth. His hands trace my body over and along the thick fabric of my corset. I allow him to explore as I revel in his taste. My bottom half is bare and waits wantonly for his touch.

Suddenly, he pulls away.

"Tsk tsk tsk, my lady. We must abide by the rules." I shoot him a seductive glance, but he drags himself away and around the corner. "I'm going to get changed out here. I can't control myself around you."

Like that's my fault.

I pull on my stockings next, then layer my petticoat over them. I can barely bend in the corset and find myself panting. How women wore these every day eludes me. I sit on the edge of the bed for a moment to catch my breath and admire my dress, which is standing upright on its own, the lush layers of extravagant fabric stiff and steady. Realizing I can breathe better standing, I wiggle into my dress. It's a nearly impossible task, and for a moment I'm lost in a tunnel of heavy fabrics. Finally, I find the neck, and emerge from the frilly detailing along its edges. I push my hands through the sleeves and straighten the lace around my wrists. I turn in the mirror and notice that half of my petticoat is sticking out the back. Despite my hearty attempts to stuff it under the dress, I know I'm going to need Parker's help. But first, I admire myself. My gown is a beautiful light champagne color with distinct golden tones and white lacing. The wrists and the chest are both punctuated with gold-lined bows with an amber jewel at the center. The dress itself is decorated with a subtle floral pattern and ruffled edging that snakes up the center. To say it's over the top would be an understatement.

I step into my gold slippers, feeling a bit like Cinderella, and grab my gold mask, white gloves, and fuzzy, brown shawl.

I emerge from my room feeling at least fifteen pounds heavier, but infinitely more elegant. Parker is finishing buttoning up his tailcoat when he turns to see me. He gives me a sexy smirk and tilts his head.

"Wow. Look at you, Lady Iris. A stunning vision, indeed."

"Thank you. I can barely breathe. And I can't button up the back on my own. Help!" I spin and reveal the mess that is the back of my outfit. Parker doesn't dare touch my skin, and instead shoves my petticoat into my dress like he's stuffing a turkey. He hastily buttons my dress. I can tell he's holding back.

"Done."

I realize I didn't really get a good look at him. I spin back around and examine Parker's ensemble. He went for a much darker look than I did. In black trousers and a black shirt, his tailcoat is a dark crimson layered over an intricate black vest. I want to rip through every single one of those luxurious layers and sink my teeth into Parker's bare skin. I'm breathless. And it's not just from the corset.

"You look incredible," I say, approaching him and running my fingers along his shoulder. "Look at all these buttons," I muse, now teasing my fingertips against the many buttons of his vest. They march south.

Parker grasps my hand in his, gripping tightly. "No. Very unladylike of you, Miss." And we're back in the game.

• • • •

I HAUL MYSELF INTO the passenger side of Parker's truck, but, unable to fit the poof of my dress in with me, struggle out and settle into the backseat instead. I fiddle with putting my mask on, but eventually find a comfortable fit. It matches the gold details of my dress, with beautiful leaves intricately decorating either side of my eyes.

"Driver - take me to the Ball at once," I jokingly demand.

"As you wish, my fair lady."

Parker pulls up the address of the Dominguez Estate and we depart. The drive is strangely familiar.

"Are you sure you have the right directions?"

"Absolutely."

"But, isn't this the way to Desi's?" I question, confused.

"It is. The Dominguez Estate is a little further, though."

"They're neighbors?" I ask, stunned. "No. There's no way. The Heads of all the Branches just happen to be filthy rich and coincidently live off the same mysterious street? How is that even possible?"

Parker sighs heavily, his chest rising and falling under the beautiful embroidered detailing of his dark vest. "Just too perceptive for your own good." He chuckles. I've caught him in something. He's reluctant to give it up, though. "They don't own the properties. They belong to Our Family."

"I see." But something still doesn't seem right. "And where does Our Family get the money to afford a million fancy mansions?" I ponder. This isn't the first time I've asked. I doubt I'll get an answer, but my curiosity is catching fire.

"That," Parker pauses, "is an excellent question. The founding Members come from old money. They were heavily invested in real estate, and have since developed their vast land holdings to create a number of private estates. Our Family has grown a lot in recent years. We try to keep the membership in each Branch relatively intimate and not exceed twenty members at any one time. Members do transfer and move periodically to keep things fresh and diverse. Thankfully we have kept within the capacity of estates available."

I think back to the invitation for tonight's event. Dominguez - Branch 15; Rachels - Branch 04. We are Branch 29.

"How many are there? Estates, I mean."

"Forty."

I choke on the words as they exit Parker's mouth. "Forty!" I scream. Forty estates. I do the math. That's around 800 members. My jaw drops in shock. Our Family must have some friends in exceptionally high places. Keeping forty extravagant properties hidden from the masses is no small feat.

"The interesting thing, though, is that every estate is identical in its layout. So, once you've been to one, you've been to them all. The idea is to make Our Members comfortable regardless of which property they're at," Parker explains. "All the main houses are the same; all the guesthouses are the same. The only real difference is that some properties have additional guesthouses to allow for larger events like tonight's. The Dominguez Estate has twenty instead of the usual ten. This means that most of us will be assigned to the guesthouses, while just a few will be in the main house. In all the Inter-Branch Mixers I've attended, I've always stayed in a guesthouse."

• • • •

PARKER IS RIGHT. THE Dominguez Estate is essentially identical to Desi's. The fake familiarity works though, fooling me into a natural state of ease. Even Sylvie is there, wearing an absurdly elaborate gown that certainly upstages my own. Parker escorts me into the grand ballroom, and my senses are overwhelmed with wonder. An intoxicating scent of warm amber seeps through the air and tickles inside my nose. Classical music fills my ears. With my arm wrapped firmly around Parker's, I inhale deeply and take it all in.

Bustling with at least fifteen other couples, we are transported into another era. Everyone is clothed in the most beautiful gowns, exquisite tailcoats, intricate masks, and the lavish accessories. Walter dressed me to fit right in. A relief.

I meet countless Members from the other Branches. There's Felicia, George, Nicole, Davin, Juliette, and Shawn. There's Vlad, Josie, Celia and Garrett. It's impossible to remember who's who. I forget their names the moment I learn them. Not only is almost everyone a stranger to me, but everyone is donning a unique mask, adding an extra layer of difficulty in deciphering the identities of my fellow partygoers.

The night unfolds as a mysterious erotic puzzle.

Matthew seeks me out, the color of my hair no doubt a homing beacon drawing him in. He's dressed just as dapper as the rest of us, and our conversation flows with more ease than I expected it to. I'm not the only redhead at the party, though, so he continues his rounds, jumping from one of us to the next.

There is one stranger who I find particularly intriguing. My heart skips a beat. At the sound of her voice, my pulse quickens under my skin. I recognize that voice. I know I do. Do I? Her gorgeous body is cloaked in the most luscious scarlet fabric. I watch as she moves with confidence, her gestures strong and her voice full of confidence in the conversations she shares among friends. Her face is entirely concealed behind a black mask, but I'm sure I already know who is hidden behind it.

A loud clinking echoes through the room. Felicia knocks a spoon against her champagne glass to demand our attention.

"Welcome! Welcome, everyone!" she announces from the front of the room. Her long black hair cascades down her sides, and her stunning jade dress spills along the floor. Her eyes are obscured by an intricate black and green mask decorated with feathers and jewels, but her beautiful, luscious lips are visible. My eyes follow them as she speaks. "Thank you, everyone, for joining us here tonight. Welcome to Our Family's Annual Masquerade Ball!" Cheers fill the room, and yet, above all the noise, Wyatt remains the most enthusiastic. I clap my hands. "It's my very special pleasure to welcome the Members of Branches Four and Twenty-Nine here with us tonight. We are honored to spend this evening with all of you." Desi and Juliette, the Head of Branch 04, stand on either side of Felicia, their smiles wide as they sparkle under the dim lights. "I'd like to take a moment to explain the unfolding of tonight's events to those of you who haven't attended a Masquerade before. We have several first timers from what I understand. In just a moment, we will reveal the selected Pairings for tonight's proceedings. There are fifty-four of us here tonight, and drawing stones would take much too long. Our tech whiz, George, has created an algorithm to randomly assign partners and ensure that all Pairings are between Members of two different Branches. After you receive your Pairing, the fun begins! We invite you to *mingle* amongst the crowd to find your designated partner." The crowd whispers and sounds of delight echo throughout. "Anything goes. Let's have some fun!"

George takes Felicia's place at the front of the room. In a stunning tailcoat with black and silver details, he has a confidence about him that commands the attention of the crowd.

"Welcome, everyone, once again. For those of you who I haven't had the pleasure of meeting just yet, I'd like to introduce myself. My name is George, and, as Felicia has so kindly mentioned already, I hold the Tech Office in Branch Fifteen." He bows and everyone laughs and cheers heartily. "It's my honor to announce the Pairings for tonight's Masquerade. Let's begin with Our hosting Branch. Ladies - listen closely!" He procures an iPad, taps away on the screen for a moment, then is ready for his big announcement. "The Pairings are as follows: Felicia and Parker..."

My ears perk up at the mention of Parker's name. He's the first one chosen. I turn to him, whispering in his ear. "She's beautiful. Have you been with Felicia before?"

"Actually, I haven't. Our Branch has mixed with hers before, but we've never been partnered. Tonight will be a new experience for both of us."

I focus my attention back to George as he continues with the assignments for Branch 15.

"Paloma and Wyatt." Wyatt calls loudly. I hope Paloma gives Wyatt a run for his money.

George continues. "Nina and Marc."

It *is* her.

Nina.

I knew it.

My chest feels like it's going to burst. I don't know why I ever dismissed the possibility that I might see her again.

Because of course I would.

Our Family is tight knit. Eventually, at some point, it's likely that we would run into each other. But I never expected it to be here. Now.

My mind swims. Nina and G were my test. When we met, connected, and fucked, it was all part of a game Parker and I crafted. Or at least I thought it was. It turned out to be a game of a completely different sort. And it granted me passage into this incredible world of hedonistic understanding. I want to scream and cry and celebrate all in one breath.

Wait, does that mean G is here, too?

I clear my throat and try to calm my racing heart. I look back to George, perking my ears to the sound of his voice. Next, he announces Branch 04, and it seems intentional torture for him to give my Branch's assignments last. My stomach is in my throat as I wait. For G's name. For my name.

"Juliette and Aki. Abbey and G."

My stomach drops. He is here, too. They're both here. Holy shit. I don't know if I'm elated, or terrified. Probably a mix of both. The feel of G's skin and the taste of Nina's femininity rush back in a blast of warmth. My lips part as I get lost in the memory of it - of them.

"Iris and Elias," George's voice rings out, snapping me back to the present.

"Have you met him yet?" Parker whispers, his soft lips grazing my cheek. His touch grounds me. I repeat my Pairing in my head. *Elias, Elias, Elias.*

"Hmm. I haven't, I don't think. It's hard to keep track of everyone, though, if I'm being honest." I laugh awkwardly.

"I'm sure he'll find you."

"Marie and Davin. Scarlett and Ant. And finally, the best for last! Mallory and Alex. Thank you, everyone, for your patience. Happy mingling!"

Expectations are a funny thing. They have the power to amaze or, conversely, the power to disappoint.

Tonight, they are the former.

I didn't really have solid expectations for tonight; I suppose I expected socializing, small talk, and getting to know more people walking the same life path as me. Then, as usually happens after Pairings are announced, the crowd would thin out and people would depart to play privately.

Parker told me things would be different tonight.

Are they ever.

Sixty-Nine

Around me, the entirely unexpected unfolds. Cloaks and dresses and trousers and corsets are discarded into a mountain of ornate fabrics. A group of five at first, but growing as the minutes pass, have shed their clothing and come together in an intimate circle. A wave of heat blasts through the room as their bodies flow together. My cheeks redden when I first notice, and I'm glad to have my mask to hide behind. The participants keep their masks on, too, as if to maintain a semblance of anonymity. I study them, their movements, their connection. It's raw and beautiful and hungry and indulgent. My eyes follow the curves of their bodies. My ears swallow the deep moans of their sounds. I bask in it, experiencing their pleasure like it's my own. I search the room for Parker and see him over to my right. His eyes are expectant.

I turn back to the orgy unfolding before us. My lips part as I breathe it in. The energy of the group seeps into my pores. It takes everything in me to not strip naked and force myself into the middle of it.

I want to. Oh, fuck, do I want to. The primal, wanton need for touch calls to me.

A warm hand grazes my back.

"Iris, is it?"

"Yes, hi," I reply to my stranger. I gulp down my arousal. I focus on the man before me. He's about the same height as I am. His eyes and hair are dark like ink. His black skin is smooth and matte.

"Hi, it's good to meet you," he says, offering a handshake. It feels oddly formal, especially considering the orgy of at least a dozen people right before our eyes. "I'm Elias."

I can't help myself. I push into Elias and kiss him. Our lips and bodies squeeze together in heat. His mouth parts and I push my tongue in, swirling it in circles around his mouth. Our kiss is a release, freeing my pent-up sexual energy, even just for a fleeting moment.

"Elias. Hi," I breathe into him, our mouths just inches apart. "You're my Pairing for tonight."

"I am," he chuckles. "Can I get you a drink, and then we can make our way to the guesthouse?"

"Yes, please," I beg.

As he pulls away from me, I glance over to Parker, who is, of course, watching. With a sly grin, he raises his glass to me.

Equal forces of relief and disappointment clash within me as Elias and I leave the main ballroom. I shake off the calling I feel, propelling me toward the hedonistic mound of flesh in the center of the ballroom. I focus instead on the sensation of my hand in Elias's. Through the exit door on the side, Elias guides me down the stairs of the patio balcony and along the pathway. We arrive at Guesthouse #12. As expected, it's identical to those on the Harold property. Or at least I think it is. My focus is entirely on Elias and how badly I want him to fuck me as hard as he can.

To my detriment, Elias is a true gentleman. His hands are gentle and soft, his touch evanescent and light. The more I want him, the more he pulls away. It's a torturous game of cat and mouse. But I'm not above begging.

First, though, these clothes have to go. I turn around and Elias slowly, brutally slowly, unbuttons my dress. He takes just as much care with the corset and its endless string of knots. I pull off my mask and make quick work of removing his layers of clothing. I don't even take a moment to admire how elegant his costume is. I want it off. Now. At last, we stand before each other, our bodies exposed. Elias is solid and toned. His sizable cock is hard and perky. I want to feel it inside me. Noticing he doesn't remove his mask, I reach to touch it, but he steps back. I stare at him, puzzled, but intrigued. I move toward him once more, offering myself to him. He steps away.

"Please," I whine, "please, I want you to touch me."

"I don't think I will," he replies, the warmth in his voice now a draft of coolness.

It makes me hot. I get down on my knees, prepared to beg with his cock in my mouth. But once more, he steps away.

"Get up. You look pathetic on your knees, begging me like a common whore."

My stomach drops. I shiver. As shame floods my body, my pussy gushes with wetness.

"Stand there. Against the wall."

I make my way beside the couch and stand with my back against the wall. My body aches with such deep libidinous desire, I'm lightheaded. Elias approaches me, and I'm giddy with expectation. He grazes my arms with his fingertips, so lightly that it hurts. I instinctively lean into him.

"Against the wall!" he hollers at me. The glorious agony. "You're going to wait right here. I'm going upstairs for a moment. You aren't to move. Understand?" I nod in compliance. "Good. Very good."

The moments pass like an eternity. What is he doing up there? I strain my ears in hopes of a clue, but the ambient music veils the air.

Elias returns in a pair of jeans and a white tee. He's even wearing a pair of sneakers. I can't hide my disappointment in seeing him fully clothed. I am, however, pleasantly surprised to see he removed his mask.

"In my Branch, our safe word is five bear circle, or FBC. Is yours the same?" he asks. I nod. "Excellent." He approaches me, getting closer. His fingers line the side of my face and I shudder at his touch. "Well, then, Iris, do I have consent to do whatever I please with you?" I nod, this time weakly, the surge of want making it almost impossible to control my desire to leap on top of him. "You have my consent, as well." I lick my lips. With his mask removed, I focus on his face. He is handsome and boyish, with a small scar above his left eyebrow. "I want you to go upstairs. I've laid out something for you. Put it on, then come back down here. Now, go," he orders. There's a harshness to his voice. I love it.

Excitement charges through me. As I turn the corner at the top of the stairs, I eye the bed. As promised, my new costume awaits: a light blue apron and a ghastly tall pair of white stilettos. I pull the apron over my head and tie it neatly behind me. The shoes go on next. Grasping the handrail firmly, I return downstairs.

Elias is settled on the couch, a pair of glasses at the tip of his nose and a newspaper in his hand. His eyes meet mine over the top of his newspaper as I descend into the living room. He tosses it aside and stands up to examine me. I feel even more exposed, somehow, with my front covered but my ass visible at the back of the apron. Elias circles me like a vulture inspecting its prey.

"Good." He returns to the couch and reopens his newspaper.

I try to decode our game. It feels very 1950's housewife with a modern twist. I wait expectantly for directions, but none come. Elias ignores me all together. I decide it's up to me to prove myself.

I go into the kitchen and tap my fingers on the counter. Inspecting the cupboards and the fridge, I'm surprised to see that the kitchen is fully-stocked, as though someone actually lives here. On the counter I notice an opened cookbook, its pages spread open the way I wish Elias had my legs. I let out an exasperated sigh. On the pages is a recipe for classic chocolate chip cookies. Dressed for the role, I take the initiative.

I flash glances here and there at Elias as I bake, but he remains completely engrossed in his newspaper, giving me no notice, let alone an indication of approval. With the cookies in the oven, I slip beside him on the couch.

"Honey," I whine, leaning into the role play, "I'm making you a fresh batch of chocolate chip cookies." Still nothing. "Is there anything I can do for you while we wait for them to bake?" I ask, my voice thick with desperation.

Elias shakes his newspaper and folds it neatly.

"My drink has been empty for ages now," he chastises. His eyebrows are crooked in disgust. My shame and arousal dance as one.

"Let me refill that for you." I whisk his empty glass away, being sure to give my ass a little wiggle at him as I return to the kitchen. "Scotch?" He nods, his eyes on me at last. In the spotlight now, I take the opportunity to develop our play. "Did you have a good day at work? How are things at..." I think fast. "At the bank?" I stutter, only slightly.

"Fine."

"Here's your drink, honey." I lower myself to the couch beside him as he takes a big swig. "You seem stressed. I'm sure there's something I can do to make you feel better."

"You bore me," he states. "You, with your chocolate chip cookies and plain blue apron."

My stomach lurches. He set me up. I've been completely fooled. I swallow hard. My mind swims as I work to find a way out of this. I have all the power in this moment - an overwhelming but exciting realization. I head to the stairs, but the timer on the oven goes off. I pull out the sheet tray and carefully place the cookies to cool, thinking hard about my next move. Elias, meanwhile, has returned to the black and white of his newspaper.

Upstairs, the possibilities are endless. I add up the knowledge I have about Elias to determine my next move. He likes a slow burn. Lots of foreplay - and power play. Nothing up to now has been particularly kinky, but he set it up that way. A sprinkling of fetish is in order.

I gather my supplies from the bins and change into a new outfit from the closet.

I'm ready.

"Honey!" I call from upstairs. "I'm so sorry to bother you, I know you're busy, but can you come upstairs? There's a light bulb that's out. Can you fix it? Please?" I ask desperately.

I hear the shuffle of newspaper and footsteps as Elias ascends the stairs. He gets closer. And closer.

"I heard a rumor," I whisper in Elias's ear as he turns the corner. He freezes. "I heard you've been stealing money from the accounts you manage at the bank." I tut my tongue in disapproval. "Naughty, naughty." I bite his ear and he gasps. "You're in trouble," I accuse, wrapping Elias's wrists in a pair of play handcuffs.

I pull him over to the chair by the far wall and push him down onto it. I pace in front of him, allowing his eyes to examine me. Dressed in an all-black, crotchless pleather bodysuit and the same stilettos he picked out for me, he nods approvingly.

"Now, what do you have to say for yourself?"

"I have been bad," he admits. "Let me prove I can be good."

Who's the pathetic one now?

"Hmm, I suppose..." I continue to pace. "Are you hungry?" I ask. "You know, I just made cookies."

"Starved," he replies.

"They're not for you, of course." He wrinkles his eyebrows in confusion. "I have something much tastier for you."

I pull Elias over to the bed and push him onto his knees in front of it. I lay, sprawled before him, along the edge of the bed, and push his face into my pussy. He's immediately covered in my juices. I hold his face steady, forcing him to hold his breath. When I let go, he gasps. "Eat," I command. Elias dives into me again, this time by his own accord. He laps my fluids up fiendishly as I wiggle my hips and pour myself all over his face. He sucks on my folds, his tongue moving into my creases and dancing along them. But, with his hands cuffed behind his back, I miss them. I want more of his touch. I kick him off with the heel of my stilettos and make quick work of removing the handcuffs. He immediately fists me, driving his hand inside my slit and filling me up with it. I wail, the shock of it a jolt of pleasure. He pumps his fingers in and out of me while greedily sucking on my nub. The smell of my sex perfumes throughout the room and I know I'm getting close. I've been waiting all night for this. I buck my hips against his hand, forcing his fingers deeper and deeper into me. They wiggle and push on my tender insides. I look down at him, hovering on the cusp. Elias is in a frenzy, urging me to come. I throw my head back and soar into oblivion.

But I'm not done with him yet. I pull him into me and scratch my fingernails along his arms.

"Now fuck me."

Elias spins me around and I grab the column of the four-poster bed to brace myself. He bites the crook of my neck and strips off his clothes. He rams into me, his full length delving deep into my hole. I yelp in the incredible feeling of fullness. Elias groans as he thrusts his hips against me, his pace fast and greedy. He pumps himself into me and taps his thumb against my clit. I come again, quivering under him, my body heavy in ecstasy. Nearing his own peak, Elias pulls out of me and pumps his fists along his shaft. He groans as his hands slide in the slickness of my cum. At last, he finds his release, and his warm load spews onto my back. We collapse onto the bed, the exhilarating intensity of our interaction pumping through our veins.

Euphoria.

Seventy

Our Family has transformed my life. It's empowered me to be myself more now than I've ever been. Parker and I have grown, both as individuals and as a couple, and together we've found a dynamic that works for us.

It has worked for us.

So far.

But cracks are forming. I can't ignore them. The wild, seductive high that has possessed me since the inception of my membership is fading. Seedlings of doubt are sprouting. I can't shake them. The questions I've let sit in the shadows are nagging at me, and when I look at Parker, I see uncertainty.

What is really going on?

October has been a challenging month. It's been busy beyond belief, bursting with commitments and big milestones. As I sit by the river with my hot coffee in hand, my mind runs through a review of the month past.

The good: I've reached four months of membership within Our Family. The entirety of it has been exhilarating, and every interaction I've had has inflated my confidence and solidified my sense of belonging. I now even have the opportunity to *deepen* my commitment through holding an Office, which I am very much looking forward to. My mom got engaged this month. I suppose that *is* good; it's the most stable relationship she's been in since dad died. The Masquerade blew my mind in all its hedonistic decadence. My interaction with Elias was gratifying in new ways, and, although the presence of Nina and G felt strange, something about it also felt right. Almost as though my journey has come full circle. I spent time with Ben and Kai, and my heart glows for them and the love they've found together. Parker has reached his ten-year milestone within Our Family. It's an impressive commitment I almost can't even fathom.

The bad: Our Family has been nothing but accepting of me, yet the secrecy is festering like a wound that won't heal. Parker's ten-year has formed the beginnings of a snowball. The blow of being disregarded and dismissed from it simply because I'm not of the same *ranking* as him, hurts.

I always have to wait for more... more information, more responsibility, more understanding. Confidentiality is one thing, but exclusion is another.

And then there's my own membership. Although I understand the lengths Our Family goes to keep membership discreet, the whole idea of recruitment seems over-the-top. The tangibility of Nina and G, my *test administrators*, at the Masquerade made my own recruitment come racing back. I was tested - evaluated on my suitability to be a Member of Our Family - which all too closely resembles a sort of deceitful manipulation in my eyes. That sour taste of deception lingers on the tip of my tongue. I was vetted for membership in this secretive organization without my consent or knowledge.

It's been one of the best things to happen to me.

And despite the joy of seeing Ben and Kai in love, Kai's judgment of my lifestyle still stings. Especially given the recent skepticism brewing in the back of my mind. The conversation with Kai has stayed with me, and not in the way I anticipated.

On top of it all, I've been realizing, bit by bit, how little I know about how Parker lives his day-to-day life. He knows mine, virtually inside and out, with a special thanks to what he learned while essentially stalking me during my membership recruitment. He admitted that we never met by chance, that it was all orchestrated by Our Family. Just how much do they know about me, exactly?

I know enough about Parker to know I'm in love with him. That hasn't changed, and it never will. He's the one for me. I know this. But I also know he has secrets, and I'm going to get to the bottom of them.

The doubts are growing. I've never met his family. Which part of me wants to dismiss, because I wouldn't say it's important to me, not really. I guess more than anything, meeting them would show me how Parker has grown and transformed, just as a caterpillar becomes a butterfly. Then again, maybe he's not ready for me to meet them. But he's never really mentioned them outside of the context of them existing. He doesn't talk about seeing them, or what they're up to, or much about their current relationship.

Then there's work. I've never been to his office. Of course, I know he works at Olahoni Financial, and when I Google the building, I see it's two cities over in a high-rise near the freeway. So it exists; he's not making it up. I play with the idea of surprising him at work one day, maybe show up for a lunch date, but it's truthfully not feasible. I can't just skip out of work to check that my boyfriend is at his office. Because even if he's not, there are a million reasons to justify him being out.

My thoughts turn in twisted circles, the doubts doubting themselves. My head begins to throb with the beginnings of a headache. I dig through my tote bag for some Tylenol but find none. I chug back the last few sips of my coffee, willing the caffeine to do its job, and rub my forehead.

Paranoia is not a good look.

There's one more thing.

How has it never occurred to me until this moment?

I have no idea where Parker lives.

I try to reason it out. We're both in our thirties now. We're both well-established. We both have our own homes, our own routines - our own lives, even, outside of each other. Yet, I have never, ever, in the entire time that Parker and I have known each other (which at this point exceeds half of a year) been to his house. In fact, I don't even know his address. I haven't seen where he lives, what he owns, or how he tackles the complexities of organizing the cupboards in the kitchen. Caught up in the whirlwind of events since joining Our Family, these were seemingly insignificant details that I not only overlooked, but ceased to be aware of at all.

Parker has always come to me. Chivalrous, isn't it? I've never thought twice about it. There's also the fact that I don't have a car and rely heavily on walking to get around. Parker lives further than is really walkable from me. At least, I think he does. I had always assumed so, but this has never been verified by Parker himself. Again, one of the many things I neglected to notice.

It makes good sense, though; it seems only practical that Parker comes to me. He's the one with the truck, after all. But as I delve more into the specifics of our relationship, recalling the little things that are only now adding up to be a really big thing, I realize Parker has intentionally been elusive around the topic. Elusive, but not deceitful.

Do I entirely know this man?

It's a fleeting thought, but a thought, nonetheless. And it scares me.

I need to know all of Parker.
Including the place he calls home.

Seventy-One

I spend the entire day at work not mentally present. I'm somewhere else, floating in a blurry space of bewilderment and foolishness. Maria, overcome with pregnancy hormones and still reeling from her husband's infidelity, doesn't notice. I'm grateful for it; the last thing I want is to be asked what's wrong. Not only can I not verbalize it *in the interests of discretion*, but I honestly wouldn't even know where to begin.

It's Tuesday - my night with Parker. I can't decide if what I'm feeling is relief or dread. I think it's relief. I spend the day reflecting and know it's time to have a serious discussion with Parker. It's time to have my doubts weeded away.

Our love can conquer all.

Can't it?

Just inside the door of my apartment, my phone rings. It's Parker.

"Hi," I say. "I've been thinking about you a lot today."

"Oh, yeah?"

"Mm hmm. Will you be over soon?"

And that's when it all shifts.

As usual, Parker is overcommitted. He tells me he can't see me tonight; an *unforeseen urgent matter* requires his attention. I am irate. This isn't the first time that Parker has been otherwise engaged - when something else has taken priority over me. Over us. I've about had it. What is it, that is so imperative, that it demands this much time from him? I almost hang up on him in all my rage.

Then, a bite.

At last, Parker tells me something. It isn't much, but I cling to it like a starved dog, ears piqued, lips trembling.

"Iris, I serve on the Executive Branch in Our Family. The Executive Branch is essentially the framework that holds the organization together. I'm the CFO, and there are several issues that have come up. I need to deal with them immediately, in the next couple of days. Before the month ends."

I'm speechless. I soak in his words, drinking them in. All I've wanted this whole time is an explanation.

431

"You are the most important thing to me in my life. I love you, so much, Iris. Trust me, I don't want to spend tonight looking at balance sheets and analyzing financial documentation. I really don't. I want to look at you, watch your body move, feel it against mine. But I have a commitment to Our Family."

I release the breath I didn't realize I was holding. I'm the most important thing to him, but but but.

All I have are more questions.

Parker urges me to be patient. With him, with myself, with the things I don't understand just yet. The way he reassures me, placates me like a small child, with a hushed voice and gentle tone, it makes my skin turn to fire. I feel my blood boil. It's almost as if he gave me this snippet of information about being CFO for the Executive Branch to simply pacify me, to subdue my emotions. His secrets feel heavier than that, and I'm not falling for this. Have I been fooling myself this whole time? Is Parker even who I think he is? What the fuck is he keeping from me?

After we hang up, Parker calls me, over and over, leaving sweet voicemails of reassurance. His voice seeps into me, like a drug charging through my veins. It's impossible to endure. He texts me to remind me how much he loves me and that nothing NOTHING could ever change that. Ever.

You and me, Iris, we're forever.

I'm a wreck. Everything I was so certain about just days before has contorted into an ugly, grotesque question mark. Am I fighting with Parker, or am I battling with myself? It hurts so much. That deep burn in the pit of my stomach. It aches in my lungs. My head won't stop pounding. My mind churns, my thoughts spinning at the culmination of things leading to this moment.

No matter how much I want to fight it, I know the only remedy for the agony is Parker.

I struggle for days before I give in to the veracity of it. In a mess of sobs and sniffs, I fall into him. Parker whisks me up in his arms, wrapping me in them and squeezing me delicately. His skin against mine feels forbidden, almost, like a violation of some imaginary rule. Parker's body is warm, comforting, and, despite my will to resist it, profoundly alluring. I fit right here, against him.

"I'm sorry," Parker breathes, his voice warm in my ear. "I'm sorry for letting you down. You mean everything to me, Iris." His voice cracks. "I know it's hard. I really know. There's so much I want to share with you. I wish I could. But it's not time, not yet." Parker's beautiful blues glow beneath a sheet of wet tears. He's hurting, too. I've been so selfish in thinking only of myself; I've failed to see how the secrecy impacts him, too. "I promise, this won't be forever."

"I'm sorry, too!" I yelp.

The guilt. The anguish. The sorrow. Parker's mouth claims mine and it vanishes.

Seventy-Two

T he weekend blissfully belongs to us. Just us. Nothing sweeps my worries away like the warmth of Parker's body next to mine. As our naked skin brushes together, electric shocks strike through to my core. We kiss, our lips joining as one, and luxuriate in the shared warmth of a world all our own.

Parker tastes divine.

We can't keep our hands off each other. We fuck on the couch first, our clothes a discarded pile on the floor. I wiggle against the heat of his skin, soaking in the sensation of our bare flesh brushing together. I slide my hands against his chest and swipe my fingertips along the outlines of his muscles. I kiss his neck and his shoulders, I taste the surface of him, I breathe in the scent of his body. Parker's aroma invades my brain. I'm drunk off it - off him. I sweep my breasts against his chest and my nipples harden at the stimulation of them. I gently rock my hips against his thigh, the slickness that's formed between my legs allowing me to glide effortlessly. I move my mouth onto his again and find myself moaning as my clit swipes against his leg. His hands find my hips and he grasps my ass with wide fingers. His touch guides my movement, and I breathlessly pant into him.

"Fuck," I whisper into his mouth.

Then, I come apart. Panting, my body shakes. I crumble into him.

We kiss again, more, still. We could kiss forever and it wouldn't be long enough. Our tongues twist and twirl and our lips press into each other. I'm lost in his mouth. He shifts, but our kiss remains. We're sitting now, his cock hard and waiting against my leg. My hand finds it, and I gently pump my fist along its length. Parker moans into me. I grasp his sack then work his shaft again. I don't want to stop kissing him, but I pull away and slide off of the couch onto my knees. I open my mouth widely and look up into Parker's eyes. The blue of them is unreal. He smiles at me and brushes the back of his hand against my cheek.

"You're so perfect, Iris. I don't know how I ever got this lucky."

With wide eyes I wait expectantly, and finally Parker slides his erection into my mouth. He runs his fingers through my hair and along my scalp, groaning as I take him all the way in. I immediately choke. He thrusts his hips gently, pushing into the back of my throat, eliciting a symphony of gasps and gags. My skin floods with goosebumps. I grab his hips and push him hard against me, desperate to feel my throat full to the brim with his cock. I can't breathe; the pleasure of it chokes me just as much as his cock does.

Parker pulls himself out of my mouth and I whimper. Moving hastily, he grabs me by the arm and tosses me over the side of the couch. He thrusts into me from behind, and having him inside of me at last overwhelms my body with endorphins. He yanks my hair as he bucks his hips wildly, marching closer to his climax with each passing second. My muscles clench around him as I wail in euphoria.

The next moment, our mouths are on each other again and he pulls me into the bathroom. Parker turns on the shower and we leap in, eager to feel the stimulation of the water beating down on us. I want to bend my knees, to consume him in my mouth once more, but his lips and mine are joined in an impenetrable seal. Our kiss flows, everlasting. Parker effortlessly slides his cock into my slit as I lean against the back wall, and he rocks slowly, his hips swaying gently. Our mouths fused still, we stand, as if under a waterfall. The flow of the water drizzles like the beginnings of a rainstorm sprinkling down on us. My nipples harden as I imagine we are in a far-off place, fucking in the depths of a secret jungle. Parker wraps his hand around my throat and groans as he pushes deeper inside of me. At my core, it blooms. I hold my breath as he penetrates me, faster now, his cock invading me at inaccessible depths. I'm breathless. As we fuck, I'm intoxicated by the sensation of our mouths weaved together, our bodies joined as one, our skin united.

On the brink, Parker pulls both his tongue and his cock out of me. I've never felt so empty. I whine, longing for that feeling of *everything* again. His lips leave mine and he backs away. Then, he's gone. He disappears out of the shower, leaving me alone in the rainstorm.

An eternal moment later, he returns. I could cry I'm so overcome at the sight of him. He presents me with a closed fist, and I peel his fingers open to reveal the purple bullet vibrator hiding in his palm. It buzzes against my nipples for a fleeting moment, then Parker guides it along my slick slit. His touch is on me again (finally!) as he twists and flicks the tender skin of my nipples. Meanwhile, Parker slides the vibrator along my crevice, teasing its entry but not granting it. His mouth finds my nipples as the toy focuses its attention on my delicate bud. I'm so aroused that even the slightest stimulation quickly builds into my undoing. I come almost instantly, thrust into oblivion, my release so profound that it makes my toes curl. I struggle for breath as my body quivers and I ride the euphoric wave of my climax.

But it's not enough. Parker slides the bullet into me, circling it within the lips of my pussy and provoking my weary muscles. His other hand finds my tender bud and I squeal at even the slightest touch of it. His mouth joins mine again, and his hands work magic. I'm easily persuaded into succumbing to another paralyzing orgasm.

My body responds immediately to Parker's every touch; I'm putty in his grasp.

Weary and weak, at last Parker heaves into me. He thrusts just a few times before his own climax overtakes him. Our lips connect, bliss expelling into the air around us, and we wrap our arms around each other. He cradles my face in his hands. "I love you," he says. The words enter into me and wrap around my soul. They settle there, where the starkest truths of my life live.

I sink into Parker's chest. Beneath his skin, the thudding of his heart dances against my rosy cheek. I smile at the comfort of it; the comfort of Parker.

Seventy-Three

Before Parker leaves me on Sunday, as he does routinely, we agree to sit down and have a mature, honest conversation. All the sex has calmed my nerves and saturated my body with those happy chemicals. I promise to keep my cool, and Parker vows to do his best to answer my questions with candor.

I'm no fool. I'm aware there's a lot about Our Family that he won't be willing (or able, I suppose) to answer. My biggest hope, though, is to at least have those blank spaces in the Parker Fact Sheet filled in.

We sit on my couch, and I try to drag my brain away from replaying our romp here yesterday. My skin grows warm just thinking of it.

Parker pushes his glasses up on his nose and smirks. "Fire away."

I take a deep breath and bite my lip. Where do I even start? There are so many things I need to know. Parker waits patiently, rubbing his thumbs against the back of my hands. My thoughts are in a frenzy. I reign them in.

"Your family. Your mom and dad, I mean. You mention them on occasion. I know you aren't particularly close with them, but do you see them very much?" I ask. My voice is light, wary.

Parker smiles. He looks at his hands for a moment before refocusing his gaze on me. "I wasn't expecting that."

"It's just... you've met my family. I mean, there isn't much to it. Just me, and my mom. Zach and Molly and the girls. Willard now, too. But you've met them all. I guess... I was just wondering if I was ever going to meet your parents? If that's even important to you?"

"It's funny you're asking about this now," Parker answers. He rubs his chin. "I talk to my parents a couple of times a month. They raised me, but I've never felt like I belonged with them. Not like I belong in Our Family. Still, we have a good enough relationship. The last time I talked to them, a couple of weeks ago, they mentioned Thanksgiving." Parker's eyes light up, their blueness tunneling into me. "They host a dinner every year. Mostly with their neighbors, a couple of aunts and uncles here and there. I've never brought anyone home with me. I told them that will be different this year."

I all but melt. I'm flattered. And smiling like an idiot.

"I told them all about you, Iris. How incredible you are. Your love for books, your passion for animals. How much you mean to me. They can't wait to meet you. That is, if you'll do me the honor of accompanying me to my parent's Thanksgiving dinner." Parker does a faux, half-bow, offering his previously withdrawn hand out to me.

"I would be delighted," I sing, biting my lip. "That means a lot to me, you know."

"They'll love you. Of course they will. You are disgustingly lovable." He squeezes my cheeks between his thumb and forefinger. I playfully swat him away. Relief sweeps over me in knowing that not only are Parker's parents very real and part of his life, but that he is ready to introduce me to them. It's awfully traditionalist, but I can't deny the draw. Meeting the family of the love of my life will somehow substantiate the realness of him. "What's next? What else do you want to know?"

I take a moment and ponder where to take the conversation next. I feel sort of dumb asking it, but I need to know about his job.

"Your work. You're at the Olahoni building, right?"

"I am, some of the time. I have an office space there, in the main building. But my hours are very flexible, for the most part, so I go in when I want to, stay home when I feel like working from there."

My eyes follow Parker's lips as they move. I hear his words, but they aren't adding up. Did he really utter the word *flexible*? I wouldn't describe anything about Parker's schedule to be flexible. I furrow my eyebrows, confused.

"My job as CFO in Our Family takes up a lot of my time, too," he offers in my skepticism. "If I'm honest, I spend a lot of my core work hours doing things for OF, which I can't do from the Olahoni office. So I do spend more hours working from home than I do at the physical office."

I nod. That makes sense. So far.

Feeling brave, I take the leap. "What are you doing when we aren't together?" It spills out of my mouth like a balloon popped open. "I mean, I only have three nights a week with you. And if you're spending some of your regular work hours doing stuff for Our Family, I assume you aren't spending all of your off-work hours fulfilling your CFO responsibilities. What are you doing for the other four nights we aren't together?"

This catches Parker completely off guard. He takes a deep breath and steadies himself. I worry that I may have overstepped. But I need to know. He wrinkles his eyes and purses his lips.

"That's going to be a more difficult one for me to answer," he admits. "Yes, I do spend some of that time doing things for the Executive Branch, or EB, as we call it. It's a huge commitment, and it requires a lot of time from me."

I watch him intently. But four nights a week crunching numbers? In addition to the time it takes away from his regular job? I'm still not buying it. I pivot. "What about Our Leaflet? Do you ever use it?"

Parker scoffs. "Not like you do," he chuckles. My cheeks turn a mortifying shade of red. "To be honest, since I met you, Iris, my hands have been exceedingly full. Even since before I met you. I spend all my spare time with you, and the rest is dedicated to Our Family and my commitments to them. Before you, I did have interactions with others through Our Leaflet, but things have changed a lot in the last year."

"It's just..." I stop myself. I'm beginning to sound whiny and desperate. I *am* desperate, but I promised to keep my composure. I take a deep breath and try again. "I understand you are committed to Our Family. It's hard for me to understand what exactly is taking up all your time, though."

Parker nods. That's all he gives me on this.

I forge ahead.

I fidget with my fingers, rubbing the tips together and picking at bits of peeling skin. I feel utterly stupid asking Parker this next question. It's so straightforward and innocent, but loaded with such ignorance. I hesitate.

"Anything else?" Parker asks in the strained air between us.

Of course there's more. We can both feel it.

"Where do you live? Like, do you have an apartment in Vista Loma, too? Or do you own your own home? Live with roommates?" The more I say, the worse I feel. My head falls into my hands. I exhale, loudly, almost laughing at myself in how ridiculous this all is.

Preoccupied once more with my own humiliation, I neglect to notice Parker. When I finally look up, I'm shocked at what I see. All the color is drained from his face. A look of terror is painted upon it, like a thief caught mid-heist. I initially laugh it off, assuming his reaction is playful, simply a part of one of our games. But he remains rooted to the spot, his gaze unyielding.

"Parker, what is it?" I ask, a wave of fear hitting me, too. My stomach falls. Panic rises in my chest. "Are you okay?"

He clears his throat, at last making a sound. It echoes between us.

"Iris, there's something I need to tell you."

Part Four
Iris

Seventy-Four

P anicked and flustered, Parker's voice rings in my ears: "There's something I need to tell you."

My heart stops abruptly, then immediately begins beating inconceivably fast. I'm sure it's going to explode. The pounding in my chest is so furious that it's visible under the thin fabric of my shirt. It aches, a sort of combustive burn rattling beneath my skin.

"I owe it to you - to be honest. I love you too much not to be," he continues. I can hear my heart in my ears now, the blood pulsing and pressure building in every fiber of my being. Flooded with panic, my brain is a useless blob of mush weighing me down. Sensing I am not alright, not by far, Parker clears his throat. "Iris, I love you." His voice reverberates around me, bouncing off every surface in the vacuum I exist in at this moment. I'm certain he expects me to echo his sentiment, which under any other circumstance I would. But, frozen in peril, I am mute.

"I... fuck. Fuck. I should've told you this sooner. But I couldn't. I honestly shouldn't be telling you at all. Fuck, I'm going to get into big shit for this." He rubs his hand along the back of his neck, as if to massage his thoughts into place. "I've already talked to Sabine about this, though. She agrees this can't go on much longer without your knowledge." He cranes his neck to the side and his eyes find mine once again. A hot, tingling sensation cakes my skin and a searing pain overtakes my brain. Parker clears his throat again and reaches for my hands, but my instinctive flight response forces me to pull them away. My body is on high alert. Parker's shoulders are slumped, his mouth dipped. Our places have reversed - he's the one now feeling desperate and defeated. I blink fiercely as though it will help me better focus on what he's about to say next.

"You have to understand. There's a level of confidentiality I am responsible for upholding due to my place within Our Family." Pausing, he groans in his own frustration. "I have secrets, Iris. Not secrets I intentionally hold as secrets, but secrets inherent to my position in Our Family. There is still so much you don't know." His voice rings like a broken record, telling me the same things over and over in different words. "But you need to. This, you need to know."

A guttural lump rises in my throat and I find my voice at last. It's deep, feral, and frightened. "Tell me," I urge, the sound unrecognizable to my own ears. Pleased to have my attention, Parker shifts his body closer to mine and lowers his voice to a whisper. His eyes dart around, as if paranoid.

What the fuck is going on?

At last, he breaks the silence.

"There's another level of membership within Our Family. I need you to listen very carefully." Parker lowers his voice even more, seeking to steady it. "After a couple of years of membership in Our Family, I never thought things could get better than they were. Being a Member - it's given me belonging, acceptance, and pleasure beyond what I dreamed possible. But then, Our Family recruited me for membership into something else - a highly exclusive, deeply secretive, and wildly hedonistic club within the organization. I had no idea it existed, or what I was getting into when I agreed to join. But, Iris, it's incredible." He pauses again, calculating his next move. I watch him, my eyes unmoving from his lips as they spill his secrets. A fire shines in his eyes as he speaks of this *other club*. My confusion is swept away by intrigue.

"I thought that being a Member of Our Family was the most gratifying experience of my life. But this club - it has allowed me to live completely as myself every day of my life; to fulfill my every indulgence and my deepest desires. It's unlike anything I've ever experienced." He pauses again. I lick my lips, realizing that I'm suddenly, undeniably, seduced by his words. "It's a fully immersive experience of the lifestyle that transcends the boundaries of personal life. Everything becomes intertwined. I became a Member a couple of years ago, first as a Devotee, now as a Superior." With each word, my mind twirls, desperate to make sense of Parker's confession. He shifts his body closer still and rubs his thumb against the bottom of my lip. "I love you so much, Iris. Keeping this part of me from you has been hell." I imagine Parker's naked body tangled amongst others, arms and legs and hips grinding together in a lascivious display of raw pleasure. I see the look of pure euphoria on his face, and think, *if this is hell, send me to the devil.*

I cast my eyes away from his endearing gaze, guilty in my own imagined indulgence. Parker's dedication and commitment to Our Family has given him even more than membership in a swinger's group - it's given him ultimate fulfillment. Parker has become deeply entrenched in Our Family in ways I never could've fathomed. My cheeks burn as the touch of his fingertips trails across them. Parker's words settle in my brain. *Devotee. Superior.* Is this some kind of BDSM arrangement, I wonder? The terms are different, but their meanings are similar. Parker's strained schedule makes sense now. He gets more, but he also gives more. Suddenly, a wave of shame overcomes me. For always wanting more from Parker. For being so hard on him, for making my needs bigger than his own.

"The experience has been incredible for me." He's beaming, his skin bright and his face glowing. He couldn't hide his elation even if he wanted to. I lean in closer to him. "It's allowed me to immerse myself fully in the lifestyle. It's meant more to me than anything. And I've found true gratification in it. But then... I met you. And everything changed." Parker chokes on the emotion in his throat, and my heart is on the cusp of bursting open. "I fell in love with you, Iris! It happened almost immediately, as soon as I met you and your clumsy ass on the riverbank." He shakes his head and laughs, and I can't help but indulge in a reluctant giggle alongside him. "You have brought a new depth of fulfillment to my life, and I've found myself struggling to keep my commitment to you and to Our Family separate. I have to uphold the confidentiality of Our Family, but at the expense of withholding things from you? It doesn't sit right." Parker is uneasy now, his earlier pride replaced with concern sinking deep into his pores.

"Our Shadows. That's what it's called. Most Members will never know about it. Just like Our Family as a whole, you have to be recruited into it. Which, eventually, I'm sure you would've been. You show huge potential, Iris. Everyone sees it." My throat tightens and I gulp down a wave of pride, hitting me at the most inconvenient moment. "The process is very complex," Parker begins again, his businesslike tone taking over. "There are two immersive roles: Superior and Devotee; I was initially assigned the latter. Through a highly personalized process, I was scrutinized, trained, and tailored to meet the exact needs of my Superior. Our unique relationship was curated and solidified by a team of specialists within Our

Shadows. My Superior and I mutually consented to a one-year term, at which point I expressed interest in becoming a Superior myself. At that point, Our Shadows assigned me a Devotee, but she unexpectedly moved due to a medical issue with her family overseas. It took some time to find me a new match, but eventually I was assigned the Devotee I currently manage." Parker's voice stalls, and the quiet is a sickening and painful reprieve from the barrage of information. "Superiors and Devotees' lives are deeply entangled together. As a Superior, it's my responsibility to care for my Devotee at all costs. My Devotee's purpose is to serve me and my needs, at all costs."

At all costs. It echoes in my eardrums.

"She lives with me, Iris."

I clench my jaw so hard my teeth squeak together. My eyes burn as I struggle to blink back heavy, hot tears. It's not out of sadness, but shock. It all makes sense: the obscurity around his home and limited time available for me. Incredible how I didn't see it sooner. I'm such a fool.

But through the swamp of my own ignorance, I find not a single shred of jealousy. Instead, my thoughts are teeming with shame and foolishness, and, admittedly, a dash of betrayal. Not of Parker, but of Our Family. For Our Family insisting Parker keep such a secret from me.

"Iris?" Parker searches for my eyes, which have been focused on a loose thread hanging along the edge of my sleeve. I want to pull it, to yank on it and force my shirt to unravel in the same way my brain is at this moment. He pulls my chin up so I look him in the eyes. His beautiful blues stare into me, and I collapse under them. I want to fall into him, snuggle into his chest, and listen to the steady beating of his heart.

"There's more."

Of course there is.

"M-my Devotee," Parker stutters, "she's not a stranger to you. You already know her."

Seventy-Five

My stomach drops as my thoughts desperately flip through a mental list of members in Our Family. How could I have been so stupid? This entire time, right in front of my eyes, not even trying excessively hard to hide it, Parker has had this secret relationship and I've been too invested in my own selfish, tunnel-vision feelings to even notice it. I dig deep into my memories, examining the instances that were blatant clues I was too confident to see.

Scarlett. It has to be Scarlett. She's quiet, withdrawn, reserved. All qualities I know Parker typically prefers in his partners. But, as I recall from Our September Mixer, not entirely silent when it comes to being spanked with a belt. Also pleasing to Parker.

"Scarlett," I whimper, hating myself for how pathetic I sound.

"No!" Parker laughs, his howl resonating in my ears and insulting every orifice of my body. "No, Iris, it's not Scarlett."

My mind swims. Who else could it be?

For some reason, Nina pops into my head. G and Nina were my test; maybe Nina's involvement in Our Family is murkier than I know. She's beautiful, experienced, and open to all kinds of interactions. I remember when I spotted Parker and G outside of Molly's gallery. That moment still sits in my mind as a big question mark. They must be close, somehow, and I wouldn't doubt that Parker and Nina have a more intimate relationship than he's let on.

"Nina?" I suggest, my voice a pathetic squeak.

"It's not Nina, Iris." Parker's eyes crease as he looks at me with pity.

Pity. How pitiful I am.

I know he's enjoying watching me squirm, seeing me struggle to figure out the puzzle. My stomach churns in disgust of myself.

"Who, then?" I beg, urging an answer to satiate my suffering.

"It wasn't supposed to be this way," Parker begins, his thumb rubbing the back of my hand. "I was supposed to vet you for recruitment, monitor your test, and determine if you'd be a good fit for Our Family. Not everyone who is selected for recruitment passes and becomes a Member. And even those who do pass don't always stay with the person who oversees their recruitment. I was assigned to you; I didn't pick you." Maybe he means to comfort me, but Parker's words sting. What's he getting at? The more he talks, the less I understand. "You were my assignment, Iris. But the more I got to know you, the more dangerous it became. I fell in love with you without even trying! If anything, I tried *not* to fall in love with you, because of my other commitments in Our Family that I knew would pull me away from any kind of meaningful partnership. But my feelings for you are undeniable. And now I'm in this awkward in-between place, where I'm committed to Our Family in a million ways, but I'm also committed to you.

"When we met, all of my attentions were on my commitments within Our Family. I didn't expect my relationship with you to blossom the way it did. It caused a lot of internal turmoil. I questioned everything. My Devotee and I have a significant partnership that I have made a serious commitment to. I owe it to her, and to Our Family, to honor it. But you've made it so complicated. You, Iris, you.

"But I know it's time that I am fully transparent and honest with you. I hope you understand that everything I've agreed to and done has been with my own consent; I've committed because I've wanted to. I deeply respect Our Family, and I feel honored to devote myself to it. But my love for you and for Our Family are not mutually exclusive.

"I trust you. I trust you with everything I am. I know that we can share in experiences in Our Family together and be better for it. I've already seen such beautiful growth in you. Your confidence, how happy you are in finally being true to who you are. You're experiencing life as the most honest version of yourself. It's been truly incredible to see that in you."

Despite my instinct to want to place blame, I know Our Family is not the enemy. It can't be. Parker's right - there's been too much good to come out of my membership thus far. And when it comes to withholding these secrets from me, I do understand it, too. There are simply policies in place in the interests of discretion. The relationship that Parker and I share is *because of* Our Family. I have no choice but to respect the rules, even though they are acting as hurdles in our ability to be honest with each other. But I truly needed to know. There's no denying it. I don't even want to imagine what would've happened between us if he didn't tell me what is going on.

I was questioning my sanity.

But one key detail is still missing: his Devotee.

"You have to tell me who she is," I beg.

"The ironic thing is - she's the one responsible for all of this. Not only is she my Devotee, but she's also the one who put your name forward for recruitment."

Now it's my turn to turn white. My stomach lurches at the thought of someone I know - who remains a mystery to me - advising a lifestyle organization to recruit me as one of their own.

"She was right. You are perfect." Parker eyes me meticulously.

"Please, just tell me who," I whine desperately.

"Her name is Maisie. Maisie Warren."

Seventy-Six

Maisie

H*ere I am.*
         For the first time.
The Ceremony.
Anticipation hammers in my chest. I'm ready. So ready.

Membership in Our Family is the most meaningful aspect of my life. My experiences as a Member have enabled me to pursue the interactions and connections I crave, while also challenging me to push my boundaries and grow in areas I never imagined. It has truly been enriching.

Every experience has been a stepping stone building the path to now - to this incredible opportunity. It's here that I will fulfill my truest potential.

Francesa meets my eye and we lace our fingers in the same way our hearts have been since I became a member of Our Family some four years ago. I take the first step. Francesa walks with me, out the doors of the Estate and down the pathway toward the first white gazebo. I keep my eyes up, raised to take in the sights around me. My green eyes drink in the beauty of the gardens, the bright blue sky of the day, and the cool freshness of the February air. The flowery scent of jasmine invades my nostrils. I smile, burrowing these experiences deep in my brain.

This moment - I never want to forget it.

The Story Will Continue In Book Two

Acknowledgments

I would like to first and foremost thank you, the reader, for believing in me enough to pick up this book. My sincerest gratitude goes out to you. I hope you enjoyed reading it as much as I enjoyed writing it.

There are countless others who have inspired, supported, and encouraged me on the path to pursue my dream to become a writer.

To my husband: Thank you for loving me for who I authentically am. Where I see my flaws, insecurities, and challenges, you see beauty, strength, and ambition. Thank you for believing in me even when I don't believe in myself. It's because of you and our love for each other that I am who I proudly am today. You've been by my side every step of the way on this insane journey, and I wouldn't be here, with this book in my hand, without you. I love you more deeply every day. Thank you.

To my two children: Thank you both for inspiring me every single day to find the joys around us and admire the beauty of the world. I'm in awe of your imaginations and love seeing you grow, create, and invent the possibilities of what can be. My greatest wish for each of you is to never stop believing, dream big, and know that you are capable of anything. Live your truth, my sweet babies. Thank you for inspiring me to live mine. I love you both with my whole heart.

To my sister: Thank you for believing in me, validating me, seeing me for who I am, and loving me unconditionally. You inspire me every day with your open mind and thirst for understanding. I can always count on you for the most genuine laughter, best pep talks, and realest conversations. Thank you for embracing me in all of my quirkiness. I admire your beautiful heart, broad mind, and kind soul. You have gone above and beyond in supporting me while I pursue my dreams. Thank you, from the bottom of my heart. I love you so much, now and always.

To my mom: Thank you for the laughter when I'm sad, the hugs when I'm hurt, and the support in every step I take in the many journeys of life. I'm deeply grateful to have known you since the day I was born and to have you play such a significant role in all the biggest milestones of my life, including this one. I love you so much, mom.

To my dad: Thank you for your understanding, patience, and support in all the years and stages of my life. You've taught me a lot about growth, second chances, and the importance of family. I admire your earnest attitude and exceptional heart. I love you so much, dad.

To my many friends...

Ferleine Bautista-Beal, Elizabeth Cho, Ruth Daly, Di, Elena, Jessica Ellis, E.V.J., and Michelle E. Lowe: Together, we've built a safe place made of love, acceptance, and deep understanding. We've shared incredible memories full of laughs, rawness, and adventure. Together, we've faced adversity, change, and grave difficulties - and triumphantly overcome each and every one of them. I am deeply grateful for each and every one of you. You inspire me to be unapologetically true to myself. I wouldn't be me without the support and understanding I've gained in our friendships. Thank you, my beautiful queens.

My oldest friend, E.B.: All the years, all the moves, all the life changes, all the struggles of childhood, all the insanity of adulthood - through all of that, we've remained friends. I value it every day. Our connection isn't one of convenience or boredom, it's one of true meaningfulness, love, and appreciation. You understand me in a way others don't, and I'm so grateful to always count on you for cat memes, sarcastic commentary, and a true understanding of who I am. Thank you for being by my side for decades past and decades to come.

Mindy Wendrick: Our connection stands out to me as one of the most inspiring I've had in my life. I want to thank you for allowing me to be me, for nurturing my vulnerabilities, and for encouraging me to live my truth. I hold in my heart a deep gratitude for you and our time together. Thank you. For all of it.

Christy J.: Thank you for being such a beautiful role model to me. Your incredible heart inspires me to love deeper, choose kindness, and seek to understand. You inspire me to see the magic of our imaginations. I am truly lucky to have you as a friend. Thank you, for accepting me, supporting me, and always being there, no matter what.

Tamima Ziemer: Thank you for being a safe place for me to be exactly who I am. Our friendship is rooted in an acceptance of and love for each other in all of our perfect imperfectness. I wouldn't have it any other way. Thank you for your unconditional friendship.

Thank you to the countless others who have impacted my life in the many ways that brought me to this point. I am grateful for everything I have experienced, as it has made me who I am. And, I'm pleased to finally say, I'm proud of myself. I'm proud of this book, and I'm proud to have created something that only ever existed in my dreams. Thank you to everyone who made this dream a reality. My gratitude is endless.

With all my love,

Ellie

Don't miss out!

Visit the website below and you can sign up to receive emails whenever Ellie Katz publishes a new book. There's no charge and no obligation.

https://books2read.com/r/B-A-JFXBB-WPSYC

BOOKS 2 READ

Connecting independent readers to independent writers.

Also by Ellie Katz

The FOUND Series
FOUND

Watch for more at www.elliekatzwrites.com.

About the Author

Ellie Katz is a Canadian author. She now resides in Southern California, where she savors the many indulgences accompanying her choice of lifestyle.

Ellie is hard at work creating the next novel in her FOUND series. She readily admits that her biggest guilty pleasure is writing, which she can never get enough of. She loves crafting stories laced with suspense, vivid imagery, and, of course, intense passion.

You can follow Ellie on Instagram @elliekatzwrites

Read more at www.elliekatzwrites.com.

Milton Keynes UK
Ingram Content Group UK Ltd.
UKHW030711041024
449263UK00001B/138

9 798224 025497